Constantine Capers

THE PENNINGTON PERPLEXITY

NATALIE BRIANNE

Immortal Works LLC
1505 Glenrose Drive
Salt Lake City, Utah 84104
Tel: (385) 202-0116

© 2021 Natalie Brianne
https://nataliebrianne.com/

Cover Art by bookcoverzone.com

ISBN 978-1-953491-13-8 (Paperback)
ASIN B08WS31F6L (Kindle Edition)

To my Mum, who is still with me.

And to my Dad, who I could never forget.

September 12TH

The sun rose in the sky over London, sunlight filtering through the leaves onto the pavement. Clouds and airships drifted about the blue, casting shadows. Mira Blayse stepped out of the shadows, the heels of her boots clicking along each cobblestone towards her destination, wherever that may be. She approached the corner, biting her lip as she considered the scenery.

Quite a bit of brick, some ivy, a few shops, but mostly residential buildings. Carriages passed her on the road, horse hooves clipping the road methodically. A paperboy stood on the corner opposite, yelling out one bit of news or another.

"Won't want to miss this! More news in the Whitechapel murders! Just a farthing for a paper!" The boy called after her as she turned down the street. She shook her head and kept going. There would always be horses, and buildings, and boys selling newspapers. Another block passed beneath her feet before she stopped in front of a cafe. It had been a week or so since she had last ventured into one. Well-placed umbrellas offered amiable shade.

She took a breath to steel her courage and chose an empty table with an ample view of the street. Ignoring the chiding glances of the other customers, she retrieved her sketchbook from her bag and flipped through it to find a new page. She scanned the area for a subject and noticed the waiter approaching her table. She closed the book and looked up at him like an angel.

"Eating alone today, miss?"

"For the moment. I'm sure my aunt will be arriving soon,

however I'm certain she wouldn't want me to wait for her." It was a blatant lie, and she knew it. Fortunately, the waiter didn't. He nodded, and the patrons at the other tables visibly relaxed. She had a chaperone coming, after all. It wasn't as if she was a young lady out in the city by herself. Oh no. Not at all. The waiter took her order and hurried inside.

As soon as he had turned away, Mira felt her cheeks flush. She just needed to breathe. The hardest part was over, at any rate. Now she only needed to ensure that no one else paid her any heed, and that was easy. One of her strengths was becoming invisible; she had only recently become more adept at drawing attention to herself.

She flipped open her sketchbook again and cast her gaze to a gentleman a few tables away. He sat in direct sunlight with deep shadows outlining his jawline, his nose was oddly shaped (like a turnip, bulbous at the base with a point on the end), and most fortunate of all, said nose was set deep into a newspaper. Really, he was the perfect subject. The news article must have been spellbinding, as he was oblivious to her gaze. Or more precisely, her sketching his facial features as if her life depended on it. She added subtle shading to the sketch as the waiter approached her table again. By the time he arrived, her sketchbook was closed, and she looked up at him with as nonchalant a smile as she could muster. He placed a plate of French toast in front of her.

"Thank you." She nodded to the waiter and handed him a few coins.

"Let me know once your aunt gets here, or if you need anything else." He pocketed the payment and nodded back before returning to the interior of the cafe. She hastily opened to the sketch again and sighed at the smudges. She'd have to fix those later. The man wouldn't be at his table forever. In fact, she barely had time to etch in the final details before the man folded his newspaper and left. She looked at the finished product disparagingly and swapped her pencil for her fork.

Even if being without a chaperone breached the norms of propriety, and her insides flip-flopped every time she told a lie, she did have French toast as a consolation. Granted, the reason why she stopped at this café had nothing to do with breakfast. And it was the same for the other twenty cafes she visited in the past three months. It just happened to be that cafes were quickly becoming her favorite place to people-watch and sketch. And if she had to break the boundaries that society had so painstakingly put in place around her? Well, it couldn't be helped, even if it was potentially embarrassing. Actually, no. It was always embarrassing.

Then again, society life was, as well. She never could remember all the rules and regulations, how to flirt with a fan, what colors matched, and when to wear what. This couldn't be more humiliating than the time she had tripped over her own skirts and spilled the punch bowl all over herself at Maureen Harris' last gala. It had been the last party she had attended, over six months ago. This was simply a way to see more of London, and to sketch new things every day. Recently, she had a growing interest in doing portraits; she just needed suitable subjects.

As if in answer to her thoughts, a man rounded the corner and leaned up against the building opposite, obviously distracted. He seemed to be looking for something. Perfect. She smiled softly to herself. He wouldn't notice her, then. She flipped her sketchbook over, drawing on a fresh page. He walked along the building, holding his top hat in one hand as he ran the other through a mess of wavy, brown hair. She waited patiently for him to turn towards the cafe again, hoping this wouldn't become another unfinished drawing. He stopped at the corner, frowning, then turned back, resuming his position on the wall. He examined the cafe as Mira examined him.

He was well built, with an angular, clean-shaven face. His piercing eyes were curtained by bushy eyebrows, and light in color. Perhaps blue. She couldn't tell from this distance. His mouth was downturned and determined, but seemed liable to smile at any moment. His grey suit had silver buttons that gleamed in the sunlight and drew the eye into his blue waistcoat and sharp white cravat. He couldn't be any older than twenty-six. She subtly finished his outline and started to shade as a carriage passed between them on the road.

Glancing up again to reaffirm the shape of his chin, she realized he wasn't looking at the cafe anymore. He was looking at her. Heavens, he'd noticed her! Blushing up to her ears, she closed the sketchbook and slipped her pencil behind her ear, looking away. Footsteps came closer, and she chanced a glance back across the street. He was fast approaching her. Biting her lip, she attempted to act nonchalant and invisible at the same time. When he stopped at her table, she could barely breathe with embarrassment, and yet her corset dug into her ribs as if she were hyperventilating. This was certainly worse than the punch bowl incident. Why had she ever thought it was a good idea to sketch in public?

Then he slipped around the table murmuring his excuses and thrust his hand straight into the shrubbery behind her. The pencil fell from her ear with a clatter, and she bent to pick it up, keeping her eyes on the man. He felt around for a moment and brought out a slip of paper. The man smiled, read the paper, then replaced it into the bush from whence it came. Mira furrowed her brow as the man once again apologized and moved back to the street. He turned in a slow circle, meeting her eyes, winked, then walked slowly in another direction. She focused her attention on the bush.

Pushing the leaves to either side, she discovered the paper. *"I have four faces yet cannot see. I have eight hands but cannot touch. I sit beside the seats of power. What am I?"* She slipped the paper into her sketchbook, the chair scraping against the ground as she stood, looking around for the man. A grey coat flap disappeared around the corner. She considered her options: she could stay at the cafe and forget this happened, she could return home, or she could follow him. As unladylike as stalking was, she opted for the latter. She hastened after him, keeping a good distance, and tracked his path towards the

Clock Tower, leaving the waiter to wonder what happened to her aunt.

The man in the grey coat strolled past shop windows and carriages, observing everything with a meticulous energy. As he approached parliament, his movements became more deliberate. His eyes roved over the scenery for a few moments before he pulled a small book out of a satchel. After consulting it, the man replaced the book at his side and proceeded to a tree. Mira slipped behind a lamppost and watched him dig around in the dirt and leaves. Soon enough he pulled a dirt-ridden wrinkled sheet of paper from the roots and took it to a bench to examine it. He made some notes, then he put it back where he found it before he ambled off in another direction. Mira rushed over to the tree and retrieved the paper.

Marjorie Castro.
E. Elizabeth Smith
Vincent Holland
Borneo Treaty

The list went on and on, with most items having some sort of note accompanying it. Descriptions of people, places to visit, questions to be asked. Some had *"Solved"* written next to it. Others had *"Resolved."* Some were vague titles, while others were names of people. There were forty-two entries listed, each with a number next to them. Her eyes flicked to the last entry. *"Airship Operator."* The note next to it read *"Motive? Witnesses?"* Airships? She glanced up at one of the steam powered balloons above her. On the back of the paper, it read *"Two more notes to go. St. Paul's West Yard."* She sat there puzzled for a moment and slipped the paper into her sketchbook. With her interest piquing past normal curiosity, she hurried on towards St. Paul's Cathedral, hoping she could catch up with this person, whoever he was.

She found him walking away from the cathedral farther down the street. Rather than nudge around for details in the moldering gardens, she sprinted to catch up to him. The man sat at a table writing in his notebook. After a moment, he ripped out small strip, set it in a potted plant and started off again. The last one! She snatched it up, disturbing a few leaves in the process.

"I know you are following me."

She was certain her face rivaled the roses in the cathedral gardens. She looked up just in time to see him give her another devilishly handsome smile before he disappeared into the crowd. Digging around St. Paul's gardens came to naught as there were no notes to be found, and she left before anyone thought ill of her. She turned back towards her rooms at Campden Grove, the diversion over, but questions still piling in her mind. Who could he possibly be? Why all the notes? Witnesses regarding what airship? She looked up at the airships drifting past above her again. Could he possibly be referring to the accident of 1870? No...he couldn't be. The disaster was over eighteen years ago. And while she had reason to be curious about it, why would anyone else be interested? Would she ever get answers to any of her questions? She hailed a hansom cab to take her back to her lodgings. Probably not.

Church clocks across London all chimed together to let the world know the sun had reached its apex. And that meant the noonday post was in! With any luck, a letter from her brother, Walker, was waiting back at her rooms!

Was this what she had been reduced to? Following suspicious strangers in the street and living vicariously through the letters of her brother? The cab stopped in front of her rooms and she paid the driver as she stepped out onto the street. Fumbling with her keys, she skipped up the steps and opened the post box. She retrieved three letters and held them close to her as she unlocked the door.

Her cat, Nero, rubbed around her ankles as she entered the sitting room. She set her sketchbook down and appraised the envelopes. One was obviously an advertisement of some kind, the next was from her brother and the last was from the Central News Agency. She bit her lip and picked up the letter opener. "Might as well get the least exciting one out of the way, right kitty?" Nero ignored her and looked out the window from the sill. She turned her attention back to the letter. The advertisement was for electric corsets. She grimaced. Corsets were bad enough without sending electricity through them. What would they think of next? She set the advertisement aside and picked up the letter from her brother with eagerness. She slid the letter opener through the top of the envelope.

My Dear Mira,

I am so glad to hear that our uncle has finally agreed to stop pestering you about moving back to Swan Walk. I believe these last three months living on your own have done you good. Although I'm sure if dear old Uncle Cyrus found out what you've been up to, he would move you back right away! I'm pleased to hear about your progress in researching Mum and Dad's accident. I always thought the story seemed a bit sparse, but with you on the trail we might find out what really happened. Let me know what the newspaper editor has to say on the story. Hopefully it will be good news to help you in your little investigation.

In my own news, my schooling is continuing to go well. Soon enough, I shall be finished with the general studies, and then perhaps I can convince our uncle to allow me to pursue engineering as a career. I am certain if you find out more about what happened to our parents, you can convince him that airships aren't dangerous in the least. In fact, if you remember, I wrote you all about the one I took to cross the channel! I love you dearly, my Mira, and wish you luck. Don't envy me too much. It doesn't suit you.

Au revoir!

Walker Blayse

She placed the letter back into its envelope and threw it on the table. Nero's ears perked up, and he jumped onto it. The slick envelope skittered off the table and onto the floor. It was hard not to be jealous of Walker. After all, he had the opportunity of a lifetime to go and study in France. If only. France was the center of the arts, and before she could even pick up a pencil she had wanted to go. Unfortunately, France was one of those irrational dangers her uncle kept on about. For whatever reason, Walker could go while she was forced to stay in London. Nero pounced on the letter again, leaving a paw shaped indent near the seal.

She blew her hair out of her face. She knew the reason. Even though she was the exact same age as Walker, give or take a few minutes, she was a lady. Ladies shouldn't go abroad, at least in her uncle's mind. Blowing a strand of hair from her face, she tugged the strewn letter from underneath Nero's lean body and deposited it in a well-worn box on the mantel. The cat watched with curiosity before finding a stray thread at the edge of her skirt to paw at. Mira sat down in her armchair and picked up the last letter. At least her uncle allowed her to have her own set of rooms. And she was doing something Walker couldn't. She hoped. The envelope felt heavy in her hand. It had been several weeks since she had sent her question to the editor. Would this letter even have the answers she was looking for? She caught the edge of the seal with the opener and held her breath.

Dear Miss Blayse,

I regret to inform you that we have no further information on the airship accident of 1870 aside from the information sent out in the newspaper around the date of the tragedy. We also do not have a copy of the newspaper available to send you. I am aware of several bound editions of our newspaper in the London Library at St. James' park. I recommend that you consult their facilities and regret that we are unable to offer more assistance currently.

Sincerely,

William Saunders

Mira replaced the letter in its envelope, picked up the advertisement, and tossed them both in the direction of the hearth.

This "little investigation" as her brother had called it almost seemed like a fox-less hunt. If it came to nothing, then what was the point of it all? She watched the letters smolder for a few moments before perusing the spines in her bookshelf. *Alice in Wonderland, Little Women, Around the World in 80 Days* were all ways to escape her reality. Her eyes drifted to her collection of Dickens and Austen. Her fingers lingered over a particularly old, leather-bound book. With consideration for the delicate cover, she pulled the tome from the shelf and brought it over to her armchair. Nero hopped up in her lap, and she stroked his fur.

Her father brought the book back as a gift for her mother just before they were married. If she remembered right, it had come from Arabia or India. Granted, this information came from her uncle. She was young enough when her parents died that she didn't remember anything directly from them. The book was small in her hands as she fondled the intricate patterns decorating the cover. She perused the novel, knowing she wouldn't be able to read it. The symbols on the page were foreign to her, but every so often she came to a word circled in red. Next to each circled word or phrase was a written translation, presumably in her father's handwriting. Her name was written in the margin on page 79 next to one of the red circles. The page was wrinkled and water splotched, but it was hers just the same. Sufficiently calmed, she set it on her side table.

It had been foolish to hope the newspaper would have any further information. She checked every diary of her parents, every stray note, asked her uncle as many questions as she had deemed reasonable. Still the same story. No. If she wanted to find any new information about what happened to her parents, she needed to find it herself. She could make the trek back to St. James' park in the afternoon, but she had already wandered in that direction and didn't fancy making the journey again.

She attempted to read, but the man in the grey suit kept entering her mind. She smiled to herself as Nero fell asleep. He might have information too. She likely wouldn't be seeing the man again, but perhaps she could give him the opportunity. Tomorrow, she would go back to the same cafe and see if he was a frequent visitor. And then, as it was convenient, she would go to the library at St. James' park. Her plan laid out in her head, she retrieved a new book from the shelf and settled into the armchair again, content to envelop herself in the world of Elizabeth Bennett for the afternoon.

The sun rose in the sky over London, attempting to beat down through the clouds and fog. Several airships swept through the mist. Mira Blayse sat at the cafe, drinking tea and sketching buildings. She had an excuse ready, just in case the same waiter attended her. Luckily, he didn't.

She finished shading the ivy that trailed up the building opposite, and then flipped through the rest of her sketchbook, examining her drawings. Most were portraits, but there were some full figures, some animals, and a few buildings. She came to a stop, looking at the face and chiseled jaw of the man in the grey coat. She looked over the notes she had retrieved the previous day. No scenario made sense in her head for why these notes would be there. She examined his face again. Serious? Yes. Determined? Definitely. Certainly a gentleman, from how he dressed and carried himself. Was there a hint of kindness? Perhaps. She smiled as her eyes roved over the sketch. His eyes looked a bit like her father's. Piercing and full of life. She looked up at where he was the day before. And there he stood. Wearing a black suit with silver buttons and a red waistcoat. His steady gaze focused on her.

No. He was looking at the bush behind her again. She looked down at her sketch of him. Dangerous? Maybe. She closed her sketchbook and swallowed. Maybe he was looking at both the bush and her. She bit her lip. He knew she had been following him. It might have not been such a good idea to come back to the cafe after all. She chanced a glance up at him. He was moving towards her. He stopped in front of the table and she held her breath, waiting for him to confront her. She should have just gone to the library. He slipped around the table and started looking through the bush. She furrowed her brow in confusion. Hadn't he already read the note? This confusion grew more and more as she realized the intensity of his anxiety. He was looking for the note, and the note was in her sketchbook.

He almost seemed frantic, searching the shrub from one end to the other. He ran his hand through his hair and looked again. When he had retrieved the note the day before, he was so calm and collected, it had seemed normal for him to be preening a bush. No one besides her had paid him any attention. Today he was at the center of it.

"No. No, no, no! It said it was here," he murmured, as he checked beneath the planter. He was bound to see her soon and blame her. She decided to beat him to it.

Clearing her throat, she attempted her best effort at confidence.

"Um...good morning, sir. I wanted to apologize for yesterday." She sounded a bit more hesitant than she would like, but it did get his attention. He stopped looking in the bush and turned around to face her, hiding his anxiety behind a facade of composure.

"Sorry?"

"First and foremost, I didn't realize you still needed these." She extended the three notes to him.

He released a breath and plucked the notes from her hand, drooping into the seat across from her.

"Thank you. Apology accepted young lady."

He read over each, placing the first note back into the bush when he finished with it. After reading all of them, he looked up at her.

"You were following me, then?" He asked. She averted her gaze, hiding the pink tinge invading her facial features.

"Um...yes. You see..." Her mind whirred to formulate an explanatory lie. Perhaps if she just omitted the full truth. "I like to draw people who pass the cafe. I was sketching someone and well, when you walked towards me, I was rather embarrassed. But when you took the note, I realized you hadn't noticed me at all. I read the note, and it was just too curious. I am terribly sorry if I caused any trouble for you."

She looked back up and met his scrutinizing stare. His eyes *were* blue. It looked as if he was studying every feature of her face. Was that how she appeared when she studied others for her sketches? She looked down and fidgeted with her hands.

"I probably ought to go." She stood, picking up her sketchbook.

"No. Wait." He fixed a hand on her arm, then dropped it. She sat back down and looked at him.

"You messed up my usual run, yes. At least I think you did. And it's nice to have something different happen." He frowned. "I think. I might not be certain." He smiled at her and shook his head. "Sorry. What's your name?"

She faltered. After all, they hadn't been properly introduced. However, they were acquainted in some respects. In this case, she decided to keep it formal. "Samira Blayse. Yours?"

He paused, thinking it over. "Byron Constantine."

"Nice to meet you, Mr. Constantine."

"The pleasure is mine, Miss Blayse."

"Apologies again for taking the notes."

"It's not a problem. You gave them back, and that is what matters."

She nodded and stood again. "Good day, then."

"Good day." He stood and started walking in the direction of the Clock Tower.

She didn't know what to think of it all. Her theories for the notes all fell to pieces, and she felt more confused than before. She wasn't sure it was a good idea to ask him any of her bursting questions, and so it was better she left. Besides, he seemed to have someplace to be. She continued to justify herself as she walked to the library. But she couldn't help but wonder: If she came back to the cafe the next day, would he be there?

MIRA LOVED the old Beauchamp House that the library was in. It had been owned by a wealthy parliament member, and upon his death it was converted into a library. Because of its long history, it was steeped in mystery and rumor. The stories quickly migrated to the supernatural when a death occurred in the library. She found the tales fascinating and frequented the place as often as she could. But this time she had a specific piece to inquire after. She turned away from the book listings and went straight to the librarian. He was a short, portly gentleman with a well-trimmed mustache and round spectacles.

"Excuse me, sir?"

"Yes? May I help you?"

"I believe you can. I am looking for a specific newspaper from the Central News Agency."

"What year and season?"

"1870, Fall."

"Just a moment."

He walked back into the library stacks, and she considered the other occupants of the library. Several people perused the library listings. Others meandered back into the reading rooms. A few minutes later, the portly gentleman returned.

"I've set up our bound copy in the fifteenth reading room. Let me know when you have finished."

"Thank you."

She wandered to room fifteen. It looked like a normal sitting room, except a bit larger and with a few more tables. One other person was reading at a table near the window. Only one other table held a book. She moved over to it.

The book had a blue leather cover and brass brackets holding it together. Golden lettering shone from the front. *"Central News Agency: Fall/Winter 1870."* The leather casing bound hundreds of newspapers together. She opened it up and glanced over the dates until she came to the one she required: October 12, 1870. Morning edition. She skimmed through the paper, looking for any sign of the accident. When she found nothing, she opened to the midday edition. Nothing of consequence. She turned the page to the afternoon edition and found it on the front page.

> *Egregious Airship Accident!*
>
> *In preparation for its maiden voyage, the dirigible designated as the* Daydreamer *met a tragic fate at ten o'clock this morning. Authorities are on the scene attempting to determine the cause of the explosion that killed and injured several crew members and passengers. Of interest are the deaths of one of the inventors of the steam powered dirigible, Octavian Blayse and his wife Rose Blayse.*

She wrote down the article in its entirety and then flicked to the evening edition.

> *Authorities have ascertained that the explosion originated from the engine room. There are only two confirmed deaths related to the accident and two minor injuries. The Silver Lining Airship Company has commented that this is "A tragedy beyond belief." The damages made to the dirigible may put Silver Lining out of business for good, especially with the loss of one of their main engineers and inventors. The Vaporidge Steamship Company has expressed interest in obtaining the corporation before, and it is possible with this setback that Silver Lining may be interested in selling. When our correspondent asked the company representative about any negotiations of that nature, he refused to comment.*

She read over each article a few times before closing the bound edition. It was the same story she had always been told, although she didn't know that Vaporidge had an interest in acquisition beforehand. They must have succeeded, as the Silver Lining Company no longer existed. Which was why she had never been told about it, as her uncle refused to discuss any subject related to her father.

She walked out of the reading room, paused to tell the librarian that she had finished with the book, and returned to the foggy afternoon. Other than Vaporidge's interest, there wasn't any new information to be found. And while the news reports varied one from another, that was bound to happen as different reporters may have been sent to document the scene. But for as much as she tried to justify it, something was off. She trusted her instincts; she just didn't know what the issue with the incident could be. Something was missing. She strolled through Kensington Gardens, and her thoughts drifted back to the man at the cafe.

Tall, dark, handsome, mysterious. His demeanor teemed with intrigue and nuance. He must be someone of importance. Or else he was insane. Perhaps both. She laughed a little to herself. Byron Constantine. Where had she heard that name before? It felt vaguely familiar, but she couldn't pin it down. She toyed with the idea of going to the cafe again the next day. He couldn't possibly forget her again after their conversation. Maybe she could ask him about the note he made about airships. If by some miracle it related to her parents' accident, then she would have another source of information. She determined to do so the next day as she sat on a bench to sketch for the afternoon.

September 14TH

The sun rose in the sky over London, even if the fog obscured it from view. Airships had canceled all flights because of the conditions. Mira Blayse sat in her usual spot, the umbrella at her table open in case of rain. She took a bite of her crepes and hoped the sun would come out so she could sketch properly. She reached a hand out and felt a raindrop. She continued to eat her breakfast and examine her surroundings. At least the waiter had bought another excuse about a nonexistent aunt. She looked across the street and saw Byron. Same place, same time. Looking past her at the bush. Wearing a smashing grey suit with a blue tie. He walked towards her, and she moved her chair out of the way so he could more properly access the bush. He picked up the note, read it, and started to leave.

"Good morning, Mr. Constantine."

He looked at her, confused. "Good morning to you as well...?" He stepped back and cocked his head. He went to move again.

"You really read these every day?"

He stopped again. "I apologize, who are you?"

It was her turn to look confused. "Samira Blayse? We spoke yesterday. And sort of the day before?"

He swallowed. "Right. Yes. Yes. I see. Well...good day." He quickly turned and walked away, pulling out his notebook and making a note.

"Good day?" She was thoroughly confused as he disappeared once again. Had he forgotten her? Except he couldn't have. She had followed him, taken his notes. Maybe he was a spy. But if he was a spy, why would he come to the same place every day? She grabbed the note from the bush and read it. There wasn't a single difference, other than a few more smudges and a water splotch or two. None of this made sense. She finished her crepes, escaped the notice of the waiter, and went to the Clock Tower, finding the paper. Only one thing had changed, a note next to *"Airship Operator."*

"See journal." There's a journal as well? Is that what all the notes lead to? Perhaps that was the book she had seen him carrying. She put the paper back in the same place Byron had left it as the rain fell in heavy droplets. She would have to investigate further on another day. She held her sketchbook close to her, sheltering it from the rain, and made a mad dash back to her rooms to find shelter for herself. If only he had stayed long enough for her to ask him about the airships.

She set her sketchbook down on a side table and shivered into the living room. She squeezed the excess moisture from her mess of curls, grimacing at the stringy tangles. Soon enough, she stoked the fire, changed into dry clothes, and set a kettle on the hob. She opened her sketchbook on the floor in front of the fire to dry the damp pages, then sat at her desk. Nero warmed her lap as she wrote a letter to her brother.

> *Dearest Walker,*
>
> *If I could convince our uncle to forget his anxieties about airships, I would have done so already. However, I shall continue to try to find out more about the accident. Thus far I keep coming to dead ends. The newspaper editor had no further information, besides directing me back to the newspaper article we've already read countless times. However, when I went to the library, I did find an article in the evening edition elaborating on the accident. Apparently the Vaporidge company may have been involved, at least in buying Silver Lining. Perhaps you already knew this? No matter. In other news there is a gentleman who has been frequenting the cafe I've been drawing at recently. His name is Byron Constantine. Do you recognize the name?*
>
> *I am sure that you are doing splendid in your studies and I do*

hope that Uncle Cyrus will allow you to continue your interest in engineering. If not, I'm sure we can both fly away! It is also quite impossible for me not to be at least a little envious of you. After all, you are in France, of all places! But I am happy for you, truly.

    With Love,

    Mira

She finished her name with a flourish and placed the letter in an envelope. She would mail it tomorrow on her way to the cafe, and if Byron was there, she would ask him about the airship before he had a chance to leave. Of course, if he didn't come, then what course of action could she take? She needed information. Maybe she could go to Scotland Yard to see if they had any files on the 1870 airship accident. She doubted that they would have anything, but following any lead was better than nothing. She took a sip of tea and smiled. With any luck, both mysteries would soon be solved.

September 15TH

The sun rose in the sky over London, and the clouds and fog dispersed. A single airship floated in the sky. The cafe hadn't opened yet that day, but Mira didn't mind. She wasn't there for the cafe. She only cared about the bush behind her chair and the spot across the street. And with it closed she didn't need an excuse to be there. She was adding color to her sketch of Byron. Why did he forget her the day before? It seemed that she appeared foreign to him, as if they were meeting for the first time. The table jolted as she added blue to the eyes. She blew a strand of hair out of her face and noticed Byron skirting around the outside edge of the table. He grabbed the note, read it and replaced it without a moment's pause. She opened her mouth to speak, but he beat her to it.

"Good morning, Miss...Blayse?" he said, hesitating.

She smiled. "Good morning. How are you today?"

"Well enough. I think. How are you?"

"Very well." She repositioned her chair as he sat across from her, closing the sketchbook to hide her rendition of him.

"Is that a journal?" He cocked his head to see the cover.

"In a way. It's more of a sketchbook, really."

"Do you draw often then?"

"Yes. Every day."

He paused for a moment, mulling something over, then looked up at her. "May I see some of your drawings?"

"I don't usually show anyone—"

"Please?"

Her fingers gripped the edges of her sketchbook. Then she

flipped to the first page and pushed it over to him. He thumbed through the drawings, eyes roaming over each page. She fidgeted in her seat, watching every movement so that she could pull it back before he reached the drawing of him.

"You are quite accomplished."

"Thank you." She pulled the sketchbook away. He gave her a confused look and then relented.

"You mentioned that you sketch a lot of people who come this way? What kind of people?"

"I don't know any of their names...except...well...never mind." She ducked her head.

"Except who?"

"Well...you."

"Me?"

"I sketch every day and I just choose random people who pass by. You looked interesting so—"

"I did?" he interrupted. She nodded and took a deep breath, feeling a steady heat spreading between her ears.

"May I see?" he asked.

Her eyes dropped to her sketchbook for a moment. She chewed on her lip, then lifted the cover again. Her fingers ruffled against the edge of the pages until she found his drawing. Her eyes darted from the sketch to him. He seemed sincere. Surely, he wouldn't laugh, would he? The material on the cover grated on the table as she slid it back to him. He studied it in silence. His eyes traced every mark and line on the surface of the page. The autumn wind rustled the papers in the sketchbook and prompted gooseflesh on her arms. Mira swallowed.

She broke the silence. "I've never talked to anyone I've drawn before."

"You haven't? How odd." He didn't look up from the sketch.

"I...I know," she stammered. "I sketch people who pass by me. Until four days ago, no one ever approached me while I was drawing them. Of course, you came over for the note..."

"Right."

"Speaking of your notes, I do have a question."

"You do?" He looked up at her at last.

"Well, I did end up reading several of yours and one of them had something about an airship operator on it."

"Yes?"

"That wouldn't happen to be about the accident of 1870 would it?" She closed her eyes and waited for his answer.

"No, I'm afraid not. May I ask why?"

"Well—"

Big Ben struck noon, and he whirled in that direction. "Dash it all. Late. I think." He turned to face her again. "We really must talk again, Miss Blayse."

"I'm sorry for making you late." She smiled. "Good day."

"I'm just late for a crime scene. Possibly. I think. That's all. Good day to you as well!" He rushed away from the table and around the corner before she even comprehended what he said.

"A crime?"

She furrowed her brow and closed her sketchbook with a snap. He didn't have any information about the accident. Of course, why would he? She didn't even know who he was. She felt like she had become Alice falling down a rabbit hole. "Curiouser and curiouser" was the perfect description of what was happening. With any luck her white rabbit, Mr. Constantine, would be back the next day and she could get some more answers about *him*. Or likely more confusion. She stood and looked at the cafe. Still closed. Perhaps the owner was on holiday.

She picked up her sketchbook and began to walk towards Scotland Yard. They likely wouldn't have anything either, no one did, but she had to check. On the bright side, it was a lovely walk through St. James' park to reach Scotland Yard, and maybe she could go to Westminster Bridge and sketch the parliament buildings afterwards.

As she approached Whitehall Place and the police station, she noticed a familiar figure exiting. Byron. Why would he be at the

Yard? Didn't he say he was late for a crime scene? All thoughts of airships and her parents disappeared as she watched him walk up the street. She bit her lip deciding whether to follow him again. He seemed to remember her today, which meant if she was caught, he would likely question her. She watched him turn around the corner. Her curiosity intensified, and she ran to follow him.

When she peeked around the corner, she saw him hailing a cab and getting in. She leaned against the wall. "He must be going to the crime scene he was talking about earlier." She muttered to herself. "And if he got the information from Scotland Yard..." She looked towards the police station and walked back. His name was so familiar to her so why couldn't she place it?

She had never been in Scotland Yard before. She hadn't had a reason until now. The exterior of the building was rather inconspicuous, but the interior gleamed. Marble columns kept the ceiling up, and gigantic crystal chandeliers attempted to pull the ceiling down. The walls were covered in wood paneling and beautiful paintings. Truly the *pièce de résistance* of police departments. Not that Mira had seen many. She hesitantly approached the first desk. A police constable sat behind it scribbling on some paperwork. He had a large forehead, and a wide, angular nose. His head was top heavy. He looked up at her and smiled when he noticed her.

"Hello, Miss! How can I help you?"

She glanced at his nameplate. Frederick Wensley. She nodded before beginning.

"I was wondering if I could look at the records for a specific case."

The constable frowned. "That is certainly an odd request. If you tell me the name of it, I can ask one of the inspectors if it's alright."

"The Airship Accident of 1870."

He frowned. "Why that one in particular?"

Mira's voice caught in her throat.

"My parents died in it." She kept her gaze to the floor. The constable's demeanor softened.

"Oh, I understand. Let me go and ask."

He left the desk and walked up a staircase to her left. He stopped around the middle stair and looked back at her for a moment before continuing. She wilted against the desk. If Scotland Yard couldn't give her the file, she would be at another dead end. Perhaps the newspaper was all that there was to be had. It probably was just an accident, and no one was at fault. She would just have to accept that. But, how could she? A few minutes later, Officer Wensley returned from the upper offices.

"I'm sorry Miss. Only records that we've had for over twenty-five years are available to the public." His shoulders drooped.

"Is there any circumstance where more recent records can be viewed?"

"Unless you work for or with the police department, or you were directly involved, I'm afraid there's nothing I can do."

"If my parents were in the accident, shouldn't I be allowed to view it?" Mira twisted her gloves.

"I'm afraid not miss."

"Thank you for trying."

She walked through Hyde Park, trying to think of another angle she could try. The only other person who knew anything about the accident would be her uncle, and she knew how well that conversation would go over:

"Oh, by the way, Uncle, you wouldn't happen to have any other information about my parents' accident, would you?"

"Why would I have any more information other than it was all because of your mother's ignorant, risk-taking, charlatan husband and his dangerous invention?!"

She sat down on a bench with a huff. Uncle Cyrus hated that topic more than anything in the world. And Walker was right. If she brought up the fact that she was investigating their deaths, she would be back in her uncle's house in no time flat. Say goodbye to freedom, Samira Blayse! It had been a miracle that she convinced him to let her go out on her own to begin with. She watched as a couple walked in the park with their daughter. She couldn't have been more than five years old. The little one held tightly to each of her parents' hands. Mira closed her eyes and saw herself between her parents. Walker holding onto her father's hand. She between her parents, each of her hands firmly planted in theirs. Laughing and skipping. Was it a memory or just her imagination wanting it to be true? She opened her eyes again. The little family moved on. Mira took a breath.

She turned herself towards home. There had to be some way of continuing the investigation. After reading the newspaper articles, she felt as if something was wrong. Why couldn't she just push the feeling aside? She opened the door to her rooms and went directly into the kitchen to make some tea. As the kettle whistled, it occurred to her that she had forgotten to ask the constable who Byron was. She pulled the kettle from the stove and drowned a bundle of tea leaves with the scalding water, chastising herself. She'd have to ask another day. Tomorrow she would go to her uncle's. And she still needed to find a way to ask him about the accident without him knowing what she was up to.

It was Sunday, and the rain tapped on Mira's window. She had returned from church several hours before. She felt around the cuffs of her coat to see if they had dried yet and frowned when her fingers touched the damp wool. She moved the coat closer to the fire. Her eyes watched the flames dance, each feathery burst of light creating a story in her head. After a few moments she realized that most of those stories centered around Byron and she pushed those thoughts aside and moved to the window.

Mira watched two raindrops race each other down the windowpane, feeling the cold air sneaking in through the crack between the sill and the window. What if Byron was at the cafe? She knew that it would be closed. Would it hurt anything for her to go and check? A heavy wind hit the house and caused the shutters to rattle. Perhaps she shouldn't brave the pouring rain until absolutely necessary. She checked the time on the grandfather clock in the hall. It was after noon. Even if she went, he wouldn't be there at this time. Something about his schedule was even more rigid and predictable than hers. Every day was the same for him, even if it made little to no sense. She didn't even know who Byron was, but her curiosity intensified with each scenario she played through her head. No. She shouldn't be thinking about him. She curled up next to the window with her sketchbook and Nero.

The grandfather clock chimed three, causing Mira to roll over. One moment she was dreaming of running through Kensington, and the next she was rudely awoken by the harsh wood floor. She blinked and looked out the window. The rain had stopped. She blinked a few more times, then felt around for her sketchbook. She found the pencil first, pulling it out from under her. She cringed at the broken tip. Her sketchbook lay in a heap at the end of the bench. She opened it up and smoothed out the sleep-caused creases and laughed at a line drawn across it. After setting it to rights she remembered why she had woken up. She jolted up, glanced at the clock to ensure she wasn't late, and dashed for a mirror, hatbox, and pins.

Her hair went down well past her shoulders and usually did whatever it wanted. Some days she was able to coax her curls into ringlets, but most days it was directly opposed to anything she wanted it to do. It didn't help that she didn't like the fashion to put your hair up or to wear ridiculous hats. But if she was visiting her uncle, it was necessary. He wanted her to be a proper lady, a respectable woman, and wearing your hair down was strictly against that. Supposedly. She had decided early on that if her hair was going to fall out of its style anyway, she might as well save herself some trouble by not bothering to try.

After stuffing most of her hair under a hat and pinning it into place, she put on her coat. The sunlight dripped through the clouds like pools of honey on the pavement as she stepped out into the wet afternoon. She paused for a moment to let the smell of the rain overtake her and then started towards her uncle's house at Swan Walk in Chelsea.

Chelsea was a more affluent part of London. Only the wealthiest members of the population could afford to live there. Swan Walk was a red brick building with a reasonably sized lawn around it and a bit of a garden. When her parents died, her uncle sold their estate out in Yorkshire and used those funds to purchase a new house closer to his work. The house quickly became the home where she and her twin brother Walker grew up, and it was a place she had come to adore.

It wasn't a long walk, and soon enough she climbed the stairs. The door opened before she could knock, and a familiar face appeared. A long rectangular face, with big, kind brown eyes that held many laugh lines in their corners. The mouth was turned up in a half smile and his greying brown hair was thick upon his head. Mira grinned seeing him.

"Hello, Landon!"

"Good afternoon, Miss! It's good to see you again."

"I come every Sunday; you know that." She teased.

The butler, Landon Tisdale, stepped away from the door, and Mira walked past him into the house. Once inside she stopped for a moment just to take in the smell of old wood and books. Oh, how she loved that smell!

"How are you Landon?" She placed her coat on a hook in the hall.

"I am doing quite well, Miss."

"I'm glad to hear it. Is my uncle in the dining room?"

"I believe he is in the parlor at the moment."

"I see. Does this mean he is in one of his...?" Mira paused to find the proper term for her uncle's brooding habits.

"Nostalgic, melancholy moods Miss? Yes."

"Thank you for the warning." She nodded to him and headed towards the parlor. She knocked on the door before entering. Light pink floral wallpaper spread across the room and a darker pink carpet swept the floor from wall to wall. There was a portrait of Mira's grandparents with her uncle and mother hanging on one of the walls, and a photograph of her mother on a shelf in a sort of memorial. Of course, any images that included her father were entirely absent. Her uncle stood at the window in a daze.

"Uncle Cyrus?"

"Hello, Mira," he said without turning.

Her uncle was an imposing man. Above six feet tall with a rigid facial structure. He had light brown hair that had greyed for some time, and emerald green eyes that matched hers and her mother's. His careworn face withered with the reality of life. Landon had told her once that he used to be a jovial and amiable man, but years of grief had taken their toll on him.

"How are you doing?" She moved over to him, hesitant. He glanced at her.

"As well as I ever am." He looked back through the window. Mira bit her lip. Today likely wasn't a good day to remind him of the accident. Of course, he was already thinking about it if he was spending time in the parlor. A stillness settled over the room. Mira moved to a vase full of roses and pulled a few out to rearrange them.

"Has Walker written you again?" Her uncle attempted to start the conversation.

"Yes. He's good about writing frequently. He's almost finished his preliminary studies."

"Good lad."

A knock on the door announced the arrival of the last of the dinner party. Mira's eyes lit up as he entered the room.

"Professor Burke!"

"Hello, little Mira." He smiled with kindness in his eyes. If Mira had been younger, she would have rushed to hug him.

Professor Edward Burke had been a friend of the family for years. In fact, he was the link between her parents' worlds. He met her father, Octavian, when they were going to school at Cambridge, and met her uncle on an expedition to India. He became such good friends with both of them that it was only a matter of time before Rose and Octavian met. Despite her uncle's dislike of Mira's father, Cyrus never seemed to lose affection for the professor.

"Good afternoon Edward." Her uncle nodded to him.

"Cyrus, my good chap! I haven't seen you in weeks. How are you?" The professor clapped a hand onto his shoulder.

"I'm fine, old friend." Cyrus forced a smile. "Shall we have dinner?"

"I was promised something along those lines." The professor grinned and walked out of the parlor. Mira followed him, glancing back at her uncle who took another look at a portrait of her mother. She bit her lip and joined the professor in the dining room.

"I wasn't expecting you, Professor! Last I heard, you were in

France. Is that right?" She stopped herself from bouncing in her seat in anticipation for his account of his travels.

"France, Italy, and Germany, my dear girl. It was wonderful."

"I'm so glad to hear it."

Her uncle entered and took his place at the head of the table. Dinner commenced with the usual pleasantries, speaking over this topic or that, moving between politics and personal news with ease. Mira waited patiently for a moment to move the conversation towards the accident.

"Now, Cyrus, I've been hearing that the mercantile business hasn't been faring too well as of late. Is this true?" the professor said before taking a bite of roast beef.

"For some, I would think. It is still a profitable business from my end, especially since I've stopped making the expeditions myself."

It wasn't exactly the topic she was looking for, but it could work if she chose the right wording. She could guide the conversation where she wanted without him even noticing.

"I've heard that they have almost finished an airship large enough to carry supplies across the continent to Russia. Would that affect the business, uncle?"

There was a moment of stillness at the table. The professor raised an eyebrow. Mira bit her lip in anticipation. Cyrus looked over at her, his voice soft and steady.

"If it stays in the air long enough, then perhaps."

"They have become incredibly safe in recent years, uncle. In fact, they may become so well-used that you'll have to work with them!"

"I won't. They are too dangerous. Men weren't made to fly."

She inwardly chastised herself. By the expression on her uncle's face she had already lost this battle. But it was too late to turn back now.

"Men weren't made to cross the oceans either," she said, testing her limits.

"Steamships are far safer than airships."

"But the last accident was—"

"Why the fascination with airships today, Mira? You haven't traveled on one since living on your own, have you?" A spark of worry flickered in his eyes.

"Of course not. I just read about it in the newspaper." She looked down at her plate. The professor cleared his throat.

"It does seem to be an impressive ship, Mira. But your uncle is right. If they don't manage the weight properly, there could be another accident. It's a tricky business. Now would either of you like to hear the story of how I rescued someone from drowning in the Seine during this last trip?" Professor Burke diverted the conversation.

The conversation was over. She wouldn't be getting anything out of her uncle. If she pushed it any further, she would arouse his suspicions. If she was being honest with herself, she was grateful that the professor intervened. So, she played along with the rest of the conversation through the remaining courses of food and dessert. Soon enough, the last plate was gone, and the professor looked over at her.

"I'm not sure if you're interested, but I do have some stereographs for you."

"You do?!"

"Oh, I was right. You don't want to see them."

"You know I do."

"Well then. I left them in the sitting room." He smiled before standing and leaving the room. She paused to look at her uncle. He gave her a nod, and she followed the professor out. He was in the sitting room setting the stereographs on a table. A large black box sat next to them. She went to open it.

"Just a moment, Mira. Remember our agreement?" He put a hand on hers.

"It's the same drawings I always have, Professor."

"Every time it is slightly different."

"Alright..."

"I'm sure they are wonderful!"

He sat on the couch and she sat next to him, exchanging her

sketchbook for the black box. She carefully removed the stereoscope from its velvet enclosure. The first time the professor had brought home stereographs, she was certain it was magic. From two similar images, a three-dimensional picture formed behind the lens of the stereoscope. In her opinion, stereographs were much better than regular photographs. Photography was still magic, but it wasn't nearly as fun as the stereographs that teemed with life and energy. She remembered the only time her picture was taken. It was almost impossible to stand still, and it didn't turn out that favorably. And yet, stereographs could take any pose, setting, or emotion and bring it to life. When she was ten, she tried to replicate them with paint and had failed miserably. After all, how could she properly imitate a photograph?

She eagerly picked up the first slide and examined the label. "Garden Party." She slid it into the stereoscope and looked inside. The lens transported her to a Parisian garden party. Fabric from extravagant gowns flowed towards the viewer. Flowers seemed to burst out of the frame. She laughed and picked up the next. Here, she was transported to a large stone building. The carvings swirled in intricate patterns and the windows were covered in a lace-like tracery. Each slide brought an adventure, and she wished for more when she finished. She set it down with a click and looked over at the professor. He was still looking through her sketches and hadn't flipped the page in some time. She leaned over to see what was so fascinating. Byron's face stared back at her.

"This sketch seems more defined. Do you know who he is?" He looked up at her.

"He's a frequent visitor of the cafe I've been going to. We've talked a few times."

"I see..." He studied her face for a moment before looking back at the sketchbook. He stopped at a sketch of an airship, hesitated, then looked up at her.

"Mira what were you thinking during dinner?"

"What?"

"You know your uncle can't stand the topic of airships and yet you deliberately brought it up."

"I...yes. I did."

"Why?"

"Promise not to tell him?"

"I promise."

"I'm investigating my parents' accident."

"You...what?" His brow furrowed with worry.

"All my life I've been told the same story, and all my life I've wondered about it. Something doesn't seem right."

"Mira, it truly was an accident. You aren't thinking someone is to blame, are you?"

"Yes. I am. I've gone to the newspaper and Scotland Yard and they couldn't help me. I thought maybe—"

"It was an accident Mira. You've been told the same story because that is all there is to be had."

"But—"

"I know it's hard for you. It's hard for all of us. I wish there were someone to blame, but there isn't."

"I can't accept that answer, Professor."

"It's the only answer." He closed her sketchbook. "I'm sorry, Mira."

She took the sketchbook from him and fondled the cover. "And what if I prove that it isn't?"

"Then I suppose I'll be a liar."

"Or just misinformed." She placed the stereoscope back into its box. "I know there is more to this than meets the eye."

"And what if there isn't another explanation?"

"Then I'll be the liar. Good evening, Professor. I hope to see you again soon."

"Good evening, Mira."

She found her uncle in his study, looking over some navigational charts.

"Uncle Cyrus?" She knocked on the doorframe.

"Hmm? Oh yes, come in, Mira."

"I just wanted to say goodbye before I headed back home."

"You're leaving then?"

"It is getting late."

"Before you go..." He hesitated for a moment. "I want to apologize. You're right. If that airship you were talking of does get off the ground it could potentially change the shipping industry."

"You don't like the thought of it though, do you?"

"No. I don't. They're dangerous and—"

"Don't worry uncle. I really was just curious."

"I just don't want to lose you ag...lose you as well." He corrected himself. Mira knew full well that he was going to say "again." All he ever saw when he looked at her was her mother. She tucked a strand of hair behind her ear.

"I know."

He cleared his throat. "You're still alright living on your own?"

"More than capable. And the allowance you're giving me is the perfect amount for my expenses."

"You don't feel the need to come back here?"

"No. I'll let you know if anything changes. Is there anything else?"

"Just stay safe." He smiled a bit, trying to reassure himself.

"I will. I'll see you next week."

"Yes. Next week."

Landon was waiting for her in the hall with her coat.

"I hope seeing the professor again was a good surprise for you Miss."

"It was, Landon. Of course, it's great to see you and Uncle Cyrus too." She smiled up at him as he helped her into her coat.

"Ah, but you see us much more frequently. Do you need me to call you a cab Miss?"

"No thank you. It isn't dark just yet. I think I'll walk." She adjusted her hat.

"Of course. Have a safe walk home."

Once again, her questions had come to nothing. No help from the newspaper, Scotland Yard, or her uncle. She stepped over a puddle. There had to be some other way to figure this out. The only other option would be to find some way of working for Scotland Yard. Officer Wensley said as much the day before. But how could she manage that? The setting sun made the houses look golden as she walked up the street to her home. She yawned as she took out her keys. Tomorrow she could make a new plan of action.

September
1888
17TH

The sun rose in the sky over London, and there wasn't a cloud to be found. The sunbeams weaved their way around the dozens of airships that dotted the blue. The cafe bustled with activity as Mira enjoyed her French toast. She had finished her sketch of Byron and decided that he did in fact have a kind face. Her gaze shifted up to him as he crossed the road towards her.

"Good day, Miss." He took a seat across from her and reached for the note in the bush.

"Good day, Mr. Constantine."

"Please, it's Byron."

"Isn't that a bit informal, as we are just acquaintances?"

"I find that sometimes formalities waste valuable time. If you don't make the most of the time you have, it will be lost to you."

"What a fascinating philosophy."

"I think so. Usually." He smiled and read the note, putting it back into the bush. She stifled a laugh.

"Well then Byron, you may call me Samira."

"Hmm. You don't happen to go by something shorter, do you?" Then he took out a journal and wrote something down. She cocked her head.

"Why do you ask that?"

"Samira is quite beautiful, but so is Mira. Or Sam. And they are shorter. Easier to remember." His gaze deepened as he trailed off, deep in thought.

"My family does call me Mira. And Sam is..." She grimaced. "I'd rather you didn't call me that."

"Well then, Mira it is, and Mira it shall be." He grinned up at her with a wink and picked up his pen to make note of something else. Mira couldn't help but smile.

"You like to write, then?" She gestured to his journal. He swallowed.

"Yes. You could say that."

She studied his face. He seemed a bit nervous. She glanced at the church clock. If she was right, he'd be leaving at noon. It was quarter 'til now. He put his pen down and flipped back a few pages in his journal, beginning to read. She opened to a fresh page in her sketchbook and nibbled on the end of her pencil. They sat in silence for a few minutes.

"You are well, then?" He looked up at her. She glanced up at him and continued to draw.

"Indeed I am. Are you?"

"I believe so, Miss Mira, of course one can never be sure."

She furrowed her brow and brought her full attention away from her sketch. "Why not?"

"All sorts of reasons. I'm glad to hear you are well."

"Your routine seems rather rigid. You won't be late again, will you?"

"Late for what?

"Yesterday you said you were late for a crime. Or something."

"Did I?"

"That is what you said."

"Ah. Well thank you for remembering."

"Is it the same every day?"

"Is what?"

"Everything you do?"

He laughed a bit. "Well of course it is impossible for every part of my day to be the same, however, I do try to stick to a routine. It's easier that way."

"Oh, I see. Then with the notes...aren't you worried that the wind will blow them away, or the rain ruin them, or someone take them?"

"I've never had that problem before meeting you, Mira."

"Oh. Sorry."

"Quite alright. Now, if I did in fact say I would be late, I probably ought to go." He took the paper from the bush and slipped it in his pocket as he stood.

"Good day, Mr. Constantine." She nodded to him.

"Good day, Mira." He gave her a kind smile and a bow, then he meandered away from the cafe. Big Ben struck twelve, and he picked his pace up to a sprint.

Her eyes followed him until he disappeared around a corner. Then she looked through the bush to ensure that he had taken the note. Her hands turned up empty. What if he didn't come back? She packed up her sketchbook and turned herself towards home.

As she approached her house, the postman made his way to the next abode. With a grin, she rushed to the post box and pulled out the one letter she had received. Humming to herself, she entered her rooms and set the newspaper down on a side table as Nero mewed at her feet. She gave him a scratch, and he wormed around her legs purring. "Well Nero, I saw him again!" She smiled down at him. The cat meowed in response. She laughed and brought the letter and newspaper into her sitting room to peruse them.

My Dear Mira,

It is unfortunate that the newspaper couldn't give you any further information, but I'm certain you'll find something. Especially if you've made the acquaintance of Byron Constantine! If I'm not mistaken, he's a detective that works with Scotland Yard. I may be wrong in the name, but either way it might be wise for you to consult a private detective. They might have resources you don't currently have access to.

Nothing much has changed on my end, other than the fact that there is a possibility that I can start an apprenticeship under Henri Giffard. You might not recognize the name, but he is the man that started the whole airship business! Father worked under him as an apprentice and then went on to perfect the technology. One of my professors mentioned Giffard, and that he is from this area of France. Isn't that marvelous? Tomorrow, I'm going to do my own investigating to see if I can't meet him. I feel as if I'm in the beginning of some Jules Verne novel. Soon enough I'll be inventing things others have only dreamed about, just like father.

In other news, it's been raining for over a week now. I know I usually refrain from speaking of the weather, but it is starting to get ridiculous.

Much Love,
Walker

She read over the first paragraph several times, thoughts swirling in her mind. Byron made sense now. Or at least he made partial sense. She still couldn't explain his notes or lack of remembrance, but if he truly was a private detective, it meant she had another way to investigate. Or rather, have someone else investigate the mystery for her. She groaned. She would much rather solve the whole thing on her own. Perhaps he would allow her to help. She determined to ask Byron about it the next morning. Except he had taken the note! How would she find him if he didn't return to the café? She set the letter to the side. Anxious questions weren't going to help. Not until she found out for certain that Byron wouldn't return to the cafe. She took a few deep breaths and picked up the newspaper.

The headlines were littered with all sorts of different stories. One detailed a new factory opening. Another documented the biggest airship that had ever been built. She had read that story the week before. One story outlining all the facts of a series of incidents in the Whitechapel district. They were gruesome things that she could do without. Still another spoke of a series of burglaries that had been happening in North London. She skimmed over a few more articles before an advertisement caught her eye.

The Central News *September 17, 1888*

Something troubling you? Are people following you in the street? Sounds that can't be explained? Mysterious letters in your postbox? Perhaps a loved one gone missing? Look no further. Come to 27 Palace Court, London. Can't miss it. Oh, and yes, I'm a private detective if you were wondering.

She had seen the advertisement before, but never thought she would ever have the need to use it. Now it appeared right as she needed it. There wasn't a name attached to the advertisement. It might be Byron. Or it might be someone else entirely. But if she didn't ask for help, her journey into Wonderland would be over. If she didn't take a chance, she probably wouldn't find out anything more about Byron, and she certainly wouldn't be able to solve her parents' mystery. Hopefully, it was Byron. She clipped out the section she needed and folded the newspaper up. She opened the blinds to look out over Kensington, then sat on the couch, Nero purring as he joined her. She wrote a quick note to Walker.

Dearest Walker,

I am so excited that you are likely going to be an apprentice to an engineer! And with Henri Giffard no less! I'll have to read up on Jules Verne, then perhaps I can better imagine how your adventures are progressing. I have decided to take you up on your advice. Just after receiving your letter, I found an advertisement in the paper for a private detective. I'll write again once more has happened on my end.

Much love,
Mira

She resolved to go early the next morning to this private detective and go from there to the cafe to check for Byron once more. Tomorrow would either be the beginning or the end of both rabbit holes. She just hoped she found something more than dirt and earthworms. She moved back to her bookshelf and took *Around the World in 80 Days* from the shelf.

September 18TH

The sun peeked over the horizon as Mira woke and stretched. The night before, she laid out an outfit after looking her wardrobe over. Normally she didn't take so much time, but she wanted to make a good first impression. She decided on a white blouse with ruffles and lace, a dark brown skirt and petticoat, and a lighter brown overlay with floral designs and clasps in the front. A simple necklace with her mother's silhouette in ivory adorned her neck. Then she buttoned up her polished boots, dressed quickly, and tried to tame her hair.

For once her hair resolved itself to casual waves framing her face. She liked it when it did that. It somehow made her green eyes more vibrant. Of course, that frame also made the freckles on her nose more prominent. Her freckles were the only things she omitted when she drew her self-portrait. She thought about drawing another one as she examined herself, and then put that thought aside as she grabbed her sketchbook and left her rooms to find number 27 Palace Court.

She moved down to the main road and waited for a hansom cab. The wait wasn't long, and soon enough she climbed into one. It was large and black, certainly spacious enough to sit two comfortably. The driver stood behind the compartment where she sat. A sleek, brown horse was attached at the front.

"Where to, Miss?" The cab driver had a rough voice.

"27 Palace Court if you please."

"Ah. Palace Court. I've gone there several times. You're looking for the private detective?"

"Well. Yes, actually."

"Odd fellow that one. If he could forget his head, he would, but he's as sharp as a tack in other ways."

"I see." She settled further back into the seat.

"Course that's just what people say. I only drives them to and from. He did help me find me horse's shoe when he threw it once. Course that doesn't take much detecting, now does it?"

"No, I suppose it doesn't."

He continued to ramble about this and that, pausing here and there to give directions to his horse. Mira didn't really mind. She preferred to listen. Before too long they came to Palace Court. She hadn't realized how close the building was to where she lived. It was certainly within walking distance. An apartment door with the shiny lettering of "27" stood in front of her. She paid the cabbie and stepped out onto the cobblestones, looking up at the building. She took a deep breath, crossed the street, and knocked using the large brass knocker. Footsteps shuffled on the inside, accompanied by the sound of fluttering papers. Then the door opened.

"Byron?" She couldn't help but smile.

"Do I know you? I do, don't I?" He turned away from the door, rifling through a stack of papers and glancing over them. He turned back, looking her over.

"Or are you here for the job offer? Come on in, either way." He stalked off into another room.

"Job offer?" With hesitance she entered, stepping over slips of paper, stacks of books, forgotten teacups, and other odds and ends.

"Ah yes. As you can probably tell, I need a secretary of sorts to keep everything in order."

"Oh...no, I didn't mean I was here about the job offer. I was just surprised that you didn't remember me."

"I do know you from somewhere, don't I?" He put the stack of papers down and looked her over again. "Have I been solving your case? I can't quite remember. I've misplaced my journal you see. I don't know what's in it, but I know it's gone. If you help me find it, the job is yours." He seemed distracted as he spoke, turning in circles and running a hand through his hair. She had never seen a man in such a state before. His suit coat was missing, shirt sleeves rolled up to his elbows. His attire was rumpled, and his hair stuck out in odd directions.

"Alright. I suppose I'll start looking. Do you remember where you saw it last?"

"That's the thing. I remember my name and that I forget things. There are some fuzzy memories in the back of my head, but they don't seem to correspond with the date in the paper. I found a note saying that there would be a journal somewhere."

"Oh...um...right. Well I'll help you find it." She turned in a circle, bewildered at the state of things. How would anyone find anything in such a mess?

"Perhaps if we picked up a little, we could find it." She started arranging slips of paper.

"Right. Yes. Sorry. I've turned the house over trying to find it."

They continued to pick up the place in relative silence other than the rustling of papers and books and the clinking of teacups. Some papers dictated cases, a few were just reminders. *"You need to buy groceries this week,"* and *"There may be people coming for a secretarial job today. Make sure you read your journal before,"* and *"Make sure to retrieve all the notes out in town. They could get lost or destroyed, and then where would you be?"* She read each note with interest and separated them into piles for later organization. Slips with reminders in one, slips about cases in another, random bits of trivia in another. She picked up a stack of books and moved to the bookshelf. There were books on physics, mathematics, history, Shakespeare, even a copy of *Alice in Wonderland*. She laughed a little at that as she placed the books on the shelves. She found a filing system full of different people and case files.

Once the sitting room was picked up, she noticed how nice it all was. There was a piano by the window. She sat on the piano bench, looking outside through the curtains. Not the best view, but not a bad one either. She looked back into the room. A few couches, an armchair, a large fireplace, and a door that she believed led into the kitchen. She could hear Byron moving dishes around in there. She moved closer to the window and sat on the window seat, her fingers brushing another book. A journal lay open on the seat. Picking it up she read the last few lines.

> *The girl at the cafe is named Mira Blayse. Scotland Yard had nothing for me today. I placed an ad in the newspaper to get a secretary. Hopefully they can help you keep things straight. Remember to write a note to remind yourself.*

She closed it and moved into the kitchen. Dishes had been piled in the sink and a chemistry set sat on the table along with several other books and papers.

"Byron, I think I found it!" She set it on the only clear space on the counter. He whirled towards her.

"Thank you." He picked up the journal to read it. He read a few pages then whipped his head back up to her. "Wait. How do you know my name?"

"We met yesterday. And the day before. And the day before."

"How well do we know each other?"

"We only met recently. I would say we are acquaintances at most."

He nodded and turned his attention back to the journal. It occurred to Mira that he must read it every day as well. It was a thick journal, but he shot through the pages, skimming through a shortened version of each day. He mumbled here and there and went out into the sitting room. She followed him, curiosity bubbling at the surface, and sat on the piano bench again. After about fifteen minutes, he closed the journal.

"Consider yourself hired. What was your name again?"

"Samira Blayse."

"Ah! Mira. Right."

"I'm afraid I didn't exactly come here for the secretarial job."

"Well, do you want it? You are the most qualified for the job it would seem."

She paused in thought. "How am I qualified?"

"Well, the job entails helping me to remember the day to day. Making sure I read my journal. Keeping me professional in front of clients when I forget things. That sort of thing. Seeing as I have..." He paused to look at the journal then cleared his throat. "Seen you every day for the last three days at least—"

"Six days actually," she interrupted. "This is day seven."

"Yes, then you know a little more about me than anyone else and you have an excellent memory yourself."

She thought about it for a moment. She really didn't need a job. Of course, this would be a change from monotony, and aside from that if she worked with him, wouldn't she technically be working with Scotland Yard? And they could work together on the case! She nodded. "I'll take the position."

"Excellent. Let me make a note of that." He took out a pencil and added that to the journal. He closed it when he finished and looked up at her, studying her again. She averted her gaze to the window.

"Well Mira, you'll have to deal with me now. We can discuss salary later. I would like it if you could get here early each morning." He stood and moved over to her, taking something out of his pocket. He took her hand and placed a set of keys into it. "Mornings are hard for me, and I probably won't remember you. You can come right in, make sure I read my journal, help me stay organized, etcetera. You'll be listening in on cases, so I expect you to act with discretion."

"Anything else I should know?" She looked up at him.

"Well, other than the fact that I forget every day, I don't think much else is important."

"What were the notes for?"

"Ah, those were a sort of exercise. I'd follow the clues until I made it to Scotland Yard. A doctor said it might help my memory to recover. Obviously, it was of little use," he said, almost bitterly. "And leaving those notes in the elements was not the wisest course of action. I realize that now."

She nodded. The pieces of the puzzle fit together now. The notes, him forgetting her, why he would always leave.

"And the airship operator case is the one you are currently working on?"

"Indeed, it is. Although I seem to have misplaced that case file."

"I'm sure we can find it."

"Hmm. Yes. But first, would you like a cup of tea?"

He made his way into the kitchen and she followed. He filled up a kettle and placed it on the hob before leaning against the counter and looking at her. She shifted her stance, trying to squelch her unease. Then he turned his gaze to the opposite side of the kitchen, still silent. She usually didn't mind silence, but this kind was unnerving. She tried to catch glimmers of what others thought but for whatever reason, Byron was impossible to read.

It was then that she realized she was the one staring now. Her cheeks heated, and she looked away. He cleared his throat.

"Mira, while I am a detective, I can't quite figure something out."

"What?"

"Why would a fashionable young lady like yourself look into a secretarial job?"

"Oh. Um..." She paused formulating her answer. After all, she hadn't exactly come looking for the job to begin with. The kettle started singing, and he turned back towards the stove to prepare it.

"Curiosity?" The word escaped from her tongue. He raised an eyebrow as he placed items on the tea tray.

"That sounded more like a question than an answer."

She followed him back into the living room and sat on a couch opposite him. "Well Byron, I didn't exactly come here looking for the job. I came to get help with a case of my own."

Byron frowned. "And you ended up being my secretary? I don't remember writing down a case in my journal involving you. Could you explain?" He handed her a cup of tea and she paused in thought. She tucked a strand of hair behind her ear and took a sip of tea.

"Do you have your pen ready?"

He looked at her with curiosity for a moment, then smiled and pulled out his journal, ready to write.

"Are you familiar with the airship accident of 1870?"

"To a point, yes. I was a bit young to be investigating it when it happened."

"My parents died in that accident."

"I'm so sorry to hear that."

A moment of silence passed between them.

"And what exactly needs to be investigated?"

"I don't think it was entirely an accident. Something about this doesn't add up. The fact that the airship had been tested once before without a problem, that only two people died in a massive explosion," She trailed off before finishing. "I don't know."

"You don't happen to have any proof or other clues?"

"I've tried looking on my own. I truly have. The last month I've been searching through my parents' journals, newspapers, I even went to Scotland Yard. Everything came to naught."

"Scotland Yard wasn't able to help?"

"Only those who work with or for the Yard have access to recent case files."

"Hmm."

Byron finished writing in his journal and went silent for a few moments. Then he looked up at her.

"I'll take it."

"You will?" Relief filled her voice.

"It's a fascinating problem. Attempting to solve a 'cold case,' so to speak. I am in the middle of a case for Scotland Yard currently, but seeing as it involves airships, we might be able to work on it concurrently."

"Thank you."

"Yes. Well, I'll see what I can do. I must warn you the original case takes precedence. I have a policy that unless there is a threat of someone dying, the case I am currently working on comes first. Understood?"

"Yes, of course."

He nodded as he picked up his own teacup and took a sip, turning pensive.

"That still doesn't answer the question of why you agreed to be my secretary." He looked up at her again.

"I suppose it doesn't. I'm not quite certain of it myself. I do need something to occupy my time, and all of this is just so fascinating. And aside from that I'd like to help solve my parents' mystery myself rather than stand on the side lines."

"Mira, this is dangerous work. You'll want to consider that. Why don't we do this on a trial basis?"

"I could agree to that."

"Cheers to our agreement then." He smiled and teasingly gestured with his teacup. She tipped her cup in his direction, and they both took a sip.

"Am I to start tomorrow then?"

"Tomorrow. Yes." He gave her another scrutinizing stare and set his teacup down. He looked around at the room.

"Thank you for helping me organize. When I can't find something, it does become a mess."

"I was happy to." She finished her tea. An awkward stillness settled between them as she set her cup down. She stood.

"I suppose I'll see you tomorrow then." She started for the door, fingering the keys.

"Indeed, you shall." He beat her to the door and opened it for her.

"Good day, Byron." She stepped out onto the street.

"Good day, Mira." He smiled and closed the door.

She moved down the street, mulling everything over. This was exactly what she had been waiting for. Not only did she know definitively who Byron was, and what he had been doing, but she had an ally. And a job, for that matter. She smiled and began the walk back to Campden Grove. It was much quieter than her journey to Palace Court, but she liked that. Her thoughts were noisy enough.

The sun filtered through Mira's window the next morning. She stirred, then jolted out of bed, dressing as fast as she could and grabbing a bite of breakfast before running out the door. "Don't want to be late!" she called back to Nero, who curled up in a patch of sunshine.

Now knowing how close Palace Court was to where she lived, she set out on foot. Her walk through Kensington Gardens was beautiful, the air a little misty, but she didn't mind. The time was about half past nine when she arrived at Byron's. She fingered the key in her pocket for a moment and then knocked on the door instead.

The door opened to reveal Byron holding his journal, a finger marking his place on the page. He was dressed, but not wearing his suit coat. His messy hair looked like he hadn't had time to tame it yet.

"If I know you, I'm sorry, I can't remember." He looked her over.

"You hired me yesterday to help you keep track of things. I'm sure if you keep reading, you'll find me," she said.

His eyes narrowed, and he looked back at the page he was on, then to her again.

"I hope you aren't lying." He stepped aside so she could come in. As soon as she stepped across the threshold, he closed the door and leaned against the wall, continuing to read. She hung her coat on a hook in the hall and went into the sitting room. Everything was as she had left it, other than a few notes pinned to the wall next to the fireplace. She moved across the room to examine them.

"Still low on food. Get some before end of week."

"The secretarial position has been taken. Mira Blayse. She might just come in."

"Meeting with witness in the airship case. 12:30. Scotland Yard."

She turned and leaned against the wall, glancing back at Byron who had moved to the doorway. He turned away as soon as her glance passed him, and he started to pace with his journal, tapping the end of a fountain pen against his cheek. Eventually he sat down in the heavy armchair near the fire, set the journal on his lap, and looked up at her.

"Alright, Mira. Just give me a second to write something down."

He uncapped his pen and opened the journal to the next empty page. But instead of writing, he first looked at her, eyes flicking from her hands to her hair, settling on her skirts, scrutinizing every detail. After a few moments he took the pen to the page, fountain pen delicately sliding over the tooth of the paper. He wrote a few paragraphs then set the journal to the side for it to dry.

"Well, we ought to get started."

"You mean just like that?" she said, surprised.

"What do you mean?"

"Well you just offered me this position yesterday, and you don't know anything about me."

"You'd be surprised."

"You couldn't know more than my name, Mr. Constantine." Especially since he never seemed to remember her.

"Is that a challenge?" His mouth turned up at the corners.

"I...suppose?"

"Hmm." He looked her over. "I know that you like to write or draw. Your left hand is more dominant, although you are ambidextrous in writing, aren't you?" He didn't wait for her to answer. "You also are painfully shy, but for whatever reason, you seem comfortable around me. Perhaps these last six...no seven days you've come out of your shell more than at the beginning, but seeing as I don't remember, I wouldn't know. I can tell just by interacting with you that you are uncomfortable talking with people, but I would say you've found a way to push past that in the name of propriety. You are probably too curious for your own good, but that should work out nicely for our arrangement. Your demeanor shows you are a young lady with some wealth." He paused and examined her again. "I have noticed you do some things quite atypical of a lady of your age. Perhaps you are a bit rebellious. Stubborn."

Her mouth hung open in an unladylike fashion and her eyes opened wide with confusion. "Stubborn?"

"Yes." He capped his fountain pen and placed it next to his journal.

"How can you possibly know all of that?"

"Observation is the key to what I do each day, Mira. All I have is what I can get with my senses in any given day. The more I observe, the more I can write down, the more I can remember. Because of the need for observation, I've become rather good at it. Now shall we move onto the case?"

"You mean, you gathered all of that information just by looking me over?"

"Exactly. I gather that I was right then?"

"Well yes, but how?"

"The fact that you draw is painfully evident by your sketchbook, and the graphite on your hands. I say hands because you use both to draw and sketch, however you have set your sketchbook to the left side, indicating a preference. Shy because of your tendency to blush. Curious because you couldn't help but read my notes. Your demeanor is obvious, I shouldn't have to say much on that, but you do go about town on your own and wear your hair down which isn't exactly what is considered proper currently."

Mira opened her mouth, but no words came. She furrowed her brow looking at her new employer. Just what had she gotten herself into? She found herself sitting on one of his couches in disbelief.

"That should be enough to be getting on with. Now, to fill you in on the current case." Byron moved to the filing system to retrieve the case file. He cleared his throat and sat down in the armchair again.

"Since you read some of my notes, you'll know that this case involves a certain airship operator. Scotland Yard has been stumped in the matter. When they are in doubt, they call me. For whatever reason, I'm really not quite sure." He looked at her and his eyes seemed to be laughing. "I work primarily with Inspector..." He looked back at the paper. "Excuse me, Chief Inspector Raymond Thatcher. How could I forget?" His voice trailed off to a sad mumble. He cleared his throat and continued. "He is the one who presented this case to me but is a bit busy with another urgent case now and so this one falls to me. Now here are the facts..." He stood and paced the room with the case file, referencing it as needed.

"About a year ago, a certain Clement Pennington applied for a job with the Vaporidge Steamship Company as an airship operator. He had previous experience as an engineer and ship builder. They hired him. Clement was employed there for several months, happily, with no complaints from passengers or coworkers. Back in March he began to be more withdrawn. In July, a little less than a year after he had started, he quit his job. Nine days ago, September 10, he was found dead in his lodgings in North London."

"How did he die?"

"He could have been killed by a blow to the head. There was a bit of blood involved and bruising. However, no weapon was found, and the amount of blood wasn't substantial enough to be fatal. He may have just fallen into a table. But they did find a hypodermic needle, suggesting drug use. The medical report hasn't been officially released so we can't be certain on the cause of death."

"Any signs of suspects or motive?"

"Possibly. The police believe that the burglar that has been terrorizing North London may have been the one to do the deed, if a deed was done at all. His rooms seemed to have been ransacked."

"They are the only suspect you have?"

"Unfortunately, yes. Of course, the first thing to look for is any familial ties, and Mr. Pennington was all alone in the world, so to speak. His mother died when he was young. His father was a civil engineer and died in an accident a few years ago while Pennington was going to school. Of course, he followed somewhat in his father's footsteps, only he was more interested in machines. Hence, going to work on an airship."

"So, he didn't have any family or connections whatsoever?"

"None at all, at least that have been determined at this point."

"Perhaps it was suicide then."

"Perhaps. The body was found by the landlord, and he might have more information on that subject. I shall be interrogating him later today."

"At 12:30?"

"Yes, indeed. Which means we have ample time for a cup of tea, don't you think?"

AFTER TEA, they hailed a cab and headed off to Scotland Yard. Byron was greeted by several people he didn't remember, but pretended to remember anyway, as they made their way to Chief Inspector Thatcher's office. Mira stayed close to him. After climbing a few staircases, they came to an exterior office with a young lady at a desk writing something on a piece of letterhead. She looked up as they entered.

"Hello, Byron." She chirped sweetly in her slight cockney accent. He cleared his throat.

"Is Thatcher in?"

"Yes, he is. Who's this?" The girl's smile went a bit sour looking at Mira.

"Miss Blayse, my secretary."

"I wasn't aware you were looking for a secretary." She scowled.

"I wasn't aware you were interested in changing positions." He walked past her towards the door to the main office. "Wait here Miss Blayse. I'd like to talk to the chief inspector alone for a moment."

Mira nodded and waited by the desk. She glanced at the nameplate. *Juliet Chickering.*

The woman that went with the name was quite petite. She had small hands and wrists that probably could be broken as easily as a pencil. Or perhaps the proper word was delicate. Her blonde hair was pulled into an updo that didn't suit her at all, and her complexion was so pale Mira couldn't imagine she had ever seen the sun. She seemed to like neatness as she arranged her fountain pen straight against the paper she wrote on. Juliet's shrill voice pulled Mira from her thoughts.

"Might I ask why you would be interested in a secretarial position? You don't look like a working girl." Juliet moved the paper onto a neat stack on the left side of her desk, refusing to look at Mira, her cockney accent suddenly becoming more prominent.

"Well, he's helping me solve a case of my own, actually."

"Oh, so you aren't interested in him?"

"I'm afraid I don't know what you mean."

"I've had my eye on him for a while. Every day he resets, they say. That means every day I get a chance. If I get put down in that journal of his, then soon enough I'll be remembered and then who knows where we'll go from there."

Mira stood astounded. "The thought never even crossed my—" She was interrupted.

"Oh good." Juliet put the paper she was holding down and opened a drawer. She took out a small piece of rouge colored tissue, licked her lips and pressed them against the paper. When she put the paper away, she had a pinkish tinge to her lip. "But you do have to admit that he is right handsome, don't you think?"

"I...I suppose..."

The door opened, and Byron came back out. "Miss Blayse?" She hurried into the inspector's office and shut the door behind her. Byron raised an eyebrow. "You feeling alright? Your face seems a bit red."

"Quite alright." She avoided eye contact and turned her attention to the man sitting behind the desk.

Raymond Thatcher was a portly gentleman whose black hair greyed along with his perfectly trimmed mustache. He had laugh lines around his hazel eyes, and a kindly face. He reminded her a bit of Landon, and Mira smiled at the thought.

"You must be Miss Blayse, Constantine's secretary?" Thatcher stood and extended a hand to her. She shook it and stepped back.

"Yes, I am."

"I certainly hope you can help him keep his facts straight. He's brilliant, I'll give you that, but his deductive reasoning is nothing without memory."

Mira glanced at Byron and noticed he was taking the compliments with a smug sort of humility. She smiled. "I'll do the best I can."

The chief inspector smiled at her response then turned to Byron. "Now, I'm sure you didn't come for pleasantries, Constantine. You're here to see the landlord?" Byron nodded. Mira noticed several case files on the desk, some with gruesome photographs she wished she had not seen. The chief inspector picked up the only file without a photograph and handed it to Byron before continuing.

"His name is Doyle Morrison. He's owned that branch of buildings for the last three years. You're welcome to question him. He was kind enough to wait for you. You'll find him in interrogation room three."

Byron led her through Scotland Yard to the interrogation chambers. A constable stood outside the door. Byron nodded, and the constable stepped aside.

A man sat at a table in the center of the small room, and another constable stood on the opposite end of the room, watching him. The man at the table seemed skittish. He sported a receding hairline and an ill-kempt mustache. His clothing teemed with intricate patterns, but the fabric was obviously cheap. Mira's stomach tightened watching him.

Byron went to the opposite side of the table and gestured for Mira to take a seat in one of the chairs across from the landlord. She did, and he followed suit. Not knowing what to do with herself, Mira opened her sketchbook and began to subtly sketch the man, pretending to take notes.

"Doyle Morrison?" Byron's voice cut the tension of the air. At this distance Mira could tell that Doyle was sweating, and she caught a whiff of alcohol on his breath.

"Yes, that's me name. Who's the girl? I was told I was getting questioned by a detective, not a detective and a lady."

"This is my secretary, Miss Blayse. I assure you she is discreet. Anything you can say to me can be said in front of her."

Mr. Morrison looked her over for a moment, shrugged, then cleared his throat, turning his attention to Byron. "I run a reputable business, Detective. It's right rude for Mr. Pennington to go and get himself killed. You know how hard it is to rent out a place when someone's gone and died in it?"

"I'm sure that is very unfortunate Mr. Morrison. However, currently, I am more interested in the facts."

"The facts? What facts? I come home from the pub after having a late breakfast. It was rent day, it was, so I set down me things in me place and I went up the stairs. I knocked, and the door crept open just a crack, and so I says, 'Mr. Pennington,' and I knock again. When I peeks me head 'round the door I see him lying there. Right awful business."

"Do you know what time it was when you came to get the rent?"

"It was in the mornin' I think. Somewhere 'round eleven o'clock, it was. Must have gotten himself killed the night before."

"And then you contacted the police?"

"Right away, sir. Didn't touch a thing."

"How often did Mr. Pennington come late on his rent?"

"This was the first time I can remember. I thought it funny that he hadn't come. Normally he delivers it the day before. That's why I went to ask him about it."

"You were worried then?"

"That's right. I was worried." Doyle attempted to shift to a more comfortable position.

"You don't happen to know of any frequent visitors to his apartment, would you?"

"No, I stay pretty much out of my tenants' business."

"Except when it comes to the rent?"

"Well we have an agreement, don't we? If I get the rent, I don't worry about any other goings on in my establishment. My tenants have the right to privacy, and so do I."

"And you didn't hear anything coming from Pennington's apartment the night before?"

"Not a thing."

"Hmm...good day, Mr. Morrison. Thank you for your help." Byron stood, chair legs scraping against the floor, and left. Mira followed close behind.

"Of course, sir! Pleasure to help," Doyle called after them.

Mira closed the door behind her and ran to catch up with Byron.

"You don't have any other questions for him?"

"Not currently. He's told me all the information that could possibly be useful to me."

"But didn't we already know when Pennington was found and how?"

"Yes, we did. But now we know that the landlord doesn't care about anything but the money. That means that he won't have been paying attention to anything else. Hundreds of people could have been in Pennington's apartment that night and Morrison wouldn't have noticed. Why continue to question an unobservant witness?"

"Is he a suspect now?"

"He always was." He glanced at her before continuing. "But I'd say he doesn't exactly have a motive. He said himself that a death in the building was bad for business."

He continued to lead her through Scotland Yard until they reached the front desk. Officer Wensley manned it again.

"Byron! What brings you to the desk of knowledge?"

"Do I need a reason to stop by and say hello?" Byron smiled.

Mira looked at Byron with surprise. Why would he remember Wensley? She looked back at Officer Wensley as he laughed. "No, but you usually only come when you need something from me."

"Very observant of you Fred. Firstly, I want to introduce you to my secretary, Miss Samira Blayse." He stepped aside, and Mira stepped up to the desk.

"I believe we've met before," she said.

"Ah yes. You were here the other day asking about a case file. I'm sorry we couldn't accommodate you."

"That's my other reason for coming. Could you possibly retrieve a case file for me?" Byron said.

"Why of course my good man! It wouldn't happen to be the file for the airship accident of 1870, would it?"

"Once again you've read my mind, old chum."

"Let me get that for you. Won't be a minute."

Officer Wensley left the desk and went directly into a records room. Byron leaned against the desk with a smile.

"It really was that easy?" She blinked at him.

"I'm a detective. I work with the Yard. Why shouldn't I have access?"

"I suppose you would. I just didn't expect it to be *that* simple."

"To be completely honest, sometimes old Fred there bends the rules for me. We've known each other since we were young."

"You grew up together?"

"You could say that. I like to think I'm the one who got him interested in becoming a policeman."

"Always with the ego, Constantine," Fred said.

Mira jumped slightly and turned back towards Officer Wensley who had returned from the records room. Byron chuckled.

"You know I'm kidding."

"I know. Here's the report you wanted. Let me know if I can do anything else for you."

"I always do." Byron reached for the report.

"It was nice to officially meet you, Miss Blayse." Officer Wensley gave a slight bow.

"You as well."

Byron bounded down the steps as they left Scotland Yard. He handed the report to her. She furrowed her brow.

"You're giving it to me?"

"Of course. It is your parents' case file after all."

"You aren't going to look at it?"

"I'm sure I shall eventually, but for now I think you deserve to have the first look." His voice softened. "You've waited long enough. Just bring it with you tomorrow."

"Thank you."

He nodded. "You think you can remember what we learned from Mr. Morrison?"

"I think so."

"Good. I don't feel like writing it all down. You can go home, Mira. Look over that report. I need to do some grocery shopping and think about all of this."

"You're sure?"

"Yes. Tomorrow we'll check out his lodgings. See if we can't find anything. I expect you to come earlier tomorrow, and don't worry about knocking. You have a key, and you are welcome to use it."

She nodded as he ordered a cab. They rode in silence back to the cafe. There, he paid the driver before parting from her.

"Good day, Mira." He smiled.

"Good day, Byron." She followed him with her eyes until he turned the corner out of sight. Clutching the report tight to her chest, she hurried home. She arrived just as the postman delivered the afternoon post.

"Good evening, miss. I've got another one of those letters from France for you."

"Thank you."

"I've noticed you've received quite a few from there. At least two a week."

"My brother is a voracious writer, and I try to keep up with him. Thank you for the delivery." She took the letter from the postman and went inside.

Nero meowed at her feet, asking for fish. She ignored him and brought her papers over to her desk. She looked between the letter and the police report trying to decide which to open first. Picking up the folder she took a deep breath and then opened it.

Officer James Davies
  October 12, 1870
  As I was walking my beat near the shipyards, I heard an explosion coming from the airship docks. I quickly made my way in that direction. Once close to the location of the incident, it was easy to see that the explosion had come from the engine room of one of the larger airships. As I approached, I noticed that people were evacuating from the main portion of the airship. By the time I reached the main dock, the fire had been extinguished. I entered the area where the explosion had occurred. The main window had been shattered. Several crew members were gathered around a half-melted steam engine. It was still smoldering. I moved over to them first and asked if there had been any injuries. They stated that Octavian Blayse and his wife Rose Blayse had been in the engine room at the time of the explosion, but they weren't anywhere to be found. I left to send a messenger back to Scotland Yard for additional constables to be sent. While I was gone, the bodies were recovered. They were burned beyond recognition—

She put down the report and swallowed. It was hard to read it in such unsympathetic terms, but even worse to read about their condition. And this wasn't even the medical report! However, she did find it odd that her parents' bodies weren't found until after the policeman had left. What if there were more clues? She took a deep breath and looked out the window. Was it just her imagination? Her false hope that somehow her parents' death was more than an accident? She paused in thought. Why would she want her parents to have been murdered? What sort of motive could there have possibly been? She slumped back in her seat again. There *had* to be more. She took a deep breath and managed to continue.

They were burned beyond recognition, but their clothing positively identified them as Mr. and Mrs. Blayse. Their bodies were found outside the airship. The explosion sent them through the main window and onto the ground below. I hadn't seen them as I approached because they had fallen behind some scaffolding. Soon enough the additional officers arrived on the scene, as well as some reporters. We brought the bodies back to Scotland Yard to be examined by the Yard physician. The bodies were further identified by a friend of the family, Edward Burke.

She blinked at the professor's name. How had she never heard about this? If the professor had been there, then he had to know something! Although, he only identified them. He wasn't at the shipyard. She just needed to find a way of contacting him.

She glanced over the medical report. It was worse than the police report. She set it off to the side when she couldn't read any more. Pushing away the folder, she picked up the letter from her brother. Thank goodness she saved it for last! At least she would end on a happy note.

My dearest Mira,

I'm happy to hear that you are getting help with this case. It certainly seemed as if every part of it had come to nothing for you.

I'm afraid my previous letter's news wasn't exactly meant to be. Fairly soon after I sent that letter, I found out that Henri Giffard died back in 1882. I would have thought his death would be more well publicized. After all, he did invent the first airship, or as the

French say "dirigible." Of course, our father likely would have still invented it if Giffard hadn't. As you may well have guessed, I am rather disappointed, but not to worry! I'll find a different apprenticeship soon enough. We'll be going on a trip to the Alps this next week, and then I'll start my search again. Of course, being in the Alps means I won't be able to write you until the beginning of October. Hopefully, my next letter will carry more favorable news.

 Love,

 Walker

She placed the letter in the box on the mantle. It wasn't particularly happy news. But at least it was a letter from Walker. The last one. For over a week. She woke up Nero from his twentieth nap of the day and brought him up the stairs to her room. Tomorrow would be another day, and although the police reports and letter were slightly depressing, nothing could stop her from being excited for it. Another day on the case with Byron was certainly something to look forward to.

September 20TH

The sun peeked through Mira's curtains, but she was already up, dressed, and breakfasted. Her excitement made it difficult to sleep. The walk to Palace Court through Kensington Gardens was uneventful, and she arrived in front of Byron's abode before the frost melted from the grass, sketchbook and police report in hand. Piano music drifted out an open window in his sitting room and Mira smiled to herself. Even if he forgot the day to day, muscle memory couldn't be forgotten. She slipped the key into the lock and entered. The piano stopped playing.

She closed the door and turned to face a pistol. Her smile disappeared. She froze and looked at the owner of said pistol. Byron stared at her, questions playing on his features, scrutinizing her once again. There was something else as well. Anger. Something she had never seen on his face before. She swallowed and took a step back, paling. Her eyes flicked between the barrel of the gun and his face. Muscle memory couldn't be forgotten. Her heart raced in her chest.

"Who are you and how did you get in?" He cocked the pistol. She tensed and tried to be confident.

"Samira Blayse. You gave me a key. Have you read your journal this morning?" Her voice cracked as she spoke.

"Journal...journal..." He shook his head. "I don't know what you are talking about."

"Your journal. The one you read every day to help remember what has happened before?" She tried to keep her voice level. He didn't lower the pistol, but he took his finger off the trigger. He looked entirely confused, and the anger seemed to be dissipating. She took a chance.

"Maybe if we found it...it would help." She slipped past him and into the sitting room to look for it. He didn't try to stop her, but he kept his gun trained on her.

The journal sat on his armchair, closed with a fountain pen on top. She picked it up and returned to the entry hall, holding it out to him.

"Read this. It might make more sense."

He looked at her, narrowing his eyes for a second. Then he lowered the pistol. "I'm trusting you." He took the journal, opened it and moved into the sitting room to read. She stood frozen for a moment then took a deep breath and followed him. After taking her usual place on the couch, she began to add shading to Doyle. After another fifteen or so minutes he closed his journal and looked up at her.

"Oh...I'm sorry, Mira."

"It's perfectly alright," she said straightening, "as long as you remember now. You do remember now, right?"

"Yes."

"Good."

"I don't know what I was thinking." He disarmed the gun and placed it back in its case on the side table.

"You didn't remember me, and I just randomly came into your house. It makes sense, in a way."

"I suppose." He watched her for a moment before shaking his head. "Now that that is taken care of, can you remind me of what happened with the landlord?"

She nodded and handed her drawing to him.

"This is Doyle Morrison. He found the body at eleven o'clock, you determined that he wasn't useful for further questioning as he seemed more interested in money than in people, and we were going to investigate the scene of the crime today." She finished, and he handed the drawing back to her.

"Is that good enough?" she asked.

"That's more than good enough. I've never had visuals to remind me before. At least I think I haven't." He grinned at her.

"Oh! I also brought the police report back. The one for my parents' case."

"Ah yes. I read about that. What did you gain from it?"

"The same story again." She blew a strand of hair out of her face. "Other than I thought it was odd that my parents' bodies weren't found until after the constable returned." She passed the folder of documents over to him.

"Hmm...that could be a clue, or just how it happened. How were they identified?"

"By their clothing. The explosion had, well, made them unrecognizable." She swallowed and fidgeted with her hands. "And I know the individual who identified them. He's a family friend. I plan on asking him about it the next time I see him."

"I see." Byron scanned over the first page of the report. "I'll give it a read through. Maybe I'll find something else of use. And I'd like to know what you find out from your friend."

He paused a moment more before setting the folder on his side table and standing.

"Let's go." He retrieved his satchel and placed his journal into it. He strode towards the door and she followed him out onto the street. He hailed a cab as she locked the door.

"Scotland Yard, if you would." He told the cabbie as he helped Mira into the carriage.

"Aren't we going to the victim's lodgings?"

"One needs an address to do that, Mira, and I believe I forgot to get that from the Inspector yesterday."

The carriage bumped and bustled over the cobblestones and they swayed with the chassis. They rode in silence for a while until it occurred to Mira that it was rather odd that Byron had relied on her instead of his journal with facts for the case.

"Byron, isn't it risky not to write down certain facts in your journal?"

"Hmm? Oh yes. I suppose it is."

"Then why did you ask me to remember what Mr. Morrison had said? I know we didn't find out much, but that doesn't mean it wasn't important."

"It was a sort of test. Just to see if you truly were up for the job."

"And what if I wasn't?"

"I wrote up my own version and put it in one of my drawers. I made a note in my journal that I was relying on you this time, and if your account wasn't satisfactory that there was another one."

"Oh."

"Don't worry. You passed."

He gave her a reassuring smile and, she smiled back. The carriage reached Scotland Yard, and he helped her out. They entered and went up to Thatcher's office.

"Good morning, Byron! How are you doing today?" Juliet chittered.

"Good morning. I'm doing well. Thatcher in?"

Juliet nodded. "Go on in."

Mira thought she saw a wink from Juliet as she gestured them into the office. Thatcher looked up from his desk as they came in.

"Constantine! Just the person I wanted to see! Take a seat. We've nearly solved the case."

"You have?" Byron took a seat with a questioning glance towards Mira. She took a seat next to him.

"Definitely. The medical report has come in. The head injury was not the cause of death. There were drugs in his system. He must have administered the drug, it took effect, he fell backwards into the table, causing the head injury."

"And the fact that the place looked ransacked?"

"There is still the possibility of burglary. We're still trying to track down the burglar to see if we can't get any other evidence. However, the landlord did tell us that Pennington's rooms were hardly ever clean. It is a clear case of suicide. Or death by misadventure at any rate. And it's a good thing, too. I've got several other cases I'm working on and it's nice to put one to rest."

"Hm. If it's all the same to you, could we still look over the crime scene?"

"Be my guest. I'd be surprised if you found anything."

"Might we have the address?"

"Didn't I give it to you when I assigned you to the case?"

"I must have misplaced it."

The chief inspector nodded and wrote the address down.

"Miss Blayse, if you could ensure he doesn't lose it this time."

Mira nodded as Byron took the paper and stood to leave.

"Just a moment Constantine!" Inspector Thatcher called after him. Byron paused at the door. Thatcher picked up a different file folder and walked over to him.

"I think you might also want a copy of the medical examination."

"Thank you." Byron took it and left. Mira followed him after offering her own thanks to the chief inspector.

They stopped for brunch at a cafe on the way to the victim's rooms. Mira added milk to her tea and Byron read over some notes he had taken.

"Shall we look over the medical examination?" She stirred the milk in, watching the swirls die down into a cloudy haze. He nodded and pulled out the file.

"Cranial hemorrhaging near the back of the head, as we already know, and high amounts of opioids in his system. There is a bruise on his left arm and a pinprick suggesting that it was administered through his left cephalic vein. There were a couple of standard bruises on his legs, but those could have come from anything. Nothing else out of the ordinary."

"Cephalic vein?" She could feel herself getting a bit squeamish, but this report was nothing compared to her parents'.

"Yes. It's the one that goes up your arm and back to your heart." He gestured to a place on his inner arm.

"So that didn't give us anything else to go off of."

"I wouldn't say that." He sipped at his tea. She sipped at hers and watched the airships float past. Just a few months ago, Clement Pennington had been flying inside one of them. What was that like? Byron brought her out of her reverie.

"Have you ever been in one?" He glanced up at a blue airship that passed overhead.

"Oh heavens, no. My uncle would never approve. He's terrified of them. He thinks they're dangerous."

"Do you?"

"Well, I suppose they are. But in the same way that sailboats, bicycles, and horse-drawn carriages are dangerous."

"So only slightly?" He took a sip of tea and searched her face.

"To be completely honest, I've always wanted to fly. It somehow terrifies and thrills me at the same time."

"Hmm."

"Why do you ask?"

"Oh, no reason." He jotted down a note in his journal before setting his teacup down. "We probably ought to get going."

They reached the place in the early afternoon and had no problem gaining access. It was a tall, rundown building holding several apartments belonging to different people. They learned from a rusting nameplate that Mr. Morrison's apartment was the door halfway up the building. Pennington's apartment was at the top of the stairs.

Byron went up the stairs first and opened the door. It creaked as it opened inward. Mira peered in. The room was in worse condition than Byron's when she had first seen it. Papers everywhere. Two bottles of champagne opened, one empty, the other still half full, but no bubbles coming from it. A box of chocolates melted on the windowsill. A glass sat on the piano; a ring left beside it by condensation. Many of the chairs were turned over. A teacup sat on a side table, and another lay in shatters on the floor. A chalk drawing of a body drawn on the floor was near the side table.

They moved into the bedroom where pillows lay on the floor, and the mattress skewed at an angle. Every drawer in the dresser lay open, the clothes all rumpled together and spilling out onto the floor. The desk seemed to be the only tidy space. Letterhead somewhat in the center. Pen on the left, straight beside a pad of paper. A vase of dead flowers on the right. Byron observed everything with deliberate thoroughness.

In the washroom, the tooth powder was upright next to a half-empty bottle of perfume. Byron moved into the kitchen and Mira followed. There was some food left out, but most of the dishes had been done and the counter was clear. All but two of the teacups hung where they should be. They moved back into the main room.

"So, Mira, what do you take from this?"

She looked at him surprised. Why would he want her input? "What do you mean?"

"What do you see?"

"I'm not the master of observation. You are."

"On the contrary Mira. You're an artist. Observation is all that you do."

Mira turned in place, looking around the main room again. Byron picked up two of the chairs, setting them to rights and sat in one. She took a seat in the other.

"Well..." She hesitated.

"I'll give you a hint. What could you tell from the kitchen?"

"It wasn't nearly as messy as the rest of the house. Which means he took better care of it or cleaned it most recently."

"And what does that tell you?"

"He likes to cook?"

"Think Mira. What about the champagne and chocolates?"

"He has expensive tastes?"

"Don't question me. Question your surroundings."

She looked around again, thinking. Frowning. "Why would he have chocolate?"

"Two teacups were missing as well." Byron stalked over to the window.

"Someone was over. A woman."

"Very good. From what I can gather, they had tea, cooked dinner, ate it, drank champagne, talked for a while, and then she left. Now, how did you know it was a woman?" He turned back towards her.

"Men rarely buy chocolate for themselves, and there is perfume in the bathroom. She must frequent the place, but she doesn't live here because there are no dresses hanging in the closet."

"Excellent. I knew you had observational skills." He smiled and picked up the handle from the broken teacup, examined it, then dropped it. Mira cringed as the china splintered even more.

"Now, Mira, do you know what causes me to believe that this is still a murder case?"

She bit her lip. "I'm afraid I don't."

He walked over to the piano, picked up the glass, examined it, then turned back, setting the glass back in its place.

"The kitchen was clean. If a man was going to invite a woman over, the entire apartment would be clean. It was ransacked. The mattress was upended, meaning someone was looking for cash. Drawers opened and rummaged through, indicating a search for jewels."

"So, you think the woman killed him, and then searched his room?"

"That is a possibility. There is one other thing that points to murder." He stood up and walked back into the bedroom. She followed. He stopped at the desk.

"Anything strike you as odd about this?" He gestured to the pen.

"No. Nothing."

"That's because you are left-handed Mira. You place your pen on the left as well. Easier to grab. To any right-handed person, it would feel uncomfortable and awkward."

"How does this point to murder?"

"The drug was administered into his left arm. That means someone else had to do it."

She sat in stunned silence for a few moments. He stepped out of the bedroom, looking over the main room once more.

"We need to talk to his neighbors. See if they noticed that he had a friend who frequented the place." He strode towards the hall and Mira followed, being careful to close the door behind her.

After knocking on a few doors without response, a door at the end of the corridor near the stairs finally opened.

"What do you want?" a crotchety voice gristled out at them through the crack in the door.

"We'd like to ask you some questions Mr....?"

Byron looked around for a nameplate. There wasn't one.

"Graham. And who are you to be asking any questions?"

"I work with Scotland Yard."

"Those policemen, trampling up and down my stairs at all hours of the day. Can't give an old man any rest. If they didn't ask me any questions, why should you?"

"Perhaps I am more thorough. May we come in?"

"Harrumph." He breathed heavily through his nose.

"We just want to ask what you have seen recently."

"And why is that any of your business?" the man asked. Byron sucked air through his teeth and let out a breath.

"A man was murdered in this building not a fortnight ago, sir. If you'll just cooperate, we'll be on our way."

Byron's voice raised in volume a bit. Mira touched his arm, and he looked at her, a question dancing in his eyes. She stepped into view of the door.

"Sir, if you'd like, we can come back when it's more convenient. We were just thinking that a man of your experience, and obvious intellect, would have noticed the goings on here more than the average person. Your evidence could be invaluable in helping to solve this case." The old man opened the door further, peering out at her.

"Mrs. Blayse?" His voice was hesitant and soft.

"Um...no. Miss Blayse. My mother passed away several years ago."

He pondered on her words for a few moments, then the door opened, fully exposing the old gentleman leaning on his silver-tipped cane. He sighed.

"I know."

His hair was entirely silver, his eyes dark brown. His skin was wrinkled and weathered. He seemed to have lived a full life; Mira could tell that from the deepness of his eyes. His suit was expensive, but worn, fraying at the edges. He looked them both over.

"You look quite a bit like your mother." His voice sounded hollow. "Come on in then." He hobbled off into his living room and took a seat in an extremely overstuffed chair. Byron looked at Mira in astonishment, and then followed her in, closing the door behind him. They both took a seat on a couch facing Mr. Graham, and Byron took out his notebook.

"You knew my mother?" Mira glanced at Byron.

"Not as well as your father. We worked together on a few projects. He was a brilliant inventor. And your mother was a wonderful woman. The accident was heartbreaking. I had wondered what had happened to their twins."

"My uncle, Cyrus Griffon, took us in."

"Ah yes. Your uncle is a good man."

They sat in silence for a few moments. Then Mr. Graham cleared his throat.

"Let me get a pot of tea going."

He stood, his back cracking, and went into the kitchen. There was the clamoring of tea things, and a few minutes later they sipped at some excellent Earl Grey. Although there was a chip in her cup, Mira didn't mind. She'd found a family friend she didn't know she had.

"Sir, can you..." Byron barely started before the old man interrupted him.

"No, I can't. Now Miss Blayse, what is it that you are wanting to know?" Byron sat silent.

"Well sir, we were..."

"Now don't start with calling me sir. Just call me David. After all, I was friends with your parents."

"Al...alright...David," she stuttered. "We were wondering how well you knew Mr. Pennington."

"Not very well at all. I keep to myself mostly. I leave in the morning, go and get a newspaper, read it in the pub with a pint, and then come back here to tend to my mums. They're over there on the windowsill." He gestured with his cane to a few flowerpots brimming with beautiful red and orange chrysanthemums. "I take a nap after lunch. After my nap I usually sit here and smoke my pipe, read the paper, have some tea, and watch people come and go. In the evenings I go out with a few old friends to get a bite to eat and talk about the old days. I keep out of my neighbors' business, and they keep out of mine."

"So, you are home quite a bit then?" Mira bit her lip waiting for an answer. Byron wrote feverishly.

"Most of the time. I don't like to wander far from where I'm planted once I'm there. Course things were different a half a dozen years ago, but times have changed and so has the functionality of my hips. Why, if I could just engineer myself a new hip the way I used to help engineer your father's inventions, I'd be able to dance a jig right there on the table!"

Mira smiled. He seemed to be warming up to them, and it was nice to hear about her parents again.

"I would have loved to see that."

"Me as well, Miss Blayse. Now were those all of your questions?"

She had plenty of questions. A hope built up inside of her that he would know what had happened the day of her parents' accident. She glanced at Byron for a moment remembering their real reason for being there.

"Just a couple more, if you don't mind."

"Fire away."

"When you watch out the window, do you see people you recognize often?"

"Yes, I do. I may not pry into my neighbors' business, but I do know them all."

"Who do you see most often?"

"Well there is Mrs. O'Neal who lives down the hall. She's got two cats that are always meowing in the night. They make a right awful racket. And there is Mr. Morrison who is always peeking his beady head in everyone else's business. I don't often see Mr. Pennington. He mostly kept to himself. A man after my own heart. From what I know he was an engineer, just like his father before him. We'd exchange a couple words here or there. Of course, when I did see him, it was usually when he was with a young lady."

"A young lady?"

"She came quite often. Started coming around in April or May. Lovely looking girl."

"Do you happen to know her name?"

"Indeed, I do. Molly Bridges. She'd come around once a week, at least. First time I noticed her, I was just leaving to go meet my gents at the pub. She asked if Pennington lived here, I said yes, and she introduced herself. That's all I know about her. I keep out of my neighbor's business, and they keep out of mine."

"Thank you." Mira looked to Byron who finished writing Mr. Graham's words.

"Of course. Anything for the daughter of an old friend." The old man softened over the course of the conversation. Mira gathered that he didn't get visitors often.

"I...I do have two more questions." She glanced at Byron again. He looked surprised but stayed silent. Mr. Graham nodded.

"Did...well were you present at the accident? My parents' accident I mean."

A sad look glazed over his eyes. "Yes, I was."

"Do you remember what happened?"

He looked towards the window. "How could I forget? We were just getting ready for the preliminary test of the *Daydreamer*. Your father was late. He often was. After all, he was always working on at least five projects at once. I waited for him on the outskirts of the docks. All at once, I heard an explosion come from the engine room. Everything after that was a blur. I ran up the scaffolding, but the door closest to me had been locked. I went back down to go around, and finally got to a place where I could get into the airship. There were so many people, it was hard to get through. I got to the engine room and found the steam engine melted and burning. Some police officer was there asking questions. Someone mentioned your parents had been in the engine room. I couldn't believe it. Not only had I thought he was late, but he *never* brought your mother to tests. But when the bodies were found..." He trailed off. Mira swallowed.

"Why would he have brought my mother to this test?"

"He hadn't mentioned that he was bringing her. I do know he thought the *Daydreamer* was the pinnacle of his career. He might have wanted to share that moment with her. I never did figure out what went wrong with the engine. They wouldn't let anyone near it at first and I was taken off the project when Vaporidge bought up Silver Lining."

They sat in silence for a few moments. Byron finished making a note in his journal and then stood.

"Thank you for your cooperation Mr. Graham. You really have been incredibly helpful," Byron said.

"As long as it means I won't be bothered about Pennington again," Mr. Graham stood, leaning his full weight on his cane. Mira stood and smiled at him.

"It's amazing you recognized me like that."

"It's hard to miss those dazzling green eyes and beautiful smile, Miss Blayse. I'm glad you grew up to look like her." He took her hand and kissed it softly before letting go. He lowered his voice. "Say hello to your uncle for me, and be sure to visit again."

"I'd be more than happy to."

Byron offered his hand, which the old man shook before hobbling over to the door. Mira and Byron left, and the door shut behind them. Byron hurried down the stairs and out onto the street, and Mira followed.

"I'm sorry about all that. I didn't realize he would refuse to speak to you."

"Well, we got the information we needed. For both cases, no less. And now I know I just need to bring you along to butter up any witness," he said without looking at her, completely serious in his manners.

"What do you mean?"

"He only let us in because of you, Mira." Byron stopped and looked at her, a strange expression appearing on his face. "I can see what he meant about your eyes."

His voice was softer, and his gaze deeper. He stared at her a moment more, then he turned and continued walking. Mira followed, dumbfounded. He cleared his throat, his voice slowly returning to normal.

"It was quite fortunate that he knew your mother, and that was an excellent line of questioning."

Mira continued to walk next to him in silence. He seemed uneasy now and continued to ramble.

"Now all we have to do is find this Molly Bridges. And I probably ought to stop at Scotland Yard to let them know this has been, and always will be, a murder case."

Mira nodded, still silent. He looked at her with slight concern, then composed his features, looking ahead.

"Have I upset you, Miss Blayse?"

"No. I'm just thinking."

"You're certain? Because if I have upset you, I'll have to write it down, so I'll remember tomorrow," he said. She shook her head, and he continued. "Then what are you thinking about?"

"Quite a few things, really. I mean, I just found out that there is someone else out there who knew my parents. I might be able to come back and perhaps find out more about them and—" She looked up at him and tucked some hair behind her ear. "I'm sorry. You probably don't want to hear all of this."

"No, it's fine. You've had quite a bit of time to think about all of this, and now you have someone to talk to about it. I understand." He smiled.

"Thank you. I just always wondered what my parents were like."

"Hasn't your uncle ever told you?"

"I've heard plenty about my mother. My uncle has no problem telling me about her. But my father is a different story."

"They didn't exactly get along?"

"Not at all. My uncle blames him for the death of my mother. 'If he hadn't come along that wouldn't have happened.' That sort of thing. So, any talk about him usually gets shut down."

"I can see why you'd be excited to find someone else who knew him, then."

"I just wanted to ask him more questions, but they aren't exactly relevant to the case."

"We'll come back, I'm sure. And feel free to ask any questions you like. After all this is *your* case."

"Thank you, Byron."

"Of course. Was that all that was on your mind?"

She hesitated. There was something else. Her green eyes. It was always her eyes. Her uncle was always commenting on them, even the professor and Landon; Mr. Graham had let them in because of them. Her *mother's* eyes. That always bothered her. But when Byron looked at her, his entire demeanor had changed, and it felt different somehow. It didn't bother her when he commented on them. But how was she to explain that to Byron? She managed to come up with a lie to tell him.

"You had just mentioned Scotland Yard, and that reminded me of something that Thatcher's secretary, Juliet had told me."

"Oh?"

"She said that if she were put into your journal, that perhaps eventually you would remember her."

"Oh, she is in my journal."

"She is?"

"Yes, marked as someone to be wary of." His eyes laughed and Mira couldn't help but laugh as well.

"So, you know of her..." She didn't know how to phrase Juliet's actions.

"Affections? Yes. I'm a detective Mira, and she doesn't have much experience in hiding evidence."

"She'll be so disappointed." Mira smiled, stifling another laugh.

"Which is why she won't find out." Byron laughed. "Right?"

"Of course, Mr. Constantine."

She was so busy laughing, she hadn't noticed that they were walking to the cafe until they were right in front of it.

"Well, I suppose this is where I bid you farewell, Miss Mira." Byron tipped his hat.

"Don't we need to go to Scotland Yard?"

"I think I can handle it, and you've had quite the day already. I'll stop there and then go home and read through your police report. Tomorrow we'll go to the newspaper to see if we can't find Molly Bridges via an advertisement. Good evening, Mira."

"Good evening, Byron."

She watched him walk down the street. He stopped at the end of the street and looked back at her with a smile before disappearing around the corner. Mira turned and walked back to Campden Grove, trying in vain to stop her anxious feelings, and to sort out all the thoughts in her head.

September 21ST

The sun rose as Mira fed Nero, buttoned her boots, and slipped out onto the pavement. She bought a croissant from the bakery down the street and ate it on her walk to Palace Court. She hesitated outside of his door, thinking of the incident with the pistol the day before. She decided to knock just to be on the safe side. The door opened.

"Come on in..." Byron was still reading his journal, and he walked away from the door almost as soon as he opened it.

Mira walked in and picked up a few scattered papers and stacked them on a side table, before going over to the piano. She played a few keys before noticing a note pinned to the wall.

"Notice of Inquiry: Seeking information regarding Molly Bridges, in relation to a Mr. Clement Pennington. Please send correspondence to 27 Palace Court, London."

She sat down in her usual place and began to sketch again. Byron paced in the outer hallway. Finishing his journal, he moved to his armchair.

"Good morning, Mira! We certainly got a lot done yesterday."

"Yes, we did. How did Scotland Yard take the news?"

"Thatcher thinks it may still be a suicide, although the left-handedness bit did sway him slightly. He isn't going to close the investigation just yet."

"Well that's good, I suppose."

"Yes, it is."

"Were you able to read through the police report?"

"Indeed. There is certainly something odd around it.

Unfortunately, the officer who wrote it died about ten years ago. Otherwise we'd be able to ask him more about it."

"That is unfortunate."

"But with the information Mr. Graham provided us, we have a bit more to go off of."

"He told us the same story, Byron."

"Except your parents weren't supposed to be there. By his account, your father was late, and your mother never came to those kinds of things. That means something was definitely wrong."

"Why wouldn't Scotland Yard have figured it out?"

"I don't know if you remember this, after all, you would have only been a child at the time, but there was a major trial involving Scotland Yard in 1877."

"I hadn't heard about that. But wouldn't you have only been a few years older than me?"

"Never mind that." He cleared his throat before continuing. "It just so happens that there was some corruption. At this point I believe it has all been snuffed out, but at the time of your parents' accident—"

"It was still corrupted! So that means—"

"There is most definitely more to this than meets the eye."

"Brilliant!" She found herself grinning, and he returned a smile.

"Now I'd say we ought to pop over to the press, send in our advertisement and then perhaps do something different today." He placed his journal in his satchel.

"And what is that?"

"You'll see." He stood, grabbed the note, and moved towards the door. He put on his hat as Mira followed him. They walked along the cobblestone street for a few blocks before Mira's curiosity got the better of her.

"Can't you just tell me?"

"I've been told that telling people things can ruin the surprise." He looked over at her with his laughing eyes, and she smiled, relenting.

"Very well."

"Besides, if you work with me, I assume you like a good mystery."

"It isn't a mystery if I don't have clues!"

"It's just a surprise then."

"You infuriate me sometimes."

"I do? I must make a note of that then," he teased. "Is this what you look like when you are angry?" He gave her a sideways glance.

"No! I mean, maybe." She paused. "Yes."

"Ah, so then I don't infuriate you. Good to know. I won't make a note of it then." She laughed at his statement and he grinned, beginning to laugh as well. Her laugh died down as they approached the Central News Agency.

He opened the door for her, and she stepped inside. The sounds of type being set, several presses printing, and newsboys running from place to place echoed throughout the establishment. Byron followed behind her and went straight towards the editor's office. She followed, but stayed outside on a signal from him. She looked around at the hubbub and overheard two newsboys talking nearby.

"You seen the front page yet? 'Cat Burglar Strikes Again!'"

"Perfect headline really, it'll sell a lot of papers."

"Funny how people get robbed and other people want to read about it."

"It's called being an interested citizen Georgie, and it's what pays them bills."

"Do you think the police will catch 'im?"

"I don't know, and I don't care, as long as we keep getting good headlines. Besides, it's better to have a burglary than another leather apron murder."

The paperboys walked out of earshot, and Byron walked out of the editor's office.

"It's in! Now we just have to wait for a response," he said.

"Did you hear that?"

"Hear what?"

"The burglar has struck again."

"Where did you hear that?" His brow furrowed. She pulled him by the sleeve over to a press that had stopped. She pointed to the headline.

"'Cat Burglar Strikes Again.' If they keep making themselves known they are bound to be caught, and then we'll have a suspect for our case!"

"Correction Mira. An additional suspect." Byron began walking out with purpose. Mira followed close at his heels.

"But wouldn't the burglar be the most likely to have done it? I mean if it was murder, maybe they came into burglarize, heard a noise, picked something up, and ended up killing him."

"That is a possible solution, yes. A rather good one at that. We just need evidence to support it. And for all we know, this could go deeper than the surface." His gaze got serious for a moment.

"So then are we going to Scotland Yard?"

"Heavens, no. That can wait. I believe that we have somewhere else to be."

"The surprise you mean?"

"Yes." He kept walking down the street, pausing to wait for a carriage to pass before turning towards the docks.

Two TYPES of ships anchored at the Mooreland docks. Ships that sailed in the water, and ships that sailed in the air. Technically speaking, both types ran on steam, however only the ships that travelled through the water were called steamships. The Vaporidge Steamship Company owned Mooreland. Their steamships carried passengers and cargo across the Atlantic to America, sailed down the coast of Africa, and brought goods back from India. Their airships carried passengers around England, and crossed the channel to France, and soon enough they would travel to Russia. There were many companies that owned a fleet of steamships, but only

Vaporidge had perfected the art of flying. That is to say, Silver Lining perfected it, and Vaporidge bought it.

The docks were divided into two sections. One went down to the waterfront of the Thames. There the steamships were moored and ready to unload cargo or head out to the ocean. The second section went to a bit of higher ground, with airships moored to a large scaffolding with staircases connecting each piece. Byron veered towards the higher docks and Mira's breath caught in her throat.

They approached the docking area and moved towards a large red balloon. Cables crisscrossed over the surface, creating a quilted pattern. The cables were connected to the main passenger chassis which looked to be almost one thousand feet in length. It was significantly larger than she had expected.

She didn't realize she had stopped moving until she noticed Byron's scrutinizing stare. Her face reddened, and she started walking again.

"Are you alright, Mira?"

"Quite. I've just never been this close to one before."

"I see." He pulled two tickets out of his pocket and proceeded up the stairs. When he reached the top, he turned and offered his hand. Hesitating a moment, she took it and he helped her up, giving her hand a comforting squeeze before letting go. He passed the tickets to the conductor and led the way into the airship.

The highly embellished interior was in stark contrast to the docks below. Mira knew of airships holding up to one hundred and twenty people, with elaborate guest quarters and restaurants, observation decks and ballrooms. The halls were carpeted in red to match the canvas of the balloon. She ran her hand along the inner walls covered in a cream wallpaper with golden fleur-de-lis accents. A mahogany chair rail ran along the wall with portrait and landscape paintings dotted along the way. The outer wall was clear, curved glass that ran all the way around the exterior of the airship to give the best view. They walked along the corridor looking at paintings or out the observation windows in silence.

Midway through the corridor there was a hallway going back into the inner wall. Countless doors led to crew and passenger quarters. They rounded the bend and came to the main observation lounge. Glass nearly surrounded the place, with armchairs and couches provided. Several people already occupied them. A hall continued past and back around to the rear of the ship. The back wall of the observation room held a door that led to the ballroom and dining areas.

As she explored, she sensed Byron's gaze on her. She made a mental note and became increasingly curious as to why they were there. He would tell her eventually, right? After looking in the ballroom she came back to the observation area and took a seat near the glass exterior. Byron joined her. She bit her lip and averted her gaze.

"This is entirely wonderful, but I am wondering. Why are we here?"

"I thought it would be a nice change in routine."

"It is nice, but don't we have a case to solve?"

"We'll have plenty of time for that."

"Shall we?"

"Yes. We shall. You see, this ship is making a round trip today. It starts here, and then it flies to Bristol. Once there it will refuel and drop off some passengers, and then it will turn around and fly back probably before seven tonight. I certainly hope you didn't have any plans." His eyes twinkled.

"I do now." She smiled. "But that doesn't answer the question about the case."

"Ah, yes. I figured that this would be ample time for you to ride an airship for the first time and do your sightseeing, and then with however much time that leaves us, this does happen to be the airship that our friend Pennington was working on. The *Horizon*. I thought we might have a friendly chat with his previous coworkers."

"I knew you had a plan."

"Always do. Course this outing was a surprise, was it not?"

"Yes. It was. A lovely surprise."

"There you have it. I'm also investing in my secretary's well-being."

"Thank you."

A megaphone crackled above them. "Good morning, ladies and gentlemen! This is your captain speaking. We have just finished our preliminary checks and shall soon be underway. Just thought I would let you know before we start up the engines. Our flight is round-trip from London to Bristol. Happy flying!"

The megaphone died down. Mira noticed that her hands were gripping the armrests of her chair. This was it. They were about to take off. Being on the airship itself wasn't much of an issue. After all, it was entirely safe on the ground. But the addition of air and height made it potentially lethal. She closed her eyes. She knew that was a lie. Her parents' accident had happened on the ground, after all. But none had happened since then. She would be fine. She felt the engine rumble beneath her, and she trembled ever so slightly. Then, out of nowhere, she felt a hand fall on top of hers.

"Mira?" Byron said. She opened her eyes and looked at him. "It's alright Mira. We'll be fine."

Her breaths became steady again. Something in his voice soothed her, and his expression was so sincere. He shifted his hand, so he held hers and gently pulled her to a standing position, then steered her to the window. The airship rose, and she felt a type of weightlessness. They drifted higher and higher until they were at eye level with the clouds. It was exhilarating. It was liberating. It was safe. She glanced at Byron and he quickly looked back out the window. She smiled softly and watched as London got smaller and smaller.

"Thank you."

He nodded, not looking at her, but at the clouds outside. Then he let go of her hand. "Shall we go and explore some more?" He grinned at her.

THEY SPENT a good portion of the day looking over every inch of the airship that they could. They ate in the restaurant, and Mira couldn't tell if the French toast really was better on the airship, or if it only tasted that way because they were flying. The views from the observation windows continued to astound her. She sketched clouds and other passengers in the observation deck while Byron searched for a steward. They needed permission to go below the main deck and talk to the crew. She just finished the shading on one drawing when he came back.

"They gave us permission. Shall we?" He offered an arm. She took it.

"Yes. We shall."

He led her around the main hallway towards the center of the ship where all the passenger quarters were. They turned onto that hallway and made their way past door after door until they reached the center. A door marked "Crew Only" stood there. Byron paused.

"I must warn you; We shall be going outside."

She nodded, and he opened the door. A gust of wind pulled at her skirts as they descended a spiral staircase.

The engines and crew quarters were slightly detached from the main chassis. The design was an attempt to eliminate noise and rumbling for passengers on the main deck of the ship. The chassis containing the engine rooms and crew quarters was suspended from heavy cables that ran all the way up to the balloon about twenty feet below the passenger deck. In order to reach it you had to take a set of stairs outside of the confines of the airship in the open air.

The wind bit at her skin and pulled her hair and skirts in every direction, but she grinned, nonetheless. Byron kept a hold of her hand to keep her steady as he led her into the belly of the beast.

The closed door snuffed out any exterior light. Sweat beaded on her forehead, and she felt queasy from the smell of sulfur. When her eyes adjusted, she found that everything was made of metal, presumably aluminum. Byron led her past crew quarters and an engine room to the front of the ship. A wheel-like helm was the focal point of the room. Foreign instruments lined the walls. A large window filled up the front portion. Several airship operators attended to buttons and switches on each wall. Byron approached one of them.

"Excuse me, do you have a moment to spare?"

"Ah yes, you are the private detective?" The operator looked up from his work. He was a bit heavyset and older. His hair was dirty blond and his face red from the heat of the control room. Mira opened her sketchbook to make a rough outline.

"Yes. Might I ask what your name is?"

"Blake Gill. Yours?"

"Byron Constantine. Mira Blayse." Byron gestured to each of them in turn.

"Right. I was told you wanted to know about good ol' Clemmy. Right sad that he's dead, but it doesn't surprise me that he's done himself in."

"You think he killed himself?"

"Well that's what the coppers say, now innit?" He turned away from his panel and grabbed a cloth, wiping the grease from his fingers and the sweat off his brow.

"For now, yes. Why doesn't it surprise you?"

"Well, when he left us, he was right depressed. I mean, he acted normal enough when he was on the job. Saying his good mornings, how are the kids, that sort of thing, cheerful enough. But I mean when you're on the job you're so busy you kind of forget things, you know? But when we would go on break, he would always go off on his own. Don't know where he disappeared to. He'd be wandering the ship for hours when we docked, and he weren't on duty. Like I said, I think he was depressed. The spark had come right out of him. Didn't have any family to speak of. I think his brother got sent off to Australia for something or other. And his father died in a tragic accident or something like that. Course, before he did, he was one of the best engineers in the business."

"Pennington or his father?"

"Oh. His father. Sorry about that. Anyway, ol' Clemmy didn't really have anything other than the airship in his life that I know about. And him quitting his job all sudden-like, what else could it be?"

"I see. And how long have you been working for this company?"

"Coming close to ten years now, I think."

"And you said you don't know where he went during his breaks?"

"Yes, it's like he disappeared clear off of the ship."

"These breaks occurred mid-flight then?"

"Some of them, yes. But of course, the breaks we have when we are docked are shore leaves often enough. Most of us go our separate ways as it is during those times."

"It just surprised you that he disappeared during the mid-flight breaks?"

"Yeah, usually everyone that is off duty goes and we all have a pint and a bite to eat together. He did that for the first few months, and then, like I said, we never saw him except in the control rooms."

"When was the last time you saw Mr. Pennington?"

"It was his last day of full labor. We all said our goodbyes. He looked cheerful enough, but there must have been some awful reason for him quitting. None of us understood it. When he first came on, he said that it was a dream come true. That 'nothing could compare to soaring among the clouds,' he said. So, when he up and left, not one year after he started, we all thought it strange. He said, 'I'm going to bigger and better things lads,' and off he went."

"Anything else you think we should know?"

"Nothing I haven't already told the constabulary, sir."

"Thank you very much, Mr. Gill."

"Of course, sir, of course. Now I ought to get back to work."

He turned back to his panel. They talked to a few other operators who all had similar stories. All of them thought it odd that he left, and none of them knew where he went during the breaks when he seemingly disappeared. They left the control room and went back towards the stairway to return to the main passenger deck.

"Now, it really is pointing towards suicide, isn't it?" Mira said.

"Not entirely. We just need to determine where he went during his breaks. He couldn't have entirely disappeared. He had to go somewhere, and someone had to have seen where he went."

"So, we are going to come back?"

"Yes. We are going to come back."

They made their way up the windy staircase. The clouds changed from white to grey and the wind picked up. Mira felt a twinge of apprehension as they climbed the stairs. She shivered from the relative cold. When Byron reached the top of the stairs, he took her hand and pulled her into the safety of the airship. He closed the door behind her, let go of her hand, and they walked back to the observation deck. The clouds loomed ever closer as they passed the grand windows. Mira measured her breaths and held her shaking arms.

"Mira, you do realize that I am a detective, and although I have memory issues when I sleep, I still have my deductive powers during the day?"

"Yes?"

"Then why are you trying to hide the fact that you are scared of the storm?"

"I...well...um..." She looked away.

"You don't have to act brave for me. I understand."

"I didn't mean—"

Lightning crackled through the clouds near the ship and the resulting thunder rumbled through the deck. She jumped with a slight shriek and he caught both of her arms, steadying her. She looked up at him and saw the concern in his deep blue eyes. Her muscles relaxed.

"It's going to be alright, Mira." He studied her face and softened.

"Byron, I—" The megaphone above them crackled on.

"Good afternoon ladies and gentlemen. This is your captain speaking. Due to the weather conditions we will have to land the airship. We aren't certain how long we shall be grounded. We will be landing near Marlborough. We apologize for the inconvenience."

"It would seem that we'll be staying a bit longer than I had anticipated. I'm sorry, Mira."

"No. It's quite alright. I'd rather we land."

As night closed in, the storm continued. They sat with the other passengers in the observation lounge and watched the rain slip down the glass. The captain announced that any passengers who did not have room accommodations would be provided them. Byron acquired two keys for adjoining rooms. He led her to the back of the ship where they would be staying. They walked in a still silence as the thunder cracked outside the ship. He stopped next to one of the doors and turned to her.

"Mira...this will be the first documented occasion since the accident that I have stayed overnight anywhere that wasn't 27 Palace Court."

"Yes?"

"I'm going to be disoriented when I wake up."

"Yes. I believe you are."

"I'm going to need you to explain everything to me. I shall be setting notes around my bed to ensure that I know of something. You will come in the morning to make sure I remember?"

"Yes, Byron."

"Good. Good." It was his turn to be nervous. Up in the sky he exuded confidence. Here on the ground he seemed scared of the prospect of staying somewhere new.

"Goodnight?" She gently touched his arm, pushing him towards his room.

"Yes. Right. Goodnight." He handed her key to her, turned, and entered his room. She watched the door close and then entered her own room.

It was small, but it fit her purpose. A door connected her room and his, only separated by a lock, really. She sat on her bed thinking about the unexpected route the day had followed. On a normal day, she would be back at her rooms around this time. And what about poor Nero? Hopefully he could fend for himself.

Her thoughts drifted to Byron. His entire day, with the newspaper and the airship, her fear and his compassion, the questions, the investigation, all of it would be forgotten. Even though this was normal for Byron, it was burdensome for her to wrap her head around. How could so much be lost in such a short period of time? What kind of accident could have happened to him to cause his memory loss? The more she thought about things, the more she realized that she knew little to nothing about Byron. And now she was, as her uncle would say, gallivanting all over the countryside with someone who was practically a stranger. She laughed a little as she got ready for bed. What did she know about Byron? Practically nothing. She knew he was a private detective who forgot. Other than that, everything was a complete mystery to her. She added "ask Byron about himself," to her mental list of things to do. Although the mystery of how he lost his memory seemed a bit of a large subject to breach. She laid down on the bed. That would have to wait until the rest of the mysteries were out of the way. And when that time came, she would help him remember for good.

September 22ND

After tossing and turning for half the night, she decided sleeping was fruitless. She determined to help Byron at the first sign of trouble, despite her lack of sleep. She waited in the darkness for any sounds to come from the adjoining door, her thoughts keeping her company as she mulled over the case. One murder. Three suspects. She spread her sketches of each witness or suspect across her bed. Some were less than satisfactory as she hadn't had time to perfect them. The cat burglar still prowled in North London but that could be a completely different matter unrelated to the murder. Pennington's place had been searched, at least. But perhaps that was something else as well. There were other reasons for breaking and entering other than burglary. Had anything been stolen? Only Clement Pennington would know. Or possibly the woman. Molly Bridges. Did she kill him after a fight? Motive. That was one of the few things that hadn't come up in her discussions with Byron. What motive could there possibly be for killing Clement Pennington? Maybe it *was* suicide. Her eyes grazed over the sketch of Doyle Morrison. He certainly didn't have motive, but he was in the vicinity.

And the accident of 1870. Mr. Graham had been surprised that either of her parents were involved. After all, her father had been late and her mother shouldn't have been there at all. But the bodies were proof of their involvement.

She heard the bed creak in Byron's room. He was awake. She held her breath listening, wondering when she should intervene. Sounds of confused mumblings and the rustling of papers came through the door. She tiptoed to the door that separated them and knocked, unlocking her side. The door opened with a bang.

"What the devil is going on?" Byron's hair was a complete mess and his suit disheveled. He, like her, slept in his clothes the night before. She stood there in shock for a moment. Wasn't he going to leave himself notes?

"Well?" he said. A smirk stirred at the corners of Mira's lips. His eyes brightened from the confusion and he looked more handsome because of it. She pushed that thought away.

"I suppose the first thing to say is, it's nice to meet you, Byron."

"What?"

"I mean, this is the first time for you at least. You've never seen me before in your life. Except I've met you every day for over a week."

"What on Earth are you talking about?"

"You really don't remember anything, do you?" She searched his face for recognition.

"I'll have you know I have an excellent memory. But I do know one thing, I don't remember *you* so if you'd care to explain what's going on."

"Right. There is quite a bit to tell you then." She bit her lip.

"Such as?"

"Well, good morning is a good place to start." She walked past him to look for his journal. She knew anything she said would likely make him more upset. His notes hadn't worked to remind him. There were too many important things she might forget to tell him, even if he did believe her. The only solution was to find the journal.

"Good morning?" He was unconvinced. "How is it a good morning? You haven't answered any of my questions! Where am I and who are you and," His face flushed. "I didn't give you permission to come into my room, if it is my room that is." He turned watching her search.

"And I didn't exactly give you permission to take me on this airship yesterday but there we have it." Her voice trailed off as she looked under the bed for the journal. "Now where have you put it?"

"I beg your pardon, but we're on an airship? And put what where? What are you talking about, Miss?"

"You usually call me Mira, and I am referring to your journal. Please sit down."

"Sit down? How can I sit down while a woman I've never met searches a room I've never seen before?" He seemed to realize the ridiculousness of his statement as he spoke.

"If you sit down, you can calm down a little, think a bit more clearly, and find that all of this is obviously a dream, if it makes so little sense to you." She moved to the other side of the room. He stood there pondering for a second before sitting down.

"Are you a dream then?" He narrowed his eyes.

"Do I look like a dream?" she responded. A puzzled look came over his face.

"This feels real. And I don't remember dreaming about you before."

"And that's precisely the problem."

"What are you talking about?"

She found the journal on the top shelf of the closet, retrieved it, and sat next to him on the bed, tracing the edge of the journal with her fingers.

"What is the last thing you remember, Byron?"

"Going to bed last evening. I had just received a lead on a case I was investigating. I was going to stop off at Scotland Yard first thing in the morning at noon to see if they had any additional information, and then I was going to go and head up the lead."

"So, you don't remember anything at all after that?"

"Not a thing. Not sure why I am telling you anything though. What is that book? And you haven't explained what is going on."

"You're always telling me to use my observational skills Byron, and now you are off the hook?" She smiled, teasing him a bit. He clenched his teeth for a moment, then broke out in an enigmatic smile. She tensed.

"Mira is it?" She nodded, and he continued. "From what I can gather, considering that I am in a completely different place than I slept last night, you seem to know me, but I don't know you...hmm. There are two options that could be at work here."

"Go on."

"Well judging by the state of your clothes, you've slept in them. I seem to have slept in mine as well. According to you, we're on an airship. You are right in saying I've never laid eyes on you before. You are acting calm and collected indicating you've done something like this before. I've been getting close to the end of this case. It's only logical that they would try to stop me, but why send you?" He stood and began to pace. "It just doesn't make sense." He stopped and turned defensively towards her, looking her over. "You don't seem to be the mercenary type."

She started laughing. "You can't be serious."

He stared at her for a few moments more. Looking her over. Really trying to determine who she was. He looked into her eyes and softened.

"No, I suppose I'm not. You couldn't be one of them."

"One of who?"

"No matter. What's your name again?"

"Samira. Samira Blayse. You hired me as your secretary."

"Why don't I remember you?"

"Well what was your other logical option?"

"I'd rather not say."

She stood and took a cautious step towards him, studying his face. His anger dissipated, but his confusion remained. "Just read this." She held the journal out to him. He stood there for a moment before he took it.

She walked into the other room, attempting to calm the butterflies again. She made the bed and cleaned up the few belongings she had brought with her. With any luck they would be returning home today. She was arranging her tangled mess of hair when Byron came in.

"Miss Blayse I—"

"Mira. Please call me Mira."

"Of course. I'm so sorry, Mira."

"Apology accepted."

He stood there for a moment in silence. She could see him in the mirror, looking at her reflection. She finished brushing her hair and put down the comb. He cleared his throat.

"Hmm. Well, if you are ready, we ought to go and see how likely it is we can get back to London. After all, your cat must be missing you."

She whirled towards him. "My cat? I never told you about Nero."

"You have cat fur on the hem of your skirt, and besides," he gestured towards the bed where her sketchbook lay open, "a drawing like that must have come from a live subject. Nero? That's a good name for a cat. Does he play the violin?" His eyes smiled at her as he turned back into his room leaving Mira at a loss for words once again.

THE WEATHER HAD CLEARED up sufficiently that the airship could take flight. They landed in Bristol, and the captain informed everyone that the ship would be grounded for a few hours to check on the canvas of the balloon and to make repairs. Byron paced in the observation lounge, back and forth along the front panel of glass.

"Shall we go for a walk? The airship isn't going anywhere for a while." He stopped and turned to her.

"Alright. Lead the way." She stood and followed him out.

At the ramp he offered her his arm, and she took it as they strolled through Bristol. The city was smaller than London, but it still bustled with activity. She could see steamships being loaded from a lower dock like the ones in London. A train sped by on a path back to London. It was nice to be in a different setting.

"Shall we get something to eat?" Byron stopped walking. A small teahouse stood in front of them. Mira nodded. She got the sense that he was trying to apologize for the morning. While they waited for their breakfast and tea, Mira decided to take a chance.

"Byron, you know we never actually talk about you."

"Hmm?" He looked back to her from the window, struck from his reverie.

"You've asked all about me, and I've told you, but you've never told me about yourself. Just that you were a detective working with Scotland Yard."

"I haven't? Well, I suppose it never was important."

"Do you have any family?"

"Everyone has family, Mira." He chuckled a little. "I have four siblings. A sister and three brothers. I don't really talk to them much. They're all older than me."

He looked at her, an expression Mira didn't recognize crossing his face. He seemed hesitant to tell her something. He looked away again and continued.

"My father died a few years before my memory loss started. My mother lives in Hertfordshire, and I try to visit her often. If I remember, that is." A sadness came to his eyes. Mira paused, not certain if she should keep questioning.

The waiter brought out two trays of food. Byron nodded in thanks. They ate in silence for a few minutes.

"Have I really never talked to you about my past?" He looked up at her for a moment then back at his omelet.

"No. I suppose I've never asked, either." She nibbled at a piece of toast.

"You can ask any question you'd like. Just know there are some questions I won't answer."

She hesitated again. "Well, I was wondering about something. Yesterday you mentioned that it was an accident that caused your memory loss."

"Yes. It was."

"Were you very young when it happened?"

"I was twenty-three. So, based on the dates in my journal, over four years ago."

"Were you already working with Scotland Yard then?"

"Hmm? Well, yes. I suppose. Puzzles had always been a hobby of mine all throughout school. When I came to London, I happened to come across a few police reports, and I sent in a few anonymous tips. Fred Wensley helped with a few, before he was an officer of course." He stopped. "You do know about Fred, don't you?" When she nodded in the affirmative, he continued. "I started coming in and talking to Thatcher. He wanted me to go to police school. I thought that was rubbish. I was eighteen when I solved my first full case. And of course, my family wasn't necessarily supportive of my becoming a detective. I suppose the chief inspector is the closest thing I've got to family at this point."

"And he doesn't know what happened to you either?"

"That's the one mystery neither of us have ever solved. Maybe one day I'll figure it out, but I just can't retrace my steps if I don't remember them."

After breakfast, they walked back to the airship. The scaffolding differed from the Mooreland docks in London. She clearly saw the side of the ship. There were all sorts of seams and rivets holding different pieces of metal together, almost like dozens of doors along the side, although they likely couldn't be opened. They went up the ramp and back onto the observation deck. Mira sat down in an armchair and Byron sat across from her.

"Have you ever had a secretary before?" She broke the silence again.

"No. I never thought I really needed one. I suppose it came on a whim one day, but I don't remember how it happened."

"Do you think I've helped?"

He paused for a moment. "My journal seems to dictate that." He went silent and looked out the window. She bit her lip and looked down.

Soon enough they were touching down in London. The airship finished its journey, alighting gracefully at the dock like a bird perching on a branch. Byron escorted Mira down the ramp to the dock. He was quiet and contemplative as they walked, while her own thoughts preoccupied her. Eventually they came to the cafe, where Byron stopped, looking up.

"This is where we met," he said in a matter of fact sort of way.

"Yes, it is." She searched his expression for meaning but found none. Suddenly he turned towards her and grabbed her arms, pulling her closer. Her eyes widened, looking up at him.

"Mira. Every day I forget you. Every day you watch me in my forgetfulness."

"Well, yes." She tensed. What was he getting at? He released her arms and stepped back.

"Am I ever a different person?" He looked away.

"A different person?"

"Every day, am I different? I'm sure I respond differently, years of my life I don't remember..." He trailed off.

"Well, I suppose, you are a little different each day. But ultimately you are Byron, Byron."

"Is it hard?"

"Is what?"

"Watching me forget. Not remember you."

"Um...well...I..." She bit her lip. He turned away from her. That was enough of an answer for him. He hesitated for a moment then lowered his head. He started walking away from her and the cafe.

"I think it's best if we continued on Monday," he called back. "Same time as always, whatever that may be."

"Byron—"

"Good day, Mira," he said firmly. "Enjoy your Sunday."

She stood there in the street for a moment as he ran off once more. It *was* hard. On one hand it was incredibly wondrous to wake up every morning and not know what awaited her at Byron's. But on the other it tortured her to only have the memories to herself. Then again, how was it for Byron? It hadn't even occurred to her how hard it would be for him. She wanted to know what he was thinking. How he was feeling. But he was unreadable and stoic. She watched until he turned the corner out of sight. She felt her stomach turn in knots. It wasn't fair. For either of them.

September 23ᴿᴰ

Mira painted over her sketch of an airship with a wash of blue watercolors. She finished the sketch in the morning before she went to St. Paul's for the midday service. It had been impossible to concentrate. Her thoughts kept drifting back to the previous days with Byron. How exciting they all had been! The exhilaration from the airship flight was exactly as she dreamed. And she met a family friend and found out more about her parents' deaths. She frowned as her sketch smudged under the wash. Why were her parents there? If it was murder... She set her sketchbook to the side with a huff. It wasn't a question of "if" in her mind. Her parents *were* murdered. Why did that give her so much peace? She stood with a huff. Why was she hoping for that? That wasn't right. But, then again, if it was the truth, it needed to be made clear. Hopefully the professor would have some answers.

She looked at the clock. Nearly time to go to her uncle's for dinner. Oh, how she wished she was going to Byron's. But he needed some time and so did she. The day before was a confusing mess. She felt butterflies in her stomach just thinking about it. No. Not butterflies. Byron was her friend; she was his secretary. She couldn't possibly have feelings for him. Could she? She stood and moved over to the window. Even if she did, they would have to wait. Not only was it foolish to think he could ever fall for her with his memory problem, but they had mysteries to solve. Was it even possible to fall in love in such a short time? Well, it was possible. But that kind of love rarely lasted. Her parents had courted over several years after their initial acquaintance.

Was that what these feelings were? Her trying to fill the gap her parents left? The one her uncle and brother and Landon couldn't even fill? If she did like Byron, was it for him or for the idea of him? She shook her head. She shouldn't even entertain those thoughts. She didn't have feelings for Byron, and that was that. She had no reason to worry. Of course, she had to keep repeating that to herself as she walked to her uncle's house.

"Good afternoon, Miss." Landon opened the door before she knocked once again.

"How on earth do you always know when I'm here?" She walked past him and took off her coat.

"I suppose it just comes with being a butler." He had a twinkle in his eye. She laughed.

"Is the professor coming again today?"

"He is already in the front room." He took her coat and hung it on the hook.

"Fantastic."

The professor sat in an armchair reading a book when she entered. It hadn't been her plan to discuss what happened in the previous week with anyone other than Byron, but she needed to talk to someone.

"Hello, Professor!" She sat in an armchair opposite from his. He looked up and smiled.

"Why, hello Mira!" He closed the book.

"I'm sorry to interrupt your reading, but I'd like to talk to you." She glanced at the door. "If possible, without my uncle hearing?"

"What is it?" His tone turned serious.

"About what we spoke about last week—"

"What about it?"

"It seems I've found a lead or two."

"You have?" He raised an eyebrow in surprise.

"With help, of course. You remember the man from the cafe, the one I sketched? He's a private detective."

"Please tell me you haven't asked him to help you."

"You don't want me to lie, do you?" Her eyes lit up. He set the book aside.

"What have you found?" He rubbed his temples.

She bit her lip. "The police report mentioned that you identified the bodies."

The professor paled.

"Is that true?"

"Yes. It is." He looked down.

"What happened?"

"Do you really want me to describe it to you?" He looked up at her with wet eyes.

She glanced away. "I suppose not."

"I assure you; it was them."

A heavy silence fell over the two of them. The professor stood and moved to the window.

"I'm sorry if I was your only lead. But that's all I know."

"No need to apologize. I shouldn't have brought it up." Mira's voice cracked.

"So, I was your last lead?" He turned back towards her, a mixture of emotions flooding his expression.

"Well, we did find an inconsistency between the police report and an eyewitness."

"You've located an eyewitness? After eighteen years?"

"Yes. Mr. David Graham. He worked with my father. He said my father was running late that day, and my mother shouldn't have even been there."

The professor paced across the room. "How does that prove that it wasn't an accident? People are in the wrong places at the wrong time quite often. And why didn't the police find anything?"

"There was a court case in 1877 that cleared out the corruption in Scotland Yard. Before then it was entirely possible for policemen to be bribed."

"Your detective told you that?"

"Indeed, he did."

"Mira, what if he's just giving you false hope?" he said, exasperated.

"The evidence is there. Any hope comes from that, not him."

"Where is the motive? Why on earth would anyone want your parents to be dead?" he shouted before sagging back into his armchair.

She went quiet. She hadn't thought about that. She went over situation after situation trying to find a reason. She took a breath.

"Well you knew my parents. Did they have any enemies?"

"No, they didn't. Your father was almost a celebrity. Everyone loved them."

"But those who run in higher circles always have enemies."

"Mira, you just have to accept that it was an accident. What happened, happened. There doesn't have to be an ulterior motive for it."

"But, Professor, we found—"

"What is the name of this private detective of yours?"

"Byron Constantine. And he's brilliant."

"Is he the one without a memory? Mira, how can you expect him to help with this?"

"He's solved forty-one cases before now without a problem."

"But if this truly is a mystery to be solved, this case is eighteen years old. No clues, no traces. What could he possibly find or remember?"

Mira's thoughts sank down around her. Maybe they did have a lead, but where would it even take them? They knew that her parents were in the wrong place at the wrong time, but without more witnesses they couldn't determine anything. She felt her hopes falling within her when Landon called them into dinner.

The rest of the evening blurred together. She knew she participated in the conversation, but she couldn't remember any of the topics. She excused herself early from the evening and walked home, the lulling sounds of the city crashing against her ears attempting in vain to stir her from her thoughts. She went over the events again and again. Nothing. Another dead end. Another blockade. And even though she had Byron to help her now, what help would he be without his memory? She trudged up the steps to her rooms.

He had given her plenty of help. Because of him, she was able to read the reports and meet Mr. Graham. But what else could he possibly do? The words of the professor echoed through her head. She tried to shake it off as she got ready for bed, but the thoughts kept coming back. What if there wasn't an answer? What if he was right? She lay down and stared at the ceiling, willing the anxiety to cease.

September 1888 24TH

The sun crept through the window, the sharp slit of light beaming on Mira's face. She stirred and pulled the covers tight over around her. The shifting blankets left her feet in the cold, and she wrestled to get them back under again. Why did it have to be morning? She snuggled further into the blankets, feeling her breath on her face. Nero found his way under the covers and nibbled on her toes, asking for fish. She grimaced at his rough, wet tongue and forced herself to get up. Nero mewed at her feet.

"Alright, alright! I'm up. Apparently, you can't do anything without me!"

She didn't care to determine whether she was referring to the cat or to Byron and pushed her frustrated exhaustion to the side as she trudged into the kitchen. She paused to look at the time. Nine o'clock. Byron could wait, couldn't he? She gave Nero his breakfast and sat down to her toast and eggs in silence. Whether or not she wanted to admit it, she'd fallen into a routine with Byron.

After breakfast, she headed out to Palace Court. Clouds congregated and blocked out the sunlight. It was quarter past ten when she arrived, and she felt a few drops of rain as she stepped into the doorway. She pulled out the key and chuckled. What response would she receive today? To her surprise, the door flung open and Byron jerked her inside, closed the door and pinned her against the wall.

"Byron!" Her key clattered to the floor.

"Where in heavens have you been? I've been worried sick!"

"What?"

"You're late."

"You remember?" she whispered.

"Er...no. I read up on my journal before you got here."

"And you were worried about someone you had never met?" She retrieved her key and pushed past him into the living room. Of course, he didn't remember! It was foolish to think otherwise. The professor's words rang in her ears. He would *never* remember. If she knew that, why did it hurt so much? Her eyes stung, as she focused on the room. Papers were strewn everywhere. A rather large address book lay open on the side table.

"I know enough about you from my journal. I know enough to know you are punctual." He followed her into the living room.

"Right."

"I'm afraid I don't have your address, or else I would have called upon you to ensure that you were alright."

"Well, let's clean this up, then." Mira knelt to pick up the papers. Byron stooped to help her. She turned away from him to better organize the notes and hide her eyes.

"You are alright, aren't you?"

"Yes, Byron. I am."

"Why were you late?"

"I must have gotten preoccupied. I'm sorry," she muttered, brushing a stray tear away when he wasn't looking.

"No, it's quite alright." He picked up the last of the papers and put them in the filing system. "Would you like a cup of tea?" he asked.

She glanced up at him, meeting his sincere blue eyes. She relented. "That would be lovely."

A few minutes later the kettle whistled, and Mira settled into her armchair as Byron handed her a cup.

"Thank you." She sipped at it, letting the warmth flow through her. He nodded, sat down, took a sip from his own cup, and opened his journal.

"What we have here are plenty of facts," he started. "All of his coworkers believe that he was depressed and that his depression is what caused him to leave the Vaporidge company. From what we can tell, he had a love life of some sort. Mr. Graham has told us about Molly Bridges. One burglar that hasn't been found. Hopefully in the last day or so I have received some sort of answer to that newspaper reply. There is still the question of the cause of death—"

"I see several questions, Byron," she interrupted.

"Well yes, of course. Which ones are you toying with now?"

"Cause of death, motive, whether the house was searched or burglarized..."

"Yes, that would be two different things in my book as well. Please continue."

"Where did he go during his breaks, why did he leave the company, and what was the state of his relationship with Molly Bridges?"

"All excellent questions. And surely we shall answer them all!" He set down his teacup and pressed his fingertips together. He looked over at her. "Where should we start Mira?"

"Well, perhaps with the post." She leaned over and picked up the letters on the table, handing them to him.

"Ah yes. To see if we have received an answer." He picked up a letter opener from his side table and slid it across the top of each envelope, reading each in turn then setting them to the side.

"Aha! Here we have it."

"A response?"

"Number 10, Caxton Street. It says we can come between noon and two o'clock on Mondays or Wednesdays."

Mira glanced up at the clock. "Well today is Monday, and it is nearly noon now."

"Yes. Indeed, it is. Let's go."

They cleaned up their tea things, and Byron grabbed his hat. Soon they were on the street. Byron called for a hansom cab and helped her into it before settling in beside her. They travelled in silence for a while, listening to the beating of the rain on the top of the carriage.

"We probably ought to stop by Scotland Yard on our way back. I haven't come in for a few days," he said.

"Will they worry?"

"Not as much as I worried about you this morning."

"It was only an hour. For someone you hadn't met before."

"You mentioned that earlier. But I had met you. I've met you almost every day for twelve days, Mira."

"But you don't remember me."

"And for that I am truly sorry."

He gave her a soft smile, and the carriage pulled up in front of 10 Caxton Street before Mira could respond. Byron stepped out and offered a hand, which she took, stepping down.

He moved up to the door and knocked. Mira moved beside him as footsteps echoed on the other side of the door. The echoing stopped, and the door opened. There stood a tall, young lady, not more than thirty years old with curly red hair tied back tight against her head and red lips that caused severe contrast with her pale skin. Her brown eyes seemed dark as chocolate. Mira could see the chain of a necklace, but it was hidden underneath her lace bodice.

"May I help you?" Her voice rang out, timid and melodic.

"My name is Byron Constantine of Palace Court and this is my secretary Samira Blayse." He gestured to Mira.

"Oh, you sent out the advertisement in the paper. You were wondering about Clement?"

"Yes ma'am. Are you Molly Bridges?"

"Yes, I am."

"In that case, may we come in?" Byron asked.

"Of course. Please do." She stepped back and allowed them past before closing the door. She led them into a sitting room. It was a simple room. The side tables sat bereft of books, ornaments, or portraits. The curtains hung limp near the window. There were several chairs of various sizes and levels of comfort. Mira did like how the light came through the window, though.

"Do sit down," Molly said as she took a seat herself. Mira sat on the couch and pulled out her sketchbook. Byron sat beside her.

"I must warn you; I have an appointment in about thirty minutes, but I'm yours until then. What do you want to know?"

"How close were you with the deceased?" Byron began.

"Deceased?" Her eyes widened.

"Yes, Mr. Pennington."

"You can't mean..." Molly's eyes filled with tears. Byron softened his voice.

"I didn't realize you didn't know. I'm sorry for your loss."

"What happened?" Molly's voice shook, trying to keep her composure.

"His landlord found him dead in his rooms on September tenth."

"He killed himself?"

"That's what we're trying to determine. Could you tell us what you know about him?"

"I'll try." She stifled a sob. "With Clement, well, we had been courting for several months. Since April." She fidgeted with her hands and looked down.

"Where did you meet?"

"Well it is rather silly now that I think about it." She gave a watery laugh and looked out the window.

"We were walking in opposite directions actually, he came around the corner just as I was approaching, and we bumped into each other. We both had papers in our hands, and they went flying everywhere. I accidentally took some of his, and he took some of mine. I was home by the time I realized, so I put an advertisement in the paper. Then we met up to exchange the papers at a cafe. We accidentally bumped into each other again the week after that and purposefully met again the next week, and then we seemed to be meeting almost every day. Until now, that is." Her voice cracked, and she looked down again. "You see, I was used to Clement disappearing for a few days without warning, even after he quit his job with the company. He'd say he needed to work on something, and I wouldn't hear from him. If you hadn't come, I probably wouldn't have known until it came out in the papers."

"Can you think of any reason why he would have killed himself?" Byron asked.

"Well, I do know he was melancholic. Working for the airship wasn't everything he had hoped for. He thought he would travel the world and see the skies, but he was stuck in a stuffy, dark engine room. When he quit, I encouraged him to get another job, but he wouldn't."

"Can you tell me what happened the last time you saw him?"

"Yes. He invited me over for dinner. It was the ninth, I believe. We made dinner and talked for a while, and ate and talked some more."

"Around what time did you arrive at his place, and when did you leave?"

Molly hesitated. "I'm not certain. I think it may have been around eight or so when I got there. I left around nine-thirty."

"And he bought champagne and chocolates for you?"

"Yes, he did."

"And this was after he quit his job. How did he pay for all of that?"

"I'm not sure. I don't know where he was getting the money. Every time I asked him, he would get defensive."

"Did you ask him that night?"

"Yes, I did. When he brought out the champagne. I hate to say this, but I was worried he was stealing, or involved in gambling or some other sordid business. I know he would have told me if he had gotten a job."

"How did he respond?"

"He got defensive. He told me not to bring it up again, and I asked if he stole the money. He said no, and then was sad that I even thought that. He told me to leave. So, I did."

"And that is the last time you saw him alive?"

"Yes." A few more tears formed. Byron took out a handkerchief and handed it to her. She burst into sobs.

"I love him. I know now that I don't care about where the money was coming from. I just want him back." She continued to cry into the handkerchief. Byron shifted in his seat, looking between the two women. Mira closed her sketchbook and moved over to Molly, putting an arm around her.

"I'm so sorry, Molly. This must be terrible for you," she said. Molly cried into her.

"I just, I can't believe he is gone."

"It's going to be alright."

"And to think if it was that night," She sobbed. "If I had stayed that perhaps he wouldn't have done it."

"It isn't your fault Molly," Mira said.

"No. I suppose you are right." Molly slowly sat up and composed herself. "I'm terribly sorry for causing a scene."

"No, it is perfectly alright." Mira pulled her arm back. "This is a hard time for you."

"Thank you."

Mira nodded to her and moved back over to Byron. Byron narrowed his eyes for a second and then leaned forward.

"Miss Bridges, I hate to continue questioning, however, do you know of anyone who would want Clement Pennington dead?"

"You think he was murdered?"

"It is a possibility."

"No. I can't think of anyone. He must have committed suicide."

"And there is nothing else you can tell us?"

"No. I've told you everything I know." She handed back the handkerchief.

"You can keep it." Byron held a hand up, and Molly placed her hands in her lap. "Thank you for your assistance."

"Of course, let me know if there is anything else that I can do. But before you go, I do have one question."

"Yes?"

"How did you know about me? Did you find a letter? Something he wrote to me?" Her lip quivered. Byron softened again.

"I'm sorry Miss Bridges, but no."

Mira spoke up. "It was one of his neighbors, Mr. Graham. We asked him if he knew of anyone that was close to Clement. He mentioned you."

Molly nodded and sniffled into the handkerchief again. "Mr. Graham has always been such a kind man. I'm grateful that he told you about me."

"We'll be in contact as we find out more, but for now we'll let you get to your appointment."

Byron's cogs whirred as he stalked down the wet pavement, the rain gone for the time being. Mira nudged him out of the way of lampposts, puddles, and uneven ground as they walked in a semi-homeward direction. Just as she thought they were going to cross back into their part of the city, he stopped, examined his journal, then turned and went up a different road. Soon enough they arrived in front of Pennington's residence.

"Let's take another look around." He climbed the stairs two at a time. Mira furrowed her brow, but followed. Hadn't they seen everything?

The living room was untouched aside from a bit of accumulated dust. Byron poured over everything like a bloodhound. After poking around for a moment, Mira resigned to watch Byron at work. He eventually sat down at the piano bench.

"I might have been wrong about him being murdered, Mira." He rubbed his hands together.

"Because of what Molly said?"

"Yes. Now, this is all conjecture, but perhaps he wasn't doing well as an airship operator. He quit and became a thief. She disapproved, he felt rejected, perhaps betrayed, and then he killed himself. If he was in a crime circle, it would be all too easy for him to have gotten those opioids. He could very well have been ambidextrous like you."

He played a couple of notes on the piano. Several of the keys didn't play, and the ones that did were out of tune. His eyes lit up.

"Hold on a moment." He stood and walked around the piano.

He picked up the drinking glass from the top and set it off to the side, and then lifted the lid of the piano.

"Aha! I thought as much." He grinned.

"What?"

"There is a place for a stash in here."

"A stash?"

"Yes, somewhere to keep your valuables. Don't you have one?"

"No. I use the bank."

"I guess it would be more of a criminal-type thing to do. And it seems Pennington wasn't making use of this one. There is nothing in it."

"Must have spent it all on champagne."

"No. It was opened after the romantic evening."

"How can you tell?" Mira moved over to him. Byron closed the lid to the piano and gestured to a round mark on the top.

"You see this ring on top? It is a condensation ring. These are left when a cold glass gathers condensation on the outside and it drips to the bottom, creating a ring."

"And?"

"There's only the one ring here, and it seems to be fairly recent. It matches the glass I moved exactly. Since the glass wasn't directly on the condensation ring, it must have been moved after it had dried. I know from my journal entry that I had made note of that before."

"So, someone got into the piano either just before the murder or just after!"

"Precisely. Whatever was in here was stolen. Find that, and we might find our killer."

They left the apartment and headed for Scotland Yard; their silence comfortable as they meandered. The leaves on the trees showed the first signs of Autumn; gold, orange, and red fringe framing each green leaf. Mira pulled her coat tighter around herself as a chill wind passed. As she did, Byron reached out, then pulled away, turning towards a news boy on the corner.

"Burglar caught in North London!" the young lad shouted. Byron turned back to Mira and their eyes met. With a nod, they quickened their pace. By four o'clock, they reached Scotland Yard. They went through the marbled halls and found themselves in front of a familiar desk. Juliet lit up when she saw Byron.

"Mr. Constantine! I've been worried."

"Ah yes, Miss..." He looked at her nameplate, "Chickering." He cleared his throat. "Nothing to worry about, really. Just hot on this case. Is Thatcher around?"

"Just one moment." She stood and knocked on the door, then entered the other room. They heard mumbled chitchat before Juliet returned.

"He has a few minutes," Juliet said. Byron nodded, and he and Mira entered the office.

"Well Constantine? I don't have much time; we've got a lead on Whitechapel. Are you here to question the burglar? We caught her, you know. And she confessed to being at Pennington's apartment."

"Her? Well, yes now that you mention it, we would. However, I thought I would let you know the latest on the case."

"And what is that?"

"Clement Pennington had a secret compartment in his piano. It was accessed either after his death, or shortly before it."

"You have evidence of this?"

"Definite evidence."

"Then our burglar must be lying. She stated that she didn't find or steal anything when she came."

"That's the other thing. It is highly likely that Pennington was a thief of some kind. It is probable that he helped with a theft and took all the cash for himself. If that is the case, our burglar may have motive for murder."

"You'll have to tell me more about the evidence later." Thatcher stood, picking up his coat. "I'm afraid I am late for an appointment with the superintendent about one of my other cases."

Mira and Byron stood as well.

"Would you mind if we talked with our new suspect?"

"Not at all." He picked up his hat and nodded to them both as he left the room. "Good day, Constantine, Miss Blayse."

Byron left the office by a different door. He was heading to the interrogation rooms. Mira knew the way now. She followed next to him.

"Do you think we are dealing with a den of thieves here?"

"I believe we may be. Two potential burglars involved with one crime? It seems too good to be true," he teased.

"But do you think that the burglar might have killed him? That Pennington was involved in the other burglaries?"

"Anything is possible, Mira."

They reached the interrogation rooms and found Officer Wensley there.

"Constantine, old friend!"

"Hello, Fred."

"Let me guess, you need something again. Or should I say, someone?"

"Did the chief inspector tell you we were coming?"

"Of course not! You think I wouldn't know you'd be here in no time flat after hearing we caught the burglar?"

"That doesn't take much deductive power, Fred."

"I'll take what I can get as a constable. You want me to get her for you?"

"Please do."

Officer Wensley nodded and walked towards the holding cells. Byron leaned against the wall.

"I will never regret not going to police school."

"Why did Fred go?"

"Well there is only a certain amount of leeway that a private detective has. If you move through the ranks of Scotland Yard, you'll have access to more."

"You don't seem to have any problems with accessing things."

"That's just because I know how to play the game. If Wensley had wanted to, he could have gone in this direction. Something tells me he'll still be bending the rules when he becomes a chief inspector."

Officer Wensley came back down the hall. "They're bringing her down now. You can go wait in interrogation room two if you want."

"After you, Mira." Byron took a step back, and she led the way.

"I'm interested to see who exactly we are working with here," Byron said as they walked. "I've never heard of a female cat burglar before." Byron paused a moment as they entered the interrogation room and situated themselves. "But I suppose that is part of the beauty of it. It's no wonder that it has taken the police so long to find her. No one would suspect, and she could get away with all sorts of things." He leaned back in his chair as the door opened and a woman stalked in.

Mira frowned. The burglar, that had supposedly been terrorizing North London for weeks, was indeed a woman. Two constables led her into the room, forced her into a chair, and then handcuffed her to the table. One constable handed a folder to Byron. The burglar quickly adjusted and sat comfortably, as if she posed for a portrait, without a care in the world. She had dark hair that probably was, at some point, pulled tight back into a bun. Wisps of hair had escaped during the time she had been incarcerated. Her eyes were dark, too. She was of a slim build, probably useful for slipping into tight places. She wore all black and sported tight-fitting trousers instead of a skirt —practical for staying hidden and climbing up buildings, if Mira had to guess. She took out her sketchbook to capture her.

"Selene Vermielle is it?" Byron looked at the case file. The cat lifted her head and examined him for the first time.

"Yes. And you are the detective they brought in to make me

talk?" She had a slight French accent. When she pronounced the "r's" it sounded like she was purring.

"That all depends. Can you think of anything worth talking about?"

Selene furrowed her brow. Mira adjusted her pencil, stretching her fingers.

"Not with you. No."

"Very well. Then I'll start the conversation. How do you do?"

"Terribly. I'm being held at Scotland Yard. How do you think I'd be doing?"

"Well, if you weren't guilty, I'm sure you would have no trouble cooperating with the police. However, your lack of cooperation means you might be hiding something. The more you tell us, the more we can help you."

Selene paused, pondering the situation. He continued. "Besides, we already know you were burglarizing a different abode. You were caught with the jewels in your paws so to speak. Conclusive evidence. You'll be locked up for that alone, but why add a murder charge on top?"

"I didn't murder him."

"Well that's a start. Why didn't you murder him?"

"Because I don't know who he is! Why would I murder someone without reason? I steal things for money. No one gets hurt, really." She folded her arms and looked away, almost disgusted.

"The police seem to think that you did."

"But I didn't!"

"Here's the scenario. You climb up the building, slip in through the open window. Move into the bedroom to look for jewels or pocket watches, or anything you can sell. You hear the door open and freeze in place. You pick up the nearest object and hide behind the door. You only mean to knock him out, but you hit a little too hard. He spins as he falls, falling onto his back. You run before he can see your face." Byron glanced at Mira, and she smiled, realizing he used her version of the story. Her attention was brought back to Selene when the cat growled in frustration.

"Except that didn't happen!"

"What did then?"

She rolled her eyes. "Very well Mssr. Detective. I was there that night. I broke into the apartment on Vincent Street."

"When you entered, how did you go about it?" Byron jotted down a few notes. A glint flickered into the cat's eye, and she smiled.

"It was simple. The latch on the window was undone, and it was easy enough to scale the alley wall. I didn't even need my tools."

"And did you find anything there?"

"No. He had nothing. I checked drawers, under mattresses. Everywhere. No jewels. No cash. There was nothing."

"You didn't see anything unusual? A body perhaps?"

"A body? Of course not! If I had seen a body I never would have entered."

"Around what time was this?"

"I believe it was ten o'clock. I knew the place would be empty then."

"And how did you know that?"

She went silent for a moment, a flicker of fear in her eyes before she composed herself into a feline state once again. "Trade secret."

Byron raised an eyebrow. "You've been forthright up to now."

"Ah, but that is because everything I have told you will not harm me more."

"Then this involves someone else?"

She looked away in silence.

"It does. Well that is good to know." Byron scribbled something else down, his pencil scratches punctuating the silence.

"I see. Well thank you for your time and cooperation." Byron stood and left the room as Mira packed up her things in a haphazard fashion and followed.

"There's someone else involved here. Someone told her when it would be empty," he said.

"Could it be the landlord, Doyle?" she offered.

"If it were Doyle, she would have told us. No. It's someone else. Someone more dangerous."

They walked out of Scotland Yard and hailed a hansom cab.

"Tomorrow, we'll check the bank. If we can determine when Clement had his influx of money, perhaps we'll be able to pin down more of what occurred that night. Obviously, someone is lying."

"Well if everyone was telling the truth we wouldn't have a mystery to solve, would we?" she teased.

"My thoughts exactly. Once we figure things out at the bank, it would probably be in our best interest to map out a timeline and then we can worry ourselves about finding out who tipped off our friend Selene Vermielle."

They reached the cafe, and the carriage stopped. Mira began climbing out, but Byron placed a hand on her arm to stop her. She looked back at him.

"May I walk you home?"

"Yes, you may." She smiled. He stepped out of the carriage and then helped her down. The lamps flickered on above them. He offered her his arm as they strolled leisurely back to her lodgings.

"Is this so you can know where I live for future reference? Or are you simply being a gentleman?"

"You may think what you like about my intentions." He smirked at her. She started laughing and his laugher soon followed hers. His eyes sparkled with mirth, and she felt a heat creeping onto her features.

"Well then Mr. Constantine, I believe that you are doing both."

"You caught me." He grinned. They reached the steps that led up to her place and she stopped.

"Is this where you live?" Byron glanced between the building and her.

"I could be lying to you."

"I like to think I can detect lies more easily than most."

"And?"

"You aren't." He smiled.

"Well, I suppose this is where we say goodbye." The white building loomed above her, and she bit her lip. The morning doubts crept back into her mind. She brought her gaze up to Byron again, attempting to steel her spirits before entering her abode.

"Is something wrong, Mira?" He cocked his head, the twinkle in his eye replaced with worry.

"I've been thinking about our second case."

"Your case you mean?"

"Yes." She looked down.

"What's the matter?"

"I suppose I've been getting discouraged. After all, what kind of clues could we possibly find for a crime that happened eighteen years ago?"

"You'd be surprised. I once solved a case that was over thirty-five years old."

"How?"

"Patience. Since it happened so long ago, it is highly unlikely that being patient will result in additional deaths. We'll keep working at it until we find the evidence we need."

"Patience." She wrung her gloves together. "I've waited practically my entire life to find out what happened."

"In which case you can certainly wait a few more weeks or months for a solution."

"I shall work on my patience then."

"Until tomorrow then?"

"Until tomorrow."

Byron hesitated for a moment, looking her over. A strange expression came over his face as he looked at her. He stepped forward and grasped her hand, kissing it. She felt her discouragement melt away as her cheeks fully heated. She glanced around the street, hoping no one was watching.

"Goodnight, Mira." With reluctance, he let her hand drop.

"Goodnight, Byron."

He tipped his hat and turned to walk up the street. She stayed on the steps, watching him walk away. His shoulders sagged, the farther away he moved. He stopped at a corner and looked back at her before disappearing into the night. She mulled over how he acted at the end of each day. Every time he said goodbye to her it was for the last time. He knew that he would meet her again, but the part of him that had met her today would be gone forever. She took out her key. What would it be like to meet him by accident again? Without him reading his journal at all or her trying to make him remember. Just meeting him by chance on the street. What would that be like? A chill wind hit her, and she came back to herself and went inside. She hadn't liked his answer to her worries, but at least he wasn't giving up. And if Byron didn't give up with day after day of forgetting, how could she?

M ira flew out the door well before her usual time. She hesitated outside Palace Court for a few minutes. The clock hadn't chimed eight yet. He might not have read his journal yet. Was he even awake? She took a deep breath, ready for guns, confusion, or a fit of worry. Whatever was behind that door, she needed to be prepared. She took out her key and opened the door.

For once, silence greeted her. No piano music, or rustling papers, or confused ramblings. Only simple silence. As she turned towards the living room, she noticed several notes tacked to the walls and littered about the floor. One crumpled beneath her foot and she picked it up. *"Remember."* Another. *"Remember."* She rushed to a wall to read more. *"You must remember."* Note after note, all saying, "remember" in some form or another. In shock, she turned to the couch to sit down, and found Byron sound asleep and undisturbed by her musings. She pulled a blanket up around his shoulders and then went back to the notes, determined to read them all. What part of the investigation was he trying to remember? Was he trying to remember her? She scarcely dared to hope. She felt her heart beating against her chest. What would happen when he woke up? She laid his journal on the table nearest him, placed a note to read it on top of him, and then took a seat in his armchair. She admired her new vantage point and pulled out her sketchbook as the light from the rising sun filtered through the window.

Byron woke after another half hour, turning over to find the crumpling of a paper in his ears. The noise was enough to give him consciousness. He picked up the note and read it, rubbing the sleep out of his eyes. Mira studied his profile in the morning sunlight. He looked more confused than she had ever seen him. After reading the note, he found the journal and flipped it open to the first page, still not seeing her. She smiled a little. He poured over each page. At one point he ran his hand through his hair and at another he blushed, then smiled. What could he possibly be reading about? After a while, he closed the journal and set it aside, closing his eyes and leaning back.

"Samira Blayse." It seemed as if he rolled her name over his tongue to get used to it. For Mira, it was an opportunity. She bit her lip in anticipation.

"Yes Byron?"

His response was more than she could have hoped for, as he let out a startled shout and jumped with such alarm that the couch tipped over. He peeked out from behind it. Laughter bubbled out of her.

"You are here already!" He caught his breath. "Wasn't... expecting that."

"Yes, I am. Sorry for startling you."

"You are not."

"Perhaps it was a little comical." She stifled a laugh. Byron's eyes twinkled. He flipped the couch back to its usual position.

"I might need to take that key back, Miss Blayse."

"Will you, Mr. Constantine?"

"No, I won't. But for future reference, if I am asleep, go and get yourself some French toast." He straightened his rumpled jacket.

"Very well, Byron. Off to the bank then?"

"Er, yes. After breakfast. Let me go put myself to rights first." He picked up the blanket and left the room. Mira left to investigate his kitchen. It was a lot cleaner than she had seen it before. She set to work preparing breakfast with the few ingredients she found in his cupboards. She set the plates on the table just as Byron came out of his room, hair wet, adjusting his tie.

"I didn't mean for you to make breakfast, Mira."

"What else was I supposed to do?"

"Not make breakfast."

"You told me to get myself some French toast."

"I..." he started, then thought better of it. "Well yes. I suppose I did."

They ate a quiet breakfast and then it was off to the bank. They learned from Inspector Thatcher that Pennington owned an account with the Bank of England. Byron also received a warrant from the department to check Pennington's bank records.

They reached Threadneedle Street, and she looked up at the large building. Massive pillars extended to at least three times her height. They entered the bank. The wood paneling, marble, and tiles that surrounded them reminded Mira of Scotland Yard. Byron strode up to one of the tellers. His name badge read Elkins.

"My good sir, would you be so kind as to direct us towards the bank director's office?"

"You have business with the bank director?" Elkins adjusted his spectacles.

"Yes. We need to have access to the records of a deceased person's account. We have a warrant."

"Well, as long as you have a warrant, I can help you sir. May I see it?" Byron nodded and handed it over.

"Ah yes. Mr. Pennington. I helped him a few times. Looks like everything is in order. Let me get his file." Elkins turned and walked out of sight for a few moments.

"That's a stroke of luck." Byron leaned against the woodwork in relief. Elkins returned with a large file and directed them to a table. Byron pulled out a chair for Mira before seating himself beside her. Elkins set the file down and took a seat himself.

"Here it is sir. Are you looking for a particular period?"

"The last year if you would."

"Of course." He flipped through a few pages. "Here you are, sir." He slid a few documents over to them. Byron picked the papers up and glanced over them.

"So, his influx of money began around March of this year. He received an increased income from March until July, but when he quit his job, he was still receiving funds, withdrawing it in smaller amounts." He trailed off in thought.

"Yes sir. From what I could tell he was a financially responsible man," Elkins added.

"How often did he come in?"

"About once a week I believe. He would withdraw the funds he needed for that week, and around March he simply made deposits once a month. I assume he got a second job of some sort. His income from Vaporidge was sent directly here."

"Thank you so much. You've been most helpful. May I keep this?" He gestured with the papers.

"Yes sir, we have a second copy. Happy to oblige you."

Byron tipped his hat, slipping the documents into his journal and soon he and Mira exited the bank.

"His sudden disappearances on the airship and the influx of money are connected, but how could he have a second job on the airship itself, especially if the paychecks from Vaporidge were separate from his additional income?"

"Then that is the crux of the issue. We need to find out where he was going," she said.

"Shall we take another ride on an airship Mira?"

"I suppose we shall."

As they approached the Mooreland docks, Mira once again felt small in contrast to the balloons. The *Horizon* was moored for repairs.

"It seems as if Fortuna is with us today Mira. We won't even have to buy a ticket or leave London this time."

Mira found her breath again.

They approached the ship and Byron focused his efforts on finding the foreman. He stopped one of the men supervising the repairs.

"Excuse me, but where can I find the foreman?"

"Right over there, sir."

"Thank you."

The foreman turned towards them as they approached.

"Can I help you?"

"I certainly hope so. You see, I'm a detective working with Scotland Yard. This is my secretary. We are investigating the death of Clement Pennington."

"Oh? How can I help with that?"

"We need access to the *Horizon*."

"I'm afraid that's not possible. We need to finish these repairs. It will be launching across the channel first thing tomorrow morning, and we can't have any distractions."

"We would stay out of the way. We simply need to look around."

"I'm sorry, but unless you have a warrant, I can't let you in."

The foreman turned back towards his workers and Byron herded Mira around a group of crates.

She said, "If it's leaving tomorrow, we don't exactly have the luxury of waiting."

"My thoughts exactly. It's also rather odd that he's so against it. The repairs the ship needs now are minor in comparison to when we were grounded at Bristol, and we were certainly allowed around the ship then."

"I wonder how late the foreman stays." Mira peeked around the crates. "He can't stay all day."

"True. Perhaps we can take a walk and check back later."

After taking a long, winding route around the docks, they returned to their hiding spot behind the crates. After watching for a few minutes, Byron turned to her.

"Play along the best you can. I'm going to determine if the foreman is truly gone."

He led her towards the back section of the ship and found one of the supervisors.

"Hello there, good sir! Would the foreman be around?"

"Not currently. He's on break. Can I help you with anything?"

"Perhaps. I'm a reporter with the Central News Agency," he pulled out his journal to corroborate his story.

"Are you wanting an interview?" The man looked skeptical.

"No, we're wanting to tour your ship. After all, the new and improved airship that Vaporidge is building wouldn't be nearly as impressive without a comparison. I've heard that this ship is currently the finest ship in the fleet!"

The man stood taller. "Indeed, it is sir! I'm fortunate to work on it."

"So, you'd let us take a look around?"

"Well it isn't exactly protocol to let anyone on the ship when it's being cleaned you see—"

"You would impede a critical newspaper article?"

"No sir, not at all but," he paused for a second, then relented, "well the foreman is out for about two hours, as long as you left before he came back."

"Good lad."

They started on the top floor and checked every room, every broom closet, the ballroom, the dining hall, the observation lounge, everywhere for a trap door or hidden passage. Nothing. They moved down into the engine area. Workers tinkered with all sorts of equipment, tightening bolts and maintaining the engines. They avoided the workers the best that they could and kept searching, working their way through the ship checking welding, bolts, and rivets in the walls. Eventually they split up in order to cover more ground.

Mira walked around the back of the ship and it occurred to her that the ceilings in the crew section were a lot shorter than the ceilings in the main chassis. It was odd because they looked to be about the same height from the outside. Perhaps there was an area with more machinery beneath them, but she hadn't found any doors or stairs to lead down to them. They must need maintenance at some point or another. She kept looking around, and she assumed that Byron did the same.

When she reached the back of the ship, she noticed a grate covering some sort of vent. She furrowed her brow. Had there been any other grates? This one matched the metal surrounding it so well that if she hadn't been looking closely, she wouldn't have even noticed it. She pressed her face against it, trying to look beyond the metal crisscrossing. Her eyes met darkness, but there seemed to be an opening of some sort. That was when she noticed the hinges on the grate, as well as the lock keeping it in place.

She left to find Byron. He was around the next bend, pushing on wood panels in the walls.

"Byron, I think I found it."

"You did? Where is it?"

She led him back to the grate and showed him the hinges.

"Problem is, it's locked. How much time do we have left?" she asked.

Byron pulled out his pocket watch. "About ten minutes. But that's only a problem for the moment."

He stood, and they moved out of the airship. Byron helped her down the ramp and the church clocks struck 4 as they strolled in the afternoon air.

"Do you have a plan?" She looked up at him.

"I always have a plan. Here's what I need you to do." He stopped, looked around, and then pulled her into an alley.

"Go on back to your apartment and don't worry about things," he whispered.

"What?"

"This is something I need to do on my own."

"Will you at least tell me what you're going to do?"

He searched her face. "Very well. I'm going to break into the airship this evening."

"Byron!"

He put a finger to her lips and looked around to ensure no one heard. "See, this is why I didn't want to tell you. Don't try to stop me."

"It's not that. I want to come!"

Byron stopped for a moment and searched her face, before shaking his head.

"Well, you aren't coming."

"Oh no. You're not sending me home at the first chance of danger." Mira crossed her arms.

"Why not? You said it yourself. Danger. I can't drag you into that."

"Yes, but it's also excitement. Something different. And how are you to survive without your secretary?"

"I have done well enough on my own for the past four years, thank you very much."

"So then shall I not come back tomorrow?"

"That isn't what I meant at all." He paused, then leaned closer to her, voice dropping to a whisper.

"Get dressed in the darkest clothing that you have. Trousers if you own a pair. Come back to my place at nine-thirty this evening. Alright?"

She smiled. "I'll be there."

He tried to look annoyed, but it didn't work. Despite his best efforts he looked incredibly pleased. He tipped his hat to her before he left. She went back to her rooms to get some food and get ready. It was likely to be a late night.

She stopped by her uncle's and tried on a few of her brother's clothes to see if they would work for the job. Unfortunately, most of the articles needed to be hemmed, and she didn't have much time. She opted for her own riding trousers and a black sweater. She had her hair up and out of the way for once. With her boots and gloves, she looked like she was about to go rob something. Her coat hid her attire well enough though, and surely a spring in her step wouldn't give her plans away. She showed up at Palace Court promptly at nine-fifteen. She unlocked the door and stepped inside, placing her coat on a hook in the hallway.

Byron sat in the living room, sorting through a mess of papers.

Mira noticed that the notes he had plastered on the walls earlier were gone. The ones spread out now were much larger. They looked like maps. She came closer. Airship blueprints.

"What are you doing?" She peered over his shoulder. Byron jumped again.

"Mira! You're early. But in a way you're just in time. I've been looking over the blueprints of the airship we explored earlier."

"Blueprints?"

"Yes. Most companies keep a record of their designs. I found a bound edition of Vaporidge blueprints from the last eighteen years at the library. No grate system to be found in any of them. Whatever it is that you found, they didn't include it in the work plans. Either it is just decor, or the public blueprints are not the real ones."

"What does that mean?"

"It means you have stumbled on something extraordinary." He smiled up at her. "And you look fantastic. Just perfect." His smile became a grin.

He wore all black as well. Black trousers, black sweater, black boots. The two of them matched almost exactly.

"Are you ready to go?" He rolled up the blueprint and stood.

"As ready as I'll ever be."

"You know you don't have to come. You can still back out."

"As if I'm going to do that now."

"Very well." He walked across the room to the side table and opened a drawer. He pulled out a key ring with some odd-looking keys and lockpicks. Her eyes widened.

"You don't mean to—" She trailed off, trying to find the right word.

"Yes. We are breaking into that grate. I thought you wanted excitement?" he teased.

He grabbed his coat and slipped it on, then grabbed hers. He helped her into it, offered her an arm and led her out onto the street. The sky misted, making the atmosphere a bit chilly.

"You'll have to teach me, then," she said.

"Teach you what?"

"How to pick locks."

"Heavens, no. I'm not turning my secretary into a criminal in training."

They headed to the docks, which lay quiet and still, a great change to the usual hustle and bustle happening during the day. They walked normally until they came close to the airship, and then Byron took off his coat and gestured for her to take hers off as well. They stashed them behind a couple of crates. Byron peeked out, looked around, then pulled back.

"Guards," he whispered. Mira shrunk up against the crate. Byron put a finger to his lips to quiet her, then picked up a rock. He threw it as hard as he could, and it made a loud ricochet sound against the hull of another ship. Loud footsteps ran in that direction. Byron put his head around the corner again, then nodded to Mira, and they snuck up the ramp. He picked the lock to the main door with ease and they walked into the warm interior.

The inside of the ship changed as well. It was still as ornate, but at night it seemed gloomy. The moonlight streamed through the windows, casting eerie shadows behind the portraits. The gold fleur-de-lis on the walls turned ghostly. Mira's thoughts drifted to the haunted Beauchamp House library, and she shivered. Byron led her to the center of the ship where the door to the crew area was. This door stood unlocked.

She decided that she preferred the moonlit ghosts to the shadowy, pitch-black interior. Byron's eyes must have adapted faster than hers as he led her down the corridor with no problem. She felt the wall as she went, trying to make sense of where they were. When Byron found her lagging, he took her by the hand to make sure they stayed together. Their fingers fit well together, and she could feel his warmth through her gloves. When they reached the darkest part of the ship, she closed her eyes, and trusted that Byron would guide her safely through. The atmosphere lightened near the back of the ship where the grate was, and Byron took out his lockpicks again. She placed a hand on top of his.

"Can't you at least explain what you're doing?"

He paused a moment then nodded.

"This ring has several tools on it that can be useful for picking a lock. Some locks can be opened using a skeleton key." He lifted several of the keys on his ring.

"Others, like this one, need different tools in order to be cracked. Picks, and a tension wrench." He lifted two tools from the ring. "These types of locks have spring-loaded pins that fall into place, locking the door. When you use a key, it raises those pins, so the lock will open. You place the tension wrench on the bottom to keep the pins you've already raised from falling down again and use the picks to raise them." He demonstrated. "After a while you can do it by sound, but you usually start with the feelings in your hands."

"Why do you know how to do this?"

"Same reason as you. I was curious. When we get back to Palace Court, I'll help you practice."

This lock took a little more time than the main door. She watched every movement with careful attention. Eventually the lock clicked. He pulled on the grate and it moved without sound. Someone must have oiled it recently. It swung open to reveal a ladder going down further into the ship. Byron slipped into the opening in the grate and started to climb down. When he was a good way down Mira started herself. How grateful she was for trousers!

About halfway down the ladder the walls surrounding them disappeared. It was dim, but she could still make out how large of an area there was. It was huge. Her steps echoed as she made her way down the ladder. She reached the bottom and found that crates lined the walls, extending out towards the ladder. Byron hid in the shadow of one. She joined him.

"What is this place?" she whispered

"A cargo hold of sorts, but not a normal one," he whispered back.

They both turned to examine their hiding spot. Sturdy wood, probably oak. It was made of slats nailed together. He attempted to open it, but it wouldn't budge. He walked around it, examining every part. While Byron engaged in that endeavor, Mira looked around. This cargo hold held dozens of crates. A whiteish-grey powder was scattered on the floor in places. She walked further in and found what looked like a door. She remembered the doorlike panels on the outside of the ship. This was likely the only real one. Probably used for loading and unloading. Near the door there weren't as many crates, but square outlines in the white powder suggested there had been more.

A rumbling startled Mira from her investigation. A squealing noise soon joined in as an opening appeared beneath the door. She stood there a moment, unsure of what to do. Then, coming to her senses, she ducked quickly behind a crate. The noises stopped, and heavy footsteps with a large gait approached. Most likely a tall man. A second pair of footsteps followed the first. Two tall men. They moved to a crate three down from hers. They grunted, and wood scraped on metal for a moment. It stopped, and the footsteps went back towards the door. Panicking, she moved to another crate. The men returned for another one, and another. She moved further and further back. She heard more footsteps returning before it was logical for the first set of men to be back. There were more of them. With the constant flow of footsteps, she could no longer move without fear of being found. She leaned against her crate and tried not to breathe too much. Her heart pounded in her chest. They lifted the crate hiding her.

"Hey now, Sam, it looks like we've found ourselves a stowaway."

She quickly found herself between two of the tallest men she had ever seen. Probably about six foot seven. Rippling muscles. Dangerous slanted eyes. One gruffly pulled her up by her arm, and she noticed tattoos decorating his forearm. She tried to struggle, but it really was no use.

"What are you doing here?" he asked her. She looked up at him in fear. Not knowing what to do she started speaking in French. He looked surprised.

"Do you speak English?" he asked. She kept speaking at him in French, nearly hysterical. Babbling about nothing. Praying that he didn't understand. He turned to his companion.

"Do you speak French?" His partner shook his head. "Neither do I. We'll have to take her back to headquarters. I bet the boss does." She struggled again, but he held her fast.

"Shouldn't we just kill her now, Joe? She's seen things she ain't supposed to."

"She must have slipped on during the last shipment from France. She's probably harmless. It's better to take her to the boss." They dragged her out of the cargo hold. She looked back towards the crates hoping to find some trace of Byron but she didn't see him.

There were six men in total, all with a similar build. They loaded the crates into a wagon which read "Schwarz and Sons Butchery," in big, red letters. Mira felt herself growing faint as they pulled her closer to the wagon. Right before they reached it, she felt a hand on the back of her neck, a slight pressure, and then all went dark.

September 26TH

When Mira woke, her head throbbed, and everything felt cold. She opened her eyes, surprised by the amount light. Blinking a few of times, she tried to sit up. Her whole body ached with a freezing soreness. She used the wall for support and then examined her surroundings.

She was in a small, stone lined room. The light came from a barred window near the ceiling that was eye level with the street. Straw and wood shavings from the floor clung to her clothes and scratched at her legs. A few crates lined the wall. The door was solid wood, with bars in a small slot near the top.

She stood, shaking. Her headache intensified with height, but she needed to determine where she was. She strained to look out the window to the street, but she couldn't recognize any signs or buildings. Footsteps echoed from the hall outside and she collapsed again, pretending to still be unconscious. The footsteps stopped at the door, the door creaked open, and she felt the presence of two people in the room with her.

"She was found on the *Horizon* then?" A woman's voice asked.

"Yes ma'am. Sam and I found her while we were moving the goods."

"And you say she only speaks French?"

"From what we can tell. We don't know who she is or how much she knows. For all we know she was just taking free passage to London."

"Either way, she's seen something. Pity she's still asleep." The woman paused and came closer to her. She leaned over and moved a bit of hair out of her face. Mira tried to stay relaxed and maintain slow breaths. The woman walked back to who she presumed was Joe.

"Let me know the moment she wakes up. We can't have any more breaches in security. After that Pennington issue we need to keep our guard up. If word gets higher up, we'll all face the consequences." She walked out. The man paused a moment.

"Of course, ma'am." Then he walked out, and the door closed behind him.

Mira didn't dare move. As soon as she did, they would know she was awake, and the questions would start. Eventually she would slip up. Her French wasn't perfect, and it was improbable anyone experienced would take her as fluent. However, she couldn't lay there forever. She had to find a way out. Why on Earth had she insisted to come with Byron?

Eventually her stiff limbs couldn't bear it any longer. Her headache faded, and her thoughts cleared. She waited until she felt certain that no one was watching her and then she sat up again and stretched. Heavens, it felt good. Once she had full circulation in her appendages, she searched along every inch of the cell for some inconsistency, any weakness. Footsteps fast approached the room. She considered feigning sleep again, but she knew she couldn't do that forever either. She resigned herself to her fate.

"She's awake!" The man called Joe opened the door, traversed the distance between them with a single step, and grabbed her by the wrist. She resisted initially, but he twisted her arm and grabbed at her hair with his other hand. She cried out, and he pulled her from the room. He led her down a few hallways. The building was smaller than she had anticipated, but she had little time to map it out. They reached his destination, and he knocked on the door.

"Come in." It was the woman's voice from before. He opened the door and pulled her in with him.

A short woman with long, brown hair sat behind the desk. She dressed nicely, but not in an extravagant way. Her stout, limber, frame made her look fit, and her facial features seemed familiar. She smiled when she saw Mira and started to speak French.

"*Ah. I see you are awake. How nice.*" The woman gestured to Joe. He deposited Mira in a chair and then closed the door, blocking it on the inside with his large frame. Mira watched his movements with caution as she nursed her wrist. The woman's voice drew her attention once more.

"*Might I ask what your name is?*" Mira faltered for a moment, translating her moment of hesitation into fear.

"S...Suzette."

"*Suzette. What a beautiful name. Suzette, what were you doing inside of that airship?*" Mira hesitated again. Her answer meant life or death. An incorrect answer could be lethal.

"*It was warm, Madame. I didn't realize it was going to take off so quickly.*"

"*Where are you from Suzette?*"

"*Lyon, France.*" Mira was surprised by how quickly her responses came out of her. Based in the woman's speech pattern, she wasn't French either. Hopefully, the woman wouldn't notice her inaccuracies. She couldn't tell if the woman believed her, and that caused her anxiety to rise. Luckily, Suzette had as much reason to be afraid as Mira did.

"*Do you not speak English?*"

"*No, I do not.*"

"*Tell me how you came to be on the ship.*"

Mira swallowed. "*It was late at night. I was wandering the streets and came to the docks. I saw men loading crates onto the ship. It was cold, and I snuck inside. I must have fallen asleep behind one of the crates. When I woke the door was closed.*"

"*You don't know what was in those crates then?*"

"*No, Madame. I do not.*"

The woman paused for a moment thinking. Then she turned to Joe. "Take her back to the holding cell for now. She knows nothing; however, I would like to question her more once I have more facts.

She dresses like a thief, so she may be lying. We can hold her until we find out. I doubt she will be missed until then."

Joe nodded and grabbed her wrist again pulling her to her feet.

"*Please, Madame, what are you going to do with me?*"

"*Don't worry your pretty head, Suzette. You are in good hands.*" The woman smiled, and Mira's stomach churned. Joe pulled her from the room, and soon after threw her back into the small, dank cell. She sprung to her feet and ran for the door, but Joe closed and locked it before she reached it. She sat down beside the door and felt her hope disappear as fast as the door had closed. She took a few deep breaths and thought of the facts before her.

1. They used the airship cargo hold as a smuggling area.
2. These smugglers probably supplied the black market.
3. Killers and scoundrels surrounded her. It was only a matter of time before she tripped up, and then she'd be dead.

These thoughts didn't offer much comfort, but it was a change to be thinking logically. She added another fact to her mental list.

4. She must escape if she didn't want 3 to come to pass.

She stood and walked to the center of the room. She didn't know when the smugglers might return, and her only tool was observation. She studied the room again. Even if the bars in the window gave way, the opening was too small for her. She already checked all the bricks for any openings. The crates were empty. The only other way in or out was the door. She blew a strand of hair out of her face and then tried to fix her hair by repositioning the pins in it. Pins. She grabbed one of them and her curls fell around her shoulders.

She slipped the pin into the lock and moved it around the way she saw Byron using his lockpicks. She moved the pin up and down, around in a circle, trying every way she could feasibly think of moving it. No matter what she tried the lock wouldn't budge. Of course! She forgot the tension. She grabbed another hairpin and used the thick end to apply pressure at the bottom of the lock. She tried again, but still nothing happened. Her vision of freedom shrunk smaller and smaller with each turn of the hair pin. She felt a snap beneath her fingers and the tinkling of metal against the stones in front of her. She dropped the rest of the broken pin, hot tears rolling down her face.

She tried to compose herself again, but her thoughts kept slipping back to her situation. She was practically a prisoner on death row, waiting for an unknown execution date to sneak up on her. A death her parents had faced, probably for similar reasons. A hopelessness settled somewhere near her stomach, rising into her chest with each sob. She leaned up against the door and closed her eyes to stop her tears from escaping. And thinking of that, she opened them again so at least something could escape. If only Byron was coming.

But he wasn't. His memory wouldn't last, and he'd forget she even existed. She couldn't count on him. If she did, she would be dead. She had to try again. It was useless to waste her tears when she had hardly tried. She'd only tried Byron's way. She had to try her own. She needed an artist's observation.

She placed her hand on the lock, feeling it. Closing her eyes, she imagined how the lock was built. Perhaps an old locksmith, doing well in his trade had made it. He probably had rough hands. She had seen the keys on Joe's belt. She imagined them. Each prong had to fit within a mechanism within the lock. She opened her eyes and took out another hair pin, bending it to match her mental key. She placed her "tension wrench" at the base of the lock. Then she slipped her makeshift key into the keyhole.

She felt each peg in the lock scraping against the hairpin and listened for the clicks. After a half dozen tries, she got it. She slipped the hairpins into her pocket and quietly opened the door. She let out a breath. She had done it. No one was in the hall. This was her only chance. If she was caught now, it would be over. More questions would be asked, and she'd slip up somewhere. No, she had to get out now. She snuck past door after door, listening before continuing to make sure that she wasn't caught. She stopped when she heard voices at one of them.

"Then why don't we just kill her now?"

It was Joe's voice. She felt herself paling. They must be talking about her. She was about to continue down the hall when the woman spoke.

"Joe, a murder is a convoluted thing. If we were to kill her now and, say, dump her in the river, there is every possibility that she will be found. It is possible that by some means she'll have connections. If she does—"

"But you just said she wouldn't be missed!" Joe interrupted.

"The problem is we don't know one way or another. Imprisoning someone is fundamentally different from murdering someone. You remember Pennington? You remember how much planning went into that? How many unconnected people had to die and will continue to die until all of this is over? All that work, for whom? A worthless airship operator. She may not look like much, but killing her might cut the delicate thread that keeps us in this game. Always be careful about who you kill, Joe. Research. Plan. And if you can, consult. That's what Circe is for. They bind us together into a grand criminal circle. And when we need it, they provide adequate distraction for the police and their bumbling private detective." Mira heard the woman take a breath, calming down before continuing.

"Besides, murder is a dirty business. It takes much more planning and has more strings attached. More moving pieces. You must come up with alibis, fake accidents, frame others. It's complicated. I'd much rather be in the smuggling business."

"But the smuggling wouldn't be nearly as successful without the airships. Didn't all of this start because of a double homicide?"

"It certainly helped. And I suppose that inventor did have connections. That's why they had to make it look like an accident." She clucked her tongue. Mira could hardly believe her ears. Was she talking about her parents?

Mira heard footsteps coming from down the corridor. She sped down the hall in the opposite direction and froze next to a different door, listening. No sound came from behind it. She tried the handle. Unlocked. She slipped inside. It was a broom closet. She hoped the owner of those shoes didn't need a broom. The footsteps came down the hallway, passed her hiding place, and then quieted as they went away. She added a few items to her mental list.

5. She now had some evidence that her parents had been murdered.
6. They knew about Pennington, so they had to have been involved there. And others had died.
7. They knew about Byron.
8. Circe had to be something of importance.

She waited until she couldn't hear the footsteps anymore and then left the brooms behind, making her way further up the hallway.

She came to an intersection, uncertain which direction to tiptoe in. She looked for stairs. Stairs would lead to the upstairs which would lead to the door and freedom. She wished that she had been awake when they had brought her in. Then she would know where to go. As it was, she didn't have a clue. She turned left and passed several other doors, all locked. She doubted the exit would be locked, and she didn't have time to pick every single one. Eventually the hallway came to a dead end. She muttered under her breath, "Of course," and snuck back the way she came.

That was when she heard footsteps coming from ahead of her, from the corridor where she had turned. Her only chance was to beat them to the intersection and find the stairs before they noticed her. She bit her lip and started sprinting as silently as she could.

Unfortunately, she ran right into him at the corner. They crashed to the ground. Mira struggled with her assailant, attempting to get up. He grabbed her by the arms and pulled her up to standing. She struggled against him, hitting his chest and speaking harshly at him in French.

"Mira, Mira, it's me." Byron held her fast. She looked up at him with surprise and relief.

"Byron, thank goodness."

"Don't thank me yet. We need to get out of here."

He let her go and took her hand to run in the opposite direction. They reached the end of that hallway and turned onto the next, finding a set of stairs with a door at the top. He let go of her hand and listened at the door before opening it and pulling her through. They were in the back of a butcher shop. She could smell the rot of carcasses, hanging lifeless for far too long. He glanced around for a moment, and then finding that it was safe, continued out of the shop.

Once on the street, he ran again, keeping ahold of her wrist. She stumbled several times, but didn't fall. He didn't stop running until they had moved at least ten blocks away. He made a sharp turn around a corner and stopped, letting go of her hand, and leaning against the wall to catch his breath. Mira had trouble catching hers as well. It was several minutes before he spoke.

"I don't think I knew that you spoke French."

She looked up at him in disbelief. "I get kidnapped, and that is the first thing you ask me?"

"Sorry, but if I knew I didn't write it down." He was disheveled and exhausted. It occurred to Mira that he remembered her.

"Were you up all night?"

"Well, I couldn't very well sleep and risk not finding you. I had to follow them."

"Thank you."

"Of course. Now let's get you back to my place. It should be safe there."

He walked with a purpose in the direction of Kensington, and Mira followed. He eventually called a hansom cab and helped her into it. At one point, he had the driver stop so he could get out and give a message to a courier. Mira turned to him as he got back in.

"What was that for?"

"I sent a message to Scotland Yard. They need to get there before the smugglers realize you've gone missing. As soon as they know you are gone, they will leave the butcher shop without a trace."

"Oh. I see."

They made it back to Palace Court, and he helped her out of the carriage and onto the street. He paid the driver and then hurried Mira inside. Only once she was sitting on the sofa with a cup of tea in her hand did he relax.

"Are you hurt?" His face had softened with concern. Or perhaps it was exhaustion. Mira wasn't sure.

"Other than a few bumps and bruises, I'm fine."

"I'm afraid I need you to tell me what you know."

She relayed everything that had happened to her and Byron wrote her account down. When she was finished, he looked up at her.

"You really are quite clever. Thinking to throw them off that way. And picking the lock."

"Well, I had just watched you."

"Still. You probably would have gotten out on your own even if I hadn't come."

"I'm glad you did."

He smiled. "I would be upset at myself for allowing you to come but you were right. I needed you."

She could feel a blush rising. He continued. "And now thanks to your brilliance, they've given away the fact that they were involved with Pennington. And Circe. And your parents' accident. Somehow." He smiled at her. She felt herself turning more red.

"I didn't mean to embarrass you, Mira."

"No. It's quite alright. I blush at the drop of a hat, really."

"I've noticed." He looked at her and his gaze got deep again. She looked down. Then she cleared her throat and looked up at him again.

"What is Circe?"

"Nothing you need to worry about at the moment."

"You weren't going to tell me your plans for last night either, Byron."

"This is different. If it comes up again, I'll tell you." They sat in silence for a minute or so, sipping at their tea. She decided to breach the silence again.

"What did you see from your end, Byron? In the smuggling hold?"

"Well Mira, while you explored, I examined the powder on the ground. It's mostly white but had some other particles in it. Traces of black, brown, and grey. I took a few samples and placed them in an envelope I had." He paused and took the envelope from his pocket, placing it on the table. He looked back at her. "That was around the time I noticed you were gone and that the door was opening. I looked around for you, hiding behind crates. I was about four crates behind you when they found you. I heard what they said, and I watched them take you out. I was able to keep to the outside edges while they were distracted, and I hid behind the wagon. From there it was just a matter of following where they took you, which was to Schwarz and Son's Butchery. I waited across the street for a while, gauging who came in and out. I knew they had knocked you out, so I had a little bit of time. Eventually, I decided that I had a chance, and I came in after you. You know the rest."

"I'm glad you didn't get caught."

"As am I. I'm afraid I'm a little more well-known than you are, and then your French would have been in vain." He glanced at her before continuing.

"Now then, back to the case. We know Pennington was disappearing to that cargo hold. That's the only place he could have been going."

"But why, Byron?"

"You're asking the right questions. He could have been helping them smuggle. Or he may have just stumbled across it as you did. He could have been curious. But that may have been his fatal mistake."

"But if he found it in March, that is the time that he started disappearing after all, wouldn't he have been killed then? Didn't Mr. Gill say that he didn't have any family or anyone? No one would have missed him." She thought back to the woman's speech about murder and shivered.

"Maybe no one knew he had found it. Or it was just that he was helping them to smuggle the goods. After all that was when the influx of money came as well."

"But Byron, the money kept coming after he quit. And he had been working for Vaporidge for several months before the influx."

"Hmm. You are right about that. So where was it coming from?"

"What about that stash in the piano? Could he still have become a cat burglar? He must have known how to use lockpicks to get down to the smuggling hold."

"I suppose. But that doesn't fit in with him disappearing, though. The pieces aren't fitting." He placed his index fingers on his temples and rubbed them in circles.

"Was he stealing whatever they were smuggling and selling it? That would be a reason for them to kill him off," Mira said.

"It would, but then why would he quit? That wouldn't make sense. He'd be away from his supply of goods."

Mira pursed her lips. They were getting nowhere. Byron yawned.

"Byron, you need to sleep."

"Mira, if I sleep, I'm going to forget."

"You were just up all night. And you were up late two nights ago as well."

"Was I? I don't feel the strain." He yawned again.

"You are yawning left and right. The case can wait for the moment. You need to sleep."

"Alright. I'll take a nap if you promise me one thing, Mira."

"Anything."

"That you will be here when I wake up again. I don't want you going home alone. Not after what just happened."

She paused and then nodded. "Very well."

Byron nodded back, then picked up his journal. He wrote a few things in it and then set it off to the side. "There is a possibility that my memory won't reset. Usually it is only when I sleep for long periods of time." He laid back and closed his eyes.

"Then I guess we'll hope for that." She pulled out her sketchbook to keep herself occupied.

"Yes, we'll hope." Byron went a bit limp. It hadn't taken much for sleep to overcome him. Mira watched as he breathed deeply. Up and down. Did he dream? Of course, she would never know because he probably never remembered his dreams. She herself seldom remembered hers, and she didn't have his problem with memory.

She drew for a while and then prepared some food in the kitchen. A famished hunger had taken up residence in her stomach. She hadn't eaten since the evening before, and it had to be midafternoon by this point.

When she was fed, she came back into the living room. He was still asleep. She went over to the filing system and pulled out all his notes on the case that weren't in his journal. She wrote down the events and then sorted them into chronological order.

- *September 1887- Clement Pennington started work for the Vaporidge Steamship Company*
- *Early March 1888- He became more withdrawn. Most likely found the smuggling quarters.*
- *Late March- The influx of money appeared in his account.*
- *April- He and Molly Bridges met and started to court.*
- *July- He quit his job. The influx of money continued.*
- *September- I met Byron. Pennington is found dead. His lodgings burglarized. We started solving the crime. I was kidnapped by smugglers.*

She looked at these events for a moment and then decided to focus in on the day of the murder. September 9.

September 9

- *Eight o'clock (p.m.) Molly Bridges comes to Clement's place.*
- *They make dinner, have champagne and chocolates. Have an argument.*
- *Nine-thirty Molly Bridges leaves Clement's place.*
- *Ten o'clock Burglar comes. Clement apparently isn't there.*

September 10

- *Eleven o'clock (a.m.) Landlord finds Pennington dead.*

She looked at everything she had written. She had to assume that everyone was telling the truth. Then she would be able to find where things didn't fit. Was an hour and a half long enough to make dinner, eat, clean up, have champagne and chocolate and then argue? And where did Pennington go if the burglar, Selene, didn't see him? Maybe he went after Molly to apologize. Perhaps he didn't pluck up enough courage to actually go talk to her. Perhaps he came back after the burglary and then he checked his stash. He moved the glass from where he had left it after the fight so that he could check inside the piano. Finding whatever was in there missing, then he killed himself?

No. Because the smugglers knew about him and his death. They had something to do with it. How? She wasn't exactly sure. But he hadn't killed himself. That much was certain. The woman in the smuggling ring had mentioned that there was a security breach involving Pennington. So, he wasn't a smuggler himself; he just found the grate and was curious.

But where was the money coming from? She leaned back in annoyance. This puzzle wasn't coming together. The picture still wasn't clear. She didn't know where they would go from what they had discovered. She looked over at Byron who still slept. She yawned. The adrenaline was wearing off. She was tired, too. Maybe she could rest for a while. Byron wouldn't be awake for a bit. She set her notes on the table and laid her head on the back of the chair.

She was vaguely aware of when Byron woke up. She could hear some rustling, some footsteps towards her, and then away again, and the opening of the journal. Somewhere in her memory all of that was there. She just didn't remember falling asleep. The sounds of glass clinking in the kitchen woke her. She stretched and then went to investigate the noise.

Byron was tinkering with his chemistry set. From what she could tell he had separated the white particles from the black and brown particles. He had several piles of each and was testing them with different chemicals, she presumed in order to figure out what they were. She came in and leaned against the counter, he saw her, and smiled.

"Hello, Mira." He frowned for a moment. "You are Mira, right?"

"Yes, Byron. I see you've forgotten again. Did you sleep well at all?"

"I don't quite remember, but I feel generally awake. It would seem we had quite the exciting morning." He gestured to the journal sitting at the far end of the counter.

"Yes. I suppose we did."

"I just thought I would check up on what these powders were. There are six distinct solids in this sample."

"Really?"

He nodded. "I've tested several of the particles. I've found sulfur, charcoal, and potassium nitrate, opium, silt, and what appears to be bone." He pointed to each small pile as he went.

"From what I can tell, that cargo hold has been used for several years and over the years it has brought several different things across. The sulfur, charcoal, and potassium nitrate lead me to believe that gunpowder and guns were likely to have been transported. There wasn't as much opium, which makes sense as the bags would be sealed tight. I'm guessing the silt is simply what clings to the crates as they are being transported. The bone is a bit tricky as well; not as much of it, only a few fragments. I would guess ivory. It certainly isn't human. My guess here is that it rubbed against the crates on the inside and the powder fell through the slats." He looked up at her. She was in awe. He grinned.

"So, then they have transported guns, drugs, and ivory at some point?" she asked.

"Yes. They can get it into the country without worry for customs or taxes because the *Horizon* is only a passenger vessel. According to the public blueprints it wasn't even supposed to have a cargo hold."

"And they unload it under the cover of night so as not to draw suspicion?"

"Exactly. There is a high probability that the captain and the crew of the ship don't even know what is below them. There is probably a ground crew here in London, and one over in France that come at night and access the hold."

"And," She scarcely could bring herself to think it. "This is a motive for murder."

"What do you mean?" He leaned against the counter.

"My parents' murder, that is. My father was the inventor. He would be overseeing the building of the airship. Uncle Cyrus, and Mr. Graham both mentioned that he usually worked on several projects at once. If he had left during construction and come back—"

"They could have finished the hold without him knowing. But he was murdered, which means he must have figured something out." Byron finished.

Mira felt several parts of the puzzle coming together inside her head. A feeling of relief spread over her, but that feeling was quickly overshadowed by more questions.

"Except, what about Pennington? We may have uncovered a crime syndicate but how was he involved?" she asked.

"I'm not sure." He placed the powders into separate bags. "But what I do know is that I need to escort you home. It's getting late and Nero must be getting worried."

Mira looked back into the living room and out the window. The sun was setting. She nodded. "Alright."

He placed the bags of powder into his satchel along with his journal. He headed for the door, and she followed. He offered his arm to her, which she took, and they walked towards her home.

"Tomorrow I think we should check back at the deceased's rooms again. There might be something else we missed," he said.

Mira nodded. He continued, "I'm going to stop by Scotland Yard before heading home this evening as well. It would be good to get a second opinion on these powders, and I'd like to find out if they caught those scoundrels." He patted the top of her hand and looked deeply into her eyes, his gaze and tone turning serious.

"I'm just glad they didn't injure you in any way. I'd never forgive myself if they had."

"Byron, like I said, I'm fine."

"They threatened to kill you and very well could have. This work is dangerous." He paused for a moment.

"I want you to seriously consider why you are doing this, Mira. If this is what you really want. According to my journal I've been in more dangerous situations than that. I don't want you getting hurt."

"I'm fine."

"Promise me you'll think hard about this?"

She hesitated. "I promise."

They stopped in front of her rooms. He seemed reluctant to leave her.

"May I walk you in?" She thought a moment and nodded. Then she led him up to the door and unlocked it, going in. He followed.

Everything was as she left it. Pencils and drawing paper on the table in the small front room. Kitchen spotless. Cat mewing at her feet. She picked Nero up and cradled him in her arms. Byron came in warily. He walked into the front room and then into the back. She followed him as he went up the stairs and checked each room. He came back into the living room again.

"No one is here." He allowed his shoulders to relax.

"I didn't think there would be anyone." She smiled at him and put Nero down. He went over to Byron and sniffed at his feet before rubbing up against his legs.

"I forgot to introduce you to Nero, it would seem. Nero, this is Byron, Byron this is Nero."

Byron smiled and picked the cat up. "Hello, Your Emperorship." He flashed a grin at Mira, and she laughed. He could always make her laugh. He put Nero down again and smoothed down his fur.

"I probably ought to go." He started towards the door, stopped once he reached it and looked around the front room again, and then to her.

"Goodnight, Mira." He opened the door and stepped out.

"Goodnight, Byron."

She went to the door and watched him go down the steps. He waved from the sidewalk and then hailed a hansom cab. It drove away, and she closed the door. She looked around at her empty rooms and felt isolated. She fed Nero and got ready for bed, keeping the lamps lit for as long as possible. It occurred to her that just twenty-four hours previous she had been kidnapped. She thought about the prospect of not working with Byron anymore. He was right. It was dangerous. But the thought of stopping brought a pang of grief to her heart. Whether it was for her parents or for Byron or for the case, she didn't know. Maybe it was all three. Her emotions were all tangled and mismatched. How could she decide in such a state? She took a few deep breaths and determined she didn't have to worry about it at that exact moment. It could wait until the morning.

September 27TH

S he woke early again and dashed around her rooms to get ready. She didn't care if it was dangerous. They had to get to the bottom of everything. *She* had to get down to the bottom of everything. And aside from that, when had her life ever been this exciting? Sure, she had been kidnapped, but she had escaped. She laughed at the thought.

Working with Byron helped her to find a part of herself she didn't know existed. And she felt closer to her parents than she ever had before. It was invigorating. It was exciting. It was freeing. And it was the only explanation she could come up with. Why else would she be crazy enough to keep going back?

Byron. He was so strong despite everything. And he had been so worried about her. She smiled to herself as she began her walk to Palace court. Under different circumstances they never would have been acquaintances, let alone friends. She felt her heart leaping again, and she frowned. No. She couldn't. He just was too...

Too what? Handsome? Brilliant? Forgetful. She sighed. Perhaps she did have feelings for him. But what use were they? He was going to forget her again. And again, and again and again until who knows when. He would *never* remember her, and that stung like cold steel. A deep-set pain, different from the grief she had for her parents. She knew that now. A surprising pain. She didn't understand it.

These thoughts accompanied her through Kensington Gardens and up the steps of number 27. They weren't comfortable companions, but she couldn't be rid of them. She pulled out her key and entered.

She heard shuffling noise coming from a room up the stairs. Perhaps his bedroom? She closed the door behind her and started into the living room. Byron peeked his head out of his room, straightening his tie.

"Mira! I didn't know if you'd be coming back. I'll just be a minute." His head disappeared again. Mira looked around for any new notes. There were none. She sat down on the piano bench and looked out the window, trying to figure out her jumbled emotions and thoughts.

A few minutes passed, and Byron entered wearing a snappy grey suit. He had a spring in his step. Mira turned back to the window to keep her emotions in check. To her surprise, Byron sat on the piano bench next to her and began to play. He started with a simple melody and then added the second hand. He reached across her to play the lower notes. The music calmed her, and she turned around to watch him play. He was completely engrossed by the music, playing from memory, which she found funny. He must have learned the piece before his accident. Whatever it was, it was beautiful. He finished and turned to her.

"Are you alright?"

"What? Me? Yes, I am."

"You don't seem like it."

"Well, I'm fine."

"Very well. I assume you are planning on continuing then?"

"Yes."

"Then let me catch you up on what's happened." He stood and walked over to the side table where he had left his journal. He picked it up and flipped to the most recent page.

"I dropped off the powders at the lab, and they should be analyzed either this afternoon or tomorrow morning. The smugglers weren't at the butcher shop when the police arrived. They made a clean break. Lastly, I believe that I mentioned that we should check over the scene of the crime again. I was looking over my notes of the objects in the bedroom and realized that I had completely overlooked something."

"You had?"

"Yes. Blotting paper. He had a desk, writing utensils, and paper. It's only logical that he would have blotting paper as well. He may have written something before he died. We need to check that."

He stood and grabbed his satchel, placing his journal into it and then headed for the door.

"Are you coming?" he said over his shoulder.

"Wouldn't miss it for the world." She stood and followed him out the door.

The landlord let them in without any trouble once they got to Pennington's place.

"You're lucky," Doyle said. "I'm having the cleaners come in tomorrow. The police have given me permission to, and I'd like to get it back on the market as soon as possible."

Byron nodded to him and took the key. "Lucky indeed." He then led the way up the stairs and into the rooms themselves. Another layer of dust had joined the first and nothing had been disturbed. Byron looked around a bit before finding the bedroom. He went to the desk and opened the drawer. After rummaging through a few papers, he pulled out a piece of blotting paper with several marks on it. It looked as if Pennington reused it several times. Byron smiled.

"We'll just have to decipher this."

He rummaged a bit more and retrieved a piece of wafer-thin paper used for tracing. Then he took a pen and the pad of paper and sat on the bed. He gestured for Mira to take a seat next to him, which she did.

"Mira, have you ever used tracing paper before?"

"Several times. It's convenient for copying drawings."

"It is also useful when you want to reverse something. These words are backwards because when you blot a letter, it bleeds onto the blotting paper in reverse. So, if we simply trace it..." He took the tracing paper and placed it over the blotting paper and began to trace the backward remains of the words on the page. She watched him work meticulously. Some words seemed to be incomplete as if the ink had already dried on the original page. When he was done, he flipped the transparent paper over, and they could read it normally.

"Brilliant." She looked from the paper up to him. He grinned.

"Now we only have to decipher what might have been written, seeing as there are several different letters that must have been written using this."

He took the pad of paper and wrote every word that was seen in the order they appeared on the blotting page. He turned it as he needed to see new sets of words.

March 11, Vaporidge, it, attention, company, blueprints, "true", police, 30, anon.
March 14, Vaporidge, identity, risk, money, box, post, details, agreed, anon
April 18, increase, stipend, pounds, oblige, police, evidence, anon.
June 6, last, increase, 70, continue, post, late, anon.

He looked at it for a few moments then handed the pad of paper over to Mira.

"What do you take from this?"

She read over each word a couple of times. "Well, we are missing most of the letters."

"But?"

"We have dates that correspond with things. The first two letters might be to Vaporidge or about it. Something about police and blueprints, maybe. We already know that he found the smuggling hold. He may have been asking Vaporidge about it. Saying that it wasn't in the blueprints and that he thought he would let them know."

"That could be a possible answer. Continue."

"I thought you were the detective?"

"I like listening to your deductions while I'm formulating mine."

She nodded and continued. "Every single one of these has a date and 'anon' in them. The date at the beginning, the 'anon' at the end, which means he must have signed each of the letters anonymously."

"Very good. Since he signed them anonymously, he doesn't want Vaporidge, or whoever it is that he is writing to, to know who he is," he said.

"Alright then. I bet Vaporidge asked him in the next letter who he was, since identity is in the next letter. He might have written that he won't tell them his identity."

"Now what is in common between the second and third letters Mira?"

"Both mention something about money, but don't have any numbers. The first and fourth have numbers." She pointed to each in turn.

"Excellent. Now here is something to consider. The second letter was sent shortly before his influx of money to the bank, meaning they could be connected."

"What do you mean?"

"Mira, he was blackmailing them."

"He was?"

"Yes. He found the secret compartment, figured out what it was, and must have made some sort of blueprint of it. Then he threatened the airship company, telling them that they needed to pay him or else he would go to the police."

"There's our motive for murder!"

"But we still don't know who did it. I would say one of your smuggler friends, but they've fled their resting spot for now. They'll be lying low for a while, I would bet."

"He must have quit his job thinking he could live off the income of the blackmail, and since he wasn't even helping them anymore, well..." She couldn't bring herself to say it.

"They killed him. Yes, I think you pegged it perfectly." He stood up, placing the stationary he used into his satchel. "We should probably inform the chief inspector of the new developments."

"Byron?"

"Yes?"

"If he had blueprints of the way the airship actually was, where are they?"

"What do you mean?"

"Well, wouldn't they have been found?" she said. Byron paused for a moment deep in thought. Then he pulled out his journal and flipped through it.

"I think I remember reading about some sort of cache."

"In the piano, Byron."

"Oh, yes. Thank you." He closed his journal and went to the piano, moving the glass and opening it. He put his hand down into the cache and felt around. His hand came back up with nothing.

"I would guess that the blueprints were in here."

Mira nodded. "So, they were stolen."

"I believe that we need to have another little chat with Selene Vermielle."

They left and took a hansom cab to Scotland Yard. Mira had since memorized the path to the chief inspector's office, but she followed Byron, nonetheless. Soon enough they were in front of Miss Chickering's desk once again.

"Mr. Constantine! What a pleasant surprise!"

"You are surprised to see me? I thought I came here on a frequent basis."

"Well...um...you do. But..." Juliet flushed.

"Is Thatcher in?"

"Yes...yes, he is." For once Juliet couldn't find her words. Mira couldn't help but smirk.

"Thank you. Mira?" He looked at her before knocking on the

door and entering the office. Mira smiled at Juliet and followed him inside.

"Constantine! And Miss Blayse! I'm so glad you're alright. The streets aren't safe for a woman at night anymore."

"Thank you, Inspector Thatcher." Mira wondered what excuse Byron had made for her kidnapping. Byron waited for her to sit down before he took a seat himself.

"Of course. Now what can I help you with?"

Byron took out the notepad and the blotting paper and handed it over to him. "I believe we have some new evidence for you."

Thatcher looked at the papers in silence for a few minutes.

"Where did you get this?" He looked up at them.

"The victim's desk." Byron replied.

"So, he was blackmailing Vaporidge over the smuggling hold." Thatcher let out a long breath. "We'll have to have a chat with the company owner."

"Not yet I don't think. If we play our hand too early, we may not find who murdered Pennington or find all the people that are involved."

"You make a good point, Constantine. But I'm not sure how long we can wait."

"Just give us a few more days. A week at the most," Byron said.

"I'll give you a week, but that's as much as I can do for you. This case is getting cold."

"Thank you. Now one more favor. Can we talk with Miss Vermielle again?"

"Of course."

BYRON TURNED TO MIRA, starting up a conversation while they waited for Selene to be brought down from the cells.

"Might I ask why you were upset this morning?"

"I thought we already discussed this. I'm fine."

"Somehow, I don't believe that."

She went silent and looked down as he continued.

"If this is about continuing the investigation, you are under no obligation to work with me, I hope you know that." He bent over to meet her eyes.

"No, it isn't that at all! I do want to keep doing this. It's just…"

He waited patiently for her response. She thought for a moment, mulling everything over. She wasn't certain what to tell him. How could she tell him that she was in turmoil because of him? It would only hurt him, and there really wasn't anything he could do to change. But if she lied, he would also know. He studied her face carefully. She looked down.

"Everything is fine. This morning was just a bit rough for me."

He lifted her chin to look into her eyes. "Mira, you know you can talk to me about—"

He was cut off as the door opened and Officer Wensley entered, leading Selene by her handcuffs. He brought her in and sat her in the chair across from them, cuffing her to the table. He nodded to Byron before moving to the corner. Selene quickly made herself comfortable.

"Ah, Detective. You have more to say to me?" she purred.

"Yes. We've found some new evidence. I'm going to ask you a few more questions." Byron took out his journal.

"Ask away." The cat folded her arms.

"Did you steal *anything* of the victim's?"

"No. There was nothing of interest. Much to my dismay."

"Can you tell me exactly your movements within his rooms?"

"I can try. I entered through the window and immediately went into the bedroom. I checked under the mattress, and then in the drawers of the dresser, and then in the drawers of the desk. Since I knew he wouldn't be there at that time, I didn't bother to keep it clean. There was nothing in the bedroom. I checked under every cushion in the living room, behind every picture for a safe, but no. There was nothing. I left through the window as before."

"You never looked in the piano?"

"No. Why would I look into a piano?" She looked confused.

"When exactly did you come and leave?"

"I came at ten o'clock like I said before. I left not more than twenty minutes after. In fact, it could have been less than fifteen, seeing as there was nothing to be found."

"You are certain of that?"

"Yes."

"Thank you. I believe that is all." Byron finished the sentence he was writing. Mira spoke up.

"Wait. I have a question."

The cat acknowledged Mira for the first time. She nodded slightly as if allowing Mira to speak. Byron looked at her.

"Have you changed your mind about telling us who told you the place would be empty?"

"No."

"Was that person, or persons involved in a smuggling ring?"

The cat's eyes narrowed. "I honestly don't know. They could have been."

Mira nodded. "Thank you."

It was early afternoon when Mira and Byron walked out of Scotland Yard. They strolled slowly down the street.

"She could be lying." Byron surmised.

"She could also be telling the truth."

"Yes, we're missing something still."

"Where did he go when Selene was there, if she wasn't the one who killed him?"

"As always, you are asking the right questions, Mira."

"Then what is our next course of action? We can't look at the crime scene again. It's been cleaned, and we don't exactly have any witnesses to talk to now."

He paused in thought. Contemplating. He stopped walking almost as a physical representation of his pause. She stopped next to him.

"We go back to Palace Court to go over everything we know. And to have a cup of tea."

He started back with a brisk footfall, his steps echoing off the building opposite. They reached his abode, and he opened the door for her.

The side table lay in pieces on the floor. She entered the living room and found that every drawer, every paper, every facet of the room had been uprooted from its normal place and rearranged into complete disarray. The entire place was turned upside down. She stood in absolute shock as Byron came in. He frowned, but didn't seem to be too upset by it.

"It would seem someone wanted to see what we knew. Let's go ahead and clean up and see what's missing."

He calmly began to pick up the papers and drawers and place them into piles. Mira stood there for a moment more before helping him.

"Byron, how can you be so calm about this? Someone has broken into your home!"

"Yes. They have. And really, I'm not too concerned. Everything that matters to me was with me outside Palace Court." He smiled at her. She blushed slightly and looked down. He cleared his throat. "After all, the most useful information I have is in my journal."

"Right, of course." She shook her head, feeling a bit foolish, and continued to pick up the odds and ends that had been flung about the room.

In the end, from what they could tell, nothing had been stolen other than a few address files and some notes that he already had in his journal. He couldn't be certain what was missing because of his memory, but as he wasn't concerned, Mira couldn't be worried about it. She brought a fresh pot of tea and some cups into the living room while he finished up the last of the papers. She offered him a cup, and he took it gratefully.

"See Mira? Everything is alright. Nothing of consequence was stolen or hurt. It just means we are getting closer to the answer and someone wants to hinder us."

"Perhaps you are right." She placed the tray on the table and took a cup and a seat for herself.

"Now, I believe we were going to go over the remaining facts." He pulled out his journal.

"Let us start with the previous suspects and then work our way through this new information to eliminate some of them." He flipped through the pages of his journal, came to a stop and put his finger down on the page.

"Firstly, we have the landlord. What do you think of him Mira?"

"Well, he seems like he cares about money more than his tenants. However, Pennington dying doesn't do anything to help him. Unless of course he is involved with the smugglers."

"Which is unlikely, but is still an option. What about his coworkers?"

"Seeing as Pennington didn't know about the smuggling hold before he discovered it, I would doubt his coworkers knew anything about it. They also probably weren't good enough friends for them to know where he lived."

"Excellent thought process. I suppose we can skip over Ms. Bridges?" He raised an eyebrow at her.

"Well, no. She's in the same boat as the landlord. She would have a motive if she was involved with the smugglers."

Byron smiled. "Which is unlikely as well, but it is also an option. Selene Vermielle?"

Mira paused in thought. "I think she is telling the truth. I don't think she has anything to do with the smugglers, but she is involved with a bigger group. One that would know where Pennington would be." Her thought process stopped.

"Just a moment."

"Yes?"

"She knew he would be gone at ten."

"Yes. She did."

"How would anyone know that for certain?"

"Well perhaps if that was his usual style to go on a walk late at night, or if the murderer had invited him out..." He trailed off. She saw his internal gears turning and felt hers as well.

She stood up. "We need to talk to Mr. Graham again. He might have seen something."

"I think that is an excellent idea, Mira. But we're going to have to do it tomorrow."

"Why tomorrow?"

"Do you see the time?" She looked over at the clock. It was well after nine. Had it really taken that long to reorganize his apartment? Mr. Graham could be up, but it would be rude to disturb him at this late hour. She sat back down.

"Tomorrow, then. First thing. He must have seen something."

"I agree. Let's get you a cab back home."

They finished their tea and then grabbed their coats from the hooks in the hall. She walked down the front steps into the drizzly evening air. He closed and locked the door behind him and came down the steps next to her. He hailed a cab, as it was raining, and they both got in, telling the cab driver in unison where to go. She laughed, he smiled, and they both sat back in the seat.

"You'll have to remind me tomorrow exactly what we'll be doing."

"Of course. I always do."

"Well, *I* can't be entirely certain of that," he teased.

"Then in that case you could always write it down in your journal."

"I'd rather hear it from you."

He looked at her, with that deep gaze that made her stomach flutter. She looked down blushing again. How did he always manage to do that? He lifted her face up slightly with a gentle hand then pulled it away. He looked forward again in thought. She found herself thinking artistically again as she thought about how strong his profile was, watching the lights and shadows flickering across his face from the lights on the street. He turned towards her again, pulling her out of her reverie.

"Mira," He stopped and ran a hand through his hair. He stuttered. "What is your opinion of me?" The question caught her by surprise. She paused to pick her words carefully and to ensure that she didn't embarrass herself.

"I think you are brilliant and kind. You're a gentleman. I, well..." She stopped herself. "I'm delighted to be your secretary and to share your friendship." He nodded considering her words. She looked away, attempting to hide the thoughts she didn't understand yet. Knowing him, her eyes hadn't given her thoughts away to him already. He sat in silent contemplation.

They reached her rooms, and the carriage stopped. She went to pay the driver, but Byron stopped her hand.

"I'll take care of it."

She nodded, and he helped her from the carriage.

"Goodnight, Miss Blayse."

"Goodnight, Mr. Constantine."

"I hope I remember you tomorrow." He smiled. She went up the stairs to her door and took out her key. The carriage stayed until she opened the door, and she hummed to herself as she came in.

There were pieces of furniture strewn across the floor. Pages of her previous sketchbooks ripped out and in shreds on top of that. Her eyes widened as she came in, walking through the main hallway and into the sitting room. It was difficult to move because of all the debris left in the wake of an unknown destructive force. A rustling noise came from up the stairs. She looked out the window. The cab had driven out of sight. She picked up a table leg and wielded it over her head as she walked up the stairs to her bedroom. The room had been darkened by a curtain that obstructed the moonlight. The folds of the fabric swayed in a breeze. The window was open. Once her eyes adjusted, she saw that the room was similarly destroyed. A hissing came from beneath the bed. Nero. She tried the light. She heard a buzzing noise, but the lights were out.

She held her weapon closer to her ready to strike. She entered the room, and a paper crumpled beneath her foot. She jolted, breath catching in her chest. Carefully, she examined the rest of her room and then knelt to look under the bed. Pitch black. The hissing continued.

"Come out little one. It's only me."

Her voice shook, and her entire body trembled. Nero didn't come out, and she couldn't see well enough to reach for him. Mira moved towards the open window. The vandal must have left through it. She pulled the curtain aside and felt the humid breeze. Her arms broke out in gooseflesh as she heard the door slam shut behind her. She turned around, pulse racing, but no one was there. She took a deep breath. The wind must have closed it.

She laughed a little and fastened the curtains to stay open. Moonlight trickled into the room. She began to move back towards the bed. Another paper crumpled. She stopped and looked around the room. Someone stood in the corner behind her bed. Dressed entirely in black. She couldn't see their face or any distinguishing features. They took a step towards her, into the light. Mira swallowed and held the table leg out in front of her, taking a step back.

"I...I...I don't know who...who you are...but..." She lost her words.

The shadowy figure kept silent, advancing. Mira kept stepping back, back pressed up against the wall. Her heart pounded and her thoughts raced. She was going to die. She looked at her table leg, and then at the knife of her assailant, glistening in the moonlight. They were mere steps away from one another. It wasn't a fair fight, but at least she could try. She took a deep breath and swung with all her strength. The figure grabbed the leg with one hand and twisted it out of her grasp, throwing it to the side. Mira backed into the corner, looking for another way out.

"Can't we talk?" Her voice faltered.

A heartbeat passed, and the shadow pinned her to the wall by her throat. Mira screamed and pulled at their grasp, to no avail. She heard a thud near her ear and turned to face a knife three inches from her face. The world turned hazy, the sound of rushing water filling her ears. Her limbs stung and then numbed. She felt her weight increase, and she fell to the ground. As black splotches clouded her vision, she watched the shadow calmly walk to the window, look back at her, and escape. The world went dark.

She didn't know how long she had been out, but her head swam. She felt something wet near her fingertips. She opened her eyes and found Nero licking her. Her breathing returned to normal. She sat up and looked around the room. It was in shambles. Worse even than Byron's earlier that day. She sat on her overturned mattress, trembling. Just the day before, she escaped from the hands of smugglers. This evening her home and Byron's had been searched. She understood why they would search Byron's place. They could steal evidence or notes he had made, thus rendering his investigation useless. But why would they search hers? She felt dizzy again. They had come to kill her.

Except they hadn't. And obviously, they could have if they wanted to. They had ample opportunity. But they hadn't. She heard her heartbeat in her ears. Nero nuzzled up against her hand. At least she could be grateful that he wasn't hurt in the process.

She yawned and remembered how late it was. But how could she sleep after escaping death? First, she went through the house again and ensured that each door and window was properly latched. Then she managed to arrange the bed in a way that facilitated sleeping. When she went to find her nightclothes, she found that they, as well as most of her wardrobe had been slashed. She sagged onto the bed. Nero curled up on top of her, and eventually she drifted off to sleep.

She woke in the middle of the night having the strange feeling of not being alone. Nero lay unmoving at her feet, but that wasn't it. She felt panic rising within her, realizing that she may have locked someone else in the building with her. She stood and walked down the stairs into her sitting room. She looked around, but saw no one. She came back into the bedroom and investigated the mirror above her bed. She saw a figure behind her, entirely dressed in black. They had come back. Except this one was different. Taller. The figure moved towards her, and she found herself frozen, unable to move. The stature of the figure made her believe it was a man. The moonlight from the window highlighted his intense blue eyes. She couldn't help but stare at them. When she was able to pull her gaze away, she saw the knife, but it was too late. She saw a glint of light as her assailant's arm quickly moved around her and the knife went for her throat, missed, and hit her heart.

September

28TH

S he woke up, trembling from the cold, around five in the morning. Her sheets clung to her skin. Nero slept peacefully at her feet, his little chest rising and falling with his breaths. She looked up at the wall. No mirrors or figures to be seen. Her room was still in pieces, but she was alone. She took several deep breaths, trying to calm herself. It was only a nightmare. But it felt palpable. She mused that it was a conglomeration of the events of the day before. After all, she had nearly been killed. Wait.

She pulled the blanket tight around her shaking shoulders, her throat tightening as memories from the night before flowed into her conscious mind. She stifled a sob, which caused Nero to stir and meow at her. Then she resolved to make herself a cup of tea and try to go back to sleep.

Most of her dishes were shattered on the floor of her kitchen, but she managed to find one undamaged teacup. She heated the water in a pot and found some salvageable tea leaves. Sitting on the floor of her living room with her tea made her feel better about things. She would go to Byron's as soon as was proper, and then he could come and examine the evidence. After that, they might be able to determine who did it and then they could get the police involved. Perhaps attacking her was their mistake. They must have left some sort of evidence behind. She sipped at her tea and looked around the room.

There were pages upon pages of previous drawings and paintings scattered across the room. All ruined. All her furniture had been smashed to bits. She thought that odd, considering that at Palace

Court, only the papers had been disturbed. Nero came yawning and stretching out of her room and curled up next to her. All the pictures had been torn from the walls. She stood up and placed her teacup in the kitchen and then came back to examine things more thoroughly.

She saw that the wallpaper had been shredded. Upon further inspection she found that the paper wasn't just shredded but cut precisely with a knife. Her heartrate picked up, and she ran into her sitting room. Her books had been strewn from the bookshelf. Some had pages ripped out of them. She knelt and sifted through the mess until she found a familiar tome. A leather cover embossed and lovingly taken care of. The pages and back cover were missing. She clutched the cover to her and searched for any remnants. Eventually she gave up, blinking back tears.

She came back into her room where the bed had been destroyed. The mattress, though comfortable the night before, had over thirty holes stabbed into it and bedding was coming out. On the wall opposite the bed, she found the knife. It was thrust into the wall halfway to the hilt and was holding a paper in place. She hadn't noticed the paper the night before. Of course, she was a bit preoccupied at the time.

The paper had a message on it, pasted together with clippings from the newspaper:

"We know who you are, Mira Blayse. Leave London immediately. Cease contact with Constantine. You know what we are capable of doing."

The note wasn't signed, and a shiver ran up her spine. It was only half past five, but she took her coat and immediately started back to Palace Court, taking a carriage because that felt somehow safer.

On the way, several thoughts crossed her mind. They had tried to kill her. They *could* have killed her. They *would* kill her if she continued to help Byron.

Anxiety rushed her senses. Even in the quiet of the morning, the noise around her was almost too much. What would happen if she stopped helping Byron? First, her parents' case wouldn't be solved.

Not that they had gotten all that far, but still. Secondly, what exactly was it that made her a threat? After all, he had his journal and—*that was it.*

She reached Palace Court, took out her key, and tiptoed into the house. After placing her coat on the hook, she went into the living room to look through his files. She had to be sure of something before waking Byron up.

She rifled through the papers and notes until she got the B section. The file she was looking for wasn't there. She checked under M next. No file. Lastly under S. It was gone. The intruders had searched his files and found her address. Her file had been there before and now it was completely missing. She felt another round of tears pricking at her eyes. The rest of the house was quiet. She hated to do this, but she had to wake Byron up. She went up the stairs to the door of his room and knocked.

There was some groaning and a bit of rustling. Some confused mumbling. Then the door opened. His white shirt from yesterday was rumpled and mostly unbuttoned. His trousers had lost their crease and were also wrinkly. He blearily blinked his eyes.

"Who are you and what are you doing in my bedroom?" He was surprisingly aware, considering he had just woken up.

"I'm Samira Blayse, your secretary. I need you to read your journal right now. Please."

"My journal? What does that have to do with anything? And how did you get in here?"

"You gave me a key." She pulled it out of her pocket. "And you have short term memory loss. Please. Just read your journal."

He considered her for a moment, his gaze settling on her watering eyes, and she saw a wave of trust cover his face. He believed her. She watched as he walked further into his room to grab his journal from the nightstand. He walked past her into the living room and sat down to read. She came in anxiously and sat down across from him. Every other time she had watched him read it seemed to only take a few minutes. Now that she was truly waiting for him, it felt like hours.

Finally, he closed the book, looked up at her, smiled for a moment and then frowned.

"Based on my journal you've never come this early or woken me up before. What's wrong?"

"Did you write down the fact that your rooms were burglarized yesterday?"

"Yes, I did. And that nothing of consequence was disturbed."

"We were wrong. Something of consequence, at least to me, was taken."

"What?" He sat forward in his seat.

"My address. When I got home, everything was completely torn apart. The perpetrator was still there, they attacked me, but they got away and, well, they left a note. Other than arranging my bed and making a cup of tea, I haven't touched anything." Her words were shaky, the events of the night playing in her mind's eye.

"They came to your rooms?"

"Yes."

"They attacked you?!"

"Yes, Byron."

"Are you alright?"

"Yes, of course I am."

"No, Mira. Are you alright?" He looked at her with a mixture of fear, anger, and concern muddling his expression.

"I'm a bit rattled. But otherwise alright. They didn't seriously injure me. Or Nero."

"Then let's get back over there. You were right not to touch anything, especially the note."

He stood and walked back into his room. Several minutes later he came back fully dressed and grabbed his journal from the armchair. He placed it in his satchel. Then he walked over to the side table and took a pistol from its case, placing it into his satchel as well. Lastly, he opened the drawer in the table and removed a box and a small bottle and placed it with the rest. He looked up at her and nodded.

"We have no time to lose."

The ride over was an anxious one for them both. Of that, Mira was made certain by the tenseness of Byron's features and the drumming of his fingers on his leg. Once there, they climbed the steps together, and she unlocked the door. Everything was as she left it, other than Nero, who was now mewing at her feet, and the fact that she could see things more clearly now in the light of day.

Byron came in and gave everything a thorough inspection. Each stick of furniture, every strewn page. He stopped entirely when he saw the cuts made into the wallpaper.

"You weren't lying when you said the place was destroyed." His tone was serious, and his face darkened as he looked at her. Before she could answer, he walked up the stairs into her room to examine the carnage. She followed him as he inspected her tattered clothing, the broken bedstead, and finally the note and the knife.

After reading the note with a look of great disgust, he took out the box and bottle he had procured from the drawer. He opened it and pulled out a small brush. He turned to her.

"Hold this for me?"

She moved next to him. He placed the box in her hand and then opened the bottle, dipping the brush into a fine powder and then brushing it lightly over the handle of the knife. He examined this thoroughly and then brushed it onto the paper as well. He turned to her.

"No fingerprints. I would guess they were wearing gloves.

"They were. And they were entirely dressed in black. It was dark enough I didn't see the length of their stature."

"Mira, you are in danger."

"I know I am. But I'm not going to stop helping you just because of a note and a death threat."

"Mira, this isn't worth it."

"Yes, it is, Byron!" Her voice had risen, but she didn't care. She was uncertain what she was saying. Thoughts popped into her head and spouted out of her mouth like fire. "This is exactly what they want. They want me to stop helping you, and I think I know why."

"Why?" He folded his arms defensively and sat on the remains of the bed.

"There are only two things between them and a complete wipe of evidence against them. Me and your journal. If I leave, I won't be able to remind you. If they alter your journal, then they can erase any facts you have written down, and even replace them with new ones that you can give to the chief inspector, corrupting the case. They could steal it and wipe your memory of the case entirely."

Byron paused before standing and holding her by her shoulders, eyes roving over her face. His touch stirred her emotions, and it took all her willpower not to hug him or start crying again.

"You're right. Of course, you are right." He turned away in silence for a few moments more.

"But you are still in danger. I can't stand the thought of you being hurt."

"And I can't stand the thought of being sent away like a child. Obviously, I can handle myself, Byron. This isn't the first time something like this has happened."

"Well, it had better be the last." Byron straightened his tie. "I'm not going to convince you to stand down, am I?"

When she shook her head, he continued. "You shall continue to work with me, but you need to stay safe. We will get you police protection. You will find a new place to stay in London and I will not put that address into a file. We might also want to meet somewhere other than my rooms."

"We can't do that Byron. If you don't read your journal you won't remember to meet me."

"Quite right again." He paced for a few more steps. "We'll start by getting you settled somewhere else and get you some protection from the police, then we'll work from there. Alright?" She nodded.

"I'm sure I can stay with my uncle for the time being."

"Perfect." He hugged her loosely for a moment, and she could hear his heart beating. The rhythm was somehow soothing and melodic, despite the situation. It was short lived, however, as he pulled away almost as soon as he had done it. His cheeks had a tinge of pink in them as he turned, looking about the room.

"Well. Shall we set you up with your uncle before going on with the rest of the plans for the day?"

She nodded again and found a suitcase that had been relatively saved from the destruction. She placed things that could be salvaged into it. He helped her, and once they had taken everything that they could, she picked up Nero and they went outside to call another cab.

"Swan Walk in Chelsea please," she told the driver. Byron looked at her.

"Your uncle is that well off?"

"Yes, actually."

"Anything I should know before I meet him?"

Mira bit her lip. "He is a bit overprotective. His name is Cyrus Griffon."

"A nice name."

"Yes. And we shouldn't tell him that I've had death threats or notes or anything like that. He will have a conniption."

"Alright. Then what should we tell him?"

"Um. That there was flood damage or something. While it is getting figured out, I need to have a place to stay."

"And if he looks into it?"

"I don't know. I'm not really good at these sorts of things."

"Hm. Well what would happen if we told him the truth?"

"He would try everything in his power to stop me from continuing my acquaintance with you."

"I'll see what we can do. If we were to lie, how would you explain me?"

"Just that you are a friend."

"Wouldn't he get suspicious of that?"

"Possibly. Probably." She groaned. "And he would probably ask you a lot of questions. Although that will happen either way."

"Anything else I should know?"

"Under no circumstance tell him about the fact that I have flown in an airship."

"That makes sense as well. After all, your parents were killed in an airship accident."

"Yes. He hates airships in general." She looked up at him.

"I'll be sure to avoid that subject; however, we may want to consider telling him the truth, as it is usually more believable."

"Perhaps he will just let me stay without questioning anything."

"Perhaps."

Nero slept peacefully on her lap, blissfully unaware of his owner's anxiety. The hansom cab came to a stop in front of the house. She bit her lip in nervous apprehension. Byron paid the driver and then helped her out of the cab. She hesitated on the sidewalk. She started up the stairs, but the door opened before she could get to it.

"Miss Mira, what a pleasant surprise!"

"Landon!" She ran up the steps and gave the butler a hug. She hadn't realized how much she had missed him. For the first time in the last few days, she felt entirely safe and protected. Landon returned the hug, surprised. Byron stood at the bottom of the steps a bit awkwardly. Landon stepped away from her and looked at Byron.

"Will you introduce me to your friend?"

"Of course. Landon, this is Byron Constantine. Byron this is Landon, our butler and one of my dearest friends." She smiled at them both.

"And how did you two come to be acquainted?"

"Miss Blayse is my secretary, sir. Originally we kind of bumped into each other."

"Well, I am astonished to hear you are a working girl now Mira! Now come in! I'm sure that your uncle would love to see you. Especially after you left so suddenly last Sunday. We've..." He cleared his throat. "Your uncle has been worried." He went back up the stairs and opened the door.

"I'm so sorry about that. I simply lost track of time and had another engagement." She followed him and looked back at Byron to ensure that he did the same.

She set Nero down on the floor, and he scampered off to find a mouse to watch. Landon glanced back at her suitcase.

"Are you going to be staying for long miss?"

"I was hoping to. Of course, I'll have to ask Uncle Cyrus."

Landon nodded and then knocked on the door to the study. After a moment, he opened the door and entered, closing it behind him. She could hear his voice slightly muffled through it.

"Your niece is here, sir, along with her employer."

"Employer?"

"Yes sir. Shall I show them in?"

"Yes Landon. Do that."

Landon returned to the hall and opened the door for them.

"Mira!" Her uncle stood and came over, arms outstretched for a hug. She placed her suitcase on the ground and embraced him. The feeling of protection remained, but her anxieties returned as she tried to think of an explanation. At the very least, he seemed to be in a good mood.

"How is my favorite niece?" He pulled back from the hug to get a better look at her.

"I'm your only niece, Uncle. And I'm well."

"Well, since you're my only niece, that makes you my favorite." He smiled. Then the smile disappeared. His tone turned serious and almost threatening. "Where have you been? Last Sunday you left without saying goodbye! I've been worried."

"I've been working. And last week I simply had forgotten about another engagement."

Her uncle looked past her to Byron. "This must be your employer?"

She nodded. Byron moved forward and offered a hand. Her uncle ignored it, but Byron introduced himself, nonetheless.

"Byron Constantine, at your service, sir."

Cyrus looked back at Mira. "I didn't realize you were looking for a job, Mira. Don't I give you enough allowance?"

"You have given me more than enough. I simply need something to occupy my time. With an allowance comes quite a bit of room for boredom, and I'd like to make more out of my life, so to speak."

Her uncle gave her half a nod and frowned turning back to Byron.

"And what is your line of work?"

"I'm a private detective sir. I work with Scotland Yard."

Byron looked at Mira and then began to tell her uncle the entire story. How they met, his memory problem, the facts of the case, her kidnapping, the death threats, most everything. Mira closed her eyes and took a deep breath. She opened her eyes again and bit her lip looking between Byron and her uncle. The only part that was left out of the narrative was the fact that they had been flying on the airship, although he did mention they had gone to explore it for clues. Meanwhile her uncle stayed silent. Pensive. Watching both of their actions and smoking his pipe. After Byron finished, Cyrus sat there quietly for a few minutes, which caused Mira anxiety beyond belief. When he spoke, his voice was soft, but angry.

"You are never to have any contact with this man again, Mira. Do you understand?"

"But Uncle—"

"Don't you 'But Uncle' me. I've already lost your mother, I'm not going to lose you by having you gallivanting all over the countryside, following this," He glanced at Byron for a moment, "Charlatan who pretends to be a detective. Haven't you been reading the paper recently? It isn't safe."

He had every right to be distressed. Despite this, she wished that she could make him understand how crucial her work with Byron was. She looked at Byron. He was taking his abuse rather well. He was stoic. But his response shocked Mira.

"I'm saddened to hear you say that sir, and I see your point. However, I think you have missed ours."

"Oh? Enlighten me then." Her uncle was still livid. Byron continued, carefully.

"First, allow me to demonstrate that I am *not* a charlatan. In fact, I am rather good at my trade, hence Scotland Yard's interest in my help. You see, I use observations to make deductions about the world. For instance, I observe that you are ambidextrous, like your niece is. I also observe that you have made several journeys to India, and that your trade is in mercantile goods. You are a merchant, and you used to take the trips yourself, but I assume that when your sister and her husband died, you stopped in order to take care of their twins. However, you have always preferred the ships that travel by water, whether the accident had happened or not. It just made you dislike them more."

"How in the world?"

"You have tobacco powder on both hands and have switched your pipe between your hands several times as we've been talking. Hence, ambidextrousness. You have several maps of the world with the trade routes to India marked and have several artifacts from India on your shelves. You are affluent, and if you have been to India several times, it is likely that you are a merchant. It was simply a guess that you stopped making the trip yourself after the accident. Also, you have models of standard ships in your front hall, and a few books on nautical travel behind you. So, no, I am not a charlatan."

"Mira could have told you all of that before you came here."

"But she didn't."

"Is this true?" Her uncle turned to her. She nodded. He frowned, thinking.

"But she is still in danger because of you. She's been kidnapped and had death threats. That's more of a luxury than many other murder victims have had recently," Cyrus gestured to the newspaper on his desk.

"Yes, and I have pointed that out to her several times sir, however she insists to continue."

"Why?" Her uncle's voice sharpened, and he turned to her. Mira cleared her throat.

"This is my decision to make. I have decided to continue despite everything because," She glanced at Byron before continuing. "If I stop that will be exactly what they want me to do. Whoever, or whatever is doing this will have won. They can break into Byron's again and steal his journal, corrupt his facts, deter the path of justice, and continue to murder and smuggle and do whatever it is that they've been doing. But if I work with him, I can be his memory. With his deductions that you just saw, and my memory, we might get to the bottom of this."

Her uncle went silent and studied them both again. Mira's voice quivered as she continued.

"Aside from that, Uncle, the whole reason why I started working with Mr. Constantine is to find out what happened to my parents."

"You already know that Mira. It was an accident."

"No, Uncle. We've found proof that they were murdered. And we," She looked at Byron and then back to her uncle. "*I* have to get to the bottom of this." She saw a light flicker in his eyes and then his visage cracked, and he softened.

"In that case..." He turned to Mira, eyes welling up with tears. "I won't even try to stop you. If you are desirous to continue this object as you have done up to now, despite the threats, then there is nothing on this fair earth that I could use to convince you otherwise. You're as stubborn as your mother." Mira's heart leapt.

"You're alright with this?"

"I never said that. I am fully against you being in danger. But seeing as you would do it whether I agreed to it or not, and if it really is true about your mother being murdered..." His face darkened, the news fully hitting him.

"Oh, thank you!" She hugged him tightly, and he hugged back.

"Don't thank me yet. I have some conditions." She pulled back and moved next to Byron again.

"One is I need to know if anything else happens. Two regards Mr. Constantine." Byron nodded.

"You are to use your ties at Scotland Yard to get police protection for my niece while she is staying here."

"Of course, sir, I already planned on arranging that."

"So...then I may stay here?"

"That is my third condition. You must stay here. After all, there is no place in London as safe as this house."

"Thank you!"

"Those are all of my conditions. Now, why don't you go and unpack?"

She went up the stairs to her room while Byron and her uncle became more acquainted. Even though she visited every week, she hadn't been in her old room in months. Knowing her uncle, he likely would have turned it into another library. Not that she minded libraries, but she wanted a bit of consistency after being nearly killed twice in the last week.

She opened the door and grinned. Everything was as she left it. Her bed up against one wall, a bookshelf full of books and art supplies on the other, and a desk covered with paint and graphite in front of the double glass doors that led out onto the roof. And it was even well kept. She supposed that Landon likely kept it dusted and watched for stray spiders while she was gone. She went over to the window and pushed the curtains aside to look out onto the street. The same view greeted her. She looked around the room once again and saw Nero curled up on a blanket on the bed. She smiled. She wasn't the only one that felt at home again. With that thought she began to unpack.

Byron and Cyrus were in the middle of a conversation about Scotland Yard when she returned.

"Why would they request the assistance of a detective without just simply hiring them?" Cyrus relit his pipe.

"I believe I originally was working towards being hired on there, however after my accident they couldn't exactly trust my memory.

They trust me well enough now to help them solve tricky cases, however, but not enough to put me on salary. I'm paid on a case-by-case basis." Cyrus nodded at his explanation and Byron smiled. Her uncle saw her and beckoned her in.

"How did your room look?"

"Exactly the way I left it. Pristine, even."

He smiled. Byron cleared his throat. "Now, I believe that Mira and I need to be going."

"You're leaving again?"

"She'll be safe, I promise you. We're just going to head over to Scotland Yard to arrange the police protection, or at least get someone to watch the house, and then I think we had plans for something else?" He looked to her for confirmation.

"Mr. Graham. We were going to talk to him again."

"Oh yes. I'm glad you remembered." He looked over at her teasing.

"Then I won't delay you. I'll expect you back tonight," Cyrus said, looking between them.

They left Swan Walk in much higher spirits than when they had come.

"I'd say that went rather well, don't you think?"

"He practically yelled at you, Byron!" She laughed.

"And called me a Charlatan. I've been called many things: brilliant, charming, debonair, but never a charlatan." He flashed a grin at her, and she could tell he was teasing again. She laughed more, and he laughed with her.

"Considering what you said before that encounter, I am surprised I left with my head attached after everything I've let happen to you." His laughter died down.

"It couldn't be helped Byron. It isn't your fault."

"Still. I wish that I could have done something to prevent it."

"Well if I hadn't been kidnapped, we wouldn't know the full involvement the smugglers had with Pennington."

"We'd have found that out eventually, and I would rather have you out of danger without a clue, than in danger with several."

"But I did speed the case up, didn't I?"

"I believe so."

She smiled. "So, first to Scotland Yard, and then to Mr. Graham's?"

"Indeed."

They entered Scotland Yard and found it difficult to navigate. People crowded the stairwells and hallways, with constables rushing between offices and interrogation rooms. Miss Chickering was up to her neck in paperwork, but she didn't hesitate to start up a conversation.

"Mr. Constantine! And Miss Blayse. Back again, I see." She wasn't too pleased to see Mira. The thought briefly crossed her mind that Juliet had a motive for threatening Mira to leave London, but Mira surmised that she wasn't a likely suspect. She may be rude, and occasionally annoy Mira with her constant attentions on Byron, but she wasn't the type to do that sort of thing. Besides, Mira highly doubted she was strong enough to have been her assailant.

"Yes Miss Chickering, just stopping in to speak with the chief inspector." Byron was cheerful.

"Are you here to help with the new evidence in the Whitechapel Case?" Juliet said.

"Whitechapel Case?"

"Yes! Didn't you hear? The Central News Agency got a letter about the murders in Whitechapel!"

"I'm afraid I don't know what you are talking about."

"Must be your memory again. I thought your new secretary was supposed to help with that." Mira looked away. Byron gave Juliet a glare.

"She is. And I believe this Whitechapel business is news to us. We are actually here about the Pennington case."

"You have new evidence then?"

"Sort of. Not exactly."

"Well, he's swamped at the moment, but," She hesitated and looked at the door, almost worried. "I think he'd be glad to see you."

"And right you are." Raymond Thatcher stepped out of his office and put on his hat.

"Thatcher, what is going on? I've never seen Scotland Yard like this before." Byron moved over to the chief inspector.

"A major lead has been found for those Whitechapel murders."

"Miss Chickering mentioned that. What are the Whitechapel murders?"

"Just the other four murder cases I've been working on. They've taken place over the course of the last few months. The first was back in April."

"Do you always have so many cases to solve?" Mira asked.

"Usually I have at least two on my hands, and these murders were like no other I had ever seen. I've been trying to track senseless clues for weeks, even months. None of my constables have found any connections to the victims, except for their living conditions and the fact that these murders are gruesome. Definitely not for the faint of heart." Mira remembered the photographs that were on his desk a few days before and paled.

"I must have not written it down, or did you tell me about this at all?" Byron asked.

"I may have mentioned it in passing. That's why I had clearance to assign you to the Pennington case. The other was deemed of more importance. But with the letter they received they aren't going to take any chances. The more experienced chief inspectors and superintendents have been put on the case. They are simply waiting for the letter to be forwarded from the Central News Agency."

"They've taken you off of the case?" Byron looked surprised.

"So it would seem." Thatcher drooped with discouragement.

"Where are you going, then?" Byron asked.

"To clarify the cause of death of an old man. Since he lived in the same building as Pennington, we have to establish that it wasn't related to that."

She felt a pang of grief hit her heart and then settle somewhere in her stomach.

"Not Mr. Graham?"

THEY ACCOMPANIED the chief inspector on his ride over to the crime scene in a hansom cab. It was a bit crowded with the chief inspector, Byron, herself, and Officer Wensley.

"We got the news about an hour before you came by. I sent Wensley, and he reported back. It wasn't until then that I saw the significance. Two deaths in the same building?"

Officer Wensley leaned forward in his seat. "Mr. Morrison let me in when I got there. It looked like a clear case of natural causes, but my gut says there's something more to it. Something seemed off. Not sure what."

The chief inspector rubbed his temples. "I'm having a medical examiner take a look just to be sure it wasn't another murder."

"And one of them a witness to the other." Byron trailed off, deep in thought. Mira sat in silence.

"We had talked to him, of course, but there wasn't much useful information," Thatcher said.

"You had determined that there was a woman?"

Wensley looked at the inspector. "Not until you brought it up, no."

"Mr. Graham supplied us with that information. We were actually going over today to ask him some more questions," Byron said.

"I see. Well, he wasn't responsive to us." Thatcher looked out the window.

"He's an old friend of Miss Blayse's uncle, I think. I'm sure that had something to do with it." Byron looked at Mira a bit worried. She didn't have the heart to correct him.

They reached the scene and Mr. Morrison, the landlord, greeted them.

"This is nasty business, this. First Mr. Pennington, and then Mr. Graham. Of course, Mr. Graham died of natural causes, didn't he?" He nodded to the chief inspector, the constable, the detective, and the secretary.

"It could be, it could also not be." Thatcher led the way into the front room. Looking around, everything seemed to be normal. Nothing was amiss at first glance. Only after venturing into the bedroom, greeted first by a stench, did they find Mr. Graham, in bed. He looked peaceful enough for a corpse, as if he had died in his sleep. The only evidence of him not being asleep was the obvious smell, his blue lips and his ashen skin. There were a few flies buzzing about in an unsettling manner. Mira found it hard not to grimace.

"Were you the one who found the body?" Byron turned to Mr. Morrison.

"Oh yes. When he hadn't given me his rent, I came to check on him. That was this morning. I knocked, and he didn't answer, so I tried the handle and found it unlocked. I came in and found him like that. Right peaceful. Of course, it's bad for business. Two deaths. No one will want to rent any of these rooms out. At least neither of 'em were bloody though. That would be far worse."

"It does appear to be natural causes Wensley. Good work. We'll have to wait for the medical examiner to be certain." The inspector retreated into the living room, and the rest of the party followed.

Mira trailed behind, taking one last look at Mr. Graham, feeling ill and despondent, as if she had lost something precious and rare even though she hadn't known him long. When she followed the others into the living room, she found Byron in his bloodhound state. Stalking about the room, examining everything, each detail, every inch of the minutia. The chief inspector leaned against the wall in deep thought. Wensley examined the door.

Byron turned back to them. "I can tell right now that this isn't a matter of natural causes."

"It isn't?" the landlord and inspector said in unison.

"No. Of course not," Wensley turned towards the rest of them.

"Well...? What is it about the room that causes you to think that?" The inspector prompted him to continue.

"Oh no. It isn't anything in the room. Although the chrysanthemums do give us some clue as to how long he's been dead."

"How long?"

Byron moved over to the flowers by the windowsill. They looked under the weather, wilting and shriveling up, the color nearly faded away. He pressed a finger to the soil.

"Three days at the least. The soil is almost entirely dry. It takes a few days for that to happen, and Mr. Graham was rather fond of these mums." With that he went to the kitchen and filled up a pitcher, returning and reviving the plants. Mira smiled a little at that. How thoughtful of him to take care of them even though Mr. Graham was dead. She looked back towards the bedroom and her smile disappeared. She was brought out of her thoughts by the Inspector.

"If it isn't something in the room, then what prompts you to say it isn't natural causes?"

"Mr. Morrison, you said you just found the door unlocked?" Wensley asked.

"Yes, it was."

"From my interactions with Mr. Graham, I have found that he is distrustful of strangers and visitors. He would have the door locked." Byron moved over to the door.

"And there is evidence in the room, seeing as there are several deadbolts on this door. Why were none of them used?" Wensley gestured as Byron locked and unlocked one of them for, what Mira thought was, dramatic effect.

"Well, I suppose we shall see what the medical examiner says," the inspector said.

The medical examiner agreed with Byron on the timeline. It was declared that Mr. Graham had been dead for three days. However, in order to determine the cause of death, an autopsy would have to be performed. The medical examiner, chief inspector, Fred Wensley, and the other constables took the body and returned to Scotland Yard. Mr. Morrison returned to his rooms to arrange for the new vacant residence to be cleaned. Mira and Byron were alone in the front room. They sat in silence for some time, she on the couch they had occupied a week or so before, and he in the chair Mr. Graham had taken. He broke the silence.

"It was nice to deduct with Fred again. He really does have the makings of a chief inspector."

Mira remained silent, encased in her thoughts. He looked around from his seat as the vibrations from his voice dissipated. He cleared his throat and tried again.

"It is a pity. He was a nice old man and probably would have lived several more years if it weren't for this."

"I know." She stared at her feet.

"I rather liked him, even if he was grumpy at first acquaintance."

"I did too."

"I can only hope that whoever did this made a mistake in their haste to cover their tracks from the first murder."

"Are you saying it would be worth it then? If we get our evidence, and solve this crime, then that makes up for his death?" She looked up at him in disbelief.

"Of course not. I would rather neither of them died. Pennington or Mr. Graham. I would love nothing more than for there to be no crime, even if it does mean I'm out of a job. But that's not the way the world is, Mira. Mr. Graham died, but that doesn't mean it has to be in vain."

She looked down. He softened and moved over next to her on the couch. He placed his hand on hers.

"I'm sorry. I can see this has really upset you."

"This is personal to me. He knew my parents, after all."

"I don't think I knew that."

"You did. You've just forgotten," she said, knowing she was twisting the knife. He winced, but for the moment she didn't care.

"I'll write that down." His voice was softer too. "And I'll try to remember."

She looked up at him, he gave her a reassuring smile and squeezed her hand. She looked down again and composed herself. Then she stood and turned, gazing about the room.

"Perhaps we should take a look around the place and see if we can find anything." Her voice cracked as she spoke.

"Yes. Let's." He stood to sleuth again. She watched him for a moment or so before looking around herself.

She started in the living room. Same overstuffed chair, same couch, carpet completely clean. The mums were looking a bit better with the water, although their colors were still faded from their original glory. She determined to take at least one of them home with her. She looked at the door. No sign of forced entry. Just several deadbolts left unused. She hoped his death was natural, but something in the pit of her stomach told her otherwise. The same something that told her that her parents had been murdered. She continued to search.

In the kitchen, she found that the counters were mostly clear, other than a tea tray with the usual things. Teapot, sugar bowl, creamer, two saucers. She paused. There were no teacups. She looked at the rack of teacups hanging above the hob. There were two missing. She furrowed her brow. They weren't in the living room. She checked the cupboards in the kitchen. No teacups. She went to find Byron.

He was in the bedroom, checking the closets, the dresser drawers, and under the bed. She cleared her throat.

"Byron."

"Yes Mira?" He appeared kneeling behind the bed.

"I found something that's off."

"Brilliant! Show me."

She walked into the kitchen and showed him the tea tray and the missing teacups.

"They have to be around here somewhere, but they aren't in the living room or the kitchen."

"And I didn't see any in the bedroom either," he said.

"Well if he was entertaining, I would venture to guess the cups would be in one of those two places."

"Are you always this observant?"

"You've trained me well."

"Then continue. Please. I enjoy watching you conjecture."

"Alright. He must have been entertaining the murderer, who perhaps poisoned his tea and then helped Mr. Graham into bed before stealing the evidence of the teacups."

"Definitely a logical conclusion."

"But if the teacups are gone, what do we do?"

"First, we make sure they are actually gone." He moved over to the rubbish bin and looked inside.

"Well, it was worth a shot." He closed the lid.

"I think the murderer is smart enough not to leave the teacups at the scene of the crime."

"Like I said, it was worth a shot. Let's talk with the landlord. Hopefully the dust cart hasn't come recently, and the rubbish will still be around here somewhere. And even if it isn't, perhaps Mr. Morrison will have seen who came to visit Mr. Graham."

"Rubbish? Why would you care about the rubbish?"

Doyle Morrison was certainly not a gentleman. Even if Mira had never talked to him before, one could simply tell from his living circumstances. Papers here, tables and chairs piled with this, that, or the other, and the distinct smell of mold greeted them. Even though he wasn't a gentleman he tried desperately to imitate one. The fabrics used in his carpets and furniture looked to be more expensive, but by one touch you could easily tell they were cheaply made. The stains on them didn't help, either. Mira imagined that this room might have once been nice if it weren't for the person living in it. It was a matter of irony that the line of questioning went the way it did.

"We just want to know if the dust cart has come in the last four days." Byron rubbed his temples for a moment. Mira could tell he was annoyed again. She suppressed a smile.

"No. It hasn't. It's due to come tomorrow. What do you need with it?"

"We're just looking for something. But while we are here...we were wondering if you could tell us some information." His tone became exasperated.

"Well, I don't know anything. And you don't work for the police so there is no reason for me to talk to you."

Mira took the helm of the conversation. "Ah, we don't work for them, but we do work with them. If you answer our questions now, it is more likely you won't have to answer any more questions later."

Mr. Morrison considered the statement, then nodded. "Alright. Ask away,"

Byron looked at Mira gratefully then took the helm back.

"Three days ago, did you see anyone come to Mr. Graham's abode?"

"No."

"Did he mention anything about a visitor coming?"

"No."

"Did you notice anything at all three days ago?"

"If I did, I've forgotten. I have a great deal to look after and no time to pay attention to this and that. I only bother my tenants when the rent is due. I allow them their privacy."

Byron took a deep breath.

"Thank you, Mr. Morrison. Now, where might your rubbish pile be?"

Mr. Morrison led them to a back alley where the rubbish was kept for the dust cart.

202 | NATALIE BRIANNE

"Don't know what your obsession is with it but go ahead and help yourself."

He left the alley and headed back into the building. Byron took some gloves out of his pocket and offered them to Mira. She shook her head and pulled out her own gloves. They started by moving the larger pieces out of their way, then sifted through the smaller bits of waste. After a bit of digging, they found one of the teacups. The handle had broken off, but it was certainly one of Mr. Graham's. It had a chip in the same place as the one Mira had used the week previous. They set it to the side and continued to look for the remaining teacup. It wasn't long before they found it and reunited the pair.

"Seems as if we've found what we came for." Byron brushed his hands off.

"So, it definitely was murder?"

"Definitely. We just need to get these to Scotland Yard, and hopefully we'll get some answers." She nodded. He frowned and picked up one of the teacups, holding it up by the handle. He inspected a spot around the rim. A red one. It looked like some sort of red paste.

"This looks promising. What do you make of that color Mira?"

"It looks a bit like lip rouge."

"Currently unfashionable, dictated as impolite by the queen, and yet we find it on this teacup. Now, who do we know that uses lip rouge?"

Mira paused and thought about each woman she'd met while on the case. Juliet certainly wasn't a suspect, but even if she was, she didn't use lip rouge. She used the more acceptable tissue paper method. Selene Vermielle didn't seem to wear makeup at all, and besides, she was locked up. She couldn't recall if the smuggler woman wore makeup or not. Only one remained. "Molly Bridges."

"Precisely."

They took a carriage back to her uncle's together. Byron planned on going to Scotland Yard on his way home.

"We'll still need conclusive evidence that it was poisoning. Hopefully there are some traces on the teacup. And I'll make certain they get you someone to watch the house as well."

"I would certainly appreciate that."

"My pleasure. Now, for tomorrow I'll come pick you up from Swan Walk around noon. Hopefully that will stop anyone from knowing you are still working with me and then we can check for the analysis of the cup, as well as go and visit Miss Bridges."

"Byron, what if you don't come?"

"Well, I'll write it down and if I'm not there by noon, then come to Palace Court and find me."

"And if you aren't there?"

"I'll be sure to make a note of it. Trust me."

The carriage stopped in front of her uncle's house and Byron helped her out. He kissed her hand gently.

"I'll see you tomorrow."

Mira watched him drive out of sight before going inside. Dinner was waiting, and idle conversation with her uncle, but she couldn't stop thinking about poor Mr. Graham. Killed just because he might have known something. She thought of the Whitechapel murders. The photographs she had seen on Inspector Thatcher's desk. She excused herself early from the table. She went up to her room to find Nero waiting for her. She sat at her desk and pulled out a fresh piece of paper. The events of the day replayed in her head over and over, stopping on the murders and the death threats. She thought about Molly Bridges crying and couldn't possibly imagine her killing her significant other. Then, her thoughts turned to Byron.

The way Byron had acted that morning. His easy trust. He was so serious about everything. It made her hope for a moment that perhaps, just perhaps, he was remembering something. Remembering her.

A knock at the door jolted her out of her thoughts. "Come in."

Landon peeked his head around the door. "Miss Mira?"

"Oh. It's only you." She looked back at the drawing she had been working on. Landon placed a tray with tea and biscuits in front of her.

"Do you want to talk?" He pulled up a chair. She sat up, giving him her full attention. He only breached his butler protocol when he was feeling especially fatherly towards her.

"What about?" She picked up a biscuit and nibbled at it.

"Well perhaps we can start with why you've been acting so strange these last few weeks. I'd like to believe it was simply your employment, but I'm not certain."

"I've been acting strange?"

"Leaving without saying goodbye, being more reserved, not showing interest in your favorite foods. What's going on?"

She paused for a moment thinking over it all. "In all honesty I'm not certain. There are so many things in my head now."

"Would it help to talk them out?"

"Perhaps."

"Where shall we start then?"

"My parents I suppose. I know now beyond a shadow of a doubt that they were murdered."

"Murdered?" Landon pulled back in surprise.

"We've been investigating it. And the evidence points to that. The Vaporidge company wanted them dead for some reason."

"I see."

"I've just felt for so long that their accident was more than that. And now that I know, I thought it would make me feel better somehow. That finding the truth would bring me closer to them. The investigation is by no means over but..."

"You haven't found the closure you were looking for?"

"Exactly."

"Closure comes with time. You need to allow yourself the time to grieve."

"Eighteen years isn't long enough?"

"Sometimes a lifetime isn't long enough." He looked down. "I don't think I ever told you about Mrs. Tisdale. After all, she died before you were born." He took off the glove on his left hand. A golden wedding band shone in the dwindling light.

"No, you hadn't. You were married?" Mira filed away this new information.

"I am married. Just because she has passed on, doesn't mean she isn't here." He placed a hand on his heart. "Every day I miss her. It's been over thirty years. She died in childbirth. Which is why I feel so fortunate that I've had the opportunity to help raise you and your brother."

"I'm so sorry."

"Don't be. It isn't your fault any more than it is mine. It is something that happened, and though it grieves me every day, I know things will be alright. It may take a lifetime for you to accept the loss of your parents, Mira. Sometimes there isn't closure." He put his glove back on.

"But that's all I want!"

"Is it, though? When you close a chapter, that means it is done. You don't think about it. You forget. It is possible to move past things in life, but if we don't keep it slightly open in our memory, it will be forgotten." He paused to pour a cup of tea for himself. "And if you hadn't kept it open so far, you wouldn't have met Byron." He took a sip.

"Well, I would have. After all, we met at a cafe before I even went looking for a private detective."

"But would you know him now?"

"Probably not." She blew a strand of hair from her face.

"I suppose that isn't a problem though. Is it?" He took another sip.

"No! It would be awful if I had never met him. I wouldn't trade these last few weeks for anything!"

"Because of the mystery or because of him?" He set his teacup down.

"Because of..." She trailed off, struck by an epiphany. "That's actually one of the things that's been bothering me."

"Oh?"

"The thrill of the mystery, the chase, tracking down clues, everything; I love it. It speaks to some fundamental part of me. I can't help but be drawn to it, but I really shouldn't."

"Why not?"

"Well it isn't really ladylike, is it?"

"Since when were you interested in being ladylike?" His eyes sparkled.

"It's just, this is so new to me. Chasing down criminals, sneaking into places I shouldn't be in, questioning people, solving murders, this shouldn't be interesting to me. Should it?"

"Perhaps not. But then again, it depends on your reasons for doing it."

"What do you mean?"

"Motive is a strong indicator of character. Why do people join the military?"

"I don't see how this is relevant."

"Bear with me. Why do people join the military?"

"To protect the country?"

"That's one reason. And an admirable one at that. But that isn't the main reason I joined the regiment."

"I didn't know you were in the military."

"There are many things you don't know about me, Mira."

"Why did you join?"

"There was the promise of adventure. Foreign lands. Scouting missions. Discovering new places. All of that was highly tempting to a brash, young lad like me."

"Why not become an explorer, then?"

"I didn't have the fortune to spend on expeditions. But by joining the military, I got my adventures as well as a salary I could send back to my wife. However, joining the military meant the possibility of coming face to face with death. Killing other men. I didn't enjoy that part at all. If I did, there would have been a major problem. I'm not a killer. But I have killed people. Ask yourself what your motive is, and then you can determine whether it is wrong or right."

"I just enjoy finding the clues, putting them together, it's all just so fascinating. It's as if my artistic observations have a new purpose beyond sketching."

"I don't see anything wrong with that, as long as you are safe. And aside from that, you are helping people by solving these crimes."

"I guess that's true, but..."

"Yes?"

"There's another part to it. Byron is just so different. In a good way, of course. He's exciting, and brilliant, and spontaneous."

"He sounds wonder—"

"But I can't like him." Mira interrupted.

"Whatever do you mean?"

"Firstly, because it would get in the way. I can't focus on emotions when I'm around him. He needs me to focus on the mystery. Not him."

"Can't you do both?"

"I don't know. But even if I could, what use would it be? He can't remember me. It isn't like he'd fall in love with me."

"You'd be surprised. But I understand. You don't want to get your hopes up in case he'll never remember you."

"Exactly. It just makes sense to keep my emotions in check."

"Then, what's the problem?"

"I can't convince my emotions of that! Every time I get around him, or look at him, or talk with him, I start getting butterflies. Often enough, I can push them to the side, but other times they are insufferable!"

"Emotions are strong beasts. It is possible to control them, but it can be difficult. Especially when it comes to love."

"They're making things too complicated. I can't be falling in love with him! It's been less than two weeks."

"And who is to say that love has a timeline? Two weeks, two years, two days? What does that matter to the heart?"

"Landon, I swear if you got that line from Wordsworth or Keats—"

"Perhaps it is a paraphrase, but does that make it less true?"

"I suppose not."

"It isn't wrong to fall in love. Even if it is unrequited. It can certainly be painful, but you can learn a lot. About yourself, and about the world. I wouldn't worry too much about your feelings. Just let them be what they are. Things will work themselves out."

"Patience isn't exactly my strong suit."

"Then this is the perfect opportunity to learn."

"There's another problem, though."

"And what is that?"

"I'm not sure if my feelings for Byron are actual feelings for him or just a longing for my parents."

"What do you mean by that?"

"He keeps reminding me of someone. I can only assume it's my dad. The way he smiles and makes me laugh. I think I remember how Dad used to make Mum laugh. But shouldn't I love him for him, not for what I've lost?"

"Oftentimes in life we are attracted to things that are familiar. There's nothing wrong with that. His familiarity is what made you like him to begin with. If you love him—"

"I don't love him! I mean, I don't think. I'm not sure. Maybe I do?"

"If you love him, it will be for him." He finished his cup of tea and set it on the tray. "Would you like me to leave this for you, or clear it away?"

"You can leave it. Thank you, Landon. I do feel better."

"I had hoped you might." He paused, with a twinkle in his eye. "I don't think I've ever seen you look at someone like that before, Mira." Mira felt her face reddening. Landon smiled and stood up.

"I'll keep an eye on him and make sure that he's worthy of you, just in case anything happens. It will likely be a while before your uncle notices anything, so for now it can be our little secret."

Landon's eyes crinkled, and he straightened a bit, resuming his stance as a butler.

"Thank you." She smiled back.

"Can I do anything else for you this evening, Miss?"

"No, I think that is all."

"Pleasant dreams then."

He walked out of her room and closed the door softly behind him. She sat there for a moment, nibbling on another biscuit. Her anxiety had lessened just by talking to him. Everything had its own time. She just needed the patience to wait for it.

Waking up in her uncle's house disoriented Mira. Looking around the room from her bed made her feel like a small child once again. This room was full of wonder, excitement, boredom, dread, sorrow, grief, happiness, and love. She could see all of it in each curve of the woodwork around the doors, in each swirl of the design on the wallpaper, and in every fleck of paint on her desk. She felt every intangible feeling of her life in every tangible picture frame, bedpost, and curtain. She picked up a long-forgotten doll and placed it with reverence on the bed, meeting it like she would an old friend. So many days had been spent avoiding the loneliness that came with the isolation of a small child on a large estate. She moved over to the window and brushed the curtains aside.

A man strolled up the street in front of her uncle's house. She watched as he nonchalantly turned, keeping a steady eye on the building. Byron had succeeded. A policeman watched the house. Anxiety crept up the back of her neck.

Her appetite was absent during breakfast. She took a few bites and could barely swallow them. She said goodbye to her uncle as he left for the day, then went to the kitchen to fill a pitcher with water. She climbed the stairs to her room, careful not to spill a drop, and watered the mums that she had retrieved from Mr. Graham's the day before. She hoped Byron was wrong. That Mr. Graham had died in his sleep. But Byron was rarely wrong, and the evidence towards his hypothesis mounted ever higher. She sat on the bed.

Byron told her that he would be there before noon. She glanced at the clock and lay back, realizing that she still had hours to wait.

Well, if she was waiting anyway, she might as well reacquaint herself with her uncle's house.

Swan Walk had seven landings and a basement. Her room was at the top and had two large glass doors that let in quite a bit of natural light. These doors opened out onto the roof and gave her a wonderful place to paint and sketch when the weather was fair. She had even made a little patio for herself.

The house was filled to the brim with wood carvings and marble fixtures. The main landing contained a library that doubled as her uncle's study, along with a parlor, sitting room, formal dining room, regular dining room, and a door revealing stairs that led to the kitchen area. The library was lined with shelves full of books and artifacts. Her uncle had a large desk with different odds and ends on it, and a few comfortable chairs. The parlor sat next to the library. The formal dining room was fully serviced through the regular dining room which had a dumbwaiter that went down to the kitchen.

The cook would come and go from an alternate entrance. The one she had known as a child married recently and moved to Wales. Mira didn't really know the new one, and she and the parlor maids didn't live with them. Landon on the other hand, lived in a small apartment in the basement and had a separate entrance to the house via a small staircase at the back of the house. On the next landing there was one bedroom and a large area that could be used as a meeting place, ballroom, or studio. Mira liked it because of the small rotunda-like bay window. There was a grand piano, and there were large portraits hanging on the walls. Lacy curtains framed the windows.

The next landing had a small seating area and a door that lead out to an iron staircase. If you took it down, you would come to a lovely little veranda, enclosed and invisible to the outside world.

Following the stairs up would bring you to a guest bedroom, then her uncle's room, then her brother's room. Her room was at the top and she had to climb seventy-nine steps just to get there from the main landing. She had counted them when she was fourteen and it always bothered her that it wasn't an even eighty.

After exploring restlessly, she returned to the library pretending to read, but really looked through the window for Byron. There was a knock on the door and she quickly looked back at her copy of *A Tale of Two Cities* sitting open on the table in front of her. Landon peeked his head in.

"Will you and Mr. Constantine be requiring tea Miss?"

"No, I don't believe we will. Not at this rate anyway." She looked out the window and stood as she saw Byron coming up the steps. She glanced at the clock. It was five minutes past noon. Landon followed her gaze and moved to the front hall to greet him. Mira sat down and picked up her book again. The door to the library opened.

"A Mr. Constantine to see you, Miss."

"Yes, I was expecting him."

Byron came in, removing his hat, completely out of breath.

"Sorry, forgot to write down the address."

She furrowed her brow. "Then how did you find me?"

He regained his breath. "I'm a detective, Mira. It's what I do."

Landon left the room hiding his smile.

"May I sit down?" Byron asked.

"Are we staying here for long?"

"Not at all, but long enough I'd like to sit."

"Then please." He took a seat across from her and cocked his head looking at her book.

"A Tale of Two Cities?"

"I had to occupy myself somehow."

"It's upside down."

"I'm practicing reading upside down."

"You didn't think I would come?"

"Well, you were late."

"By five minutes. But I came."

"And I'm glad."

He paused and smiled softly, then his smile turned to a frown.

"We do need to go to Scotland Yard. I'm sure they've looked over the samples we gave them. Hopefully they found some sort of poison."

"And then on to Caxton Street and Molly?"

"Yes." He smiled. "We're getting to the end of things. The light at the end of the mystery keeps getting brighter."

They took a carriage back to Scotland Yard. Things bustled, but it wasn't as hectic as the day before. Perhaps they had found something to help with their Whitechapel case, whatever *that* was. She overheard two constables talking about the witnesses they had called into the station for the day. Things seemed promising on all fronts. Juliet was away from her desk when they reached it, and so Byron simply knocked on the door to the inspector's office.

"Come in."

Thatcher's office was cleaner than it normally was. He finished stacking a group of files before looking up.

"Ah. I wondered when you'd come in. We tested the teacup. You were right."

"I had thought I was." Byron tried not to look smug.

"It was poison then?" Mira faltered.

"Most definitely. Arsenic. We'll be doing the autopsy later today and we'll check for certain that it was in his system. Of course, that only matters if these truly were his teacups."

"They were." Byron straightened his tie. The inspector cleared his throat.

"If these were his teacups, then there is no question. It is murder."

"Perfect. That was exactly what we needed to know." Byron stood.

"What, do you have a suspect now?" Thatcher asked.

"Molly Bridges. I have reason to believe that her lip rouge was on one of those teacups."

The chief inspector stood, his chair nearly toppling from his energy. "Then we can put an end to this case!"

"Indeed, we can. Shall we go on to Caxton street then?"

Raymond Thatcher's spirits resembled a puppy on the ride over to Caxton Street. He bounced his leg up and down and couldn't keep his eyes from the window. His mustache hid the start of a smile.

The carriage pulled up to the residence, they all stepped out, and Raymond Thatcher himself knocked on the door. There was a silence for a moment or so before footsteps approached the door. It opened, and a woman with two small children appeared. She had blond hair and blue eyes. Mira's heart sunk.

"Yes?" the woman stepped onto the front step.

"Are you Molly Bridges?" the inspector asked.

"Molly who?"

"Bridges," Byron said.

Mira cleared her throat. "It isn't her."

Byron and Thatcher turned on her.

"It isn't?" they said in unison.

"Might I ask what's going on?" All of them looked back at the young woman.

"I'm terribly sorry madam. It's just we are looking for a Molly Bridges who used to have residence here," Thatcher said.

"Well she hasn't had residence here in five years at least. That's how long me and my husband have been living here." Byron closed his eyes and turned away from the door. Thatcher turned to Mira. "You are certain this is where she lived?"

"Positive. She was here, at this address, at twelve-thirty on Monday."

"Oh, I wouldn't have been here then. The house was empty, so you must be mistaken." The woman readjusted the child on her hip.

"Where were you?" Byron asked.

"Every Monday and Wednesday from Noon 'til two o'clock I take a long walk and make visits with my littles. I'd do it on Fridays as well, except that's my husband's day off."

The young woman allowed them to look in the sitting room for confirmation. The only difference from when they visited before were the odds and ends scattered throughout the living room. A child's teddy bear lay abandoned near a couch. A blanket was strewn over an armchair. There was no sign that Molly even existed.

Thatcher's mood resembled a drowning duck on the drive back to Scotland Yard. His complexion dulled considerably, and he slouched back in the seat. Byron was contemplative. For once, all Mira wanted to do was talk, but she stayed silent as well. The carriage stopped in front of Scotland Yard and they trudged up to the office again. Juliet sat at her desk.

"Inspector Thatcher! Where did you go? I went to file something, and when I came back, you—" She stopped, seeing Byron. "Oh! Hello, Byron." She smiled at him. Thatcher rolled his eyes and continued into his office mumbling something Mira didn't quite catch. Byron nodded to Juliet before following the inspector. Mira met a glare from Miss Chickering before she entered and closed the door behind her.

"It appears that the criminal class has become cleverer. This is the fourth case since April that I haven't been able to solve." Thatcher slumped in his seat.

"Except this case is solved, isn't it?" Mira looked between Byron and the Inspector.

"We don't know where Molly Bridges is, or where to start looking for her," Thatcher said.

"But we know she did it. Every piece of evidence points to her," she said.

"If we can't arrest her, the case isn't solved. I'm going to take a break and think this over. I would suggest you two do the same." Thatcher rubbed his temples and gestured for them to leave.

Byron continued in silence as they walked out. Mira wasn't sure if she should worry or not. She was used to his absentminded walking at this point, but he seemed tenser than usual. He stopped at a cafe, sat down, and took out his journal.

"Byron, are you alright?"

"Hmm? Oh. Yes. Of course."

"You don't seem like it."

"Then why did you ask if you already knew?" He snapped at her. She went silent. Eventually he relented.

"Alright then. No, I'm not alright."

"What's wrong?"

"My memory. That's what's wrong. I'm missing something. Something would have fallen into place, two things that are connected, some way to track down this killer. But I can't remember. I never can. No journal or secretary is going to keep all of the facts straight in my head."

He closed his journal with a snap, stood up and walked away, running a hand through his hair. Mira stayed sitting, unsure of what to do. She hesitated, then pulled the journal towards herself and looked at the cover. It was made of leather and well-worn. She looked up again. Surprisingly, Byron was nowhere to be found. She looked back at the journal and lifted the cover.

The pages were thick. The lettering in the journal was much different from the lettering of his notes. Smaller, closer together, neater. There was a loose piece of paper just before the first page.

Your name is Byron Constantine, and you have befallen an accident. Don't bother investigating. I don't remember and so you won't either. You see, this accident has caused you to have anterograde amnesia. I know you think that yesterday you came across a new clue to lead you to the end of the Circe case. You had plans to follow up on it today. Unfortunately, that day was years ago. You'll find yesterday in the last entry in this journal. If you want to function like a normal human being, I suggest reading through the entirety of this book. Don't worry, you've written in short sentences. For now, it shouldn't take too long. Eventually you'll have to choose what to forget so that you don't spend the entire day, every day reading through this blasted thing. You'll find earlier journals in a chest in your bedroom. Choose your memories wisely, and if you can, don't forget.

-*Byron Constantine*

Mira read over this first page a few times, appalled. Circe. She knew that name. It was the thing Byron didn't want to talk about. That she didn't need to know. Obviously, she *did* need to know.

Aside from that, she couldn't imagine having to choose what to remember every day. Did he ever skip over parts of his life the way she would sometimes skip over parts in books to find her favorites? How would he know what his favorites were? What was important? Every day he must have such anxiety about what to remember and what to forget. She flipped through the pages.

Every entry had a heading with the date and the word *Remember*. She imagined that the book must contain hundreds, if not thousands of these. The synopsis told about the things that were important to him from that day. When he worked on a case, the entries were longer. When he wasn't, they were significantly shorter. She skimmed over each page, trying to find something to help him. Every so often she would look up, expecting him to be there watching her, but he wasn't.

She found that she didn't truly read the journal. Just a word here or there until she came to an entry she knew.

The girl at the cafe is named Mira Blayse. Scotland Yard had nothing for me today. I placed an ad in the newspaper to get a secretary. Hopefully they can help you keep things straight. Remember to write a note to remind yourself.

She looked over it with fondness. The first time she was mentioned. The only entry she had ever read before today. She hesitated, placing a finger on the page as she flipped forward to see how many more pages she had. Only a half dozen. She came back to the first entry about her.

The next few entries were of medium length, talking about the fact he had a secretary, about the medical examination, about the evidence at the flat, about Mr. Graham, about her eyes, about putting something in the newspaper...wait.

She went back a few lines. His sentences were getting longer.

In case you never see her again, or you are reading through this after saying goodbye to her for the last time, you should know that Mira has the most beautiful green eyes. I hadn't noticed them before, but Mr. Graham called my attention to them.

She felt heat rise in her cheeks and her heart rose within her. She closed her eyes. This was *his* journal. She shouldn't be reading it. But he had left it. Perhaps it wouldn't hurt to keep reading, at least until she found something to help him. Right? She kept skimming. The entries got longer.

The next entry talked about going to the newspaper and everything that had happened on the airship. He had written about how happy he was that she enjoyed her first flight in an airship and about how worried he was about her when the storm picked up. Of course, there was something about Mr. Gill, but that was only the basics.

The next one was shorter.

I didn't remember her again. She mentioned that I am a little different every day. I think I may be hurting her more than I thought.

She read about his worry at her being late, and then something about Molly Bridges, the stash in the piano, and then Selene. Her eyes widened, and she smiled, reading over a paragraph again.

Person told Sel V would be out at ten.

She knew *Sel* would be Selene. *V* was what he used for victim. Someone told Selene that Pennington would be out. Molly knew when he would be out because she left Pennington's at nine-thirty. He must have left with her. That was their connection. Maybe Selene knew where Molly went. They just needed a clearer timeline of what happened, and then maybe, just maybe they would be able to finish the case once and for all.

She reluctantly closed the journal. She didn't have time to waste on her vanity. But she knew that Byron had some sort of feeling towards her, even if he didn't remember her. She picked up the journal and headed back to Palace Court, hoping to find him there.

She knew she was right before her feet reached the door. The dulcet tones of the piano rang out the window. She found the door unlocked and came into the living room. He didn't look up, completely enveloped by the music.

"Byron." He shook his head and put a finger up to silence her, before continuing. She sat on her couch and waited impatiently, until she recognized the melody. She stood and moved over to the window, closing it and then stood behind him. He didn't react. And then she began to sing.

He faltered on the keys for a moment and looked up at her. She kept singing a cappella. His expression flickered between awe and confusion for a moment before he turned back to the piano and continued to play along with her. For a split-second Mira felt intimately and completely connected with him through the music.

The song ended, and she looked over at him. He looked at his hands on the keys. Silent. He took a deep breath and pulled his legs around the piano bench, so he could look at her.

"I don't think I knew that you could sing."

"Well, anyone can sing."

"Not everyone sings well."

"I usually don't sing at all when I'm in front of people."

He cleared his throat and went silent. She set the journal down on top of the piano. "You left this."

"I know." He stood up, grabbed the journal and walked to the other side of the room. He threw open the drawer to the side table, put the journal inside and shut it with a snap. She moved over and opened the drawer again.

"I found the connection." She picked up the journal and handed it to him. He paused for a moment, looking at it and then up at her. He seemed to realize the danger of leaving it with her.

"You read it then?" he stammered.

"Skimmed. I stopped once I found what we needed."

He paused, nodded, and then brought the journal back with him to his armchair. She stood across from him.

"Did you read about when we were wondering how Selene knew that Pennington would be gone at ten?"

He nodded slowly and then his eyes lit up. He rushed to her, grabbing her shoulders. He was inches away from her and his gaze turned deeper, looking into her eyes.

"What would I do without you?" Her heart skipped a beat before Byron moved into the front hall. She rolled her eyes and moved to the doorway.

"Where are you going?"

"Scotland Yard! We have no time to lose!" His arms flew into his coat and he grabbed hers. He held it out to her so she could slip it on. She found herself smiling and helped herself into it before following Byron out the door. He called for a cab, bouncing on the sidewalk.

"I don't think I've ever seen you so excited before."

"You've never seen me near the end of a case before." He radiated excitement, and it made Mira glad.

"Are we so close?"

"We know who the murderer is, we have an idea of how to find her, and we know how she did it."

"You know how she did it?"

He stopped and looked at her. "Well, I have a hypothesis."

"How did it happen, then?"

He smiled and cleared his throat. He was in his element. "Imagine the night of the murder. Pennington and Bridges have arranged to have an evening together. Mr. P has used his ill-gotten funds from blackmailing to get her flowers, chocolates, and champagne. They meet, make dinner, eat, and have a lovely conversation. At nine-thirty, they decide to go for a walk. They leave the place together. Previously, Miss Bridges has communicated with Selene in order to have the rooms burglarized." He trailed off and as his voice dissolved so did his good mood.

"What is it?"

"Molly doesn't have a motive. And we still haven't connected it to the smugglers. They knew about his death."

"Well, why don't we talk to Selene before finishing this story? She might be able to help us." Byron nodded, and they continued in silence the rest of the drive.

Only one interrogation room was available for them to use. The rest were full of careworn women chattering to police officers about the Whitechapel case. Mira overheard a conversation about some brown apron chap all the witnesses were talking about. She heard another about a suspect called Jack. They made their way to the one open interrogation room. Byron paced. Mira sat in one of the chairs waiting for Selene to be brought in.

Selene had dark circles under her eyes and red marks on her wrists from where restraints had been cutting in. However, the dress she wore made her look incredibly feminine in comparison to her tight black attire. She came in with a constable who handcuffed her to the table.

"Back again so soon, Detective?" she purred. Byron glanced at Mira, furrowing his brow.

"It's been several days. We thought we would check in on you," Mira answered for him, and he relaxed.

The cat sneered. "How thoughtful of you. As you can see, I am doing quite well here. If that is all, I give you leave to withdraw."

"We do have some questions for you." Byron sat and pulled out his notebook.

"I had thought you might. Get to it then."

"Tell us what you know about Molly Bridges."

The color drained from Selene's face. "Um. Molly? I'm afraid I don't know anything about her."

"Your complexion says otherwise."

"I don't think I know what you mean."

"On the night that the murder of Clement Pennington took place you burglarized his rooms."

"We've already been over this. I did not murder him."

"We know you didn't. But you did burglarize his apartments."

"I did. I found nothing. You know this." She fidgeted with the handcuffs.

"Someone told you it would be empty at ten. That person was Molly Bridges." The cat went silent. "So, we are right on that. Excellent. Now if she is the murderer, why won't you help us bring her to justice?"

"Because it is dangerous!"

"What? More dangerous than being in prison?"

"What are you suggesting?"

"We have ties with the police department. If you help us, we may be able to help you." The cat quieted. Determining her options.

"I will help you. Under some conditions."

"Name them and we'll check to see if they can be done."

"One: After I help you, I get safe passage to France. Two: While I am helping you, I am under protection."

"We'll check with the chief inspector. Those seem like reasonable conditions."

"You told her what?!" Raymond Thatcher flushed to the color of a tomato.

"Thatcher, her crimes are minor in comparison to murder. And if she wants to go steal things in France, how is that injuring Britain?"

"You can't just offer a prisoner freedom like that. She hasn't even been on trial yet! And we don't even know if she can help you."

"We have to find this murderer. She's our only lead." Byron shrugged.

"My superiors aren't going to like this."

"Trust me."

Raymond thought for a moment then nodded. "Alright, Constantine. I'll make sure she is released into your care the moment you ask. I'll have Ms. Chickering take care of the paperwork as soon as possible."

BYRON NEARLY RAN down to the interrogation rooms. Selene reclined in her chair.

"Do we have a deal?" She leaned forward and offered a hand. Byron shook it without a second thought.

"Yes, we do. Now tell us about Molly."

"That isn't her real name. Of course, only she knows her real one. Most of her personas have the initials MB. She's a mercenary for hire. Everyone knows her as the Shadow."

"So that's it then," Byron said.

"She approached me about a month and a half ago about this job. She said that she cased it for a few months and that she knew the patterns of this man. Pennington was it?" Byron nodded, and she continued. "She told me that if I were interested, she would give me more details about it. She said that she would pay me for the burglary and that I could keep anything I found. We met up a few weeks later, and she gave me the exact date and time. You know the rest."

"Where did you meet, and did you ever get the money from her?"

"I'd have to take you there, and no. I didn't have the chance."

"And why did you refuse to tell us who she was before? Is she that dangerous?"

"She is, and the people w—she works with are. I was afraid that she'd find some way to kill me in here. But if this means my freedom, I'll risk it."

"We'll make sure you are protected. Write up a letter to Molly, and we'll make sure it gets posted. We'll plan on meeting with Molly the day after tomorrow. That will give her enough time to respond to you and give us enough time to prepare. We'll come retrieve you before heading out."

"You don't mean you are bringing your secretary with you?" Selene narrowed her eyes.

"Miss Blayse is invaluable. She's coming."

Mira averted her gaze. The cat looked her up and down.

"No offense, but where I am taking you is no place for a lady. She will be obviously out of place."

"We'll manage. Where are we going?"

"Into the Pit."

"Not a problem." Byron's face darkened.

They walked out of Scotland Yard together, and Byron turned his gait down to the Thames. The calm evening caused the water to gently rise and fall. Yellow and orange pastels danced across the waves. Halfway across Westminster bridge, Byron stopped and leaned over the side. He took off his hat and ran a hand through his hair. Mira stopped beside him.

"We are so close, Mira. So very close to the end."

"You think Selene can help us track down Molly?"

"I'm positive. Day after tomorrow this case will be closed."

She nodded and went quiet for a moment.

"Byron, what is the Pit?"

"A place I haven't been to since before my accident. That I remember, that is. It's the very lowest, darkest, filthiest part of this city." He set his hat on the edge of the bridge and sighed. "She was right. It's no place for a lady."

"I'm still coming."

"The more I think about it, the more I feel like you shouldn't."

"Byron—"

"According to my journal, the last time you talked me into letting you come, you got kidnapped."

"And?"

"You aren't coming."

"Yes, I am."

He turned to her and took her hand in both of his, earnestly pleading.

"Samira, you are an artist. You see the world through a gilded lens. Everything you see has beauty and worth. Even if it wasn't dangerous, I wouldn't want you to come. If you go with me into the Pit, your view of London and the world will shift entirely. There are things in this world that are dark, ugly, and impossible to get out of your head, even when you have a memory like mine."

She paused for a moment, considering his words. She looked out over the Thames. "Do you think you'll need me? To remember?"

He let go of her hand and leaned over the edge of the bridge again.

"Yes."

"Then I'm coming."

He paused for a moment.

"That's what I thought you would say." He gave her a half-smile and then put his hat back on.

"Let's get you home. We have our work cut out for us if we're going to disguise the fact that you are an upper-class lady. Would you be able to come tomorrow? I know it's Sunday, but we have an awful lot to do before Monday's meeting."

"I'll come directly after church."

He walked briskly back towards Westminster and Parliament. She trailed behind for a moment, looking over the glinting water. She smiled and made a mental note to paint it later. Byron waved down a cabbie, and they were soon rumbling back towards Swan Walk. She could tell something was on his mind. Plenty was on hers. She absentmindedly rubbed the hand he had held. Suddenly, he broke the silence.

"You are planning on continuing this occupation with me after the mystery is resolved, yes?" He avoided eye contact.

"I was planning to, yes. After all, we still have the mystery of my parents to solve. Unless you don't—"

"No! I mean, I do want you to continue."

She nodded, and they traveled a bit longer in silence. He turned to her again.

"Mira, how much of my journal did you actually read?"

"Just enough."

"Enough to know the connection or?"

"Enough to know what you think about my eyes." She smiled. "No further than that, really."

He looked away. "I see."

They rode on in silence until they reached Swan Walk. Once the cab stopped, he stepped out and offered his hand to her. She took it and exited the carriage. He kept ahold of it and left a gentle kiss on the back before letting go.

"Goodnight Mira. I..." He cleared his throat. "I look forward to seeing you tomorrow."

"Am I coming to Palace Court or are you coming here?"

"Why don't you come to Palace Court? We have an awful lot to do tomorrow, and it would be good to get a head start."

She nodded. "Goodnight, Byron."

He nodded to her, and she went up the stairs to the door. She opened it and looked back. His head turned away from her as he got into the carriage. She went inside and gently closed the door, leaning against it. Her stomach held a mound of excitement and dread for the next day. She went up the seventy-nine stairs to her room.

After a bit of searching through her things, she found a large, unused piece of watercolor paper and placed it on the desk. She wetted the paper and dropped splotches of color onto it. They swirled and danced into one another, mixing and turning. Tendrils of color slinked across the page, following where the water had been placed. Her brain followed a similar dance, slipping from one thought to another. She tried to grasp hold of her emotions, but they kept slipping away. Based on what Byron had written in his journal, and how he reacted, he must have some sort of feelings for her. But he didn't know of hers. He couldn't. After all, she hardly knew how she felt.

Or did she? She smiled thinking of him. He was brave, and kind, and intelligent. He had a sense of humor. He cared for her, and she cared for him. And they were nearly to the end of the Pennington mystery. By the end of the week it would be resolved and perhaps then they could figure out their own relationship. She captured the bridge and the Thames in watery pigments and then took her thoughts to bed.

September
30TH

S he woke early the next day and spent a bit more time getting ready than normal. She made certain her curls were tamed into submission, and she wore the very nicest of her dresses that hadn't been shredded. She rode the banisters down the staircase and grabbed a piece of toast from the kitchen, humming to herself. Landon peeked his head out of his quarters.

"You are awfully cheerful for this time of morning, Miss."

"It's a beautiful day, Landon!"

"It's raining. Make sure you take a heavy coat."

She was grateful for the coat by the time she got to the church. Her clothes soaked through before she found the sense to call for a carriage. She twitched through the service, mind constantly shifting back to Byron and her feelings. As soon as she could, she rushed to Palace Court. She shivered on the front step as she fumbled for the key. The entry hall welcomed her with a gust of warm air. Still dripping after removing her coat, she stepped into the living room and wrung out her wet hair.

"Byron?" The living room held an eerie silence. One new note was posted on the wall.

Examine 'Pit' file.

She cocked her head and went over to the cabinet holding the files. She riffled through them to the 'P' section. Pit. She pulled it out and sat on the couch.

The Pit is the common name for a street on the far east side of London. Usual place for thieves, vagabonds, murderers, mercenaries, slave traders, and smugglers. Connected with Order of Circe.

Circe? There it was again. First the smugglers, then the journal, now this file. That was the case he was working on before his accident. She put the file back and looked at the C's. 'Circe, Order of.' Her hands shook with anticipation as she pulled it out.

The Order of Circe connects every case I have solved thus far. It is some underground criminal agency. Little is known at this time. Definite evidence includes th—

"Enjoying yourself?" Byron came up behind her. Mira jumped and papers flew in every direction.

"Sorry!" She dropped to the floor to pick up the scattered pages. Byron put the tea tray he was carrying on a side table before moving to help her.

"Mira, right?"

"Yes. I'm sorry I was just..."

"Curious. I know." They gathered up the pages and he looked at the subject matter.

"Order of Circe, eh? Going right to the deep stuff, I see." He put the file back in his system, closed it, and locked it, placing the key in his jacket pocket.

"It was associated with the Pit. Your note said you needed to read it. And the smugglers mentioned it. And it was in your journal." She gestured to the note and sat on the couch again.

"It isn't something you need to worry about."

"That's what you told me last time. I don't believe you."

He sat there for a moment, studying her face. Then he relented.

"Alright. What do you know?"

"I know the smugglers mentioned something about it when they kidnapped me. Something about them being a group to consult before murdering someone. And in your journal, it said that you were going to follow a lead on it. And it is related to the Pit?"

"Yes." His countenance dimmed. "Circe is a plague that has infested the darkened streets of London for years now. Their members are everywhere and nowhere at the same time. It is like trying to stop water from slipping between your fingers. They have control over the murderers, thieves, and smugglers in this country, and potentially others. I was so close to coming to the middle of it all!" He stood and paced in front of the fireplace.

"And then you had your accident?"

"That's what the inspector tells me. All I remember is going to bed the night before. I was going to follow a lead in disguise to find the people at the center of Circe. But I don't remember what happened. The chief inspector found me half dead, nursed me back to health, and here I am."

"You haven't tried to find them since?"

"Last time I went after them I was nearly killed. And at least at that point I was in full control of my faculties. Now, I don't have a memory."

"You have me." Her voice was quiet, but he heard her, nonetheless.

"No. I'm not bringing you into that kind of danger."

"You're taking me to the Pit."

He closed his eyes. "That's only because you are so stubborn."

She nodded with a smile. "I know."

He handed her a cup of tea and seemed to make up his mind on something. "Alright then. I'll take you to the Pit. But we won't be going after Circe. This time. If you are going to come with me, we must make you unrecognizable. I spent some time last night procuring some items for you. After tea perhaps, we can role play our way through what shall happen tomorrow."

"Is it really that dangerous?"

"Not if we prepare." He took a sip of tea and then set down his cup and saucer. "Excuse me a moment." He got up and walked out of

232 | NATALIE BRIANNE

the room. As soon as he turned out of sight, Mira slipped over to the cabinet of files and tried to open it with no luck. When he returned with a large bag, she was back in her seat, sipping at her tea.

"I'm afraid if you want to infiltrate them, you'll have to look like them." He set the bag in front of her. She opened the bag and pulled out a raggedy black dress. It had deep tears in the skirt and a low neckline. It looked as if it had been dragged through the shallows of the Thames from the back of a boat and then stuffed up a blocked chimney to dry.

"You want me to wear this?"

"There's a shawl in there as well. It should give you some warmth and coverage. I found you some shoes as well. Why don't you go try them on to see if they don't fit? There's a spare room up the stairs."

In slight shock, she did as she was told. She went up the stairs, past Byron's bedroom, and found a cozy little guest room across from what looked to be his study. She changed into the dress and found that it was far too tight. The shoes were far too big, and the shawl barely covered any of her. Looking down at herself, she could see the start of a blush climbing up her neck. Steeling herself with a breath, she left the guest room. When she reached the bottom of the stairs, a grisly old man greeted her, hunched over in a tattered suit. He turned to her and straightened as she stopped on the last stair.

"Oh! Byron. I didn't recognize you."

"I'm glad. Unfortunately, that outfit does little to mask your beauty. Tomorrow we'll have to use soot to dirty your features." Byron took a seat in the living room, picking up his journal. He flipped to the last written page before continuing.

"Now to put the pieces together. I believe we have enough to finish this story."

"We know Molly is a mercenary. That doesn't mean we have all the pieces." Mira took a seat across from him.

"Which is why this is still just a theory, but bear with me. We are back to the night of the murder. We had just reached the point where

Molly left with Clement Pennington, yes?" He marked a place in his journal and looked up at her.

"Yes. You just determined that Molly must have talked with Selene beforehand, which she did, but then you stopped."

"That's because we didn't have motive or a way to tie it together with the smuggling and blackmail. Now we do. If Molly is a mercenary, then she must have been hired by the smugglers to kill him."

"Then why didn't she kill him back in April when they first met? Why kill him in September? Why court him at all?"

"All good questions, Mira. That would have been the way to go. The only problem is the thing he was blackmailing them with. The blueprints. If he died who knows where they would end up. They might end up in the possession of an honest person who would turn it over to the police. According to my notes, she told us herself that she asked him over and over where the money was coming from. She was trying to get him to trust her enough to show her where he hid the blueprints. But that didn't happen. And when he quit his job, he was more of a threat."

"So, she waited until she knew where the blueprints were?"

"Not exactly. She created a situation that would make Pennington show her where it was. Burglary. When your home was broken into, what did you think of first?"

"Nero. I wanted to make sure he was okay."

"Very admirable of you. When Palace Court was ransacked, I assume I immediately thought of my journal, and then remembering I had it on me, I thought of my files. You think of what is most important to you. Now if you were Clement Pennington, what would be the most valuable thing?"

"His livelihood. The blueprints!"

"Exactly. Selene burglarizes, Molly and Pennington come back, he makes a beeline for the stash in the piano, moving the glass from the piano leaving the ring on top. He sees the blueprints are safe, relaxes, maybe explains it to Molly and puts them back. Molly hits him on the back of his head to knock him out and gives him a syringe full of opioids making it look like an accidental overdose. Pennington is dead, Molly is free to take the blueprints back to the smugglers and get paid. Simple."

"Except we found out about her."

"Yes. From Mr. Graham. She sees the advertisement in the paper and finds a house convenient for us to meet her in. We go there, she cries and makes a scene and tries to convince us of suicide. She finds out who told us about her. Now she knows that Mr. Graham had been watching. He might be able to tell us or the police that she had come back after leaving with Pennington. He had to go, and so—"

"Poor Mr. Graham."

"Arsenic in his tea. Probably under the guise of thanking him for telling us about her and reminiscing about Clement. He let her in because he recognized her. Now we just hope that Molly takes the bait with Selene."

"And if she does? What then?"

"We will go with Selene to the Pit. From there, you will stay close to me no matter what happens. We probably follow her at a distance, trying to look inconspicuous and blend in. Speaking of which, how is your cockney accent?"

"My what?"

"Irish maybe?"

"I don't think I understand."

"Mira you are going to have to stop speaking so properly. People will question it. You can't be a lady of fortune down there. You must look, act, and sound the part. For example." He stood up and hunched over, stuffing something into his cheeks and furrowing his brow.

"Wha' might' ya be doin' 'ere lass?" His voice turned rough and scratchy, something like a ridged coin scraping on pavement. He was unrecognizable. He straightened and pulled two handkerchiefs out of his mouth.

"Alright. Your turn."

"My turn?"

"If you are coming with me into the Pit, you have to play the part. Respond to what I just said."

"Alright. Um." She stood up and hunched over slightly. "I'm... um...just looking. Lookin' round...'Ere."

Byron hesitated for a moment and looked her over. "You know what, if we cover you in soot and you clutch the shawl around you and keep close to me. Hmmm."

"Will it work?"

"You'll have to pretend to be mute. We can't risk your accent."

"What?"

"There is no other way around it. Your voice is too silvery and aristocratic. No amount of soot or practice will hide it."

"You want me to be mute?"

"Yes. I can pretend to be your husband or your brother or—" He glanced at the mirror in the hall and grimaced. "I suppose I could be your father with this makeup on."

"I suppose I could be mute."

"Perfect. With any luck we won't have to talk to anyone." He seemed satisfied with himself and set his journal next to his teacup.

"Go change out of those clothes. I can tell you are uncomfortable, and you'll be wearing them for long enough tomorrow."

She nodded and went back up the stairs to the guest bedroom. She was speechless, which she surmised was good since she needed to be mute the next day. Her own clothes felt smoother against her skin after wearing what was the equivalent of a giant dead rat.

She came back down the stairs and found Byron adjusting his tie. He looked entirely like himself again, and she preferred that.

"You certain you still want to go through with this?" He looked up at her.

"I...I'm positive. We need to see this through to the end."

He slumped again, disappointed. "Very well then." He came back into the living room and sat down in his armchair. She came and sat across from him. He scrutinized her again, and she looked down. He cleared his throat.

"And what about after we get to the end? Are you still willing to be my secretary?" She looked up.

"Of course, I am. I told you that yesterday."

"After being kidnapped?"

"Yes."

"After your home was broken into?"

"Yes."

"After reading my journal?"

"Yes."

"Why?"

"Why do you think?" She regretted the words as soon as they left her mouth. He took a breath and then stopped. She looked down. "This is the first time I have felt like I was truly my own person." She looked up at him. "I have my own life. I'm making something of it. It's exciting and invigorating and..." She trailed off.

"Intoxicating?"

After a moment she nodded. He cleared his throat again.

"You must realize that is exactly the reason why I don't want you to come with me."

"Byron, you need someone to be your memory."

"I..." He sighed heavily and looked down. "Yes, I do. But you can't throw yourself into danger for the thrill of it!"

"Well, isn't that why you do this?"

"Of course not! I'm just good at it."

"Oh really? You don't get any enjoyment out of the danger?"

"Alright. Fine. You got me. But I know what I'm doing."

"And I don't?"

"I didn't say that!"

"You implied it." She folded her arms.

"You are more than capable, Mira. I just..."

"Just what?"

"Perhaps we can talk more about this after we are safely on the other side of the Pit."

"I can come then?"

"Yes."

They sat in silence for a few minutes. The quiet of it all was like a blanket, smothering the breath out of Mira. She struggled to find something to talk about. He moved over to the window. She fidgeted with her hands. He turned back to her.

He broke the silence. "I think we have planned out our disguise, but we still need to determine what we'll do once we get into it."

"Won't we just be following Selene?"

"At a distance." He sat down at the piano bench and began to play chords as he continued.

"We'll meet up with Selene at the police station in the morning. She'll tell us the time frame for when she is meeting with Molly. We'll get into our attire and follow her into the Pit." His tune took a minor key and went into a lower register.

"She'll take us to Molly, and we'll arrest her?" she asked.

"Not yet. We'll watch what happens with Molly and Selene. From there, we'll follow Molly. Hopefully she'll lead us to more of the smuggling ring."

"And then we'll arrest her?"

"At that point we'll probably get a message to the chief inspector to bring his constables and arrest the whole lot of them. Then, our job is done, and the case is cracked." He played a scale and then closed the cover of the piano.

"That easy?"

"Well nothing is that easy, but in theory it could be."

"When do you want me to come tomorrow?"

"A bit earlier. I'll need to remember if we're going to be able to do anything."

She nodded. "I'll be here. But for now, I need to be getting back to my uncle's. He'll be expecting me for dinner." She stood up to move towards the door. He followed her to the front hall.

"Mira, for as much as I don't want you to come with me tomorrow, I am glad you'll be with me."

"Thank you."

He helped her into her coat and opened the door. The sun filtered onto the rain-soaked pavement. "I'll see you tomorrow then. Rest up today."

"I will. You should as well."

"I will. Good day, Miss Blayse." He kissed her hand.

"Good day, Mr. Constantine."

She decided to take a walk through Kensington Gardens before going home. It was always more beautiful after the rain. The trees shone with a greener hue, the water a more vibrant blue, and mist rose from the dew-tipped blades of grass. She walked around the pond as swans swam in circles around each other. Despite the serene atmosphere, she felt uneasy. Her mind was on tomorrow and what the Pit might bring. Could they trust Selene? Or was this all a trap?

A man and his young daughter walked by the side of the water. They threw breadcrumbs in for the swans to peck at. One swan reached out its long neck and pecked at the little girl causing her to cry. Why did things that were so beautiful and wondrous have to hurt? The girl's father picked her up and walked away.

"Unfortunate, isn't it?"

Mira jumped and turned to find a tall man with a long face and sharp features looking at her. He wore an elegant top hat and carried a cane. His demeanor made Mira's stomach turn. A feeling of discomfort and caution swept over her.

"Apologies, I didn't mean to startle you. I was referring to the young girl with the swan." He gestured with his cane.

"Oh, yes. It is unfortunate. I hope she wasn't injured too badly."

"Yes. You would think she would have heeded the warnings."

"What warnings?"

"Perhaps they aren't as obvious to some people. But they have been made very evident to you, Miss Blayse."

Mira bristled and took a few steps back. "Who are you?"

"If I said a friend, would you believe me?"

"Not especially, no."

"Someone who shouldn't be reckoned with, then."

"Are you threatening me, then?"

"Of course not. Obviously, threats don't work on you. However, I am inviting you to rethink your acquaintances."

"I believe that is up to me to decide."

"Indeed, it is. Just remember, all decisions have consequences. I would consider those consequences before something tragic happens."

He tipped his hat to her and disappeared as quickly as he had appeared. Mira felt ill and hurried back to her uncle's house as the clouds threatened rain again.

"Back so soon Miss?" Landon looked up from his feather duster when she came into the front room.

"We finished what we needed to do for the day. He told me to get some rest." Mira trailed off, still processing what had happened in the park.

"You don't seem as happy as you were this morning."

Nero came in and jumped onto her lap. She stroked him gratefully.

"I'm just worried."

"About what?"

"About tomorrow."

"Doing something dangerous then?"

"Well..."

"I don't need to know. Just stay safe."

"I'm not entirely certain what I am getting into."

"Does Mr. Constantine?"

"I don't know if he does."

"Hmm."

She went into the parlor to wait for dinner to be served. She moved over to the far wall and knelt in front of a cabinet, opening it. She looked towards the door. Her uncle was likely in his study.

Gently she pulled a small box out of the cabinet and lifted the lid. A small frame with a photo of her parents, herself, and Walker lay on the bottom. She took it out and dusted it off with a piece of her dress. Sometimes it felt like that time in her life was only a dream, that she had always lived with her uncle. But this photograph proved the opposite. She found it in a box in storage when she was sixteen and hid it in the parlor where her uncle wouldn't find it. Her parents looked so happy in it. *She* looked so happy. The photo had been taken only a few months before their accident. Their murder. Even if it wasn't for Pennington, she had to keep investigating for her parents.

The door opened, and Professor Burke walked in. "Good evening, Mira!"

"Oh, hello, Professor." She quickly placed the photograph back in the box and placed it in the cupboard. The professor frowned and walked over to her.

"What's wrong?"

"Oh nothing." She stood and walked over to the window.

"I can clearly tell that something is the matter. Is this about you investigating things with that private detective?"

Mira folded her arms. "Yes. To a degree."

"Your uncle told me about what had happened with the kidnapping and death threats. I'm very surprised he's allowed you to continue."

"I am, too."

"What's happened now?"

"I just received another warning. I man I've never met before stopped me in the park."

"Mira, this is serious. After all of this, you are still continuing?"

"Yes, I am. And don't try to convince me otherwise."

"You could get hurt, and I'd hate to see that."

"I'll be careful. I promise."

"Mira, I—"

The door opened, and her uncle came in to invite them to dinner. The professor sighed slightly, then smiled at his friend as they went into the dining room. The meal was tense despite the topics being relatively benign. After dinner Mira quickly excused herself. She reached the stairs when she heard the door to the dining room open again.

"Samira." It was the professor. He rarely used her full name. She turned to face him.

"Yes, Professor Burke?"

"Does my advice matter at all to you?"

"It does, but—"

"I'm advising you to stop this. It's too dangerous."

"You don't think I can handle myself?"

"No. You are very capable. But if anything happened to you, I could never forgive myself. And I don't think your uncle could take it. Please just consider that."

He went back into the dining room. Mira stayed on the steps for a moment thinking it over, then climbed up to her room and moved over to the window. The policeman strode up and down the street still. Probably a different officer than before, but he represented the same thing. Working with Byron meant danger. She didn't need Byron, or Landon, or Professor Burke to remind her. This all started with her investigating her parents. At the time, it seemed harmless enough. But they all were right. She *had* been kidnapped. Her home *had* been ransacked. That man in the park somehow knew her. This whole mystery involved an underground crime syndicate. Why on Earth did she keep going back? It was insane. And this wasn't just about her. Doubt clouded her mind. About the plan, about the theory, about Byron? No. He was one thing she was certain of. And if she didn't doubt Byron, why should she doubt or be afraid at all?

Nero meowed and curled around her feet. She sat on the bed, and he jumped up into her arms. She doubted herself. Doubted her abilities. Doubted her safety. Her reasons for coming back. Her feelings for Byron. Anxious thoughts clouded her mind. She lay back on the bed. That man had something to do with the death threats. The notes carved with a knife. The devastation of her property. She was certain if she had met the man walking home at night that he would have killed her.

And yet tomorrow she was going to willingly walk into more danger? If she didn't know better, she would say that she was going mad. Except, does one know when you are losing your sanity, or does it just happen? Why would she want to go into danger? Then again, why would Byron? He had understood exactly why she kept coming back, because he felt the same way. He felt a thrill every time they found a new clue. It wasn't her reasoning that made him want her to stay at home. He just didn't want her getting hurt. The passages in his journal came to her mind, and she smiled. He liked her. Despite his memory problems, he liked her. And if he could go into danger and not have a problem, she could too. She just had to prove to him and the others that she could keep herself safe. The more she knew about Circe, the more she would be able to protect herself. She needed to get to the end of this. She needed to know what happened. And that meant going with Byron, no matter what. Nero mewed and brought her out of her own head. She went to the window and closed the curtains on her thoughts.

M ira left the house before sunrise. She wanted to tell Byron about the man in the park. Perhaps he had made a note of him at some point before, or maybe he had a file on him. Of course, it would be difficult to figure out who the man was if she didn't have a name. Nonetheless, he might know something, and then they could figure out who the man was.

The carriage came to a stop, and she headed up the stairs. None of the lamps were lit. She frowned. Didn't he ask her to come early? She unlocked the door and came inside. The door closed behind her, shutting the early morning sounds outside. She went into the living room, sat down, and relaxed. It was early enough she could let him sleep a while longer. She looked over towards the stairs that led up to his bedroom. She thought of him sleeping. Him forgetting. He'd wake up and come out. What would she say to him this time? She heard a rustling coming from the room. She'd see his response soon. Her anxiety rose with each passing minute. The light filtering through the window intensified. The clock on the mantel ticked bit by bit, bringing the future into the present. The door to his room opened.

He came out with bags under his eyes and a bit of an unsteady gait. His messy hair fell into his eyes. He fiddled with his tie, trying to straighten it. He looked up from it and saw her. His brow furrowed.

"How did you get in here?"

"Through the door." She glanced over at the front entry. She blew a strand of hair out of her face. Once again, it was going to be a harsh remembering this morning.

"Are you a client of mine?"

"No. I'm your secretary."

"I don't have a secretary."

"Well, you do. You see if you just read your journal—"

"I don't keep a journal. It's easy enough to remember things from day to day. Anything important can go into my filing system."

"Well actually—"

"I'm afraid I have a case to solve so I'm going to have to ask you to—"

"Listen to me!" Her voice rose higher than she meant it to. She could feel her face flushing as she stood. Based on the stunned look on Byron's face, his attention was fully on her.

"You have a problem with your short-term memory. You think you are going to go follow a lead to find the Order of Circe today, but you aren't! It's been years since that time. You hired me several weeks ago to help you with your memory. To make sure you read your journal every day. That is why I am here." He considered her for a moment and then shook his head.

"You are either mistaken or, forgive me for my brashness, insane."

"Insane?" She laughed. "I thought about this long and hard last night and I concluded that I'm as sane as you are Byron. Read your journal."

"I don't have one."

"Let me find it for you."

"You won't find anything."

"Then will it hurt for me to look?"

He pondered on that sentence, studied her face and then shook his head.

"Then excuse me while I do so." She started at the piano, checking inside of the bench and then on the windowsill. Then she checked around the armchair, under the couch, in the side tables and on the mantel. He watched her with a sort of peeved curiosity for a few minutes before stepping forward and grabbing her arm.

"I'm guessing you aren't finding it. Why don't we—"

"I'm not finished yet."

She pulled away from him and went into the kitchen. She checked every cupboard and counter before moving up the stairs and into his office. She checked every bookcase for it, every drawer. She checked the guest room. She came back down the stairs and found him standing in front of his bedroom door.

"Excuse me, Byron."

"If you haven't found it yet, then you won't. I've been a good sport and let you have your fun, but I'm afraid I can't allow you to search my room. I must ask you to leave before I contact the authorities."

"Go ahead and get Inspector Thatcher here. He knows I'm telling the truth."

She pushed past him into his room and started to look. He grabbed her shoulder to pull her back and then thought otherwise. He stepped back against the wall to watch her. She checked in his closet, his dresser, under the bed, on the side table. Then she saw the trunk. She moved over and pulled on the lid. Locked.

"Where's the key to this?"

"Now you are going too far."

"Byron, this is important. Crucial even. If we don't find that journal you will have lost all your memories from the last year. All your memories of each case. Of the people you've met." She thought of herself as she spoke, and her voice cracked. "Please." He studied her again and then went to his dresser. He opened a drawer and pressed a loosened piece of wood on it. The bottom of the drawer popped open, and he grabbed a small key. He moved over and opened the trunk. "Look, but don't touch."

She looked inside. There were several leather-bound journals on the top of some old clothes and papers. His eyes widened.

"These weren't here before."

"These are your journals, Byron."

He picked one of them up and looked through it.

"This doesn't make any sense. How did you know about this?"

"As I told you before, I'm your secretary. Now we just need to find your current journal." She picked one of them up and started to look through it. He grabbed it out of her hands and snapped it shut.

"I think if these are mine you shouldn't be looking through them."

"Byron—"

"Who are you?"

"Mira. My name is Mira." She could feel herself getting desperate and tried to keep her voice steady.

"Very well, Mira. Now you say that you are my secretary. You also say that I have short term memory loss. But that doesn't give you leave to look through my journals."

"I just need to see the first page of each. Then I can tell you which one is your current one."

"Just the first page?"

"Yes."

He thought about it a moment and then stepped aside. She picked up the first journal and looked at the first page. No note. She picked up the next one. No note. She looked at the first page of each. None of them were right. She set the last one back into the chest.

"Well?" Byron looked annoyed.

"It isn't there."

"That's what I thought. I'm afraid I really should turn you over to the police. Obviously, you—" She interrupted him.

"Then let's get there quickly. Get ready. I'll wait in the front room." She walked past his stunned silence and closed the bedroom door behind her. She took a deep breath. He didn't remember her. He wouldn't remember her. His journal was gone. She went down the stairs and took a seat on her sofa in the sitting room. Of course, he didn't know it was hers. He didn't remember anything. The case or her. It was up to her to remind him. It was up to her to make sure that he saw the case to the end. Everything was on her.

Byron's door opened, and he stepped into the room, scrutinizing her. Gathering her courage, she spoke.

"Byron, seeing as you think I am insane, could you humor me?"

"How, exactly?"

"Can you listen to a case that I believe we were working on together?"

"I really think we ought to get to the police station."

"It won't take long. I could even explain it on the carriage ride over."

"Very well. But we need to get going."

She grabbed her sketchbook and the bag of clothes from the day before. He walked to the door and opened it, waiting for her to leave first. He glanced at the bag and frowned.

"What is that?"

"Something we'll need for today's investigation."

"Hm."

She walked down the steps and he joined her, waving a carriage down. He paused before telling the driver where to go. Mira swallowed and took a deep breath, recounting the case once again. Byron stared out the window. Was he even listening? She continued, hoping that something would spark his memory.

"How long have we been investigating this Pennington issue?" he asked once she was finished.

"I've been working with you on the case for almost two weeks. I don't know how long you've been investigating it. But he died on the tenth of last month."

"Hm."

"Do you believe me?"

"Not entirely. It seems implausible that I forget so much every day. But perhaps if Inspector Thatcher can corroborate your story, then I will believe you."

She nodded and went quiet. Why couldn't he just remember? Not even the case, but her. The acceptance she often saw in his eyes faded away to nothing. His demeanor constructed a chilled wall between them. Mira shivered and looked away from him to hide the tears forming in her eyes. What happened to the blind trust they had built over the last few weeks? What if he never trusted her before? What if he only trusted what he wrote about her?

The carriage slowed to a stop in front of Scotland Yard. He offered a hand to help her out. She stepped down, ready to pull away, but he kept a firm hold on her wrist. He marched her right in and up the stairs but turned down the wrong hall.

"Byron! It's this way." She tried to pull him in the other direction.

"I know the way to the Inspector's office. That hallway takes you to the main offices. The chief inspectors are there."

"But he is a chief inspector!"

"You're delusional. I don't know how you know so much about my life, but I've known Raymond Thatcher for years. I would remember if he got a promotion." He dragged her down the hall and she attempted to keep up with him. They reached the end of the hallway and he stopped with a frown. Releasing her arm, he turned slowly in a circle and examined the nameplates. Mira rubbed at her wrist.

"It should be here." He turned and paced back down the hall, face flushing. They came to the Inspector's "new" office. Juliet stood as they approached.

"Mr. Constantine! Is something wrong?"

"I need to talk to Inspector Thatcher. Who are you?"

"Juliet Chickering. His secretary?" She gestured to her name plate. "You've always recalled me before."

"Where's Ms. Adams? Did he change secretaries so quickly? She was here yesterday."

"Er, no. I've been working here for three years, sir."

"Is Thatcher in?" His voice rang hollow.

"Yes. Just knock before entering." Juliet picked up a stack of papers and rushed off in a huff.

He moved past the desk and knocked without another word.

"Enter."

Byron rubbed the back of his neck and took a few deep breaths before opening the door. The chief inspector glanced up from his paperwork as they came in.

"Good morning, Constantine. Good morning, Miss Blayse."

"You know her?" Byron whirled back towards her.

"She's your secretary. Did you not read your journal this morning?"

"We couldn't find it, Inspector. It's nowhere to be found." Mira took a seat and rubbed at her temples.

"That is a problem. I assume she has filled you in on the situation?"

"She has." Byron paced behind her.

"Do you believe her?"

"I think now I have to." He threw up his hands and sat down.

Thatcher softened. "I hoped I'd never have to see you like this again, Byron."

"Again?"

"I was the one who found you. The first person you saw when you woke up the day you didn't remember. I've seen you this way many times over."

"Exactly how long have I had this problem? This girl says it's been years." Byron gestured to Mira. She didn't like being called "this girl." The little hope she built up continued to fracture as she lost her composure. She turned away from them.

"It's been about four," Thatcher said.

"Four years? I have forgotten four entire years?" Byron stood again, running a hand through his hair and walking off his nervous energy.

"You've written all of them down. In fact, you've managed to solve nearly forty-two cases on just the facts from your journals. Miss Blayse has helped immensely with this last one. But if you've misplaced your most recent journal there could be a problem."

"Could be? I don't know anything about this case except for what she has told me. How can I deduce anything from that?"

"Maybe you can start by *trusting* me." She stood to face him. Tears threatened to fall again, but she didn't care. Her voice resonated with an unyielding determination as she approached him.

"You've trusted me in the past, Byron. You've helped me through deductions. You've listened to my perspective on things. Every day I come, and I don't know what you are going to do. You've pulled a gun on me before. You've threatened me. But I still come. You could trust me as much as I trust you."

He swallowed and looked away from her. A tear rolled down her cheek. The Inspector looked between them both and offered her a handkerchief. She didn't take it.

"I didn't know if you would come when I was kidnapped by Circe's smugglers. I was certain that you would forget." Byron looked back at her, eyes widening. She continued. "And so, I found my own way out. But you still came." Another tear followed the first. "Byron, I won't let you forget. Even if you don't believe me, I will always come. So, just trust me." Her eyes met his, and his resolve cracked.

"I'm sorry Miss. But I'm afraid I don't remember you."

"That's alright Byron. You never do." She sat down.

He nodded and looked down for a moment in silence. Then he moved over and knelt next to her chair.

"But you remember me. And more importantly, you remember the case."

She nodded. "I have all the things we need right here." She pulled out her costume and handed the bag over to him.

"Ah. Disguises. One of my favorite ways to go about detective work." He hid the guilt in his eyes with a smile.

THE REAL TEARS came as soon as Mira entered the spare offices at Scotland Yard. She could only be grateful that she hid them until she was alone. Or at least out of sight of Byron. "It's not his fault," she reminded herself. If anything, it was *her* fault for letting herself fall in love with someone who would never truly remember her. She laughed a bit through her tears. This couldn't be love. It was silly. Ridiculous.

Her shoulders shook as she took another breath and took the

ragged dress in her hands. She didn't have time to focus on her feelings now. She slipped on the grubby garments and tightened the corset, keeping her heart in its place.

Today, she could be a different person. She would have to be. She knelt by the fireplace and gently lifted some soot, the particles soft and fine between her fingertips. The soot mixed with her tears as she smudged it on her face and down her neckline, then sprinkled some in her hair. Hopefully that would be enough to disguise her. She came back into the chief inspector's office and he did a double take.

"Miss Blayse! I could hardly recognize you."

"I believe that's the desired outcome of this." She pulled the shawl tighter around her shoulders as she set her own clothes down in a chair.

"I'm sorry about Constantine. It really is hard to see him like that."

"At least he remembers you."

"Ah, yes. That would make things more difficult."

"I'm convinced he quite nearly brought me to a mental institution this morning."

"He distrusted you that much?"

"I still think he doesn't trust me. I'm starting to believe he never has." She felt another round of sobs bubbling beneath the surface and she turned away.

"I think he trusts you more than you realize. Just give him some time to warm up to you today."

"I just wish I knew where he had left the journal. It truly was nowhere to be found."

The door opened, and Byron strode in. She could only tell it was him by the way he walked, he was so well disguised.

"Well?" He turned for inspection.

"Unrecognizable, save your voice my friend." The chief inspector smiled.

"Excellent. That means we can get going." He paused and acknowledged Mira for the first time. His eyes widened.

"Goodness! Your transformation is incredible." He walked around her. The layer of soot hid her blush as he looked her over.

"Good enough?"

"More than good enough! No one will recognize you."

She smiled. "Glad to hear it."

"Now to free our jailbird."

They drew several odd looks from people as they walked through the police station. Officer Wensley escorted them.

"Byron, my good chap, I hate to say it, but you've been letting yourself go," he teased.

"It's been a rough few weeks, so I've been told." Byron glanced at her. She looked away.

"You're wanting access to the cat burglar, correct?" Wensley fiddled with his keys.

"Indeed, we are."

They came to where the cells were, and Fred unlocked Selene's door. She stretched and walked out, graceful as always. She wore her original clothing again.

"Hello again, Detective." She smiled sweetly. "You are the detective, right? I almost can't tell under your disguise."

"You've guessed correctly. Now I believe you were going to lead us to Miss..." He stopped and drew a breath through his teeth, looking to Fred for the name.

"Bridges. Molly Bridges, or MB. The Shadow," Officer Wensley said.

"Yes. Her." Byron looked back at Selene.

"Having memory troubles again?" the cat sneered.

"Just ensuring I have the correct information. Now I assume that you were able to get correspondence with her. Do you have a meeting time?"

"Yes. At noon. It's, what? Ten o'clock now?"

Byron checked his pocket watch and nodded.

"That should give us enough time to get into the Pit. That is if your secretary shows up any time soon. Or is she not coming?" the cat said.

"I'm already here." Mira folded her arms. The cat grinned.

"Oh! How dreadful! Look at you. You are practically common."

Mira narrowed her eyes. Selene was almost too comfortable with her freedom. Byron cleared his throat.

"Shall we?"

They must have made quite the spectacle coming out of Scotland Yard. The ever-graceful cat burglar, the grisly old man, and the wretched beggar woman. Byron signaled for a carriage, but none would stop. With a simple change of clothes, they looked, and now were treated, like the working class. Selene led the way down backstreets heading east, and eventually south. The buildings became more decrepit as they walked deeper into almost unrecognizable territory. They passed Schwarz and Son's Butchery and Mira shivered. She did not like this part of town. Byron barely noticed her discomfort.

Soon enough, residential buildings replaced the shops and marketplaces, although the houses looked barely livable, even for rats. Haggard faces stared out from cracked windows. She tripped over an old woman dressed similarly to herself.

"Oh! I'm so very sorry."

Byron pulled her by the wrist, and away, his voice a harsh whisper. "You're one of them now. Don't you dare speak like an aristocrat. If you can't manage then don't speak at all." He let go of her wrist. Mira silenced herself but walked closer to him being more aware of her surroundings.

A putrid stench of rotting food and meat with stale urine and fecal matter surrounded them. At first, she found it hard to not grimace, but eventually her senses gained immunity to it. The sounds of crying babies and wet coughing filled the air. The buildings closed in on either side, the walls so close to each other that Mira could reach out and touch both sides of the alley at the same time. Her breath became rapid as claustrophobia entered her mind. Selene led on.

Farther down the alleyway, a large animal lay still on the side of the street. Mira stepped to the side so as not to trip on it, as she had the old woman. As they approached, she realized something was wrong. The squalid air brought on a new scent, which grew unbearable. The animal was unrecognizable, the chest cavity open, and face disfigured and rotting. Rats gnawed at the decaying flesh, and maggots crawled under what was left of the skin. Bile crept up Mira's throat, and they walked deeper into the Pit.

After about two hours of walking, Selene stopped them just before they reached a tunnel and pulled them into an alcove.

"The meeting place is down there. It's a small club, and you need to have the password. I'll go in first so as not to arouse suspicion," she purred.

"Seems like you've done this before." Byron raised an eyebrow.

"I've had some time to think about this since you first offered me my freedom, Detective."

"What is the password?"

"Ordered Chaos. Say that and they'll let you right in. No questions asked."

Byron nodded, and Selene nodded back before heading down the tunnel. Mira squinted trying to see through the darkness. Then a small shaft of light appeared. She could faintly make out Selene's face. She heard muffled voices, and then a larger shaft of light illuminated her whole body. Then it went dark again. She took a step forward and then Byron stopped her with his hand.

"We need to wait a minute or so before going in."

Mira nodded and leaned up against the cold, brick wall. Byron looked at her, studying her features.

"I'm sorry I ever doubted you, Miss Blayse."

"Please. Call me Mira."

"Of course. Mira. It would seem you were right about everything."

"I don't blame you. If I were in your same situation, it would be rather hard to believe." She looked up at him and realized how close they were to one another. He was less than a foot away from her and staring deeply into her eyes. Her heart threatened to burst from her corset.

"I do have to say, despite not remembering you, there is something familiar." He brushed a strand of hair out of her face, and she held her breath.

"There is?"

He took a small step closer, and she felt his warmth. "It's less of a memory and more of a feeling. I can't really explain it." He shook his head and looked back towards the tunnel. Mira opened her mouth to speak and then thought otherwise. They stood for several minutes; the silence punctuated by the sounds of rats scurrying in the darkness. He cleared his throat, and she jumped, startled.

"It's time to meet with Selene and the evasive Molly Bridges."

He stepped away from her and out of the alcove, starting down into the tunnel. Mira's breath returned, and she followed him, hoping she knew what she was getting into. The tunnel turned out to be a larger alcove with a brick wall blocking any passage to the other side. A door was placed in the center of that brick wall. Byron knocked on it. A slot in the door opened and a blinding light shot through. Mira blinked a few times and tried to make out the figure standing at the door. Just two slanted brown eyes.

"Password?"

Mira frowned at the familiar voice.

Byron slipped into his cockney accent. "Ordered Chaos." The man with the slanted eyes nodded and closed the slot in the door. The door opened, and the man stepped to the side. Mira swallowed. Broad shoulders, tall stature, shirt sleeves rolled up to reveal a rippling tattooed forearm: Joe the smuggler. She ducked her head hoping he wouldn't recognize her and followed Byron into the club.

Concentrated fumes from cigars, pipes, and hookahs bathed the room in a hazy fog. A mixture of perfumes added themselves to the air, creating a distinct floral note amidst the stale putridity of smoke. Mira found herself gasping for air.

The room bled shades of crimson which drenched carpets, crept up walls, and slipped through female lips. At first glance it seemed to be nice, but once Mira's eyes adjusted to the haze, she found bare spots in the carpet, drooping wallpaper, and stuffing spilling out of the mismatched chairs. An unsettling yellow light flickered out of the gas lamps on the walls.

A large bar with many types of alcohol, cheap and otherwise, stood at one side. A case full of glass needles and vials of multicolored liquids sat next to it. A rickety staircase led to a door, presumably an office. She could just make out the inside through the window that looked out onto the club floor. Someone would always be watching. Another staircase robed in red carpet led up to another unknown door. Laughter could be heard coming from it. Couches and overstuffed pillows lay on one side of the room, the occupants seeming to not be aware that the world even existed. Another room towards the back contained tables surrounded by men. She couldn't quite make out what they were doing.

The people varied as much as the types of smoke. Some dressed like Byron and Mira, but those were few and far between. A few people looked like Selene, only they had knives strapped to their legs and pistols at their belts. Women in varying degrees of nakedness roamed through the joint, talking to anyone who would give them time. Men in expensive suits sat at enclosed booths and whispered to one another.

Byron spotted Selene sitting alone at a table with a small glass of alcohol. She seemed perfectly at ease. A booth sat empty near the table. He ushered Mira in that direction, let her slip in before him, and then sat down next to her. They had a perfect view of the door. They waited, listening to the din of people talking and laughing.

He subtly pulled out his pocket watch and Mira looked over his shoulder. Ten minutes to noon. Molly Bridges would be here any moment. Mira's eyes drifted over to the door. Joe stood threateningly in front of it, the only path to freedom blocked by the smuggler who had kidnapped her. She looked up at Byron. He wouldn't know that. His eyes carefully catalogued everyone in the room. Silently calculating. She looked back towards Joe, whose back was turned to her now. He opened the slot, and then the door. Molly Bridges strolled through as if she owned the place.

At least Mira thought it was Molly. Her face was the same, but her entire demeanor changed. The crying lover persona was a thing of the past. Her hair cascaded in waves of brown instead of red. She wore a black dress with off-the-shoulder sleeves, and carried a fan. A necklace prominently shone from her alabaster neck, a triangle enclosed in a circle. At each point of the triangle was a small gem. She looked around the establishment, saw Selene, smiled sweetly, and made her way over. Mira lost sight of her behind the booth.

"Selene Vermielle! So, it seems that you were telling the truth. Look at you! Free again."

"Cut the sweet act, Shadow. You owe me payment," Selene hissed.

"Do I?"

"We previously agreed that if I burglarized a specific set of rooms that you would compensate me."

"I specifically remember telling you that the things you found in the apartment would be your compensation."

"Even if that were true, there was nothing worth stealing."

"Perhaps you didn't look hard enough."

"I've heard tell through the grapevine that you used my burglary to kill someone. I really don't appreciate being a scapegoat. I'd like to be compensated."

"I suppose I can't argue with that." There was the sound of muffled coins crashing onto the table, and a shuffling and clinking as Selene picked them up and counted them.

"This is barely enough." There was a pause before a nervous, "but I'll take what I can get."

"Your gratitude is inspiring."

"So, is it true?"

"Is what true, kitty?"

"You killed the man that lived there?"

"And if I did? What do you care? I've killed plenty of people."

"I'm just curious."

"And curiosity killed the cat. I'd consider the consequences before asking questions. Anything else you wanted?"

"No, that's all." Selene's voice trembled.

"Good. I have places to be." Chair legs slid across the carpet and then the Shadow was visible once again. She directed herself towards the door, then she stopped and turned back towards the table that Mira and Byron sat at. She smiled, and Mira felt the bile returning. Selene practically ran to the door and escaped past Joe.

"Ah. The little private detective and his pretty sidekick. I almost didn't recognize you. Pity for you that I make it a point to know everyone who enters this club."

"I presume I have the pleasure of speaking to the Shadow?" Byron dropped the act, straightened and resumed his normal voice.

"Indeed, you do. We have met before, you know. In a small house on the other side of town. Of course, I looked a bit different then. But you wouldn't remember, would you?"

Byron bristled at her comment but stayed quiet.

"Of course, *you* do, don't you little Mira Blayse?" She smiled at her. Mira felt cold all over.

"I certainly didn't recognize you in that attire. Your posture is the only thing giving you away. Everything else is simply perfect, down to the soot in your hair. I'm very impressed," the Shadow crooned.

"You and I both know you didn't come over here to congratulate us on our disguises." Byron gritted his teeth. Mira could tell that he didn't like not remembering his previous interactions with Molly.

"No? Well perhaps you are right. I came to extend an invitation."

"What kind of invitation?" Mira managed to keep her voice steady. Her insides tied themselves into knots. The Shadow, formerly known as Molly, slipped a piece of paper across the table. Byron picked it up and glanced at it.

"The Order of Circe requests your presence at a meeting of its members later this evening. I'd suggest that you come."

"And if we don't?" Byron clenched his fist around the message, crumpling it beyond recognition.

"Well, at least one of you knows about the consequences." The Shadow stared Mira down and smiled. Mira swallowed and looked at Byron. His face continued to be stoic and unmoving.

"And if you need a hint, you need only to look at today's paper." She made a show of examining her nails before turning back to Byron. "Besides, I'm sure you'd like to get your journal back."

"*You* took it?" Mira's anger boiled to the surface.

"After getting into an apartment once, it's easy to infiltrate again. I had hoped to get it the first time, but the address I found also proved useful."

"What is it that you want from us at this meeting?" Byron slipped the paper into his pocket.

"We need to come to an understanding. An agreement. This is us offering you a chance. Hopefully, you'll take it." She stood up and took a few steps towards the door, then stopped and looked over her shoulder.

"Oh, and by the way, Samira, my sister wanted me to tell you that you impressed her with your French. She truly thought you were a native." With that, she slinked back to the door, Joe opened it, and she disappeared. The din of the Pit crashed over Mira's ears.

"Byron?"

"Hmm?"

"Are we going to follow her?"

"No. There isn't a reason to at this point."

"She's a murderer, Byron. We can contact Inspector Thatcher and arrest her."

"What good will that do us when we are dead?" He looked at her, a serious shade crossing his face. Then he stood with a start and stepped away from the booth so that she could get out. He offered her an arm and escorted her towards the door. Joe smiled when he saw them.

"Au revoir, Miss Blayse."

Mira felt the color draining from her cheeks. He opened the door and Byron pulled her out of the club and onto the putrid street. He continued to pull her, leading her out of the wastes of the human experience. Past the dead, the rotting corpses. Past the crying children, half-starved and coughing up blood. Past the rats, and the lice, and the refuse. Out of the soot-covered darkness and into the light. She didn't allow herself to breathe fully until they were past the butchery. She looked up at Byron, face still a stone. His other hand clenched.

They paused long enough in Scotland Yard for them to procure their clothing, but not long enough for conversations with Thatcher or Juliet. He eventually convinced a carriage to take them the rest of the way to Palace Court. He continued in silence up the steps and unlocked the door. He waited for her to enter before coming in himself and closing the door.

"Go change."

His voice sounded hoarse as he went into his own room and slammed the door. She forced herself up the stairs and into the guest room. She stripped down to her undergarments and poured water into the washbowl. It felt cool on her hands, cooler on her face. The water turned grey, and then black. Her face became distinguishable again. She dressed in her own clothing and looked in the mirror. Everything was back to normal.

Oh, how she wished that was the case. It wasn't normal. She wasn't normal. Byron was anything but normal. The little stability he had was lost, and the only way to get it back would be to go right into the middle of the Order of Circe. Her emotions welled up within her. She sat on the floor and felt all of it burst out of her. Hot tears rolled down her face, her hair clinging, itching, biting at her skin. She pulled her legs into her chest and sobbed into her arms. The tears kept coming, and she felt herself shaking. It felt like if she moved, she would be torn to pieces. Some ravenous harpy was eating her from the inside out. She couldn't believe that anyone could live like the people in the Pit. That anyone could kill like The Order. She thought of the children in the Pit, of the squalor, and the refuse, and she burst into a new set of sobs.

She heard a knock on the door and immediately quieted. She swallowed and wiped the tears away.

"Yes?"

"Are you..." Byron's voice was heard through the door. He hesitated and cleared his throat. "I was...going to go out and get something. A croissant or some pastry to go with tea. Would you like me to get you anything?" His voice, though muffled, was warm, and real, and incredibly grounding.

"I'd like that, yes." Her voice was hoarser than she anticipated.

"What would you like?"

"Surprise me."

She heard his footsteps head back down the stairs, hesitate in the hall, probably to grab a coat or something, and then leave the building. She took a few deep breaths and looked around. She was in Byron's house. In one of his spare rooms. She came back to the present, calming herself down. He had been right. The Pit was exactly as Byron had described it. It changed her worldview. But that didn't mean she couldn't do anything about it.

She poured the sooty water out and refilled the basin, rinsing her face of the remaining tears. If she was going to beat the Order of Circe, survive, and solve the cases once and for all, she needed to know more about them.

She crept down the stairs and left her bundle of sooty torn fabric on the floor near the entryway. She moved straight to his files and tested it. Locked. Her eyes darted to where his jacket from the day before draped over a chair. She reached into the pocket and smiled when she felt a key. She came back to the filing system and unlocked it. *Click.* The drawer opened easily, and she pulled out the file. *Circe, Order of.* Mira closed the drawer and sat in her favorite chair.

> *The Order of Circe connects every case I have solved thus far. It is an underground criminal agency. Little is known at this time. Definite evidence includes the necklaces, bracelets, and tattoos that several in the criminal circle wear.*

The necklace that the Shadow wore was drawn in the margins of the paper. She studied it for a moment before continuing to read.

> *There is also the mention of Circe from several criminals caught and brought into custody. All criminals mentioning Circe have been found dead in their cells shortly afterwards. All pronounced as suicides. Few and far between, hence the lack of obvious connection between the cases.*
>
> *Further research and investigations have proven that there are three distinct sects of the Order. The Smugglers, The Thieves, and The Mercenaries. Often, they work together to pull off larger crimes, committing smaller crimes leading up to a major one in order to keep the police distracted from the main objective.*
>
> *Smuggler group intensified its efforts shortly after the airship accident of 1870.*
>
> *First known event caused by the Order is the Great Fire of 1666. Arson offered cover for stealing part of the crown jewels.*
>
> *Unknown at this time how widespread the order is. Unknown how many members. Unknown who is in charge. Unknown how the organization works. Probable meeting place: The Pit.*

The smugglers, thieves, and mercenaries all worked together. That explained why the Shadow came in to take care of a smuggler's problem, and why Selene was involved at all. Circe connected them through an underground network. Her eyes drifted back to the lines about the airship accident. The year her parents died. The crash they died in. She knew the smugglers were involved, but now they were directly connected with Circe. Find the smugglers, find the truth. Mira closed the file and put it back in the filing system before replacing the filing key in his jacket pocket. The door opened in the front hall. Byron came into the living room and set his coat down on top of his jacket. He carried a small package wrapped in brown paper.

"Let me get some tea going." He trudged into the kitchen. She followed him and leaned against the counter as he filled a kettle with water and set it on the hob.

"Do you need any help?"

"Not with this I don't think." He turned towards her and studied her. He opened his mouth to say something, shook his head, and went to a cupboard to get out some teacups. He set them out on a tray along with the other tea things. She watched as he meticulously prepared everything. He opened the brown paper package and pulled out a few different pastries and placed them on the tray. The kettle whistled, and he transferred the hot water into a waiting teapot before picking up the tray and walking into the living room.

"We need to talk," he said.

He set the tray down on the side table and sat down in his armchair. She sat in her chair across from him. He hesitated as he poured her a cup of tea and looked her over again. He opened his mouth and then closed it, unsure of what to say, and then silently gave her the teacup.

"We're in danger, aren't we Byron?"

"The short answer is, yes."

"And the long answer?" She took a sip of tea. He sighed and looked down.

"One or both of us may die tonight."

"I'm aware of that, Byron."

"I'm afraid it might be you."

"I know."

"Once I go to sleep tonight, I forget all of this ever happened,

Mira. They have my latest journal. But you are," He stopped mid-sentence and stared at her. "Wait. You know?"

"These people are dangerous. I've interacted with them before, and they have certainly threatened me on more than one occasion."

"Then you shouldn't come."

"I think that is exactly why I should come."

"Mira, no."

"You and I are both in this together, Byron."

"Maybe not this time."

"And why not? If I don't come, they'll just find another way to keep me quiet. This way, at least, we can have some sort of expectation."

"Mira, I may have just met you today, but I am not going to let you die."

"Then don't let me die. But let me come with you."

He went silent. She simply sipped at her tea and kept her eyes level with his. He eventually looked away, setting his teacup down, leaning forward and rubbing his temples. She finished her tea and nibbled at a croissant. Silence filled the room until the bag of pastries was empty, and the teapot stood cold.

"For now, let's get you home." He stood and offered her a hand. She took it and he pulled her to standing. He tucked a stray piece of hair behind her ear, paused as if to say something and then went quiet again, dropping her hand and heading for the door.

He led her outside and down the steps, calling for a carriage. They got in and he hesitated.

"I'm afraid I don't know the address." Byron looked at her.

"Swan Walk please."

The driver nodded and urged the horses forward. The cab bounced back and forth down the cobblestones to her uncle's house. Mira's stomach lurched, her anxiety returning. What on Earth were they doing confronting a crime syndicate? How were they going to get out of this? Byron must have taken notice as he took her hand and held it in his, squeezing it reassuringly. But Mira saw fear in his eyes.

Something she hadn't seen since Circe kidnapped her. Part of her felt relief that he cared again.

He helped her out of the carriage once they got to her uncle's and went up to the door with her. Landon opened it.

"Miss Mira! You look so pale. Is everything alright?"

"I think she just needs to lay down," Byron said.

"No, I'm fine."

She let go of Byron's hand and pushed past Landon. She faintly heard Landon telling Byron to come in. She went into the parlor and took a seat near the fire. Byron closed the door and came to sit across from her.

"You aren't fine. Halfway over here you turned white as a sheet and started shaking."

"Landon doesn't need to know. Neither does my uncle."

"This is your uncle's house?"

"Yes. Mine was destroyed a week or so ago by the Shadow."

"You didn't tell me that."

"Not today. No. Usually you read your journal. And it just didn't seem important for today."

"Everything is important, Mira."

"There were death threats. I was kidnapped before that. There have been warning signs all along. Even yesterday a man came up to me and warned me. You've tried to get me to stop time and time again." She felt her voice rising.

"Then why do you keep coming back?"

"I just want to know what happened to my parents!" she yelled. She looked up at him with more conviction than she felt. And then the tears formed. He stood there searching her features again, and she turned away.

"I just want to know. I know they were murdered, but I don't know how or why, or anything." She paced. "That's why I came in the first place, that's why I've stayed." A few tears escaped. She walked to the side table and picked up the picture of her mother.

"I'm so sorry," Byron faltered, "but I don't remember talking about this."

"I know. I know you don't. You don't remember me, or my case, or this case, or anything. How can I let you go alone when I'm your memory, Byron?" She whirled towards him.

"Because I won't let you this time."

"What?"

"You say you've been kidnapped, had death threats, Circe knows who you are, and that you've been helping me. You're in danger, Mira."

"You think I don't know that? For all I know, I'll end up just like my parents, and I'll never know why. I'm scared, Byron. But I must do this. You have to let me come."

"Mira, I can't." His voice shook. He took a step towards her and then turned towards the fireplace, leaning on the mantle. He stared into the flames.

"You what?" She folded her arms.

"I can't let you come."

"Why not?"

He took a deep breath. "I don't know what's happened to me. At first, I thought it was chivalry or some innate part of me designed to protect. I'm not certain what it is." He began to pace. "Logic dictates that even if I had a memory, things couldn't have progressed this fast. And seeing as I don't have a memory, that makes this even more ridiculous. I don't even know what I have written in that blasted journal you keep talking about."

"Makes what ridiculous?" She set her mother's portrait down and moved back to the armchair, leaning on the back. He moved towards her and took her hand.

"I remember you."

"You what?"

"I remember you."

"But you didn't. This morning you—"

He interrupted her. "Alright, perhaps not in the exact meaning of the word." He dropped her hand and started pacing again. "If I could explain it, I would, but no amount of thought, no amount of deduction can bring a solid conclusion in this case."

"Which case? Pennington's?"

"No, my own." He turned back towards her. "Something about you. It just drives me absolutely insane."

"What?" A look of surprise crossed her face. A look of instant regret crossed his.

"No, no, no, that's not what I meant. Insane in a good way. If that's possible. What I mean to say is," He took another deep breath. "It isn't a tangible memory. I honestly had no idea who you were this morning. I don't remember anything we've ever done together or when we first met. But something inside me remembers you."

"I don't think I understand."

He hesitated. "Perhaps it is my heart that remembers you. A fondness. There's an attraction. Or something." He turned a light shade of pink as he got flustered. Mira gave him a soft smile, tears forming again.

"You have feelings for me?"

"That's it. That's it exactly," he sighed in relief before continuing. "And I know it is foolish for me to say that, that this is entirely a professional relationship to you, but you need to understand where I'm coming from. I care about you, Mira. Deeply. I don't know how. But I do know why. You are such a brave, kind, considerate person. You're beautiful and intelligent and a joy to talk to. You're a breath of fresh air and—"

"Byron?"

"Yes?"

"I appreciate the compliments, but now isn't exactly the time to build my ego."

"Ah. Right. Yes. Well. Knowing that, you'll understand that I can't stand the thought of you getting hurt or, heaven forbid it, killed when I could do something to prevent it."

"But I can help. We just need to get your journal back."

"My journal is not as important as you are."

"But without it you can't remember."

"Do I really remember when I have it? No. It's just memorized. It would have to be. It isn't a reminder. It's a record to be studied."

"But Byron—"

"I wish I could remember you. Truly remember you. For now, we need to keep you safe."

"I don't know if that's possible."

He paused for a moment and opened the crumpled piece of paper the invitation was scrawled on. Then he moved over to her.

"That's why I've decided that you need to leave London."

She stared up at him. "What?!"

"You heard me."

"No, Byron. We are going together. I'm not letting you go by yourself."

"Well, you are going to have to. It's far too dangerous. Do you have anywhere you can stay outside of London?"

"Yes, but I'm not going to leave."

"Yes, you are."

"Byron, I can't let you go alone."

"And I can't let you come with me."

"Yes, you can. You have in the past."

"But this is now. I don't know what kind of idiot I've been before, but *this* time I'm not letting you get hurt." He threw the paper towards the fire and turned towards the door.

"Byron, I haven't gotten hurt before. Please," she pleaded. He paused at the door and looked back at her.

"And you won't get hurt this time either. Not if I have anything to say about it." He opened the door and left the parlor, the door closing behind him. She heard him and Landon speaking in the hall. That meant he was telling Landon the circumstances. He would tell her uncle. Soon enough she would be on a train out to Yorkshire and to safety.

Safety. Safety meant she couldn't do anything. Safety meant

being stuck in her uncle's house until she got married off to someone. Safety meant playing by society's rules. Safety meant believing lies. She rushed to the fireplace and found that the paper had landed very near an ember, but not quite in the fire. She used a poker to pull it further from the flames and then picked it up and smoothed it out.

You are cordially invited to a meeting of the Order of Circe. It will be held in number 6 on Vale Street in South Kensington starting at nine o'clock PM. Do be prompt.

Beneath it the symbol from Byron's files appeared, scrawled in red ink. At least, she hoped it was ink. She grimaced and folded the paper back up. She knew the location. Now all she needed to do was get there without anyone knowing. Time for a plan. She looked at the clock. Five o'clock. Four hours to figure something out. She heard footsteps at the door and moved to sit down, hiding the paper in the folds of her skirt. Landon came in, followed by Byron.

"Mr. Constantine informed me of the danger. I believe he is right in suggesting that you leave London."

Mira hesitated. She still needed to put up some sort of resistance even if she knew it wouldn't get her anywhere.

"And I disagree. I need to come with."

"Goodness gracious. Has she always been this stubborn?" Byron looked at Landon. He nodded.

"She takes after her mother."

Byron came over and took her hands in his. "You're taking the seven o'clock train to Yorkshire and that is that."

"You're certain?" She measured her words carefully and pulled her hands away. He nodded.

"I'll go pack." She snatched the paper from her skirts and stood.

"I'll send a telegram as soon as I get this all sorted out. I promise. We'll arrange for the ticket."

She hesitated at the door, searching his face. The trust had returned to his eyes. Unfortunately, there was no reason for him to trust her now. She was going with him.

He just didn't know it yet.

October
1ST AFTERNOON

Once upstairs, Mira took a suitcase and placed it on her bed. Opening it, she looked around the room. Nero jumped inside of it and meowed.

"You're not coming with me, kitty. I'll just say that you don't really like trains and that you're staying here." She picked him up and placed him on one of her pillows. He jumped back into the suitcase.

"Alright, you can stay there for now." She looked through what remained of her wardrobe. None of it would work. She needed something lighter. Something easier to move in. Perhaps her riding trousers? No. In broad daylight she would look ridiculous.

She bit her lip and grinned. If Byron could plan disguises, so could she. Mira tiptoed down the stairs to Walker's room.

She opened her twin's door to be greeted by the smell of dust and memories. She turned to his closet to look through the clothes he left behind. A pair of sturdy trousers, a shirt, vest, jacket, hat, pocket watch, socks, and shoes. Everything she needed. Hopefully he wouldn't mind her borrowing them. She could ask forgiveness later. She took several of each article of clothing and brought them back into her room to try them on. She needed to ensure that they fit before she packed them.

She laid each piece on the bed and looked them over. Her brother had quite the fashion sense. She locked the door and smiled to herself as she tried on each article of clothing. The trousers were a bit long and needed to be hemmed, but otherwise they fit fine. The shirt could be tucked into the trousers to hide the length. The vest was a bit snug, but it was nothing like a corset. The jacket needed to be hemmed at the cuffs but fit around her shoulders nicely. The shoes didn't fit her feet at all, being far too large. But how could she adjust that? Instead, she found the most masculine pair of shoes that she owned and tried them on with the outfit. Adequate. She pulled her hair up into a tight bun and put the hat on. Passable. She couldn't hide her facial features, but that wasn't exactly the point. From a distance she looked like a man.

She quickly changed into her own clothes and packed most of Walker's clothes into the suitcase, grateful that the top hat was collapsible. Then she set to work hemming the trousers and the jacket. It didn't take long, and they soon joined the rest of the outfit in the suitcase. She closed it, locked it, and sat on the bed, feeling incredibly pleased with herself. She looked at the clock. Quarter to six. Forty-five minutes. The next course of action was to ensure that she survived the night.

She went to her writing desk and pulled out several fresh sheets of paper. Every little detail of the case poured out of her pen. She made a timeline. She mentioned every name connected with the case. She outlined the motives, the events, the clues. Every address that could be of any relevant importance. She made it as clear and succinct as she possibly could. Then she took her sketchbook and tore out the drawings of everyone involved and placed them with the papers. She then worked on two new drawings. One of The Shadow and the other of the man she met in the park. She added them to the stack. Once she felt certain she included everything, she placed the stack of papers into the largest envelope she had, addressed it to Scotland Yard, and stamped it. That way, even if something did happen to her or Byron, the case would still be solved, and perhaps the police would still catch the perpetrators.

She looked up at the clock. Six-fifteen. She would have to leave the house by six-thirty to catch the train. There was only one thing left to do. She tiptoed down the stairs to her uncle's room and listened. She heard three distinct male voices coming from her uncle's study below. She hesitated and then creaked open the door to

Cyrus' room and stepped over the threshold. The floor squeaked beneath her, and she prayed that no one heard. She went to his bedside dresser and opened it, taking out a small box from inside and opening it. The dwindling light from the window glistened off the metal barrel of a pistol. She wrapped her fingers around the carved handle and lifted it out of its velvet enclosure.

She turned it over, examining it. It looked like Byron's. Probably a flintlock or some other term she'd heard her uncle talk about. If she pulled the trigger, it would shoot. Of course, she didn't know if it was loaded, and didn't even know how to load it. She took the small package of rounds from the case and a bottle of gunpowder, nonetheless. She closed the box and placed it carefully back in the drawer. Hopefully, her uncle wouldn't miss it. The pistol was the last thing she placed in her suitcase.

Her uncle, Byron, and Landon stood waiting for her downstairs. Byron looked relieved that she had packed. Her uncle and Landon looked increasingly worried.

"Mira, I know this will be hard for you, but I can't begin to tell you what a relief this is. Ever since you've come back, I've been worried sick. I just—" Her uncle stopped.

"I know. You don't want to lose me, too." She looked up at him with a slight smile.

"I don't think I could handle it if...well, if anything were to happen to you." He cleared his throat. "I'm sure there are quite a few things to draw out there, and the new surroundings will do you good. I've arranged for you to stay in a hotel in Bradford until we can find other accommodations."

"Of course."

"Aren't you taking Nero?" Her uncle looked at her and cocked his head.

"He doesn't like trains, you know that. He can stay here until we get everything sorted out."

Her uncle nodded. "This is for the best, Mira. Especially with the recent rise in crime. Two more murders in Whitechapel just yesterday morning," he muttered.

Byron came to the foot of the stairs and extended a hand to take her luggage. She shook her head and kept ahold of her precious cargo. Byron stepped back and studied her. She tried to keep her face unreadable. Her uncle embraced her, hiding her expression.

"I would go with you if I could, but unfortunately business keeps me here. Landon will escort you to the train station. You'll be able to manage from there on your own?"

"Of course, Uncle." She started to move towards the door and then hesitated and looked at Byron. He continued to study her. He mustn't suspect. She swallowed, set her suitcase down by the wall, and moved over to him.

"Byron, please be careful."

"I will, Mira. I will."

"No, I mean seeing as I might never see you again."

"Yes Mira?"

She hesitated for a moment and looked down.

"Byron, I..." Her voice cracked. She couldn't bring herself to say it.

"I know." He brushed her cheek with his hand.

She looked up at him, noting worry in his eyes. No longer suspecting. Completely trusting. Even recognizing. She gave him a soft smile. Byron leaned in closer and whispered into her ear.

"I'll find a way out of this situation *and* get that journal back as well. I'd like to read more about the girl that I'm in love with." He took her hand and gently kissed it. Her face flushed as she glanced at her uncle. Byron smiled at her.

"Miss Mira, it's time to go." Landon picked up her suitcase and opened the door.

"Byron, promise me."

"Yes?"

"Don't do anything foolish." She gave her uncle a final hug and followed Landon out the door. Landon called a carriage and set the suitcase down in the bottom when it stopped. He helped Mira in and then sat next to her. The carriage rumbled towards the train station.

"I'm surprised, Miss."

"That I gave in so easily?"

"Yes, actually."

"You all have good reason to want me safe. Even if I don't agree."

He nodded and went silent. She peered out the window at the street. "Landon, what if he dies?" Her voice cracked again.

"He won't."

"But what if..."

"He explained the whole situation to me, Miss. If they truly know of his memory problems, he isn't a threat to them. You are the only one in danger here."

"I find it difficult to believe that."

"We'll contact you as soon as he sends us any news. I'm certain he has a plan. And I'm guessing you do as well?"

"Why would I have a plan?"

"I like to think I know you better than just about anyone, Miss. I can see the scheming behind your eyes."

"No. I'm going to Yorkshire," she lied.

"I also picked up your suitcase." He gave her a pointed look. "It seems a bit light. Just don't let me see. After all, I have a duty to your uncle."

"You aren't going to stop me?"

"I've known you long enough. I might as well save my breath rather than try to stop you. If you follow your own advice, I'll try not to worry."

"My advice?"

"Don't do anything foolish."

They rode on in silence until they reached the train station. He helped her out of the carriage and took her suitcase to the ticket desk. He returned with a ticket and walked with her into the station. The air filled with steam from the waiting train.

"I suppose this is goodbye for now, Landon."

"Yes, it is, Miss. Just remember your first stop is in Bradford. You'll stay the night there before going on to York."

"I remember. Don't worry."

"I'll always worry about you, Miss." Wetness filled his eyes. She hugged him tight.

"I'll be fine."

She pulled away and gave him a smile. He smiled back and then helped her onto the train. She would be traveling first class if she stayed on the train. Except that wasn't in the plan. She moved to a window in first class and waved goodbye to Landon through a gap. She waited until he left the station, and then began her journey to the back of the train. It wasn't moving yet and wouldn't be leaving until seven o'clock. She checked the time on the train station clock. Ten to seven. She didn't have much time. She moved past the dining car and past the people sitting in second class. A conductor stood in front of the door to the baggage car. She took a breath and walked up to him.

"Excuse me sir, a server in the dining hall told me that a conductor was needed. There is a passenger making a disturbance."

"There is?"

"Yes sir. I was just moving into second class, and he asked me if I could pass the message on."

"I'm afraid that I need to keep to my post here."

"Several other passengers were complaining about it, sir. It is becoming quite a riot in there. We wouldn't want to delay the train. I also heard that Lady Devonshire was getting quite upset with it all."

"Ah! We can't have that then, no. I'll see what I can do about it."

He sprinted up second class towards the dining hall. As soon as he ran out of sight, she slid the bolt out of the lock and slipped across the gap between the cars. She tested the handle and found it locked. She sighed and pulled out two hairpins. Her hair fell around her shoulders. The simple lock was much easier to crack than the one at the smuggling hold, and as the pins slipped into place, the door handle turned.

It was quiet and private. The perfect place to change. That is, if she could find her suitcase. Unfortunately, her luggage looked very similar to everyone else's. After looking through a couple of stacks, the train whistled, and the car lurched as the train began to move. The tower of baggage swayed in its restraints, and Mira lifted her hands to steady it. With the train moving, she had very little time to find her suitcase, change, and jump off the train before it hit full speed. After a few minutes, she found her suitcase and began to undress. She found it difficult to keep herself upright as the train continued to pick up speed, and her petticoats weren't helping. After about ten minutes of wrestling with her clothing and corset, she managed to get dressed in her brother's clothes. She found the trousers to be slightly too short after hemming, and the jacket still a bit too long, but overall everything seemed to fit adequately. She tied her hair up the best she could without a mirror, placed the pocket watch in her vest pocket, put on the hat, and buttoned her shoes. She put the pistol in one pocket and the envelope in the other. They made her pockets bulge, but if she kept her hands in her pockets, she hoped no one would notice.

She packed her own clothes into the suitcase and stacked it on the other luggage in the car. She didn't need any extra baggage going into this, especially if she had to jump. She didn't know how to get off the train, but logic dictated that the end of the train would be the best place to start. She made her way to the back of the baggage car, grateful that she didn't have to worry about her petticoats getting stuck between the luggage stacks. She sped across the car and opened the door at the end. The ground passed beneath her like a river. The coupling swayed back and forth. One misstep and she would be pulled beneath the train. The train slowed, approaching a turn. She hesitated, took a breath, and then prayed that the next door would be unlocked. She hopped onto the coupling and grabbed a hold of the handle.

It opened with ease, and she slipped inside the last car. Windows lit the room and several bunks lined the walls on either side. A guard lay on one of the bunks. She froze before realizing that he was asleep.

She let out a breath of relief, then tiptoed past. She opened the last door and stepped out. A wave of fresh air and light overcame her senses, and she smiled. She held onto the railing and looked out as trees moved past. The train slowed again, approaching a new curve, but she still didn't like the prospect of jumping from a moving train. A mossy clearing between the trees appeared around the bend. Despite her reservations about jumping, this was her chance. It was foolish, but it could be her only opportunity. She took a deep breath, braced herself, and jumped from the train.

At first, she only felt exhilaration. The wind against her skin and filling her lungs. She felt the top hat fly off her head, and she pulled her arms up into her face as she hit the mossy ground and rolled, gasping for breath. For a few moments it was all grass and moss and dirt. Rolling over and over. She slowed to a stop and laughter bubbled out of her. She just jumped from a train! The adrenaline overpowered her. Then she felt a sharp pain in her shoulder, and sharper pain near her hip.

She stopped laughing and tried to sit up. The pain in her hip dulled a bit. She landed on the pistol. She moved each of her limbs and found that they weren't broken. Her shoulder landed on a rock which tore a good-sized hole into her jacket. She was covered in a thin layer of dirt and grass stains. She stood up, aching, but alive. She gathered the things she had lost in the tumble, her hands shaking. Soon enough, she found everything, including the top hat, and walked back towards the station.

She hurried through the station, ignoring the people staring at her, and made her way to where the carriages stood waiting for passengers. She paused to check the time on the train station clock. Seven-fifteen. She set her brother's pocket watch to match, then approached a carriage.

"The Vale, South Kensington please." She kept her voice low. The driver nodded, and she got inside. The carriage rumbled down the cobblestone street, and Mira relaxed and watched the city pass. Getting there was the easy part. Deciding what to do from there was much more difficult. How could Byron go in on his own? What would Circe do? Most likely they would talk for a good period. The Shadow mentioned that they wanted to offer them a chance. What kind of chance would that be? Was this a blackmailing situation?

She realized she still had two bulges within her pockets and pulled out the envelope.

"Driver! Pull over for a moment, if you would." The carriage slowed to a stop. She got out, moved to a post box and slipped the precious parcel inside. Her own blackmail. Or rather, brightmail to shine a light on the case should anything happen to her or Byron. She smiled to herself as she climbed back into the carriage. She checked the pocket watch again. Almost quarter to eight. An hour and fifteen minutes to figure out what to do. How was she even supposed to get in? The carriage came to a stop in front of Vale street, she paid the driver, and then walked down to number 6.

In the middle of this dull residential area stood an unimposing building. Red brick, white trimmings, obviously a wealthy person lived here, but it looked exactly like every other house on the street. She walked past it and looked through the window. A young girl sat on a couch drawing. Mira smiled. She reminded her of herself. A younger boy ran into the room, followed by what seemed to be the mother. This couldn't possibly be the meeting place for Circe.

The daughter closed her sketchbook and put on a hat. They were leaving. Mira smiled. That was it. Circe wouldn't use a house that was theirs. They would use one that belonged to someone else as Molly Bridges had done. This family would leave and then the Order of Circe would come. And if she was there before Circe, that meant that she had a chance to get in. She ducked into the alleyway near the house and waited until she heard the door click and the family move down the sidewalk. Then she looked around for a way in. Going through the front door would probably get her arrested for breaking and entering. She walked around to the back. A staircase led to a small veranda at the back of the house. Perfect. A large iron gate separated her from the stairs. She took off her brother's top hat and pulled two hair pins out. Her hair fell around her shoulders once again as she picked the lock. Soon, the gate creaked open, and she snuck up the stairs to the veranda.

The setting sun created a lovely view over London, but she didn't have time to look at it now. She needed to get in. She went to the door that led onto the veranda and tested it. It opened without a sound. She smiled and stepped inside the house.

Quiet. The last filtered rays of sunlight came trickling through the windows, giving the darkness a hazy glow. She tiptoed through the house, listening occasionally, to make sure that she truly was alone. She came into the front room. They would likely meet here. The fewer rooms they touched, the more likely it would be that no one would know they were even there. She looked around the room for somewhere to hide. If Byron came alone, he would tell Circe as much. They wouldn't be expecting her.

Large couches and chairs cluttered the living room. Shelves of books stood on either side of the fireplace, every book matching one another in its cover. A small door sat in the eastern wall. It had been papered over, but the seams of the door were cut in. The room must have been sealed off at some point. She opened the door and found shelves filled with linens. She smiled. It would be perfect. She took the linens and shelves out and brought them to a guest bedroom up the stairs. She hoped the occupants of the house would forgive her.

As it originally led to another room, there was a handle on both sides of the door. Mira determined that would be nice in case anyone tried to open the door. She could hold it closed and pretend it was locked. Everything seemed to be falling into place. She needed to take that place before the Order of Circe decided to show up. She just needed to be able to see. She went into the kitchen and looked around for something she could use.

After opening a few drawers, she found a corkscrew and brought it back to the living room. She felt the wood of the door. It seemed soft, but sturdy enough. She took a deep breath and began to work. The point ripped through the paper without a problem, and although she had to work harder on the wood, it wasn't long until she had a hole to look through. Better still, it was small enough and positioned in the pattern of the wallpaper so well that it didn't attract attention. She cleaned up the shavings and put the corkscrew away. The sun set. They would be coming to get ready any minute now. She checked the clock on the mantle. Eight-sixteen. It really wouldn't be long. She stepped into her cupboard and waited.

It couldn't have been ten minutes before she heard noise at the back of the house. The Order of Circe had arrived. They lit the lights, causing Mira's accustomed darkness to vanish. She blinked a few times, then looked through the hole.

The Shadow entered the living room. She wore a pitch-black dress and carried a brown satchel. Behind her came Joe and Sam, the smugglers. At the back came the woman from the smuggling den. Presumably the Shadow's sister. She spoke first.

"Are you certain they won't be coming back tonight?"

"Positive." The Shadow's words flowed like honey. "I have several families I keep tabs on just in case I need a house. The family that lives in this house is going on holiday this week. They are meeting the husband at the bank and then–"

"Alright, alright I get it. You're brilliant. You don't need to show off." The sister sat in an armchair and folded her arms, entirely annoyed.

"I was simply stating the facts, Angelica." The Shadow closed the curtains then sat on one of the couches, leaning back into it.

"If it's all the same, I'd like to have the boys search the place." Angelica glanced around.

"It's fine by me." The Shadow smiled. Angelica snapped and Joe and Sam left. Mira heard their lumbering footsteps going up the stairs and into each of the rooms. She didn't want to find out what would happen if they found someone.

"Now, are you going to give me the blueprints, or not?" Angelica crossed one leg over the other and folded her arms.

"Oh, I will."

"Tonight would be nice. After all, I've only been waiting for them for *weeks*."

"I've been holding onto them as collateral until I got my payment."

"I gave you your payment days ago. What's keeping you now?"

"Perhaps I'd like to achieve complete and total victory first."

"What do you mean by that?"

"You know that detective? And his secretary?"

"Yes." Angelica's eyes narrowed.

"I've invited them here tonight."

"Have you gone completely mad?!"

"Not completely, I'm certain. Because I'm going to do what the Trio hasn't been able to do. I'm going to kill the detective."

"You...what?"

"Yes. He's been bothering the Order for long enough. They tried once, failed, and although his memory loss does make things a bit simpler, he is still quite the little thorn in everyone's side. Especially with the help of Miss Samira Blayse."

"If the Trio hasn't killed him yet, there is a reason. You know that."

"I think he is too dangerous to our cause."

"And Circe has been taking care of that. You know the pains they've gone to in order to make the Whitechapel distractions."

"The police can be led by the nose to the wrong clues, but he's not so easily persuaded. Now that he has an assistant, we can't throw him entirely off track."

"Can't we just steal his journal? We've done that before."

The Shadow reached into her satchel and pulled out a very familiar book. Byron's journal. She flipped through it, not actually reading, then closed it and set it on the table in the center of the room.

"I've stolen it. I stole it before he even came to the Pit this afternoon. And you know what? He still came to the Pit. Because of her."

"Then why not just find a way to get her to stop?"

"I'm planning on that. But don't you just think that victory would be much more complete if we got rid of him too?" The Shadow reached into the satchel again and pulled out a small glass syringe. She tapped it with her finger, and it made a resonating clicking noise against her fingernails.

"What does this have to do with the blueprints?"

"When he and Miss Blayse get here, I'll invite them to sit down. Sam and Joe will guard the exits. You and I will sit and have a chat with them. My end goal is to have him administer the drug to himself and then watch as I hand the blueprints and the girl over to you."

"How do you plan on doing that?"

"I've read his journal. Thoroughly. He may not always remember, but he certainly has feelings for her. Even if he doesn't remember, he'll want to be the hero. And so, I'll give him the option. He can take my 'serum' and forget all of this and her, with the promise that we set her free afterwards. Or she can die, and he can report all of his findings to the police."

"That is an incredible risk."

"I know. This is what is called the illusion of choice. No matter what he chooses he will die, and she'll be in your hands to do whatever you like. After all, you have more blood revenge with her than I do."

"And what about the Trio? Won't they disapprove of this?"

"They'll congratulate us on neutralizing the threat. I know from my sources that, as usual, the detective has kept most of the facts out of Scotland Yard's knowledge. Everything will be wrapped up."

"You've killed someone before they gave us the go-ahead, and you had specific instructions from Number Three not to touch Miss Blayse. She has too many connections. You'll be suspended from the Order."

"Graham's death was a decision made in haste and panic. This is different. This is revenge. I'm sure Number Three will understand."

Mira felt her breath quickening. The closet stifled her. The men came back down the stairs.

"Did you check everywhere?"

"Yes ma'am. All is clear."

Mira felt her head go heavy; her knees shook. She was about to faint. She crouched down quickly to try to lose the light-headedness. As she did her knee hit against the door making a knocking sound.

"What was that?" Angelica turned towards the closet. Mira's heart rate quickened, and she held her breath. Footsteps approached the door. She grabbed hold of the door handle and pulled to hold it shut. A hand grasped the handle on the other side as the clock on the mantle chimed nine.

A knock came at the front door and the hand on the other side of the closet door released. Mira let out a short, quiet breath and stood to look through the hole again. Joe moved towards the entryway, almost out of sight. She heard the door open.

"Oh, hello there. Pardon me, but I believe I have an appointment here for something or other?" Byron's voice sounded almost cheerful. How could that be? She squinted trying to see better. She could only see the members of Circe. Joe blocked any view of the door.

"Come in." Joe stepped away from the door, allowing Byron to come in. He strode in, dressed in a sharp suit and tie, his top hat perfectly positioned on his head. He took off his hat and coat and hung them on the hooks in the hall. Then he came into the living room.

"Now, I'm afraid I don't quite know what I am doing here."

"You...what?" The Shadow's smug look melted away.

"I'm afraid I woke up from, I believe a nap. I was a bit confused seeing as I had just gone to bed the night before. But seeing as I woke up around eight o'clock it must have been a nap. When I awoke, I found a note telling me to come here. So here I am."

"You don't remember anything?"

"That's what I said. I gathered from the evening paper that the date was a bit different from what I expected. Perhaps I have some sort of memory loss?"

The Shadow's face contorted in such an expression of disgust and anger that Mira felt certain it would fall off. It took all her discipline not to chuckle. The Shadow picked up the journal and handed it to him.

"Read this," she snarled. Byron shrugged, sat down and opened the journal, perusing the pages. All others in the room focused on him. He read to about a quarter of the way in, then looked up.

"Do I need to read *all* of this? It is a bit lengthy." He flipped back and forth between a few of the pages. The Shadow groaned in frustration and took the journal back from him, skipped forward a dozen or so pages and shoved it back.

"Read from there." Byron nodded and continued. As he read, his face softened, and he seemed to read certain passages a few times over. He reached the end and looked up at them.

"Where is this Mira Blayse? I'd rather like to meet her." A twinge of a smirk shadowed his lips.

"She was supposed to come here with you." The Shadow's honey-smooth voice turned sour and raw as she glared at him.

"Well, obviously, she hasn't. She seems like a smart girl based on what I've written about her. Now I'm guessing you are the smugglers and mercenary that I've been trying to track down? How nice of you to give me an invitation to your meeting."

"We invited you here to tie up some loose ends."

"Loose ends?"

"Yes. You know a bit too much about the Order of Circe. You and Miss Blayse. We were going to go with the theatrical for this, but seeing as things haven't exactly gone according to plan, we'll have to forego them."

"Oh?" Byron sat in his chair, completely unimpressed. In fact, he yawned.

The Shadow's face contorted again, and she gestured to the two smugglers. They hoisted him up to standing, each holding one of his arms. A flicker of recognition crossed Byron's face, and he struggled. They pulled his arms back.

"Take off his suit coat." The Shadow picked up the needle and flicked it a few times. Joe took a knife from his pocket and cut the back of Byron's suit and shirt open. He pulled hard on the sleeves of both, and they came ripping off, the buttons of his shirt shooting off one by one. Sam did the same to the other side. Mira noticed a few scars on his chest. She fingered the gun in her pocket.

"Do you know how many lives have been lost because of curiosity, Detective?"

"I'm afraid I don't. Would you care to tell me?"

"Countless. In this case, eight people have died thus far because Clement Pennington decided to find out what was behind a mysterious grate."

"Eight people? You seem to have miscounted. I only count two murders. Mr. Pennington's and Mr. Graham's."

"Ah, but that is where you and the police would be wrong. You see, the Order tried something new with this murder. Normally when an important killing is about to take place, Circe plans several robberies to take place around the same time. That way the police are distracted, and the killer has a bit more time to cover their tracks. This time they used the same principle and experimented with murder."

Mira's stomach churned. All the facts of the Whitechapel case came back to her. The first case popped up back in April, around the same time that Molly Bridges first met Clement Pennington. Several others in August and September. Her uncle mentioned two murders occurred just the day before. The Order of Circe connected them all.

"You say there have been eight deaths connected with this case?"

"Eight. Six of them were women of no importance or great wealth. Unconnected. All are perfect fodder for a gruesome killing spree spread across several months and taken out by several killers with a bloodlust. Untraceable."

Byron gritted his teeth and the Shadow just laughed. "Once the distraction of a mass murderer was set into motion, I murdered Clement Pennington. Then, of course, you had to get involved, and that led to the death of Mr. David Graham."

"He didn't have to die. Enough people have died," Byron clenched his fists.

"Perhaps you are right. But death can be so useful. And in the case of these 'Whitechapel murders,' as the police have been calling them, there are so many killers, they will never be caught. And who knows? Perhaps there will even be copycat killers that will be even worse."

"How dare you toy with human life and treat it as if it is nothing?" He seethed.

"And what are you going to do, little detective?"

"Fight 'til my dying breath."

"Oh, how cliché. Luckily for us, we don't have to wait long."

Byron pulled harder against the two smugglers, to no avail. They held him fast, and the Shadow moved closer to him, tracing a finger beneath the line of his jaw. Her voice lowered. Mira could barely make it out.

"I planned on killing Miss Blayse in front of you before you died. But seeing as she isn't here, I'll just take the consolation that you'll know that she will die and leave this mortal world without ever knowing what happened to you. She won't even know the full extent of why she is dying. Just like her parents."

Mira opened the door and cocked the gun pointing it straight at the Shadow's head.

"What about my parents?" The room stood in stunned silence, staring at her. Byron spoke first.

"M...Mira?"

"I told you I was coming with you, Byron. Now Shadow, or Molly as you are sometimes called, if you could please set the syringe down and step away from Mr. Constantine?" The Shadow slowly stepped away and placed the syringe on the table.

"And hands above your head if you would?" Mira gestured with the pistol. The Shadow's hands rose.

Mira smiled. "Thank you very much."

"You're bluffing. Surely, you're bluffing."

"I may not look it, but I've been fully trained on the use of firearms, and I'm more than ready to demonstrate. In fact, all of you, step away." Mira moved her aim between each of the members of Circe in turn.

Joe and Sam let go of Byron's arms and he brushed himself off. He moved over to where Mira was. Angelica stayed seated right where she was. The Shadow glowered.

"I should have just killed you that night in your rooms. Death threats weren't enough to keep you away."

"And good thing, too. Otherwise you would have gotten away with murder."

"Again, you mean? I've been at this a long-time, sweetheart." The Shadow cocked her head and smiled, bringing her hands down to her hips.

"What, did you murder my parents too?" Mira's voice shook, and she cleared her throat to get her confidence back.

"Oh, no. That wasn't me." The Shadow chuckled. "Do you want to know how they died?"

"I..." Mira swallowed.

"Let me tell you, princess. History always repeats itself. Pennington's story is your father's. He was killed because he found out about the smuggling hold that Circe secretly built into his precious airship. Of course, in his case, he was decent enough to forego the blackmail." The Shadow took a step around the table.

"Stay where you are!"

"You wouldn't shoot me before you find out what happened to your parents, would you?"

Mira hesitated. The Shadow smiled. "Your father was rarely alone, but he needed to be taken out of the picture. So, when he and your mother took a walk by a particularly vacant bank of the Thames, they were both taken. And I'll let you know; their deaths were far more painful than Pennington's. To mimic the effects of an explosion on the human body without a real explosion, now that takes skill.

290 | NATALIE BRIANNE

After they were dead, it was a simple task to fake an explosion and move their bodies into position."

"Shut up! I've heard enough!" A few tears escaped.

"You know it's true, though. If your family would just mind their own business, it would be better for everyone." The Shadow took another step forward.

"No! Move back."

"You're no murderer sweetie. If you were, you would have brought a different weapon. Flintlock pistols only have one shot." Mira felt herself paling. Joe and Sam turned towards Byron, who took a defensive stance. Mira's hands continued to shake. The pistol went off.

The shot hit Joe in the knee, and he fell to the floor in agony. Byron flew into action, picking up the knife that Joe dropped, and wielding it against Sam. Mira turned her attention to the Shadow, who leapt over the table. The Shadow tackled her to the floor, hands melding around her throat.

The Shadow's nails dug into Mira's skin. Mira tugged at her wrists, trying to get free. Her grasp was too tight. Mira felt herself getting faint. She remembered the gun and felt around with one hand until she found it. She hit the Shadow squarely in the face with the butt end of the pistol. There was a loud crack. The Shadow's hands relaxed as she tried to recover. Mira scrambled out from under her, gasping for breath, dropping the gun.

She saw Angelica moving quickly out the back. Mira looked over at Byron. He had a deep cut in his arm that was bleeding, and barely held out against Sam. They both wielded knives and were keeping each other at arm's length, trying to get a swipe in where they could. Joe writhed on the ground due to his knee.

She felt a blow to the back of the head and fell to her knees, the world becoming fuzzy, and noise filling her ears. She put a hand to the back of her head and felt something sticky. Blood. Anticipating another blow, she turned to protect herself. The Shadow wasn't there. She turned and saw her retrieving her syringe. She turned back towards Mira with a smile on her face. Blood dripped down from her forehead. Her dress was ripped off at the knees. Mira stood and looked around for something to defend herself. The pistol had been tossed clear across the room. There was no weapon in sight. Byron was losing to Sam. Mira felt nauseous.

"Not so heroic now, are you?" The Shadow cackled. Mira backed into the wall, trying to think through the fog of her brain.

"No gun, no detective, no protection. Just you against me. I think that's fair." The Shadow came closer.

"You have a weapon though." Mira's voice faltered. The Shadow looked at the syringe she clutched in her hand and then at Mira. She grinned.

"Completely fair."

With that, the Shadow pounced, kicking Mira's feet out from under her. Mira felt the wind rush out of her as she hit the floor. A weight came down on her back, and she quickly turned before the Shadow pinned her to the ground.

"Now, just hold still." She pulled at the tear in Mira's jacket, ripping the sleeve off. The needle came dangerously close to brushing her skin. Mira's hands wrapped around the assassin's wrists, trying to push back and away.

She heard a shuffling pain as Joe continued to try to get up and heard a table crack as Byron threw Sam into it. Her eyes shifted from the Shadow's hands to her face. So full of anger. Twisting, writhing, seething. Determined to kill her. She shifted underneath her, pushing with all her might, feeling her muscles burn. One of the Shadow's hands moved to her throat, pinning her. The needle came ever closer. She had to think of something fast. Running out of options and oxygen, she pushed back with all her force, and got her legs underneath the Shadow, kicking as hard as she could. The Shadow was knocked back, losing her grip. Quickly Mira sat up, grabbed the hand with the syringe, and slammed it into the wall.

The Shadow let out a blood-curdling scream as the syringe shattered and glass penetrated the mercenary's skin. She recoiled and let go. Mira clawed her way out from under her, gasping, and frantically looked around for the gun. She spied it by Byron's foot. She pulled herself up to standing, staggering and nearly falling. Her whole body ached, and her head and neck bled. She used the wall for support and moved over to Byron. He was at a standstill with Sam, pushing back and forth again. Byron's foot kicked the pistol closer to her as he dodged under Sam's arm. She stumbled for the gun, bending down. Her weight was pulled out from under her as Joe grabbed her ankle and brought her crashing to the ground. She stretched for the gun, just out of reach as he pulled her back. Boot cracked against jaw as she kicked him squarely in the face and struggled away. She grabbed the gun just in time to see the Shadow recovering to come for her again. She stood, and futilely cocked the gun, aiming, knowing there wasn't a bullet, but trying just the same. She pulled the trigger.

A shot reverberated through the room, and the Shadow fell to the floor clutching her shoulder in pain. Mira looked at the gun and then back to where Byron and Sam fought. Sam lay unconscious on the ground. Byron stood near his coat in the entryway, holding his own pistol out. He breathed heavily. He saw her, a look of relief passing over his face, and stumbled over to her. Mira collapsed onto the floor, catching her breath. She started to shake, and then the tears came. Quiet, and soft, but still there. A pained moaning sound came from one of the remaining conscious members of Circe. Byron came and scooped her up in his arms. His eyes studied her tear-stained face.

She felt certain she was bruised from head to toe, blood clotting in the hair on the back of her neck. Her lip was split, and there were fingermarks on her neck. Her head ached as she tried to read Byron's face. She rested her head on his chest and heard his heartbeat. She finally relaxed.

"I'm sorry about your parents. She had no right to be so cruel."

"No, it's alright. I'm glad to finally know the truth." A few more tears escaped. He held her closer to him. All she wanted to do was sleep. He kissed her forehead and brought her over to the couch, setting her down.

"Thank you for coming," his voice came, soft and loving. He gently brushed the tears away. She smiled and nodded, melting into the couch, breath returning to normal.

She jumped as the door was kicked in from the outside. Six policemen filed into the room, pistols at the ready. Seeing the scene, they pointed them all at the only person left standing: Byron. He put his hands in the air. Mira looked around at the carnage. Broken table. Curtains pulled from the windows. Books strewn on the floor. Blood from various bodies in blotches and patches. She closed her eyes. This did not look good. Then she heard a familiar voice.

"Constantine! What in blazes is going on here!"

"Chief Inspector Thatcher. You have no idea how glad I am to see you."

Byron sat on the ground in front of the couch, finally able to relax.

"Would you care to explain?"

"This was formerly a meeting of the Order of Circe. You know? The one I've been telling you about for years?"

"Yes. The one that by every account doesn't exist." Thatcher lowered his gun. Byron groaned and painfully stood, walking over to the Shadow. He crouched down and tore her necklace from her. Her growl turned to a pained whimper as she finally accepted defeat. He brought it back over to the inspector.

"Exhibit A. This is their symbol. I would venture to guess that something similar is on all of them." He looked around. "One of them is missing."

"The one called Angelica went out the back. I doubt she went far, and I have a description for you, Inspector. A picture, too, if the post hurries up." Mira sat up and immediately regretted it as her head exploded in an aching pain.

The chief inspector snapped, and several constables ran out the back. The inspector turned his attention to the Shadow. "That still doesn't explain all of this, Constantine."

"That woman over there is your murderer. She's a mercenary that goes by the name of the Shadow. Recently her alias has been Molly Bridges. She was hired by the Order to kill Clement Pennington in order to get the blueprints." Byron furrowed his brow.

"Where did the blueprints go?" He moved to the remains of the coffee table and kicked some debris out of the way to search.

Mira's stomach sunk. "Angelica. The sister. She must have taken them. She is the one that left by the back entrance during the fight."

"So that's Molly Bridges, eh?"

"Yes. These men are involved with the smuggling. And I or Mira can fill you in on everything else tomorrow. For now, I need to get her home."

"I'll take care of things here, then. You heard him lads, arrest the lot of them."

The officers quickly apprehended each of them and led them out to the police wagon. The Shadow managed a glare at Mira and Byron before she was taken out of sight.

Byron watched the police leave. Once they were gone, he moved to the couch and pulled Mira to standing, putting his coat around her. When she stumbled after a few steps, he scooped her up and placed his journal in her lap. She closed her eyes and relaxed into him again, holding the journal close to her. She felt his steady steps moving towards the door and then the chill of the cold night air against her skin. He walked to the street and managed to hail a carriage down. He set her gently in the seat and told the driver to take them to Palace Court.

"I thought you were taking me home," she said.

"Let's get you cleaned up a bit before bringing you home to your uncle. After all, someone was supposed to be on a train to safety earlier today." He touched her nose and smiled.

"I *was* on a train to safety earlier today."

"And then you got off of that train and ran right into certain danger."

"I didn't just get off, Byron. I jumped."

"You what?!"

"I jumped from a moving train. Aren't you proud of me?" She found herself grinning and trying not to laugh.

"And you were telling me not to do anything foolish."

"Like walk into a criminal meeting and *pretend* like you had lost your memory again?"

"How did you know I was pretending? I could have just read up on it when the Shadow gave me my journal."

"You recognized me, Byron."

"I'll have you know that I have excellent descriptive skills in my writing."

"I've read quite a bit of it, Byron. At most you would only know that I have green eyes."

"And what beautiful green eyes they are, too."

"I save your life and now all you do is compliment me?"

He laughed, and she melted. Oh, how she loved that laugh.

"You make it too easy." He smiled.

The carriage pulled up to Palace Court, and he lifted her out of it after paying the driver. They soon found themselves inside. Byron set her down on the couch in the front room before going into the kitchen. He returned with some warm water, bandages, and salve. Laying there, she saw bruises forming up and down his torso, a cut on his arm that had stopped bleeding, and a cut on his chest. He had a black eye and his hair was tousled. She was so grateful he was alive.

He knelt next to the couch and wet down a cloth. He handed it to her.

"Place this on the back of your neck. It should soothe the cut."

"Thank you."

"It's the least I can do after you saved me."

"You probably could have handled it on your own."

"Au contraire, Mademoiselle. If you hadn't come, I would have had to fight all four of them simultaneously. I hadn't expected there to be four of them, and they would almost certainly have killed me. You took out two on your own and scared off another one, giving me a fighting chance."

He put salve on the scratch marks on her neck. She flinched at first and then relaxed as a soothing sensation replaced the sting.

"I didn't know the gun was loaded!"

"But you had it, nonetheless. You planned, you prepared, and you acted. Now, I've been curious, so tell me; where did you get gentleman's clothing on such short notice?"

"They belong to my twin brother, Walker. We are about the same size. I'm just grateful that it worked."

"Oh, it most certainly worked. I couldn't believe my eyes when you walked through that door."

"You certainly looked surprised."

"I was." He pulled his hand away from her wounds and rinsed it in the water. She sat up.

"Now it's my turn."

"What?"

"You have wounds, too." She picked up a cloth and wet it in the warm water.

"I can take care of those."

"I have a better angle." She smiled and wiped the blood away from the cut on his arm and then moved onto the one on his chest.

"You really are stubborn, Miss Blayse."

"I've been told I take after my..."

"Mother. Yes. I remember." He smiled and looked into her eyes. She felt a surge of happiness flow through her, and she hugged him, joyful tears threatening to fall.

"That is the most wonderful phrase you've ever said." He groaned a bit in pain, and she let go.

"Sorry."

"It's okay. Just be gentle. Which phrase is wonderful?"

"'I remember.'"

"In that case, I hope that someday I can say it more often."

She nodded and continued to clean his wounds. She wetted down the cloth again and reapplied it.

"Tomorrow you won't remember any of this." She paused and looked up at him.

"I'll have the wounds to remind me, but, yes. I won't remember."

She looked down. He lifted her chin to look into her eyes again.

"But that only means I get another day to fall in love with you."

"And what if you don't?"

"How could I not?" He smiled. She felt her pinkness return, and she looked away, smiling.

"There's my Mira. Red as a rose."

"That's my middle name you know."

"Is it really?"

"Samira Rose Blayse. Named after my mother."

"Ah, but it suits *you*."

"Does it?"

"Well you certainly have a habit of blushing like a rose whenever I'm around. And you are beautiful, and sweet, and when threatened you have proven to have thorns." He tucked a stray hair behind her ear. She smiled and laughed a little, then picked up a bandage to wrap his arm. He watched silently as she did so, carefully lining up each edge of the bandage, binding it down. Then she took a fresh bandage and wrapped it around his chest, covering up the cut.

"There." She tucked the end of the bandage underneath the rest of it. He smiled at her.

"Thank you. Now there is only one thing left to do."

"What's that?"

"Take you home."

"Byron, my uncle..."

"Will have to understand that you are safe and sound, and badly in need of a change of clothes." He stood and offered her a hand. She took it and stood. He kept ahold of her hand and led her towards the door.

"Um...Byron...you still don't have a shirt." She glanced away. He looked down then back up at her.

"So, it seems. Give me a moment." He soon emerged in a fresh shirt and suit, with his hair combed. She smiled a bit as he offered his arm to her. "Shall we?"

She took his arm. "Yes, we shall."

They walked out into the cool night air, the streetlamps and stars flickering.

"Today has certainly been eventful." Byron smiled at her.

"Yes, it has. This morning seems so long ago. Today you've forgotten me, we went to the Pit, we've solved two mysteries, I've jumped from a train..."

"You must allow me to apologize again for my conduct this morning. It was unforgivable."

"Not quite."

"I hope I have made up for it."

"You've made up for it tenfold."

"You're certain?"

"Positive."

"I can only hope I don't do it again tomorrow."

"You know, that is part of the fun of it though, don't you think?"

"What do you mean?"

"For as much as it pains me to have you forget me, it is quite exciting to never know how you'll greet me each morning."

"I hope tomorrow I'll greet you as a man who is impossibly in love with you." He smiled at her as he continued.

"Impossible because I can say that and have it be the truth, even though I've only met you today."

"I wonder, how is that possible?"

"It doesn't take a brain to love someone, Mira. The Order of Circe may have taken my memory from me, but they can't take my heart. That belongs to you." He kissed the top of her head, and she smiled.

They walked a bit further, just enjoying one another's company until she yawned. Then he called for a carriage and helped her in, settling into the seat next to her. They rode in silence back to Swan Walk, but neither of them minded. They only minded once it pulled up in front of her uncle's house and their time together came to an end. Byron paid the driver and helped her out of the carriage. The dark household loomed above them. She looked up at it and sighed.

"I don't want today to be over yet."

"Neither do I." He squeezed her hand. "But it has to be. Both of us need rest."

"You'll forget all of this."

"I'll be certain to write as much of it down as possible before I turn in for the night. I promise." She nodded and let go of his hand. He pulled her hand back.

"But just in case I don't remember, just know that I love you, Samira Rose Blayse." He kissed her hand softly before letting her go.

She paused and studied him for a moment before heading up the stairs and slipping into the house. All seemed still and dark. She crept up the stairs to her room counting to seventy-nine. Nero greeted her at the top of the stairs with a rub around her legs and a contented mew. She looked out the window onto the street. Byron stood looking up at the house. Then he trudged down the road. She let herself drift into the void.

T he next morning, the sun crept over the windowsill and woke Mira from her slumber. Weary from the night before, she sat up, every inch of her aching. Nero jumped onto the bed and mewed. He wanted fish. She slipped off the edge of the bed and realized she still wore the remains of Walker's clothes. She groaned and dressed in her own clothes, examining the bruises she'd accumulated from the day before. She blinked, remembering. So much happened, it was hard to keep track. It felt like it had been a week's worth of days crammed into twenty-four hours.

She brushed through her hair and winced as she touched the injury on the back of her head. Byron's injuries would be worse than hers. Was he even up? He would be so confused if he didn't remember anything. After all, if she felt sore, he likely felt ten times sorer. And he had a black eye. Perhaps it would help corroborate her story if he didn't read his journal before she got there. Hopefully, he could manage until then. She laughed a little to herself. She never would have thought Byron could have fallen for her. But if he could, she would have to figure out her own feelings. Did she love him back? When she determined her hair would not cooperate, she steeled herself and went down the stairs.

Her uncle could be a reasonable man. She knew that. Landon even more reasonable. Despite that, she knew if she told either of them that she had jumped from a moving train, broke into someone's house, shot someone, and then got into a fist fight, that she would never be allowed to leave the house by herself again. Gratefully, most of her bruises were out of sight and her hair covered her neck. She just needed some explanation as to why she was back.

She walked into the dining room and sat down quietly. Her uncle read the newspaper and didn't notice her come in. Landon brought a tray of breakfast food out and looked at her with a knowing glance. She smiled and helped herself to some food. Her uncle absentmindedly placed some toast and eggs on his plate. He glanced up at her.

"Good morning, Mira." He immediately went back to his newspaper without a second thought.

"Good morning, Uncle." She quietly nibbled on some toast and hoped he would continue to not completely notice her presence. He paused in his reading for a moment and then folded the newspaper and looked at her.

"What are you doing here?"

"I came back."

His eyes narrowed. "You are supposed to be in Bradford."

"I know, Uncle, I just—"

"No. It isn't safe for you here." He interrupted.

"It is now, Uncle."

"You received word from Constantine then?"

"...yes. The suspects were all arrested."

Her uncle relaxed. "Good. Good. In that case, welcome home." He picked up the newspaper again and looked through it.

Mira smiled and finished her breakfast.

As she walked out of the dining room and into the front entryway, Landon stopped her.

"Lying to your uncle, hmm?"

"I didn't lie. All of the suspects have been arrested."

"But you were involved, weren't you?"

"Well, yes. But will it hurt him not to know?"

"I assume you won't be telling me what happened either?"

"It won't hurt you not to know."

"Very well. Oh! Before I forget, a letter from your brother came for you." He handed her the envelope, and she placed it within her sketchbook.

"Now, off you go. Just don't get into trouble," he said.

"You know I will." She smirked and walked out of the house. Landon shook his head and went back to dusting.

She decided to walk to Palace Court. The cool fall day glistened, the leaves crisped under her feet, and Kensington sounded marvelous to her. She walked past the reflection pond in front of the palace and watched the ducks playing in the sun-speckled water. The air smelled of dirt and frost, and she loved it. Sounds of geese flying overhead caught her attention. She sat on a park bench to read Walker's letter.

> *My dearest Mira,*
>
> *We have returned from the Alps! And I'm rather disappointed to see that you haven't been writing. I'm hoping that it is because you are so busy that you have forgotten, rather than you not having anything to do.*
>
> *My professor suggested another inventor for me to apprentice under. After my final exams, I'll have my certificate and be able to join you and Uncle for a little while. I look forward to that. I hope neither of you have touched my room or my things. I'd like to come back and find everything how it was.*
>
> *I love you, my dear Mira, and hope you've gotten further in our case. Write me as soon as you are able!*
>
> *Much Love,*
> *Walker Blayse*

Mira laughed a little and placed the letter back in the envelope. She'd practically shredded some of his clothes the day before. Hopefully they wouldn't be missed. Even if they were, she could ask for forgiveness when he came to visit. She stood and continued her walk across Kensington.

About halfway across, she caught sight of the mysterious man who stopped her the last time she walked through Kensington alone. Her high spirits dwindled. He sat on a bench feeding the ducks. She walked a bit faster and shot another glance at him to make sure it was the same man. He looked directly at her and then stood, throwing the rest of the bread into the pond. She tried to calm herself, but her thoughts jumped to and fro. What if this stranger was one of the Whitechapel killers? Of course, he couldn't kill her here in broad daylight. And he hadn't killed her when he had talked to her before. There were people around, and they were her safety. She turned towards a couple walking their dog. Running footsteps followed her and soon the man walked at her elbow. He put his hands in his pockets in a nonchalant fashion.

"I hoped you would be walking through here, Miss Blayse."

"What do you want?"

"Is that any way to greet a friend?"

"I thought we established that you weren't?"

"Will acquaintance do, then?"

Mira stopped and looked at him. "I don't even know your name. How could we be acquaintances when we haven't even been properly introduced?" She turned back on her course across the park. He followed.

"Perhaps another time. I do need you to do something for me though."

"And why would I do that?"

"It concerns Byron Constantine." She stopped again and turned towards him. He smiled.

"I thought that would get your attention. I need you to give him something."

"Something?"

"This." He handed her a small envelope that was sealed shut with wax.

"Just a letter?"

"Just a letter."

"Alright."

He tipped his hat to her and walked back towards the pond. She watched him for a few moments and then looked at the envelope. It seemed normal enough. She turned it over and looked at the seal. A standard floral pattern decorated it. She placed it in her sketchbook and continued to Palace Court.

Music flowed from an open window. She smiled as she unlocked the door and walked in. Time to meet Byron once again. The piano continued, and she walked into the front room. He looked up at her and smiled. She saw the journal sitting on the arm of his chair. The room looked just as she had left it the day before, except for some roses sitting on the table and several new notes pinned up to the wall. She went to examine them.

You solved a crime yesterday. Thatcher will likely come visit you today.

Buy roses early tomorrow.

She smiled and took a seat in her own chair to listen to the music. She opened her sketchbook to sketch the roses. Everything felt right. The music swelled and then it came to its resolution. Byron closed the lid on the piano and took a seat in his armchair across from her.

"I know this sounds ludicrous, but I have to make sure you are—"

She interrupted him. "Mira? Yes." She smiled, and he took a breath of relief.

"For a moment I thought a beautiful stranger had entered my house."

"You've read the journal then?"

"Indeed, I have. It was very informative."

"I suppose even if you didn't, the notes on the wall are the most important things."

"Especially the second note." He smiled.

"The roses are nice. Although it is rather exciting to have solved a case."

"That was your first one, was it not?"

"Yes, it was. If you count my parent's case, I've solved two."

"It only gets better from here."

"How many cases have you solved?"

"According to my journal these two make forty-three from the time I lost my memory."

"And before that?"

"I lost count. Well over a hundred."

"Brilliant."

He smiled and nodded, then walked over to the window, pensive. He turned back towards her.

"You seem to have become more than just a secretary, Mira. You really are an extraordinary girl."

"I'm glad you think that."

"I'm serious. Not many women would be willing to go through what you have."

"It's worth it just to know what happened to my parents."

"So now that that case is solved...?"

"Oh no. Don't think you can get rid of me that easily." She smiled.

"You'll stay on then?"

"Of course. After all, I'd like to learn more about the man who is in love with me." She gave him half a smile as he turned a bit pink.

"I did say some rather ridiculous things yesterday, didn't I?"

"Who is to say that they are ridiculous?" Her smirk softened to a smile.

"You are alright with them then?"

"As long as you understand that I'm still trying to understand my own feelings."

"Of course."

"I see no problem with them, then. As long as what you told me was true."

"I hope you know by now that I would never purposefully lie to you, Mira."

"I do."

"Why don't we go out for a little bit? You could show me the cafe that we met at, and we can get brunch."

"I would love to."

He stood and offered her an arm. She took it happily, and they left Palace Court en route to what had become her favorite cafe. They each ordered a plate of French toast and a pot of tea to share and talked about all the happenings during the last few weeks. When they finished their French toast and conversation, Byron checked his pocket watch.

"Chief Inspector Thatcher will be coming to Palace Court soon. We probably ought to get back."

"How do you know he'll be coming now?"

"I'd love to say that it was my deductive reasoning and brilliant observational powers..."

"But?"

"He sent me a telegram this morning saying he would stop by around one. It is around noon now, which means we can have a nice leisurely stroll through Kensington Gardens on our way back." She laughed a little and then remembered what happened earlier that morning.

"Oh! I nearly forgot. On my way to Palace Court this morning, a mysterious gentleman stopped me. The same that had threatened me on my way home two days ago."

"I didn't read anything about this gentleman." His tone turned serious.

"I forgot to tell you about it yesterday. Things were a bit hectic."

"Did he threaten you again?"

"No, and I suppose the other time was just a warning. He gave me a letter to give to you. It's back at Palace Court."

"Then it can wait there until we arrive." He held onto her arm protectively and kept his guard up as they walked through Kensington.

The sun rose high in the sky over London, melting the frost away and warming her back. She leaned into Byron a little. She felt entirely content. They watched squirrels running up and down the trees, the birds flying south for the winter, and the other couples walking past. They reached Palace Court and found Inspector Thatcher waiting outside.

"Good afternoon, Detectives." He smiled and his eyes sparkled.

"Good afternoon, Inspector Thatcher! How are you doing?" she offered him a smile. Byron took out his key and unlocked the door.

"Very well. Very well indeed. We've gotten confessions out of the Shadow and the two men found with her, and apprehended the other woman you mentioned. She did, in fact, have the blueprints."

"Wonderful news, Thatcher!" Byron opened the door. They all walked into the house and made themselves comfortable in the living room. Byron went to the kitchen to make some tea.

"And how are you, Miss Blayse?"

"I am quite content." She smiled.

"I am very glad to hear that. I need to thank you. Your work has been invaluable in helping to solve this case."

"I was more than happy to help."

Byron returned with the tea things and poured them each a cup. Inspector Thatcher sipped at it gratefully.

"So, Thatcher, have you been able to make any headway on the smuggling part of the case?"

"Indeed, we have. My men were able to uncover quite a few clues this morning. We should have the whole thing broken open by the end of the week. The inquest is planned for the middle of next week."

"Marvelous!"

"Of course, that wouldn't have been possible without that package you sent us, Miss Blayse."

"Package?" Byron looked at Mira.

"Before I came to Vale street, I made up a letter with all the facts, addresses, portraits I had drawn, practically everything I knew. I sent it to Scotland Yard in the hopes that if something happened to either of us that the case would still be solved."

"And the post was faithful. We received it this morning." The chief inspector set his teacup down in the saucer.

"I'm so glad it helped."

"It is likely the link that will have solved this entire mess. I can only hope that the 'Dear Boss' letter that was received in relation to the Whitechapel murders will prove as useful. Then Scotland Yard can take it easy for a little while."

"'Dear Boss' letter?" Byron's curiosity piqued, and his gaze turned serious.

"Yes. It was a letter from the killer. Signed Jack the Ripper. Quite a chilling title for a mass murderer. But we'll have caught him soon enough, now that we have a handwriting sample."

Byron looked at Mira, recognition crossing his face. He picked up his journal and rifled through it, looking at his last entry. Mira felt a chill go up her spine, a feeling of nausea spreading through her.

"Inspector, I don't know if the letter will solve this particular case. There are several killers." Byron read the final page.

"Several killers?"

"Yes. Molly, the Shadow, she mentioned that there were multiple killers."

"Oh! The letter!" Mira remembered and looked around for her sketchbook. She found it on the side table. She opened it, took out the mysterious envelope, and looked it over again. Thatcher leaned forward.

"What letter is this?"

"A man gave it to me in the gardens. He told me it was for Byron." Mira handed it to him. He examined the seal and turned it over a few times. Then he stood and went to the mantle to retrieve his letter opener.

"Now let's see."

Byron slid the letter opener delicately into the envelope and tore through the seal. He hesitated before pulling out a single piece of paper and turning it over. He frowned and handed it to Mira. On the page was a triangle with a circle around it. Three smaller circles were drawn at each of the points of the triangle. The symbol of the Order of Circe. Below it there were three words.

We live on.

Acknowledgments

Thanks to the mystery authors who came before me. You've written significantly better murders and gotten away with it. However did you manage? Agatha Christie, Arthur Conan Doyle, and Dorothy L. Sayers, I hope I've lived up to your legacy. Of course, you're dead, so unless you haunt me there isn't much you can do about that. Did the lights just flicker? Do it again so I can be sure!

Next, Mason, my RPG buddy! Byron started with you, and I thank you for giving him to me. I hope I did you proud. This book wouldn't have made it far without your idea of an amnesiac detective.

My dear Jane, or is it Becca? Or in this case, you must be my Diana Barry. I never would have sent this book off to Immortal Works without your gentle, "what do you have to lose?" So, I have you to thank for this tome as well. I don't think you needed tissues for this one, but I hope you read it with ice cream. (Yours truly, Lizzie)

Julie, I can say that at the moment you are my number one fan. You'd think my mother would be in that spot, but your excitement over reading my books makes me giddy. There are some days when I don't have motivation. Then I remember you are waiting with bated breath, and I manage to write a few more words. I love you dearly and hope I'll keep you as a beta reader for a bit longer.

I have to throw some praise to the BYU study abroad program and Professors Horrocks, Mason, Howard, and Swenson. Thank you for giving me the experience of a lifetime at the London Center and beyond. And for not chiding me as I wrote my book on bus rides, in alcoves, and when I probably should have been writing papers. The richness of my story couldn't have been possible without living in Europe. Also, thanks to Thais for feeding me.

Now, Richard Jones, you've probably never heard of me. I hope that you'll end up reading my book because without you I wouldn't have had most of my research. Your site (jack-the-ripper.org) has been invaluable for writing the period. You have no idea how long I've spent perusing the old newspapers on your site. I've checked and double-checked facts about events to make sure everything lined up perfectly with the calendar. Do you like my hypothesis for how it happened and, more importantly, why?

This book also wouldn't have been possible without Mackenzie Seidal-Guzman, who found me at the Life the Universe and Everything conference and introduced me to my publisher.

Speaking of which, thanks must be given to my amazing publishing team. Rachel Huffmire, you darling person, thank you for being so excited about my book and for giving it a chance. Holli Anderson, thank you for agreeing with Rachel that my book was worth anyone's time. John Olsen, your edits made Constantine even better and made me a better editor. And everyone else who worked on the book behind the scenes or in front of them, I thank you ardently.

As for Tabitha...well, you've said in the past that I seem to be able to do anything I want to. While I don't always believe that, it looks like I've written a book! Thanks for joining me in my insanity, throwing Andes Mints at my face, listening to me talk about things that aren't real, and being my sister in all the ways that matter. You've been with me through highs and lows and I can't express how much our relationship means to me.

To all the teachers I've had over the years, this one's for you too. Particularly Mr. Wix and Mr. Beeson. Both of you have had an enormous impact on my writing career. Perhaps I don't write papers as well as I could and this book isn't exactly what is considered "literary," but I'm proud of it anyway. Thanks for pushing me to my limits and teaching me how to fly. Not with wings, but with words.

Thanks to Jacie and Carly for dealing with me in these last months before publication. I've probably been a bit of a nutjob, ranting about book blurbs, author bios, and the enormous number of edits I've been doing. I make no promises to be better the next time around, but at least you are getting acclimated to my special brand of insanity.

I believe thanks and a can of tasty chicken are in order for da Bunter. You beautiful boo, I don't think I could have written this if you hadn't sat on my keyboard and warmed my lap. Too bad you can't read.

I must also give thanks to those strange people who raised me and were raised with me.

First off, can we get a round of applause for my mother? Thanks, Mum! Everything great in my life has started with you. I'm serious. From my own birth forward, you always knew what was best for me, even if I didn't. You said, "Maybe you should do art as your career," and I rebelled against that, but now I'm illustrating. You bring up that maybe I'd like to pursue humanities as my degree. I finally look into it and find that it is everything I've ever wanted to study. You mention off-hand that maybe my story could become a book. Poof! My book is in your hand. Thanks for everything, Mum. You're the best rubber duck I could ask for.

Alex, even if you didn't program my website, you'd still be here. I look forward to talking with you every day. I love our banter and how we just seem to get each other. I like to think my first friend was you, even if you threatened to eat me when I was five.

Brent, it's your fault that Byron and Mira didn't kiss at the end. And I thank you for that. You, of course, were right about that. This is much better for the overarching storyline. Granted, us hopeless romantics are now hanging off a cliff. Do you think they can kiss in the next book? Asking for a friend.

Stephan, you've given me a steady stream of quiet, sweet support. I'm proud to be your favorite artist, and while I may not be your favorite author, I hope I'm up there.

Heather, you beautiful human. I may have not included murder floofers and it might not be as clever as Lord Peter Whimsey, but I hope the book at least made you smile. I'd settle for a laugh because laughing with you is one of my favorite pastimes.

And finally, dear old Dad. I like to think that you could read my book in heaven. Before you pined for the fjords, there wasn't even a hint of authorial intent in my body. Or, perhaps there was. Perhaps you knew. Here's to the times long since passed when we would grab popcorn and watch an old mystery. To bunny rabbits, the monkey run, and walking hand in hand. I blame you (and Mum) for me identifying more as a Brit than a Yank. I wish that you didn't have to die for me to realize how much I love you. But, because of you, I think I understand how to live. Daddy, I've reached for the stars, and I've caught one. Thanks for watching over me.

If I've forgotten anyone, and surely I have, I'll blame it on Byron, our forgetful detective. Perhaps next go around, Mira can help us both remember everyone.

About the
AUTHOR

Natalie Brianne's love of writing might be traced back to an old Rainbow Macintosh Laptop she received for her 8th birthday. Perhaps it came from years of storytelling and the discipline of wonder. Or maybe, she was born to write and didn't realize it until a book sprung out of her fingertips somewhere between a house in Pleasant Grove, Utah and a bus on its way to Edinburgh, Scotland.

She received her degree in Interdisciplinary Humanities from BYU. While she could have studied English or Creative Writing, she opted to learn more about culture, distant lands, and people in hopes of writing better stories. Much of her first book, *Constantine Capers: The Pennington Perplexity* was written when she lived at 27 Palace Court, London, walking the streets as if she were her characters.

While her interests in writing spread across genres, you can always expect her work to be imaginative, clean, and clever.

When Natalie isn't writing, she's illustrating, voice acting, playing the guitar very badly, traveling and forgetting that she has vegetables in her fridge. You might find her in a cute little ivy-covered house in Provo, Utah. You'll know the place by the immense flock of finches that nest there. If she isn't there, try looking for her on Twitter, Facebook, or her website https://nataliebrianne.com/.